Ginger Cat
Office 65287
PO Box 6945
London
W1A 6US

Email: gdharper@gdharper.com

Printed and bound in Great Britain by Clays Ltd, Elcograf S.p.A

Typeset in Caslon

ISBN 978-0-9935478-7-4

British Library Cataloguing in Publication Data. A catalogue
record for this book is available from the British Library.

The Maids of Biddenden

GD HARPER

ABOUT THE AUTHOR

GD HARPER is a past winner of a Wishing Shelf Red Ribbon for adult fiction, and was shortlisted for the Lightship Prize for first-time authors and longlisted for the UK Novel Writing Award.

The Maids of Biddenden was shortlisted for the 2021 Impress Prize, longlisted for the 2021 Flash 500 Novel Award and was a 2021 Page Turner Writer Award finalist.

For more information visit:
www.gdharper.com

ALSO BY GD HARPER:

Love's Long Road

A Friend in Deed

Silent Money

The Maids of
Biddenden

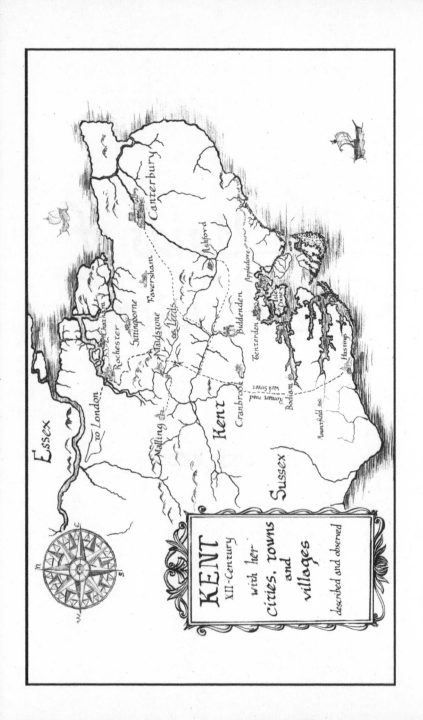

1106

~

Chapter 1

AVICIA KNELT AND PRAYED. Prayed for wisdom, to know what action would be righteous and true. For strength, to cope with the horror of what she would shortly be forced to witness. Above all, for compassion towards the unfortunates now in her care; compassion sufficient to displace any revulsion her face might betray when she saw them for the first time.

She stood up and looked around the abbey chapter house. Mid-morning prayers were over and the room had been decorated with wildflowers to celebrate her arrival. Celebrations could wait, however. She had felt elation at her appointment – for the first time, Malling Abbey would have its own prioress – but later, Bishop Gundulf had told her of the abbey's dark secret. And, since then, the thought of it had accompanied her every waking moment. Today she would see it in the flesh. It. She. They? What was best? Soon she would know.

The door opened and a sturdy-looking woman bustled in. She gave a curtsey, her eyes on the floor as she spoke.

'I bid thee welcome, Mother Avicia,' she said. Her words had a cold formality that belied the greeting. 'I am Sister

Margaret, the senior obedientiary, here to see you are well. I trust your journey was not too taxing?'

Avicia's smile was lost on the nun, who continued her downward stare. The prioress presumed the woman was a widow, like her, who had turned to the Church after bereavement. She strode over, took the nun's hands and clasped them together, forcing an upward glance.

'Most uneventful, Sister Margaret,' Avicia said, her pious smile broadening into what she hoped was a friendly grin.

The nun looked down again and started picking the sides of her fingernails. Avicia looked around the room.

'You have prepared well for my arrival. Will the other sisters be joining us soon?'

'They are awaiting my call, Mother Avicia. Shall you greet them now, or do you first need to perform your ablutions?' Sister Margaret eyed the door leading out to the cloisters, like a trapped church mouse planning a dash to freedom.

'I think it best to see them now. How many sisters have we at present, Sister Margaret?'

'Seven and twenty, Mother Avicia, including the novices.'

'And how many others?'

A chill breeze crept into the room, causing the candles to flutter. Sister Margaret made the sign of the cross and clenched the crucifix around her neck.

'Others?' She tightened her grip on the plain wooden cross.

'Yes,' Avicia replied. She tried to keep the reproach from her voice.

'There are only a score and seven of God's souls doing His work here,' Sister Margaret said, her body tensing. 'It would not be God's will to count the abomination.'

'It is not up to us to judge God's will, Sister Margaret. And this "abomination" of which you speak. They have names, do they not?'

Sister Margaret nodded, her cheeks burning red, her chin trembling. 'Forgive me, Mother Avicia. I cannot conjure the sight of it into my mind without reflecting why God has chosen to bring such a thing into this world. But when in its presence we do not speak of it in these terms. May God forgive us, we speak the names with which they were baptised. Eliza and Mary. Eliza and Mary Chulkhurst, from that respectable and God-fearing family, the Chulkhursts of Biddenden.'

Sister Margaret's voice choked with tears and Avicia decided it best not to probe any further. 'I will meet them in short order and form my own view,' she said, clapping her hands in an effort to clear the air. 'But I should not keep the sisters waiting. Bring them forth. Other matters can wait until after I have made their acquaintance.'

Within minutes, the nuns were all assembled. Avicia greeted every sister in turn, repeating their names despite the impossibility of remembering them. Each woman, according to custom, was dressed in an identical floor-length tunic, with a wimple covering her entire head bar the face. It should have been a joyous occasion, but a pall of gloom hung in the air. The obedientiaries, the senior nuns, were introduced first, strictly in order of their length of service. Then she met the oblates, or novices – young girls in their mid-teens sent by their parents to gain an education by the only means available to them. Throughout the whole process, there was no glimpse of a smile, no flicker of excitement in recognition of this key moment in the abbey's history.

Avicia recognised a darkness had to be lifted. 'I will see my chambers now, Sister Margaret. Please lead the way.' Without valediction to the others, Avicia followed Sister Margaret out of that chamber of despair.

They arrived at her quarters – a spartan cell with one small window high in the corner. Dust particles danced in a shaft of light that shone onto a bedside table. Avicia picked up her Bible and placed it in the light. Sister Margaret muttered a request to depart, but Avicia stepped past her and closed the door.

'I have met all my charges now, save for those we talked of before. There is deep pain in this house of God and I need to see the reason without further delay.' Avicia walked back to touch the sunlit Bible with the tips of her fingers. 'Take me to meet them.'

Sister Margaret looked at her with dull eyes, then spoke in a monotone: 'If that be your desire, Mother Avicia. I bow to your command. They are ready for the day and should be at play. Come, follow me.'

They walked across the abbey courtyard to the stables. At the last of them, the half-door had been replaced with a sturdy wooden door haphazardly studded with wrought-iron roseheads. As Sister Margaret slid back the bolt, Avicia felt a wave of nausea. She closed her eyes briefly to compose herself.

The door opened and Avicia stepped inside and gasped. Not in horror, but at the normality of what was before her. A windowless room, ten feet square; reeds for sleeping, scattered on the floor to the left; a latrine trench to the right. Gaps in the wooden-plank wall let light into the room and in the centre, two young girls faced them, sitting cross-legged side-by-side, each playing with a small rag doll. Their skin was pure white, like an alabaster statue come to life. Their dark brown hair reached down to the same point on each of their shoulders, but the symmetry was spoiled by one being plump, the other much thinner. As they moved their arms to play with the dolls, each anticipated the other's actions, an unconscious dance performed between them.

They glanced up and chanted in unison, 'Good morrow, Sister Margaret.' Then they spotted Avicia behind her. Each squeezed the rag doll they were holding, one cradling hers to her chest, the other staring with a probing gaze. They untangled their legs, and simultaneously, without communication between them, shuffled backwards to the farthest wall.

Avicia cleared her throat and spoke softly.

'Good morrow, young maidens. I am Mother Avicia, and I have travelled from Rochester to come and live with you in this fine place. Will you tell me your names?'

The girls looked to Sister Margaret for guidance.

'Speak to the good prioress,' she said, her voice harsh and insistent, like that of an authoritarian schoolteacher. There was silence. One of the girls started fidgeting and the other stroked her hair to comfort her. They had pushed themselves hard against the wall, and held their knees and legs tightly together. Sister Margaret's face tightened as she shook her head in exasperation. 'I'm sorry, Mother Avicia, they are not used to strangers. Speak, girls!'

'Hush, Sister Margaret, it is we who are disturbing their play.' Avicia knelt beside them. 'Can I see your doll?' She held out her hand towards the one closer to her.

The girl turned, causing the other to grab her shoulder to keep her balance, and Avicia noticed their clothing for the first time. Two calico smocks, much too big for them, sewn together at the side-seam. They disguised what was beneath, but when the children moved together they remained perfectly aligned, side-by-side but facing slightly away from one another. Avicia forced herself not to stare, instead focusing on looking the girl straight in the eye.

The girl who had comforted the other thrust her doll into Avicia's hand and the prioress detected the smallest of murmurs from her lips.

'Pardon?' she said, continuing to gaze into the young girl's eyes. 'Were you saying your doll's name?'

'Edith.' A little stronger this time.

'Edith. What a lovely name.' She looked over to the other girl. 'And what's *your* doll called?'

The girl bit on her hand and started shaking her head vigorously. The action caused them both to shake.

'Stop it, Mary, stop it!' the first girl cried. She turned to Avicia. 'Her doll's called Maud. But it's stupid, like her.'

'I don't think she's stupid, just shy,' Avicia replied. 'So, if your sister is Mary, you must be Eliza.'

Eliza bit her bottom lip. Avicia spoke again, more crisply this time. 'Well, girls, I would like to stay and talk, but I have a busy day ahead.' She clenched her teeth, and her smile, she felt sure, turned into a grimace. 'Enjoy your playtime. I will ...'

Unable to finish, she hastened from the room, Sister Margaret following behind.

Outside, Avicia closed the door and leant against it. Then she began to sob – silently, reluctantly. Inappropriately. She caught Sister Margaret's look of concern and it gave her the resolve she needed.

'I shame myself with this display of weakness. You will not see the like of this from me again.' Avicia inhaled deeply, holding her breath for a few beats of her heart before breathing out. Then she spoke in a steady, low-pitched tone. 'I have many questions that need to be answered. What is the nature of their predicament? Are they in good health? The quiet one – is she an imbecile?'

Sister Margaret waited until they had crossed the courtyard and entered the cloister before replying. 'They are a hand's length joined together. Their corporeal selves are hale and hearty, and they are of sound mind. Mary is the quiet one. She lets Eliza do the talking for her. But when they are alone, we hear them converse, often with striking animation. Their minds are wholly separate, but they are destined to be together until God has mercy on them. We pray every day for their release into Heaven.'

'And until that day? What life do they have here?'

'They pray six times a day. They are made comfortable in their confinement. They want for nothing.' There was a long pause, as though Sister Margaret was willing herself to speak further. 'Gundulf says we must do nothing to hasten the end.' Her eyes darted back, towards the locked door of the children's cell. 'But he has never set eyes on them since their arrival here. I hope that you will be more merciful, that you will petition Gundulf to let us assist them in their journey to God's side.'

Avicia shook her head. 'Gundulf has given me no counsel as to what the fate of these children should be. He bade me come here, see their predicament for myself, and with that knowledge take the path that is the most just and righteous. I do not know yet what that path should be, but I saw nothing of the Devil's work in this first encounter. I will talk more to the Maids, then convene a council of the obedientiaries.'

They had reached the door of Avicia's quarters. Sister Margaret stood to one side, her pose submissive, betraying no reaction to Avicia's words.

'I will listen to all views with an open mind,' Avicia said, trying to sound reassuring. 'There is much I need to learn about this terrible responsibility that has been thrust upon us. I will talk to the physician who treats them. It may well be that God will decide for us.'

'No physician has set foot in their chamber since they arrived in their swaddling clothes,' Sister Margaret said. 'That was six summers ago. Sister Agnes is our infirmarian, and she is skilled at laying balm on them, to cure them of any childhood ailments. No outsider has ever been told of their existence.'

'And for six years, the girls have flourished? Save for the normal afflictions all growing children have to bear?' Avicia did not wait for Sister Margaret's confirmation. 'Then we have two robust children in our care, who seem to be of sound mind and body. Let me dwell on that fact. My destiny may be to create some joy out of the misery that seems to surround us all in this place.'

Sister Margaret's silence eloquently conveyed her view of Avicia's optimism.

'I will take my leave of you now,' Avicia said eventually, reining in her words to hide her frustration. 'We will talk again, when I've reflected on the events of this day.'

With that, she entered her chamber, closed the door behind her and collapsed onto her bed. She replayed these last few minutes over and over again in her head. Nothing she had been told by Gundulf could have prepared her for what she had encountered. Nothing she had experienced in life could tell her what actions to take. But she must decide what to do next – and decide wisely.

The lives of these young maids depended on it.

Chapter 2
Eliza

MARY IS THE MOST boring, annoying and stupid person in the world.

Why do I have to be joined to *her?* She cries all the time and she never talks to anyone but me. I have to speak for both of us, and I always say something wrong and get into trouble. Mary never gets punished, even though it's usually her fault. It's not fair.

And she always gets the hiccups. They're even more annoying. They go on and on and she doesn't even try to stop them. I punch her in the stomach to make them go away, then she burps and they sometimes stop. If they don't, I hit her again and then she cries because she says I hurt her. And that makes the hiccups worse. It's not *fair!*

Sometimes I get so angry at being joined to her that I pull her hair and scratch her with my nails. It serves her right for being so annoying. I only do that when I'm really, really angry, because the scratches make her ugly face bleed and then Sister Margaret sees them and hits me with the broomstick and tells me it's a sin and I'll go to Hell if I do it again and I say I'd like to go to Hell if it means I don't have to be joined to Mary and Sister Margaret says that is blasphemy which is an even bigger sin and she hits me even harder. And all because Mary is so annoying.

But I know I'm not going to Hell because I talk to God six times every day. It's different when you talk to God, it's not like talking to a normal person. You have to pray to God, which means saying exactly what the nuns tell you to say, and it's all about thanking God for things and asking him to look after us and forgive us for our sins. So that means I'm not going to Hell, no matter how many times I hit Mary.

But I want to ask God other things. Like what is on the outside and what Heaven is like. And most of all, I want to ask God to make it so I don't have to be joined to Mary anymore. He does it for everyone else, so why won't He do it for us? Sister Margaret tells me to be quiet when I say I want to make my own prayers to God, but Sister Agnes explains that I can only say the prayers the nuns tell me to say. God is very busy hearing prayers from people all over the world and so we can only say the ones that Jesus tells us to say. Jesus is God's son.

Sister Agnes is the nice nun. When she saw a bruise on my arm after Sister Margaret hit me with the broomstick, I heard her tell Sister Margaret that we only fight because we are bored and frustrated. Frustrated must be the same as bored, because the next day Sister Agnes brought two dolls for Mary and me to play with. I chose the pretty one and called her Edith and Mary had to take the ugly one. That gives me a nice tingle in my chest and I feel all puffed up.

The new nun who came to see us yesterday hasn't been back today. She said that Edith was a lovely name. That's because I thought of the name. Mary called her doll Maud but the new nun didn't say that was lovely.

'I wanted to tell her more about Edith,' I say to Mary. 'But you were so stupid. I couldn't before she ran away. You always spoil everything.'

'Her name is Mother Avicia,' Mary replies. 'And she said I wasn't stupid, just shy. And being shy isn't a sin.' She crosses her arms, holding Maud against her chest. 'I can be shy if I want to.'

'Nobody will want to be friends with us if you're stupid and boring. And you are boring.'

'She didn't say I was boring.'

'But you are. Boring.'

'Am not.'

'Are. *Boring, boring, boring!*'

We have another fight and forget all about Mother Avicia. Then we stop and wait for someone to come and do prayers with us. But no-one comes! God will be getting angry. He might send us to Hell if we don't do something.

Because I'm clever, I come up with an idea.

'Let's do a prayer ourselves. We say them so often, we know the words.'

Mary lets out a gasp. 'It is a sin to pray alone.'

'Better to pray alone than not pray at all,' I reply. I feel my chest tingle again. Sometimes I could be so, so clever.

Mary's shaking tells me she isn't convinced. I start anyway.

'Oh merciful God, fill our hearts, we pray Thee, with the graces of Thy Holy Spirit, with love, joy, peace, long-suffering, gentleness, goodness, faith, meekness, temperance.' Mary joins in now and we speak the rest together.

'Teach us to love those who hate us, to pray for those who despitefully use us, that we may be the children of Thee our Father, Who makest Thy sun to shine on the evil and on the good, and sendest rain on the just and on the unjust, through Jesus Christ our Lord. Amen.'

Mary claps her hands in excitement at what we've just done.

I am so excited, I can't help myself. 'And, oh merciful God, please split us into two on the morrow. Please. Amen.'

Mary bursts into tears. 'You mustn't say that to God. You mustn't! Sister Margaret said it is a sin to burden God with silly things and now you've done it. Jesus never said to God to split us on the morrow. God will punish us and it's all your fault.'

I don't hit Mary, I'm so worried. We play with our dolls for the rest of the morning and I keep thinking about God's punishment. At noon, we hear our door open and we both scream and stumble to the far away wall. But it's only Sister Agnes.

She looks at us in surprise. 'Eliza, Mary, whatever is the matter?' Then she smiles. Sister Agnes is the only nun who smiles. 'Ah. The visit of Mother Avicia has unsettled you. Shush, shush, my dears. The day has been busy and I have neglected my care for you, but there is nothing to fear from her. I have met her only briefly, but she is a godly woman, honest and kind. The abbey will gain much from having a prioress.'

Sister Agnes explains what a prioress is, that we are to call her Mother Avicia and that she is going to be in charge of the abbey and can tell all the other nuns what to do.

'Even Sister Margaret?' I ask, open-mouthed.

'Even Sister Margaret,' she replies and she laughs. I sometimes hear the nuns laughing as they pass by our room, and when I do I feel my heart beat faster. It is the nicest sound you can ever hear.

We say our prayers and I am so scared Mary is going to tell Sister Agnes that I did a terrible thing and we prayed on our own. But Mary must have forgotten because she doesn't say anything. Then we eat our rye bread and onion.

'Slowly, Eliza,' Sister Agnes says to me, shaking her head as she wags her finger. 'Remember what you promised.'

I haven't forgotten, but I have been so nervous I can't help but gulp my food. I always eat much faster than Mary and when I feel full, Mary says she does too, even if she's only had a few mouthfuls. She got thinner and thinner but said she was never hungry and was sick if she tried to eat more. Sister Agnes told me I had to eat really, really slowly so we both stopped feeling hungry at the same time. Another annoying Mary thing.

After Sister Agnes leaves, Mary asks me what is going on. 'Mother Avicia is very important,' I explain to her. 'And Sister Agnes told us she was very busy, which is why she had to leave so quickly.' My breath sticks in my throat as I have my next thought. 'But she's not as busy as God,' I say, clasping my hands under my chin. 'Maybe she can do our splitting.'

I feel I am floating on air. Mary is nodding and wriggling and squirming. I don't find it annoying – I get excited by it and start wriggling too.

'Do you think so?' she asks, taking deep breaths.

I go to say yes, but I can't. It is just too big a word to say out loud.

'Maybe,' I say instead.

I play with Mary for the rest of the day and we never fight once. After I am split from Mary, I am going to love her.

That night, as I wait to fall asleep, I remember my prayer from earlier. I gather up all my courage and say another.

'Oh merciful God,' I whisper, the words hardly coming out of my mouth, too soft for Mary to hear. 'I'm sorry I bothered you today. Please help Mother Avicia to split us. It doesn't have to be on the morrow, if you're too busy. But soon.'

I hear an owl hoot. God has heard me.

Chapter 3

THE SOUND OF the abbey bell roused Avicia from a fitful sleep. A heavy weight of despondency pressed down on her as she lay motionless on her bed. After a few minutes, she closed her eyes and a waking dream started to overshadow her. That caused her to sit up with a start. It would be unforgivable to miss Lauds.

When the early morning service was finished she spoke to Sister Margaret with newfound strength.

'It is important that we conclude our conversation, I know,' she told her. 'But first, I need to get to know Eliza and Mary better. I will break my fast, then I will spend the morning in their company. What is the best manner in which to garner their trust and confidence, so they will speak openly to me?'

Sister Margaret shrugged. 'Sister Agnes spends her time with them freely, even when not required to tend to their ailments. You will find her under the north abbey wall, where she cultivates her healing herbs and remedies. That is, if she has not stolen away to see her charges again.' She paused for a moment, as if considering whether to say more. Finally, she said: 'You might do well to remind her of her primary duty to the abbey.' There was a pinched expression on Sister

Margaret's face. 'The coughing season is upon us, and no linctus has been prepared.'

Avicia found the small rectangular garden, sheltered against the abbey wall but able to catch all the morning sunlight. Sister Agnes was tending a cluster of plants with spikes of small blue flowers. She turned as Avicia approached and jumped to her feet.

'Good morrow, Sister Agnes,' Avicia said, nodding a greeting. 'This is a fine physic garden you have created here. Tell me, what is that fair flower in your hand?'

Sister Agnes bowed her head a little and gave a nervous curtsey. Her soft round face and deep brown eyes gave her the appearance of youthful innocence, though she was doubtless close to Avicia's age.

'The blue hyssop, Mother Avicia. It is in flower, so time to collect the petals to infuse the syrup. It will warm away the travails of winter.'

'Sister Margaret will be pleased. She bade me mention that it would soon be greatly needed.'

Sister Agnes bit her lip and stammered an apology. 'The hyssop is only this day in bloom, Mother Avicia. I am not late in preparing the linctus, and no bad humour has been visited upon us. Please do not punish me for my tardiness.'

'Hush, dear Sister, I am not here to chastise. I mentioned its need as honour for your talents, not to censure you. But though your skills as an infirmarian are of much value, it is not for those that I came to seek you out. It is another matter that weighs heavily on me.'

Sister Agnes touched her hand to her chest and her eyes widened. 'I cannot help but want to care for these poor creatures,' she said, her voice trembling. 'Sister Margaret told me we must let nature take its course, but I cannot bring myself to do that. Please do not instruct me thus, Mother Avicia. Until your arrival no-one in the abbey had the authority to issue such an instruction, and I have been fearing the coming of this day. Fearing the moment when I had to choose to follow my conscience or my orders.'

Avicia placed a hand on Sister Agnes's shoulder. 'God has not spoken to me on this,' she said. 'Sister Margaret has indeed entreated me to take what she thinks is the most merciful path, but I must make up my own mind. You are the one to whom the children are closest, I believe. Let us spend some time with them, so I may know them well also.'

Sister Agnes wiped away a tear. 'Forgive me, Mother Avicia. When you sought me out so soon after your arrival, I feared the worst. When will you want to attend to them?'

'I saw them briefly upon my arrival. Take me to them now, and let us stay until their true selves become known to me. Can your garden await your return?'

A faint, transient smile lit up Sister Agnes's earnest face. 'Nothing is too pressing. Let us call on them without delay.'

They went over to the stable yard, Sister Agnes knocked gently on the rosehead-studded door and stepped inside. Avicia heard screams of delight and a shuffling sound as the children stumbled forward to embrace the nun. Avicia stepped quietly into the room. The girls' faces were buried in the cloth of the nun's habit

Sister Agnes disentangled herself from the mass of arms and legs as Eliza and Mary looked up at her adoringly. Avicia couldn't help but be moved by the joy on their faces, so different from the muted welcome shown to Sister Margaret the day before.

'Eliza, Mary, your new prioress has come to visit you again.' Sister Agnes spoke with evident eagerness. 'You should be very honoured. Many tasks await her attention, and she has spoken to no more than a few of us sisters, yet here she is, back to see you once more. Please welcome her.'

Eliza and Mary turned and hugged Sister Agnes again, a hug of comfort rather than fear. She gently unpeeled their embrace and stroked Eliza's neck as she spoke in a reassuring whisper. 'Come, come, Eliza. You speak first. Bid Mother Avicia good morrow.'

Eliza gazed up at Sister Agnes, a look of anxiety but also of wanting to please. Mary moved in such a way as to half-hide herself behind Eliza, forcing Eliza to fully face the prioress.

Eliza started yelling. 'Mary, stop doing that! You always want to hide, it's not fair. *You* speak to her!' She whacked Mary on the side of the face.

Mary burst into tears. 'You hit me! Sister Agnes, Eliza won't talk to the prioress. Tell her to talk to her.' She attempted to wrestle Eliza with her left arm, which caused the two of them to fall over, four legs waving in the air.

Avicia burst out laughing. 'You will not be able to fell her without consequence to yourself, young Mary. You should know that by now.'

The two girls sat bolt upright, straining their necks to look at each other.

Eliza spoke first. 'Mother Avicia does not cry, Sister Agnes.' She was frowning as she looked at the nun. 'Everyone cries when they see us. Why does she not cry?'

Sister Agnes gave a little shrug. 'Thank you, Mother Avicia,' she said, 'for bringing joy here today.'

Avicia thought it best to revert to speaking with a dignity more fitting to her position.

'I did not desire to bring unwarranted attention upon myself,' she said, straightening her back and adjusting her wimple. 'I bid you good morrow, fair maidkin Eliza. Now be so kind as to bid me the same.'

'G-g-good morrow,' Eliza replied, blushing with pride at being addressed by such an affectionate term. She twisted round to address Mary. 'See? I am a fair maidkin, and you are a cry baby. Cry baby, cry baby.'

'Hush, hush,' Avicia countered. 'Now, Mary, you too may be a fair maidkin, but I cannot know for sure if you remain hidden behind your sister. Come, present yourself to me, so I may also bid you good morrow.'

There was a long silence. Eliza went to move, to force Mary to reveal herself, but Avicia rested her hand on her shoulder. Finally, Mary shuffled forward an inch or two and pulled her hair across her face. An indecipherable sound left her lips.

'And good morrow to you,' said Avicia, giving her the benefit of the doubt. 'Now when I saw you yester-morn, there were two dolls you were playing with. Maud was one, wasn't she? Where is she hiding? I want her to bid me good morrow.'

Eliza grinned. 'Silly,' she said, stretching out the word. 'Dolls can't talk, don't you know that?'

Mary nodded agreement.

'Don't be contrary with the prioress,' Sister Agnes blurted out, instinctively defending Avicia's authority despite the ridiculousness of her request. Avicia gave her a wink. Sister Agnes's jaw fell in astonishment.

Avicia turned back to Eliza. 'When I was small, I had a doll and we talked every day. In a silent tongue that only the two of us could hear. Don't you do that with Maud?'

Eliza frowned. 'You were small like us once? So, you have done the splitting?'

Avicia glanced over to Sister Agnes, looking for an answer. She received a helpless, panicked stare.

'Every grown-up was small once,' Avicia said. 'If you eat all your food and pray to God every day, you will grow up too.' She caught Mary's look of dismay. 'And you too, Mary. That's what happens to all good children.'

'And the splitting. When does that happen? Is it painful? Mary is so annoying, I hate being with her.'

Mary started sobbing at this and Avicia seized on the distraction to avoid answering the question. 'See what you have done, Eliza,' she said, feigning annoyance. 'We'll have no more talk of splitting today. Let us talk of laughter instead. You brought much merriment to me when you tumbled over with your legs in the air. The two of you looked for all the world like a playful puppy, wanting someone to tickle its tummy.'

Eliza wrinkled her nose. 'What's a puppy?'

Avicia tried not to show her surprise. 'A young dog. Sturdy, the abbey's mastiff, was one once. All animals are small when they are born and grow bigger.'

Avicia saw that this too was a novel concept for Eliza. She turned to Sister Agnes and beckoned her to the far side of the room, away from the children. She spoke in a whisper.

'Tell me, good Sister, what do these girls know of the outside world?'

'They know nothing, Mother Avicia,' Sister Agnes whispered in reply. 'This room is their world, a few playthings their only possessions. Sister Margaret allows me to take them for a walk the length of the abbey walls once a day, and I show them the birds in the sky, the plants in the ground, the farmyard animals that roam inside these walls. They know no other children and thus speak more in the manner of the sisters than that of others their age.' She turned to look at the girls, and her voice grew louder. 'I visit them after Vespers, and I read from the Bible or tell them a fable I remember from my childhood. All they know of the world comes from this.'

'Oh, yes,' Eliza said, bouncing up and down. 'Sister Agnes tells us all about baby Jesus. Tell us of the wise men's journey to Bethlehem tonight, Sister Agnes. Please?'

Sister Agnes smiled at Eliza's enthusiasm. 'We will see,' she said. She looked at Avicia and shrugged. 'I have to do extra penance to get this dispensation from the other sisters. But it is worth it to see the joy these few moments bring to them.'

'They seem strong of word and mind for such little stimulation.' Avicia pursed her lips in thought. 'How can it be?'

Sister Agnes raised her chin high. 'They are remarkable beings, Mother Avicia. When on their own, they are in constant discussion with each other. Even Mary, who is so quiet in the presence of others, has a lively tongue when alone with her sister. They debate, explain, question each other every waking moment of their day. The smallest grain of learning is seized upon and expanded by their inquisitive minds.'

'There is so much I need to learn about them. What is their daily routine? Do the other sisters care for them also?'

Sister Agnes's face clouded over. She moved towards Avicia and whispered in her ear. 'I will speak no ill of the women of faith in this good place. These children are bathed every morning, kept nourished by our garden's bounty, and taught the path of righteousness. But the sisters pray every day for them to be released from their mortal torment and pass into God's kingdom. When they first arrived, it was thought that they would be here no more than a few days. But they are still with us and grow stronger every day.' Her voice became even quieter. 'There is talk of what must be done to aid their passing.'

Eliza led the scuttling to be near them. 'Tell us, Sister Agnes, tell us what you say. Are you talking about us?'

Avicia smiled at the girls. 'She was telling me how clever you two can be. It was whispered so you do not become vain and conceited, for that would be a sin.'

There were squeals of delight from the two girls.

'May we be excused for a moment?' Avicia said to Eliza and Mary. 'I need to hear of some pressing matters from Sister Agnes, but we will return soon.'

Eliza struggled to hide her disappointment. 'You won't come back. No-one ever does.'

'I promise, in God's name,' Avicia replied. 'A few minutes, not more. Prepare your dolls for me to inspect on my return.'

She stepped out, Sister Agnes following, and they walked briskly away from the room until they were out of earshot.

'I have heard this talk,' she said to Sister Agnes. 'Gundulf has been petitioned on this very topic and he awaits my thoughts on the right path to take. It is costing the abbey dear that it can receive no visitors while the secret of these maids is hidden in its midst. Tell me more of their torment. How much do we know of how they share a body?'

'The join is at the waist, towards the spine. That is why they face a little away from each other. I am no physician, but I can see all the vital organs are separate – heart, lung, stomach, each maid has her own. They have developed a way of walking where they co-ordinate their legs after a fashion, but they stumble if one of them forgets or their concentration lapses. They put their arms around each other for balance; Eliza makes the most use of her right hand, Mary her left. Mary is slightly larger, so she has to bear some of Eliza's weight. It puts a lot of strain on her, so she is the frailer of the two. If one is to become sick, it is always Mary. This creates the imbalance in Eliza's blood, and she quickly succumbs to the same ailment.

'Their blood is shared? It flows freely between them?'

'Of course. Eliza eats quickly and when she feels full, Mary tells us she feels the same. But it's Eliza's body receiving sustenance and Mary does not know she is starving. Every day there is a danger Mary could waste away and take Eliza with her.'

'Some, it seems, would call that a blessing.'

'True, Mother Avicia.'

Avicia saw a tremendous seriousness in the depth of her eyes.

'When they were babes,' continued Sister Agnes, 'no-one thought they would be long for this world. Now that all can see they grow strong, some would encourage Eliza to eat more than plenty, to do harm to Mary. But they are survivors, these two, and intelligent. They know of this consequence and Eliza makes sure Mary matches her for every mouthful of food.'

'They know this consequence because you enlightened them. Am I right?'

Sister Agnes flushed. 'I could not stand aside and see them die in a manner that could be avoided. But I am their sole advocate amongst the obedientiaries. When it was noticed they had started to co-ordinate their eating, there was an inquiry. I was almost banished from the abbey as a result.'

Suddenly, there were screams and crying.

'We will talk more of this,' Avicia said. 'Come, let us find out the reason for this commotion.'

They entered the room to find Mary clinging to the two rag dolls, Eliza trying to wrest them from her.

'Girls, girls!' said Sister Agnes. 'Why this uproar? Eliza, leave poor Mary alone.'

'I don't want Eliza to have Maud,' Mary sobbed. 'She's my doll.'

It was the first time Avicia had heard Mary speak. She was struck by how delicate her voice sounded, like the chiming of a silver bell.

Eliza's face was set in a petulant scowl. 'I wanted to play at splitting, but I need Mary's doll for that. We sew the two dolls together in all sorts of funny places and see what happens when we pull them apart. Sewing the heads together is best.'

'But Maud doesn't like it,' protested Mary. 'Every time, *she* gets ripped, not Edith. I don't want to play anymore.'

Sister Agnes shook her head and bent down to face Eliza. She spoke with a sweet sincerity. 'Eliza, that's a mean game to play with Mary's doll. What is Mother Avicia going to think?'

Eliza glanced over to Avicia, her chin raised in defiance. 'It's me that should be splitting. Mary is always tired and stupid. When will you do the splitting, Mother Avicia? On the morrow? Today? I don't want to wait any longer. If you don't do it now I'll kill Mary and you'll have to cut her off. I hate her.'

Mary burst into tears and Avicia tried to defuse the situation. 'Your blood is getting too hot, Eliza. Sister Agnes will give you some camomile to cool it down. My presence has upset your balance, and some soothing herbs will fix your humour. Do you agree, Sister Agnes?'

'Of course,' she replied. 'There has been too much excitement for one day.' She knelt down to speak to the young girls. 'I want you to draw Noah's ark with your sticks. When I come back this evening, we can recite the story together.'

Mary picked up a stick and began tentatively to scratch on the earth floor. Eliza immediately rubbed out the marks with her foot. The girls started to fight, tearing at each other, frustrated they couldn't strike a proper blow.

Avicia slipped silently out of the room. An ill-formed dread had begun to crystallise into thoughts. Maybe the other sisters were right after all. What kind of life was this?

Chapter 4
Mary

I HATE IT WHEN Eliza plays the stupid splitting game. Maud is always getting ripped, and I have to sew her back afterwards. I feel sad for Maud and hug her and promise I won't play the game again. But Eliza always grabs her when I'm not looking and sews her to Edith and holds her in her far-away hand so I can't reach.

Poor Maud.

Eliza is mean, mean, *mean*. She always takes things that are for both of us and keeps them. Sister Agnes tells her to share with me and calls her selfish.

I want to be selfish sometimes.

Eliza says I'm boring, but that's because The Room is boring. There's nothing to do all day except play with our dolls and when it starts to get dark the light stops coming in through the cracks in the door. And if Maud keeps getting splitted I'm not going to have a doll to play with.

I wish Eliza wouldn't be mean.

She hits me all the time. I used to hit her back, but she's stronger than me and my punches don't hurt her as much as hers hurt me. So now when she starts hitting me I curl into a ball and wait till she stops.

Then it doesn't hurt so much.

Mother Avicia likes Eliza more than me. I can tell. She asked her lots of questions about Edith and when Eliza said she would kill me if we didn't get splitted, Mother Avicia didn't hit her with a broomstick, she asked Sister Agnes to give Eliza some camomile. Even though camomile tastes horrible, Eliza says that means Mother Avicia isn't angry at her for hitting me and that means she likes her more than me and that's why she called her a maidkin.

But Mother Avicia says I might be a maidkin too.

Eliza says that Mother Avicia knows that she is clever and I'm boring and stupid and that's why she likes her and not me. But that's not true. I'm not boring and stupid. I know I'm not, because I have a secret. Eliza says we can't have secrets from each other, but we can.

My secret is called Gerald.

Gerald is the little mouse that lives in our room with us. He's a very nice mouse, but very shy. He only comes out when he knows we are far away, and if we try to sneak over to him, he runs very fast back into his hole before we can catch him. The first time we saw him, Eliza tried to whack him with the broomstick, but now she also thinks he's nice and just wants to catch him so she can play with him.

Eliza doesn't know his name is Gerald. And she doesn't know that I play with him. That's my other secret. When we get our rye bread, I break off a little crumb and drop it at Gerald's mouse hole with my far-away hand. Gerald pops out and gets it and goes into his hole again. Then he pops out again and looks at me to say thank you.

Gerald is a polite mouse.

Eliza says that the reason Mother Avicia has come to visit us is that we are going to be splitted soon and that makes me happy. When we are splitted, Eliza won't be able to hit me anymore and we won't have to live in The Room. I hate The Room. We have to stay in it all day, except in the afternoon, when Sister Agnes takes us for 'the walk'. The walk is the best thing in the world, it's when we get our exercise, which Sister Agnes says is important to make us grow up strong and healthy.

I love the walk. We both do. We come out of The Room and follow the abbey walls all the way round until we get to The Room again. Eliza is much fatter than me because she eats her food so quickly, but I'm taller, so I have to have some of her weight on my side and it gets sore about halfway round. But I don't tell Sister Agnes in case she says we can't do the walk any more.

We've found the best way to move together is to put our arms round each other's shoulders. To start off, Eliza taps me on the shoulder so we both move the same leg at the same time. She usually forgets and stops after a few minutes and then one of us will go too fast and we'll get in a tumble and she always says it's my fault. But she never hits me when we stumble in case Sister Agnes won't let us do the walk again. All the animals in the abbey have their second pair of legs behind the first pair, not side by side, so they don't stumble. But that would mean Eliza was in front of me all the time and I wouldn't see anything.

So it's better we're joined our way.

This is the only time when I do as much talking as Eliza. I ask Sister Agnes about everything, like what would a cow say if it could talk, what do the clouds smell like, where does the sun go at night. Sometimes she tells me, sometimes she says only God knows.

God must know lots of things.

I like the pigs the best, but don't like goats. A goat came up and bumped me with its horns once. Eliza thought it was really funny, but I was scared. I saw a little animal with spikes on one walk, which Sister Agnes said was a hedgehog. She said the big animals can't eat it, because it curls up in a ball and all its spikes stick out.

I wish I had spikes, so when I curled up Eliza couldn't hit me.

But the best, best, best things are the plants. The flowers look so beautiful and Sister Agnes told me that God had given some plants special powers to make people better. There's a garden where she grows the ones that we use in the abbey. I remember she gave me some mint boiled in water the last time I was sick and it made me better.

There's a stream that goes through the middle of the abbey and we have to cross it twice, once where it comes into the abbey and once where it goes out. I like the stream and I used to ask Sister Agnes if we could stop and play in it, but she always said no. It's because there is a Rule the other sisters made that says we can't stop on our walk.

I don't like the Rule.

There were two frogs joined together in the stream once. One was on the other's back, so they hadn't split yet. It looked really uncomfortable.

I'm glad I'm not a frog.

We're usually all excited when we finish the walk and Sister Agnes takes us back to The Room, and it always feels sad when we hear her slide the bolt outside the door and she goes away. Eliza made up a game called Guess Who, where we have to say out loud who the next person to open the door will be, and the winner is the one who gets it right. One time Sister Roesia came instead of Sister Agnes or Sister Margaret so neither of us was right.

That was funny.

But ever since Mother Avicia arrived things have been different. Yestermorn, we missed praying twice and had to pray to God ourselves and Eliza did a bad thing. And today Sister Agnes said we couldn't do the walk because she had to talk to Mother Avicia. Eliza says it must be the splitting and she chooses Mother Avicia for Guess Who because she is important and she will be doing the splitting. But I choose Sister Agnes because she is kind and will tell us what is happening. But it is Sister Margaret who brings us dinner and says prayers with us, and she won't answer any of our questions.

Tonight is even worse than last night for trying to get to sleep. I hear Gerald scurrying around the room and smile as I think about my secret.

Soon, I will have lots of secrets.

Chapter 5

AVICIA CALLED an obedientiaries council the next day. It would be best to determine the Maids' fate quickly, she had decided, before sentiment could cloud her reasoning and stop her from seeing clearly what action should be taken. Sister Margaret, Sister Agnes and the four other senior nuns were already assembled in the chapter house.

They celebrated Mass, then Avicia started the discussion.

'Remind us, Sister Margaret, of the story of the Maids. How did they come to be in the abbey?'

Sister Margaret frowned. 'Their story is known to all of us, Mother Avicia. Is there a need for a fresh account of it?'

Avicia tried to hide her displeasure. 'We are discussing the fate of two human souls, Sister Margaret. We will spare neither time nor distress in making our deliberations. The story should be told again, so we are all of one mind in knowing the facts before us. You were the only one amongst us who was here for their coming. Tell us the circumstances.'

Sister Margaret tugged at the hood of her habit before replying. 'The Maids, as you call them, were born in the village of Biddenden, in the Lathe of Scraye, just over a day's journey from here, in the summer of the year of our Lord 1100. They were born to the Chulkhursts, a respectable family of that village, who own a large longhouse and a sulung of land, one hundred and sixty good acres. The land was granted by Walter de Meduana, who came to England with the Conqueror, when Thomas Chulkhurst married de Meduana's daughter Juliana.'

'And Juliana?' Avicia asked. 'What became of her?'

'She died from the ordeal of the birth. By all accounts, she was spared from knowing what was plucked from her womb.'

One of the sisters started sobbing. Avicia silenced her. 'We cannot allow ourselves the indulgence of expressing our sorrows in these discussions,' she told the nun. 'Only by being strong of heart will we conclude matters today. Go on, Sister Margaret.'

'A great madness descended on the family, and Thomas Chulkhurst forbade any visitors to the estate, save for a wet nurse to care for the infants and the village priest to baptise them with due haste. They were admitted into the family of Christ, and there the story should have ended. But in his madness, Thomas Chulkhurst petitioned Bishop Gundulf to spare them having their lives ended at the hand of man.'

'And the petition succeeded, did it not?' Avicia said. 'And the abbey we have today is the result of Thomas's generosity.'

Sister Margaret gave a grudging nod. 'Gundulf sent word to Thomas that any knowledge of the Maids would bring terror to the hearts of the simple villagers of Biddenden, who would fear a monster was living in their midst. He sought to assuage Thomas's madness by inviting him to take over the sponsorship of this abbey, so our sisters would have their own order and not provide temptation to the monks of Rochester. Thomas agreed to hand over all that remained of Juliana's dowry to bring this to pass, and promised an annual stipend for as long as the Maids remained here. We prepared for the infants' arrival with all possible haste, and they were moved here in secret once a secure place of accommodation away from prying eyes had been prepared for them.'

'And good Thomas Chulkhurst's benefaction has provided not only for the Maids' sustenance but also for the growth of the abbey these last six years, has it not?'

Sister Margaret glanced uneasily around the room. 'Thomas Chulkhurst has indeed been generous. But now he has taken a new wife, and I fear the alms we have been receiving will cease when she bears fruit. There is not only a compassionate reason to release the Maids from their suffering.' She looked around, as though seeking support from the other nuns, then continued: 'They are a cost to this abbey which we will no longer be able to bear.'

The starkness of this last comment left a cold silence in the room. All the nuns knew the abbey had precarious finances and the recent cut in rations had left everyone weakened by a lack of food. Faintings during manual labour, and even at prayers, were becoming more and more frequent. The celebrations for Avicia's arrival had exhausted their meagre reserves. Consternation at this news – that things could get still worse – was writ large on every face.

Everyone waited for Avicia to speak.

'The pecuniary affairs of the abbey should not be talked of so freely, Sister Margaret,' she said at last. 'And speculation on its future should have no bearing on the decision here before us.'

The two nuns glowered at each other, their stares meeting like crossed swords.

'Forgive me, Mother Avicia,' Sister Margaret replied, 'but I beg to differ. It was easy to keep the Maids hidden when they were babes in arms. But now they have grown, we are forbidden to have merchants visit the abbey, lest they discover what is in our midst. Our school has had to close also, with the loss of many handsome stipends, in case the pupils hear the sounds of the Maids from their room. The Chulkhurst alms can no longer compensate. Our buildings are falling into disrepair, we cannot put sufficient food on the table, and still we provide every day for two unfortunate souls who live a life of the most wretched torment. As they grow bigger, the demands the Maids will make of us will grow greater and greater. It cannot be right, Mother Avicia, that this state of affairs is allowed to continue.'

The assembled nuns ventured a low murmur of agreement, but Avicia set her jaw in defiance.

'"Suffer little children to come unto me, and forbid them not: for of such is the kingdom of God." That is what the Good Book tells us. We must accept whatever hardship this life of ours forces us to endure. I will not do evil to alleviate it. You are right, Sister Margaret. The status quo cannot continue. The Maids are innocent of all sin, yet they spend their life with no more freedom than a caged animal. As long as they are on this Earth, they should be loved, and be allowed to flourish and grow. We need to plan for their freedom, that they might see even a little of the world outside these four walls.'

There was a collective gasp. Avicia silently remonstrated with herself. She had said more than she planned. She had promised herself she would secure the Maids' position before venturing to improve it. No matter, she told herself. What's done is done.

Sister Roesia was the first to speak. 'The abbey is dying, Mother Avicia. We are failing in our duty to provide help to those who come to our door. I feel sorrow for the plight of the Maids, but their predicament should not be allowed to cause the suffering of others. If they have to remain in the abbey, then I must beg leave to move to Syon Abbey, to join the order there.'

Sister Margaret seized the moment. 'Mother Avicia, I too would wish to depart for Syon. And many other sisters, all pious disciples, good and true, have shared with me their confidences that they are of the same mind. The consequences, should the Maids stay in our care, will be grave indeed.'

'I will stay with Mother Avicia and provide guardianship, even if I am the last to remain,' Sister Agnes said quietly. 'To banish the Maids from our care would be sentence of death. They cannot fend for themselves, and even if a home could be found for them, they would be set upon by the superstitious and the fearful and be slain most hideously. Good sisters, find mercy in your souls. Do not sentence these blameless innocents to death.'

There was silence. Avicia waited, hoping at least one of the other nuns would support Sister Agnes's plea.

But there was nothing.

Finally, Avicia spoke. 'If this is the will of you all, then I have to acquiesce. It must be a collective decision.'

Sister Agnes began sobbing as Avicia continued, 'I will write to Gundulf this day, telling him the future of the abbey is in doubt, and I will abide by whatever decision he may make. Trust me to write in good faith, dear sisters, and let us all await his reply before precipitating any action. For my part, I will sanction no changes to the Maids' routine until we know of their fate.'

Avicia feared what Gundulf would say. The Bishop was a good man, famed for his ability to instigate and guide many of the great building projects of the age. He had overseen the construction of the White Tower, the keep of the Tower of London, then built his church in Rochester and, soon afterwards, Colchester Castle and Rochester Priory. He had founded the abbey at Malling eighteen years earlier, but only through the generosity of Thomas Chulkhurst had it grown enough to justify its own prioress. With the prospect of the Chulkhurst funds drying up, and the presence of the Maids hampering any attempts to generate commerce with the outside world, Gundulf would be forced to choose between safeguarding the Maids and seeing one of his lifetime projects wither and die. Knowing his pride and ambition, Avicia was certain what his decision would be.

In her letter to Gundulf, Avicia forced herself to spell out in the starkest, clearest terms the consequences of the Maids remaining in the abbey, adding her own view that continuing to keep two otherwise normal, lively and inquisitive children locked up and unable to experience any glimpse of the outside world was heaping further cruelty on top of their already desperate plight. The current situation could not continue. The Maids deserved either their freedom or an end to their ordeal. She, his loyal prioress, would abide by whatever course of action he decided upon.

Avicia sealed the letter with her signet ring for immediate despatch, fearing in her heart that she had signed the Maids' death warrant.

Gundulf's reply, when it came, was a shock. He would journey to the abbey to inspect the workings of the convent straight away, he wrote, and during the visit would hear representations concerning the fate of the Maids and make his pronouncement. Avicia's brow furrowed as she read his words. This made no sense. If the Maids' fate were to be sealed, Gundulf would not want his name and reputation associated with such a heinous atrocity. Avicia had expected a circumspect message whispered discreetly from one of Gundulf's trusted couriers if the Maids were to meet their end, or a written edict pronouncing their salvation if they were to be saved. Why Gundulf was involving himself so personally was a mystery.

ONE OF THE OBLATES brought news of Gundulf's imminent arrival a few days later, and when he appeared without ceremony Avicia was horrified.

'My lord Gundulf, we have had no notice of your visit, and no preparations have been made or festivities organised. I feel only shame at this lack of respect.'

'I chose to come without ceremony or fanfare,' the Bishop replied. 'I even dismissed my guide when we caught sight of your walls, so that I might talk to you alone. He waits at the village. There are urgent matters we need to discuss and any ceremony would be an unnecessary and time-consuming distraction. I was deeply troubled to receive your missive, by which you placed the fate of two innocent souls in my hands.'

'That was not my intention, Bishop Gundulf. But I find myself torn as to what path to take. The Maids grow stronger every day, confounding all expectations. They have the minds of two normal six-year-old girls but are imprisoned here, seeing nothing of the outside world. Their presence prevents the abbey receiving visitors, and now there are rumours that Thomas Chulkhurst taking a new wife could mean his alms may soon come to an end. Things cannot continue as they are.'

'Then my course of action has been the right one,' Gundulf replied. 'I summoned Thomas Chulkhurst to meet with us here because only his deep pockets can prevent the tragedy of the Maids' demise. His choice will be a simple one. He must make a fivefold increase in annual payments to remedy the abbey's finances and also construct a permanent home for the Maids here – hidden behind the chapter house so no visitor would ever suspect their presence ...' Gundulf paused. 'Or he must shoulder the responsibility of dealing with them as he sees fit.'

'As he sees fit?'

Gundulf ran his fingers through his long beard. 'It must be his decision, Mother Avicia. The Church baptised these poor creatures and gave them sanctuary. I saw them then, and the sight has haunted me ever since. You say they are now of strong mind and body. If that is so, things have changed since the dark days of yesteryear. New provisions will have to be made.'

'No father would sanction any action that could lead to the deaths of his daughters, no matter how unfortunate their lot in life,' Avicia said. She took a deep breath. 'Bishop Gundulf, your plan has shown yet again your wisdom and compassion. With God's help, the Maids can be saved.'

Gundulf smiled. 'Your sweet words may also play a part, Mother Avicia. Now, I must return to the village. It is not seemly that a man, even one who has taken his vows, should spend a night here. But first, I need to see for myself how the Maids have grown since I saw them last, these six years ago.'

Avicia bit her lip to prevent her own smile turning into a grin. 'I would be honoured to present them to you, Bishop Gundulf. But you should be prepared for the upset your visit may provoke.'

Gundulf's eyes narrowed. 'I do not need counsel from my prioress to summon courage to cast my eyes upon the Maids. I have seen the horrors of the battlefield, Mother Avicia. I think I can cope with whatever sight awaits me here.'

Avicia swallowed, her smile faltering. 'I do not question your fortitude, Bishop Gundulf. It is the Maids who may be fearful, not you. They have only ever been visited by the nuns of the abbey. They have never seen a man. It is they who need to be warned of the uncommon sight they are about to behold.'

Gundulf barked a laugh. 'How arrogant we are, to say what is fair and what is foul. Tell them of my presence, and reassure them I am a man of God, not some demon come to harm them. For my part, I will take care not to alarm their virtuous souls.'

'I will have Sister Agnes tell them of you. She is the one the Maids trust more than any other. Shall I summon her?'

'You forget protocol, Mother Avicia. I should greet your senior nun first before I meet with a more junior obedientiary.' He narrowed his eyes. 'From your words, am I to understand that all is not well here in the abbey?'

Avicia felt herself blush. 'Forgive me, Bishop Gundulf, I forget myself. There is indeed discord amongst the obedientiaries in respect of the Maids. Sister Margaret holds opinions that differ from mine.'

Gundulf shrugged. 'I expected that there would be discord. Let me greet her as briefly as respect demands, and then proceed to my audience with the Maids. I cannot stay long. I need to return to the village before nightfall – I hope by then to have news of Thomas Chulkhurst's arrival.'

The formalities with Sister Margaret were performed briskly, then Avicia summoned Sister Agnes to prepare the Maids for their audience with Bishop Gundulf. Avicia and Gundulf waited outside the Maids' room while Sister Agnes went inside to tell them the news.

Avicia entered first, followed by Gundulf. The Maids gasped in astonishment at the sight of Gundulf, then Eliza burst out laughing.

'His face is upside down,' she cried. 'Look, his chin is on the top!'

Sister Agnes froze with embarrassment for a moment, then ran over to Eliza, her hand raised to smack her for her impudence. She made a show of delivering the blow, but pulled back her hand at the last moment so it was no more than a gentle tap.

'Eliza, shame on you for your disrespect,' Sister Agnes said, wagging her finger. 'Bishop Gundulf is a great man, who has many demands on his time, yet he has travelled all the way here to check on your wellbeing. He will be shocked by your insolence.'

Eliza cried and Gundulf stood tall, stroking the top of his tonsure, common to all monks after taking their vows. Avicia detected a twinkle in his eye at Eliza's indiscretion. But when he spoke, his voice boomed authority. 'Eliza Chulkhurst, bow down to me and I will forgive your lack of respect.' In a gentler tone, he added, 'And you, young Mary, bow with your sister also. I will lay my hand upon you and give you my blessing.'

'Do as the good Bishop tells you,' Sister Agnes said to the Maids, her eyes wide with anxiety. Eliza's cry softened to a snivel as she and Mary clumsily attempted a bow.

Gundulf stepped over, laid a hand on each girl's shoulder and gave them a blessing.

'Now, young maids, let me hear you recite the Lord's Prayer.' He turned to the nuns. 'I trust you have taught them the word of our Lord, Sister Agnes?'

Sister Agnes nodded and turned to the Maids. 'Do as Bishop Gundulf says, my charges. "Our Father, Who art in Heaven …"'

The Maids picked up the verse and recited in unison. Avicia could see Sister Agnes's relief when they finished.

Gundulf nodded his appreciation. 'Well remembered, for ones so young,' he said.

Emboldened by the praise, Eliza glanced at him shyly and spoke in a whisper. 'Would you like to hear it as Jesus said it?' Her sister squirmed in embarrassment and whined her disapproval. Eliza shushed her.

Gundulf nodded, as though unsurprised by the request. Avicia gave a helpless shrug.

'You have a confidence that belies your years, Eliza Chulkhurst,' said the Bishop. 'Let me hear it.'

'*Pater noster qui es in caelis, sanctificetur nomen tuum, adveniat regnum tuum …*'

When she finished, there was a stunned silence.

Gundulf gave a half-breathless murmur of incredulity. 'I have witnessed a miracle here today, Mother Avicia, Sister Agnes,' he said. 'We need tarry no longer. I have seen enough.'

Gundulf departed for Malling village and Sister Agnes could barely disguise her glee, wringing her hands at the performance of the Maids and the news of their father's imminent arrival.

'The Maids have done themselves proud, have they not?' she said to Avicia.

The prioress nodded, but she didn't share Sister Agnes's optimism.

'Gundulf is truly a saint amongst men, Sister Agnes, and he could not have been more impressed by the Maids' intelligence and piety. But he is also very astute when it comes to managing the treasuries of the church. Thomas Chulkhurst's benefaction was, by all accounts, very generous, and Gundulf will want to make sure a wealthy patron is not dissuaded from making further restitutions to guarantee his place in Heaven. His visit may have more to do with matters of commerce than we might think.'

'I know our coffers are empty,' Sister Agnes replied. 'But one look at the Maids and Thomas Chulkhurst will open his heart and dig deep into his purse. Then you can offer more schooling to tempt other fathers to send their daughters here as oblates to become the new obedientiaries, replacing any that might leave. We can construct a fine building to allow the Maids to grow and flourish and learn a little of what lies outside these walls. They and the abbey will survive.'

Avicia shrugged. 'Thomas Chulkhurst has taken a new wife. She will want to bear him children and put the Maids furthermost from his mind. We might represent a shame from his past that he now thinks it best to forget. Sister Margaret will be persuasive in convincing him the Maids will feel no pain in the manner of their passing and their death will be a blessed relief. It is only when I meet him that I will know what sort of man he is and whether he is strong enough to resist such temptations.'

And with that, she knelt and prayed.

GUNDULF ARRIVED BACK at the abbey mid-morning the next day. His face was grim.

'Thomas Chulkhurst will arrive on the morrow, and it was important I met with you again before our deliberations.'

'What of his arrival could alarm you so much?' Avicia said, her stomach tightening.

'He travels not just with a guide as I instructed, but with his new bride, Gudrun. I hear she has been a boon to him and that she has finally cured him of the melancholy that possessed him after Juliana's death. But I have also heard tell that Gudrun is a woman of ambition. She came from a low rank in his household and is trying to establish herself, to be accepted by the local elders and esquires as being fit to be the new lady of the estate. They have been married for two years, but so far she has proven barren. No new offspring. I fear her presence will not be conducive to any attempt to persuade Thomas Chulkhurst to take more responsibility for the future of the Maids.'

'Indeed,' said Avicia. 'It is not good for the Maids. But a second wife knows it is her duty to care for the family of her predecessor. We can but hope she is of strong enough character to honour and fulfil her marital obligations.'

Avicia tried to speak with confidence, but she knew her words sounded hollow. Gudrun had not been invited to the meeting; Gundulf had made clear it was for Thomas Chulkhurst alone to decide the Maids' fate. She must have forced her will upon her husband to be allowed to attend as well. That meant she was persuasive, and determined to influence the outcome.

The Maids were a dark secret of which she would want no part. Avicia feared that Gudrun had come to make sure that secret remained buried forever.

Chapter 6
Eliza

Mother Avicia gives Mary and me a hug when she visits with Sister Margaret for morning prayers. Nobody has ever done that before except Sister Agnes, and she has a little cry afterwards. But Mother Avicia doesn't cry. I like that.

I tell Mary it is because Mother Avicia loves us very, very much and doesn't like to say goodbye and lock us up in The Room again. It is funny to have someone who's not *us* touch me; it is so different from when Mary does it. I know the stroke of Mary's hand like it is my own. But when Mother Avicia touches me, my mind jumps out of my body and I believe I can run and skip and fly through the air. Maybe that's how birds are able to fly.

Mary laughs when Mother Avicia hugs her, and that's when I like being joined to her. She gives these little shakes and they come over into my body, like someone is tickling me, tickling me from the inside. And I can't help it, I start laughing too. Mary's not joined to me. She *is* me. I like it when she puts tickles inside me.

But after the prayers, Mary makes us stumble so I do my backward whack, the one where I hit her on the back of her head with my far-away arm. She deserves it, but she screams so loud into my ear I have to scream back to stop my head from exploding. Then Mary tries to scream even louder, which I know is because Sister Margaret and Mother Avicia are there. So I hit her again, to get her to be quiet.

Sister Margaret hits me with the broomstick three times and Mary twice, before Mother Avicia stops her. It's the first time I've seen Mother Avicia grumpy. Sister Margaret is grumpy with us all the time. It's Mary that Mother Avicia should be grumpy with. It's all Mary's fault we had a fight, because she stumbled and then screamed so loud.

The prioress doesn't hit Sister Margaret with the broomstick. That would have been funny. She does a yelling, like when Sister Margaret yells at us, but not so loud.

It is so amazing to see that Mary and I stop screaming. Then Mother Avicia tells me I need to stop hitting Mary or I won't go to Heaven. I ask her about Mary and she says Mary will go, because I hit her first. I say that is good, because that means God will have to split us and I will stay in The Room all on my own and Mary will be all on her own in Heaven.

Mother Avicia says no-one is going to heaven just yet and I have to learn to be kind to Mary and stop hitting her.

When the door to The Room opens in the afternoon, Mother Avicia is there on her own. She always comes with Sister Margaret or Sister Agnes and I worry they might have gone to Heaven and not said goodbye. But what she tells us is even more amazing.

Our mother and father are coming to visit us!

I haven't ever thought about having a mother and father. Mother Avicia told us Sturdy had been a puppy and she herself had once been a little girl. The other sisters must have been maids too, before they became nuns, and they

must have mothers and fathers, but nobody has told us we
have ones.

Mother Avicia explains that Mother is not our real
mother. Our real mother was very tired after we were born
and so God took her to Heaven to have a rest. But Father is
our real father and although Mother isn't our real mother,
she loves Father very much and he loves her too and they
are both coming to see us. Bishop Gundulf liked our Lord's
Prayer so much he told Mother and Father to come and hear
us do it. I feel very clever I thought up the idea to say it the
way Jesus says it. I don't tell Mother Avicia all these things,
in case it makes Mary feel stupid.

I've been so busy thinking all this, I don't hear what Mother
Avicia says next and it is only when I feel Mary's tickling that
I realise I've missed something good. Mother and Father are
coming to see us this very day! I wonder if Father will have
hair on the bottom of his head like Bishop Gundulf ...

Mother Avicia tells us it is very, very, *very* important
we are good girls at the meeting, and we must not get too
excited. She gives us a strange look and says she has to rush
off to get things ready, and tells us that once Sister Agnes
has finished her urgent tasks she will come and prepare us
for the meeting. As we hear the door lock, Mary and I both
fall on our backs and wave our legs in the air. We do that
when we are excited and we always know exactly when we're
going to do it, without any signals or anything. We do it for
the longest time.

Mary spoils it by starting to cry.

'I'm scared, Eliza, about meeting Mother and Father. They
won't like me, only you. You're the pretty one. You think of
the clever things to say. I'm ugly and stupid.'

I know this to be true, but now I have to be nice to Mary so she doesn't spoil everything by screaming again when the time comes.

'You can sing a lullaby. Sing *Lalla, Lalla, Lalla*, that's your favourite. You can sing that, can't you?'

Mary smiles suddenly. 'I *can* sing that. Will they let me? *Lalla, Lalla, Lalla, aut dormi, aut lacte, nisi*— I can't remember the rest …' Her voice is trembling.

'You can stop there,' I tell her. That is very clever of me. Now she'll sing that one single line and that will make her feel good and not start screaming. And I can say the Lord's Prayer like Jesus and they'll know I'm the clever one.

'Why do you think they're coming to visit us?' Mary asks. 'First Mother Avicia, then Bishop Gundulf, now Mother and Father. What does it mean?'

'We must be getting ready for the splitting,' I reply, nodding very fast. 'Yes, that must be it. Bishop Gundulf is going to split us in two, so we can go and live with Mother and Father. He'll probably do it before Mother and Father arrive, so we're all ready for them when they get here.'

Mary sends me a giggle. 'I hope so, I hope so, goodbye, goodbye, boring old *room*, boring old *room* …'

'Goodbye, goodbye, boring old *room*.' We chant together. 'Boring, boring, boring. Splitting, splitting, splitting.' We sing the words over and over until our throats are sore.

But it isn't Bishop Gundulf standing there when the door is unlocked in the afternoon. It's only Sister Agnes, who bustles in like a startled hen.

'My dears, my dears, they have arrived and are awaiting you. Oh, Eliza, what have you done to your hair? Come, child, let me attend to you.'

There's nothing wrong with my hair, but Sister Agnes fusses away, running a comb through it until I think she will never stop. Mary has a proud look on her face and I can tell she's pleased that it is me Sister Agnes needs to get ready. I don't tell her not to be so boastful because then she'll cry and spoil everything. Sometimes I can be so, so clever.

When we arrive at the chapter house we see the most amazing sight. Every one of the nuns is there, even old Sister Wymarc who seems to live in the infirmary. Sister Agnes sits us down, facing everyone. It's strange, and a little frightening at first, seeing all these faces. Most of the nuns glance away when I look at them, but the young ones stare at us with big wide eyes, waving their hands to fan their faces, even though it's not at all hot. It looks so silly, it makes me giggle. When Sister Margaret sees that, she gives me the look she has when she uses the broomstick. But we're safe. There is no broomstick, and that makes me giggle all the more.

I try to stop when Mother Avicia comes into the room with Bishop Gundulf. Behind them are two people who look like a king and queen. At least that's how a king and queen look in my head. The man has a short tunic lined with fur, that fits much more tightly than Bishop Gundulf's robes, and a hooded cloak. He has the same hair on the bottom of his face that all men must have, but his is short and he has hair on top, so it doesn't look as silly. The woman has a long blue gown and is not wearing a wimple and veil, so her red hair is all past her shoulders and it moves as she walks. She looks like a tall, flickering candle. Mary gasps, and my own skin tingles. Could this be Mother and Father? I can hardly breathe. Suddenly I feel very ugly and want to burst into tears. No mother and father this beautiful will want children like us.

The woman covers her mouth and starts choking. I wonder why she hasn't finished eating – maybe she had to hurry to get here on time. She presses her hands to her stomach and at first I think she is going to be sick and spoil everything, but the man puts his arm around her and turns her away. He is saying something. I try so hard to hear what it is, but he speaks too quietly. Sister Agnes produces a cup with steam rising from it. I sniff the air. It's mint. She walks over to give it to the woman, who takes one sip, then gulps it all down. The woman looks at the man, but he stands there, not helping her at all. Finally, Mother Avicia takes her by the hand and motions for her to sit on one of the seats at the front that has been kept empty. The woman looks at the man with wide, starey eyes. He holds the seat for her and she falls into it, as if she's tired. The man sits down slowly in the other seat and takes the woman's hand. She looks away, shielding her eyes with her other hand.

Perhaps beautiful women have delicate eyes and don't like the light.

My heart is bursting with excitement. Mother Avicia will inform us they are indeed Mother and Father and we will tell them our names and they will jump out of their seats and give me a big hug and tell me how much they love me and I will tell them I love them and they will give Mary a hug after me and she will say the same and not scream and all the nuns will clap and cheer and Mother will start feeling better and everyone will be happy and Mary will sing her song and everyone will clap and I will say the Lord's Prayer and everyone will clap even louder and Father will make a fine speech about how wonderful it all is.

But no.

Bishop Gundulf says a prayer. It's in Latin and I don't understand it and it goes on for ages. Mother Avicia stands up and says our names, but there is none of the usual gaiety in her voice. Mary sings her lullaby line and when she finishes there is silence. I say the Lord's Prayer and try to sound very grown up, but once again nobody says anything. My heart shrinks inside me. For a moment, there is silence in the room.

Gundulf speaks. 'So, you can see they are not imbeciles ...' His voice echoes off the wall of the chapter house. I don't know what that word means, but it sounds nasty so I'm glad I'm not one. 'The Maids are ready and prepared to submit to any interrogation, at your pleasure. Come forth with your questions, good Thomas Chulkhurst.'

That means for sure he really is Father. I wait for him to speak, hoping I'll sound clever when I give him my answer. And suddenly I feel scared he'll ask Mary a question and she'll go into one of her stupid silent moods.

Finally, Father clears his throat and speaks to us both.

'Tell me your names, good Maids, so that I may tell which of my daughters you are.'

Mother starts crying. She must be sad we are not her real children.

'I am Eliza and this is Mary,' I say quickly. I smile at how clever I've been, answering for us both. I pause and then add, 'Most noble Father.'

There is a gasp from the room. Mother squirms in her seat and turns even further away from us. She must be shy, even shyer than Mary. I didn't know big people could be shy.

Father acknowledges my address with a nod and pats Mother's arm. She pulls it away and runs out of the room. Father stands up and looks at Bishop Gundulf.

'We need stay no longer, Bishop Gundulf. I have seen enough.'

Mother Avicia claps her hands uncertainly and the nuns start to walk in silence towards the door, one by one.

Mary turns and stares at me in confusion and I too am surprised. Is that it? Surely Father will want to know lots more about us, and tell us all about Mother and himself? But no. Without pausing to bid us farewell, Father rushes off after Mother. Perhaps he loves her so much he cannot bear to be a moment without her.

Soon it is just Mary and me and Mother Avicia and Sister Margaret. Mother Avicia looks worried. I don't like that.

Mother Avicia tells Sister Margaret to take us back to The Room and we are dragged there by her to get us locked in as quickly as possible. I call out questions all the way there. What does she think of Mother and Father? Do they love us? When will we see them again? But she never speaks once. As I hear the bolt sliding into place on the other side of the door, Mary begins to weep. I can't help myself – I start weeping too.

'Don't worry,' I tell Mary. 'Sister Agnes knows all the healing herbs. Once she fixes Mother's stomach, Mother and Father will come and visit us again. On their own this time. They will tell us all about their fine house and when we can go to visit them there. You'll see, Mary. Everything will be all right.'

There. Now I've said it, it must come true.

But they don't come to visit. When Vespers are completed, Sister Agnes comes with our supper and tells us that Father has left with Mother for the village inn and they are going to stay there until Mother gets better. But she won't tell us when Mother and Father will come to see us again. She does promise everything will be all right, just as I said to Mary. Then she makes the sign of the cross.

That's good. Now God knows she's promised too.

Chapter 7

Thomas Chulkhurst arrived back at the abbey the next morning to meet with Bishop Gundulf. Gundulf took him to the sacristy, a separate room attached to the main abbey building, explaining that there was less chance their conversation would be overheard. Thomas kissed the Bishop's ring, then steadied himself against the wall. Gundulf adjusted the lie of his cassock. Thomas had no wish to be the first to speak, and it seemed he was not alone.

In the end, Gundulf broke the silence. 'I trust the humour of your good lady wife is improved?', he said, running his fingers over a tapestry that hung from the wall, clearly unwilling to meet his visitor's gaze. 'She saw something to which no lady of tender sensibilities should be exposed.'

'Gudrun is no delicate flower who needs protection from the misadventures of the world,' Thomas replied. He felt the colour rising in his cheeks. 'She was raised from humble beginnings, the daughter of a cotter from the wasteland north of the Outbounds of Smithsditch. She fears nothing.'

'Yestermorn, she buckled at a sight she knew to expect, did she not? And fled the room, causing our consideration of the Maids to be ended prematurely.' Gundulf paused, and still refused to meet Thomas's eye. 'A husband might have wished to … shield his wife from such horrors. Women do not have the constitution of men to behold such things and stay strong. Even when they have the strong heart of a milkmaid.'

'It was that strong heart that made her insist on accompanying me, knowing the horrors that awaited us here,' Thomas replied, forcing himself to speak in a measured, respectful tone. 'Yestermorn was a momentary lapse of decorum, from which she has recovered. She awaits the results of our deliberations and I will seek her council on whatever we propose. There are many in Biddenden who have expressed scorn at a man of means marrying a cotter's daughter and having her at his side when deciding on matters of the estate. I did not expect you to be among them, Bishop Gundulf.'

Gundulf gave a dismissive snort of laughter. 'You defend her faithfully, Thomas Chulkhurst, and I meant no disrespect to your good lady's name. But the incident served us well, I do believe. If one strong of fortitude reacts so badly to the sight of the Maids, it tells us much as to how best they should be cared for. The sisters of the abbey feel they have discharged their obligation to care for them while they were weak and vulnerable. The burden of keeping them hidden is costing the abbey dear, and it rises by the year. The Maids have confounded every expectation by showing they can survive, despite their affliction. Time has come for them to leave the abbey and be cared for by others. Or to fend for themselves unless provision be made for their tenure here to be permanent. And the cost of that provision would be great indeed.'

'I have been dreading these words,' said Thomas, 'and I knew they were the reason you summoned me to this meeting. You are right, Bishop Gundulf: I do not doubt that the mere sight of the Maids would cause disorder and commotion to follow them wherever they went, even into my family home. But can a man of God sentence them to the fate of death they would surely meet, were they to be banished from the safety of these abbey walls? They would have no means of fending for themselves and would be struck down by the first fearful peasant they encountered. Cast them out in the morn and they will be dead by nightfall.'

Gundulf grimaced, turning to face his visitor for the first time. 'That is nature's way, Thomas Chulkhurst. The nuns of Malling Abbey could be caring for scores of deserving souls, but instead they have to care only for the Maids. That is not just, nor is it fair. Sometimes, the few have to sacrificed for the many. My conscience would be clear were I to issue such a fateful order. It is up to you if you wish to halt it.'

'Halt it? How?' But Thomas already knew the answer.

'A hermitage needs to be built, separate from the abbey, to house the Maids. That will allow the abbey to open its doors again, to partake of commerce and to help the deserving poor. The Maids will need a servant, a cook and a guard at the hermitage, and to be visited by the abbey infirmarian when they become unwell. It will cost ten pounds to build, and a stipend of two pounds a year to ensure its safe and secure operation. That would be the cost you would have to bear to keep the Maids in comfort until the end of their days.'

Thomas felt his heart quicken. 'I am a man of means, Bishop Gundulf, but these sums are vast. Five pounds is the total income of my estate and I have no two-pound purse ready at my disposal. I would have to borrow coin to make a stipend of that size.' He gave Gundulf a pained stare. 'Is there no other way?'

'The Maids could reside with you in Biddenden. But yestermorn we saw what the reaction would be to that proposal.' Gundulf sighed and his lips formed into a thin line. 'Or, we send the Maids forth from these walls before the grip of winter is upon us. You are right to say there is a choice of life or death for the Maids. I do not envy you in making your decision.'

Thomas closed his eyes and leant back, tapping his head gently against the wall.

'There is no choice to make,' he said, as muscles jumped under his skin. 'I will not have blood on my hands, especially not the blood of kin. Let me apprise my dear Gudrun of the sacrifices we will have to make for every day the Maids remain on this Earth. I vow to ensure that, however many days that may be, each shall be a day of Christian charity, of succour to these innocent sufferers.'

Gundulf's eyes glistened and he nodded, almost bowed, to his guest.

'You have secured your place in Heaven with this act of selfless charity, Thomas Chulkhurst,' he said, laying a hand on Thomas's shoulder. 'Go forth and inform your good lady wife. I will prepare a protectorate, written in my own hand, that the Maids are not to be harmed or to be shown ill will by any who come into contact with them. I cannot promise every man will obey my words, but hopefully the authority of my office will provide safe harbour to them for the rest of their days.'

Thomas headed back to the inn a worried man. Finances on his estate were already tight after his spending in the two years since his wedding. Thomas had been determined Gudrun's humble past should be forgotten as quickly as possible and had spent lavishly on fine garments for her to wear on social occasions. When they had entertained the neighbouring franklins, reeves and haywards, they had served the choicest cuts of meat and poured the finest wines imported from France. The expense had been worth it. Gudrun had charmed all with her poise and beauty, and the initial scurrilous murmurings that Thomas had married beneath himself had all but died away. Now these extravagances were about to come to an end. He steeled himself to inform Gudrun of his decision.

Thomas climbed the ladder to the small chamber room above the Malling Inn. He called to his wife from outside the locked door, and tensed as the large bolt slid open. A stout woman stood at the entrance, glaring at him. Thomas recognised her as the inn's alewife. Gudrun sat behind, stroking her hair with an antler comb.

The woman turned to Gudrun, who gave a quick nod.

'Come in here quickly, Master Chulkhurst, and be with your wife at last,' the woman said, shaking her head and making some undecipherable mutterings. 'The day's drinking is underway and more than one amorous fool has already scaled that ladder to try to force himself into this bedchamber. Be grateful the last of them caused such a disturbance that my husband was alerted and bade me sit with your wife until your return. He needs no scandal to blot the reputation of the orderly establishment we run here.' She brushed her hands down the front of her tunic. 'Some would say it is no business of a wife to travel with her husband when he ventures to foreign parts. But all would say he has no business leaving her alone, to be assumed a harlot by those who come here hot of blood looking for some cunny. I have had to spend the evening here and we have lost much custom as a result, being shorthanded to say the least. My husband will want to have words with you on the morrow, to have you make amends.'

Without waiting for a reply, she pushed past him and descended the stairs.

Thomas felt himself flush. 'Gudrun, have you been harmed? I should not have left you alone. What does this alewife speak of? Tell me the worst.'

Gudrun gave a dismissive wave of her hand. 'A few village boys in high spirits, their drink giving confidence to their words, not their actions,' she said. 'I have known far worse at harvest day celebrations and have never needed a protector to guard my virtue.' She fixed Thomas a piercing stare. 'Your conference with Bishop Gundulf was of much more importance. I disgraced myself yestermorn by my display of weakness towards those poor unfortunate creatures. Tell me, good husband, what was the upshot of your discussions?'

'Gundulf said the Maids were to leave Malling Abbey. They have outgrown the facilities made available to them, and the prioress has told the Bishop the nuns will leave for other convents if the Maids stay, with the increasing provision that would entail. They are to be cast out before the harvest moon, to wander the woods and meet whatever fate awaits them.'

Gudrun shook her head. 'The poor dears. Their end will not be long in coming.' She turned away and started combing her hair again.

Thomas was taken aback. 'I could not leave matters like that. I implored Gundulf to reconsider and he gave me two options.'

Gudrun stopped combing and turned to face him. 'Two?' she said.

'We care for the Maids ourselves in Biddenden …'Thomas saw his wife's eyes widen in horror. 'Or, we pay his price to keep the Maids here in Malling, with a more permanent – and more costly – arrangement to care for their needs.' He paused before continuing. 'I told him the Maids must stay here; that we would find the means to let them live out whatever days they have left in this world with Christian charity.'

'But you said the burden was such that the nuns would rather move elsewhere than endure the hardship. What coin would Gundulf need to deal with these issues?'

'Ten pounds for a hermitage, and two pounds every Easter for the upkeep,'Thomas replied. He avoided Gudrun's gaze. 'It is a painful price to pay, but I cannot countenance sending them to their death. It was my seed that brought them into this world. I am responsible for their fate for as long as they both have breath.'

'Painful? It is more than painful, Thomas.' She spoke almost in a wail. 'We have nothing like such a fortune to lavish on these poor souls. How could you make Gundulf such a reckless promise? We will be ruined.' These final words snapped like a whiplash as her sobbing continued. She started clutching at herself, shaking her head in a maniacal frenzy.

Thomas went to embrace her, but she pushed him away.

'I have thought long and hard on my ride from the abbey,' he said, his words barely more than a whisper. 'If we sell the longhouse and move into a … more modest home near the boundary of the village, that would provide the ten pounds for the hermitage and a little more besides. Gundulf could issue an edict to set up an assarting. The villagers could fell trees, haul out stumps and cut brush to create new arable land which we could plough and sow ourselves. If we worked a yoke of land with two oxen, we could provide for ourselves and pay the annual stipend to the abbey until the rest of our coin runs out. With God's grace that would take many more years than the Maids have left on this Earth.'

Gudrun flailed at him with her fists. 'You are a dreamer and a fool!' she screamed. 'A yoke of land is a quarter of what we have now and those who partake in an assarting will expect the new land to be divided up and shared by its creators. We will have resentful neighbours if Gundulf instructs otherwise, and we will be living in a stinking hole for the rest of our lives, praying for the Maids to die before we become truly destitute. And for what? To spare the lives of those we will never see again, or speak of in other company? Ride to Gundulf's lodgings on the morrow and tell Gundulf the foolishness of your decision. God willing, you may reach him before this folly has a chance to take root.'

Thomas pushed her away so hard that she fell backwards onto the floor. He made no effort to help her up. A hot anger burned in his heart.

'I will not be spoken to thus by a woman, even if she is my wife. The Maids are part of me, and I confessed their existence to you before we became betrothed. I will not be their murderer. If you do not understand that, then I do not recognise the woman I love. Many a cotter's daughter would be happy to live in a sunken hut and plough her own fields.'

It was the first time Thomas had ever reminded Gudrun of her background, and the sting of the words shocked her out of her rage. She went limp on the floor, her hands covering her face as sobs racked her body. Thomas stood over her, standing stock-still, his jaw set in stern determination. The sobs subsided into sporadic whimpers.

Eventually, Gudrun pulled herself upright and rubbed the tears from her eyes.

'I have dishonoured myself again, good husband,' she said, her voice faltering as she tried to get her words out. 'Not only by my disrespect to your authority, but also by being so unsupportive of your Christian charity.'

She bit on her bottom lip as she stared at the blue gown hanging on a wall peg. Her eyes traced the elegance of the embroidery on the sleeve and came to rest on the sumptuous fox fur collar.

Thomas crouched down and hugged her close.

'You shame me with your selflessness,' she said into his ear, 'in supporting those you brought into the world. I will be a dutiful wife and help you do right by your responsibilities.'

Gudrun stood up, dusted herself down and took a deep breath. 'If you want to know what is best for the Maids, it is not to keep them locked up, never to have a moment's love in their tragic lives. Let us take them to Biddenden, and show them a family life as well as we are able. It is a sacrifice I will be honoured to make.'

She looked away, and Thomas pulled himself to his feet.

'You are a saint amongst women,' he said softly. 'And wiser than your headstrong husband. This is the best course, and it has taken a feminine heart to see it. I will send word to Gundulf of our decision and we shall return to the abbey on the morrow to make arrangements for our daughters to come home.'

Gudrun winced, then seemed by some act of will to compose herself.

'It is you,' she said, 'who have chosen wisely.' Her voice was calm and steady. She walked over to her robe and ran her fingers through the fur collar. 'Let us banish this eve from our memories forever, and think only of our future. Our future with the Maids.'

Thomas made to hug her again and she stiffened.

'I'm sorry,' she said. 'I am a little tense after the strong words that have been spoken this evening. I—'

But she said no more, and instead buried her head in her husband's chest.

He looked down at her, but he was unable to see the expression on her face.

Chapter 8

Thomas and Gudrun arrived early at the abbey the next day. Avicia welcomed them into the chapter house, a wary look on her face.

Thomas got straight to the point.

'Mother Avicia, I have talked long into the night with my good wife. I would be failing in my duties as a father if I allowed my daughters to remain under your supervision, denying them the chance of a normal life and the loving care that only a family can provide. Let me return to Biddenden to make preparations for their arrival. We have a handmaiden staying with us, a young orphan who can assist my wife with their upbringing. Would that be agreeable to you?'

Avicia shot a glance to Gudrun, who looked away. Avicia smiled instead at Thomas, and clasped her hands in prayer.

'This is wonderous news, good Thomas Chulkhurst. The Maids have been most listless since your visit, and I know they await word of when they might see you and Gudrun again. It would have broken their poor hearts to know you had turned away from them and they were to live out their days in our care. Shall I take you to them now, so you can tell them these glad tidings?'

'In a moment, Mother Avicia. Let us consider the manner of their departure, so we have to hand the answers to any questions they may have. My plan would be to depart for Biddenden forthwith, to prepare accommodation for when they arrive. Gudrun would stay on here, to await Gundulf's protectorate and to aid their safe passage. Granted they will have the protectorate, but I would want to make doubly sure nothing befalls them on their journey. I think it best they travel out of sight of prying eyes. A wagon will need to be procured, and two stout oxen to draw it. Could all of this be arranged?'

Avicia laughed. 'Forgive me, Master Chulkhurst, your news has left me as dizzy as the most junior of our oblates. Bishop Gundulf has already departed for Rochester and promised to send his written protectorate with all haste on his arrival. Gudrun is welcome to stay here as our guest until then.'

Gudrun spoke, her glassy eyes displaying no emotion. 'That is most kind of you, Mother Avicia, but I would not want to intrude on your daily order. The inn at Malling can give me all the comforts I need.'

Thomas was puzzled. 'You forget the unwelcome attention your presence attracted, my dear. Those hot of blood who frequent the place are undeserving of your tolerance – believe me, they will come calling again. This is a far more suitable arrangement and one that will allow you to spend time with your new charges, to develop the bond every mother should have with her children.'

Gudrun remained silent.

'It is agreed then,' Thomas said. 'Thank you for your generous offer, Mother Avicia. Gudrun will stay and await

Gundulf's protectorate. When it arrives, she has my full authority to take any action she sees fit.'

Avicia stared at Gudrun, as though trying to fathom her thoughts, but Gudrun gazed blankly into the middle distance. Then Avicia clapped her hands once and said, 'Now let us make haste with these arrangements so we can bring joy into the hearts of these two young innocents. I will task Sister Agnes with this responsibility – she is the one who knows how best to prepare the Maids for the journey. Let me call on her.'

AVICIA FOUND SISTER AGNES working in the abbey under-croft and told her the news. The nun remained silent for a few moments before speaking.

'It is surely a great blessing, Mother Avicia. But my heart is nevertheless troubled. Mistress Chulkhurst was so distressed by the sight of the Maids, it seems fanciful to suppose that in the next moment she would open her heart to let them into her life. Are you sure all is well?'

'Hush, Sister Agnes. Thomas Chulkhurst is a good man, and he has provided generously for the Maids over the years. I had no doubt he would continue to do so, even with Bishop Gundulf's new demands. But now we see he is compassion-ate as well as generous, welcoming his own children into his home, no matter how ... otherworldly they are to behold. And Mistress Chulkhurst is of sound peasant stock, she has done well to wed the owner of a longhouse with a tidy parcel of land. Like any good wife, she will choose to honour and obey him. Let us not cast doubt on their motives.'

Sister Agnes slowly paced three sides of the room before turning to face Avicia.

'Forgive me, Mother Avicia, but I know what my heart tells me to do. The shock to the Maids of their new life will be very great indeed, and they have many needs which their new parents will take long to learn how to perform. Let me travel with them as their guardian, live with them in the Chulkhurst household, help teach them the ways of the world until they are able to fend for themselves. It is too great a task for those who do not know them, no matter how pure their hearts.'

Avicia was the first one to break eye contact. 'You are needed here, Sister Agnes. It is the duty of a mother to care for her kin.'

'Gudrun is neither mother nor kin to the Maids,' Sister Agnes replied. Her tone was even, firm. 'It would be a burden to love another woman's brood at the best of times. You saw the horror on her face at her first sight of them. She needs help and support to bring love for them into her heart.'

'Young Sister Peony has been of assistance to you in tending the physic garden, certainly … Come, Sister Agnes, it is I who have been too hasty to judge. Let us put your proposition to the Chulkhursts and see if they would welcome your support.'

Sister Agnes touched her index finger to her lips. 'When we plant a seed, it needs time to grow; it must be fed and nurtured before it is able to flower. Let Gudrun get to know me first, and I her. Let her observe me with the Maids, so she can see the worth of my caring for them. Offer that I should accompany them to Biddenden, no more. I can use the journey to press for a more permanent invitation when we arrive.'

'You have much wisdom, Sister Agnes. A prioress should have the humility to learn from an obedientiary. Your plan is a good one. Let us present it to the Chulkhursts.'

The two nuns went back to meet with the Chulkhursts. Sister Agnes was right to expect Gudrun's reluctance.

'Gundulf's protectorate and a strong cart to secure the Maids are all you need provide,' she said sullenly, '... and a guide to lead the way. They will be hidden under blankets. I will walk beside the cart. There is no need for any other encumbrances.'

Thomas shook his head. 'It will be a trying journey for Eliza and Mary, dear wife,' he said. 'We should be guided by those who know them best as to how to undertake such an endeavour.' When Gudrun remained silent, he gave a little cough and went on: 'Let us leave this decision until we can gauge their reaction to the news. It may be that all of this plays lightly on them and all will be well.' He turned to face the nuns. 'That is a good plan, it not, Mother Avicia?'

Avicia gave a thin smile of acknowledgement.

THE SQUEALS OF THE MAIDS had continued for five minutes or more, and showed no sign of abating.

'Eliza, Mary, be quiet!' Sister Agnes shouted again. A feeling of doubt, almost of panic, had come upon her. 'If you do not stop this commotion, your mother and father will surely reconsider their plan for you to stay with them.'

The Maids looked simultaneously towards Thomas and Gudrun, who stood together awkwardly in a corner of the room. Sister Agnes's threat caused both girls to stop for an instant, then Eliza let out another yelp of joy. Mary joined in, and the two of them tumbled and rolled around on the floor.

Sister Agnes appealed again for calm. 'Hush, hush now, my dears,' she implored them. 'Settle yourselves down and thank your mother and father for their decision. Show them how polite and well-mannered you can be.'

Eliza composed herself first.

'Mother, Father, I will be a dutiful daughter to you.' She clambered to her feet, forcing Mary to do the same. 'Thank you for taking me ... home.' She made a small curtsey, almost causing Mary to fall over.

Mary muttered something inaudible and quietly sobbed. That calmed the room. Sister Agnes seized the moment. 'Good, girls, good. Now sit quietly while we talk further. Master Chulkhurst, are there any words you wish to say?'

Thomas cleared his throat and glanced around. 'We will have plenty of time for talk when we meet again at Biddenden.' He coughed again and then spoke with more authority. 'I must go ahead of you to prepare for your arrival. There is much to be done. Be good until I see you again.' With that he took Gudrun's hand and they abruptly left.

Gudrun had said not a word.

As they stood watching the Chulkhursts ride off in the direction of Malling village, Avicia confided to Sister Agnes, 'Your fears were well-founded, my sister. I have never seen a woman show such coldness to those she is to mother. I fear for what sort of life they will have to endure when they reach Biddenden. You can expect much opposition to your plan to stay on as their guardian.'

GUDRUN RETURNED to the abbey in the late afternoon and was shown by Avicia to the guestroom reserved for visitors.

'I expect Gundulf's protectorate to arrive on the morrow or the day following,' Avicia said. 'He is a man of great energy for his years and has accomplished many noble deeds in his lifetime. It is less than a day's march to Rochester, so he will already have commissioned a scribe to prepare the document.'

Avicia made to leave, but Gudrun raised a hand and took half a step towards her'. 'I know little about this Bishop of Rochester,' she said deliberately. 'What are these noble deeds you talk of?'

'He is known as Gundulf the Builder and age has not diminished his ambition. Only last year he founded a leper colony in Chatham, a short ride from his abbey at Rochester.'

Gudrun raised an eyebrow. 'What, pray, is such a place?'

'A building to care for those who are afflicted with that terrible curse, those who are shunned by their villages because of their affliction. Lepers are left at a monastic cell, the length of an arrow's flight from the colony, and guards collect them from there. All who live in the colony are forbidden to venture forth, but are given some comfort and succour while they await being called to the Lord.' Avicia crossed herself. 'It is a place I fear I would never have the fortitude to visit.'

Gudrun listened with rapt attention. 'But if the lepers are so afflicted, how can they take care of their basic needs?'

Avicia sighed. 'They are tended by the guards, the poor and destitute of the neighbourhood, who have neither coin nor kin to help them, and who can find no labour and have no roof over their head. These unfortunate souls have to choose between the certainty of perishing from hunger and cold, or the hope of being spared from the lepers' afflictions. Many guards do perish, but some live out their days in a modicum of comfort. That hope is all that they can cling to. It is a cruel choice, but the colony is their only hope of survival.'

'Gundulf is indeed a great man,' said Gudrun. 'I am honoured that he troubles himself with such trifles as the Maids.' She gave a little nod. 'Yes indeed. I await his protectorate with humble patience.'

Gudrun spent the next day in her room, passing the time by working on the embroidery of a handkerchief. Sister Agnes visited her after Sext prayers at noon, asking if she would like to visit the Maids, but Gudrun politely declined. The nun visited again after Nones prayers and this time was more insistent.

'Eliza and Mary have been most agitated today, knowing of your presence in the abbey and waiting for your visit,' she told Gudrun. 'Could you spare them some moments of your time to talk to them and join them in play? It would bring them much joy.'

'I did not ask that they be told I am here. There will be time a-plenty for such fripperies when I have them in my care. Until that time, please let me enjoy the peace of the last few days before I take on my obligations to them.'

'Being responsible for the care of the Maids should be a joy, not a burden,' Sister Agnes replied. 'I plead with you, open your heart to them. You will find they will give you much gladness and fulfilment, just as they have blessed me with their love.'

Eventually a compromise was reached. Gudrun and Sister Agnes recited the last prayers of the day, Compline, with the

Maids in their room. As soon as it was over, Gudrun said she must leave. The Maids said nothing.

Gudrun overheard the nun's whispered words as she left the room.

'One day at a time, my dears, one day at a time.'

GUNDULF'S EMISSARY, Alard, arrived the next day with the protectorate. The nuns assembled in the chapter house and the emissary read it out in a loud, clear voice.

'*Haec baptizatis, Eliza et Maria Chulkhurst, libere et absque pavore habitabitis in vobis invitis. Parentibus oboedire, Thomas Gudrunae Chulkhurst, in omnium premissorum …*'

His words bounced around the walls.

Avicia gave him a blessing and the nuns dispersed.

As Alard handed the document to Avicia, Gudrun shuffled over, her head bowed in a rare gesture of humility. 'I am not schooled in the Latin tongue, Mother Avicia. Can you tell me the meaning of the emissary's words?' Her face reddened.

'He did not think to repeat the text in the vernacular,' Avicia replied, 'as even the most junior oblates are familiar with Latin. A farmer's wife has other demands on her time than learning the language of the Scriptures.' She glanced at Gudrun's almost finished handkerchief, then studied the goatskin document for a moment, running her fingers along the lines. Finally, she said, '"*Let these baptised children, Eliza and Mary Chulkhurst, pass freely and live safely amongst you. Obey the wishes of their parents, Thomas and Gudrun Chulkhurst, in all matters concerning them.*" If you are required to show this to ensure the Maids' safety, you will need a man of the cloth to read and understand these words.'

Gudrun asked Avicia to repeat the words, and then said them back to make sure she had memorised them correctly.

GUDRUN THANKED THE PRIORESS and headed back to her room, rubbing the back of her neck as she walked, adjusting her gown as if it was chafing. Twice she stopped and turned to look at Mother Avicia, who was heading off in the other direction. Gudrun entered her room and lay motionless on the floor, staring at the ceiling. There was a churning feeling in her stomach, and her throat was parched and dry. Despite the cool late-summer air, a sweat developed on her brow as her insides trembled.

She lay there in fretful anticipation until almost noon, then made her way back to the chapter house. She was already kneeling at the altar, deep in contemplation, when Avicia arrived for Sext prayers. She rose and said to the prioress, 'Mother Avicia, now that Gundulf's protectorate has arrived, I need take advantage of your hospitality no longer. Let us make plans for my departure with the Maids.'

'Excellent,' replied Avicia.

Gudrun closed her eyes in an attempt to remain calm. 'There is to be a change in the plan for the Maids' destination,' she said. 'My husband recognised his decision to take the Maids into our home was of necessity made in haste, and he charged me to determine if there were other arrangements that would be more suitable. I have prayed for guidance on this matter and I'm pleased to say God has spoken to me, giving me His wisdom as to the best path. The Maids will be transported to the leper colony founded by Bishop Gundulf, where they can live out their days safe from prying eyes and be a burden neither to you and your charges here at the abbey, nor the Chulkhurst's at their farm in Biddenden. I am grateful you shared with me the knowledge of Gundulf's great work, so that what is best for all concerned could be discovered.'

Avicia lifted her hands to her mouth. 'Life in a leper colony is a terrible fate for any poor creature. It would be cruelty beyond belief to commit two children unafflicted by the scourge of the disease to such an unspeakable existence. The Maids must travel to Biddenden or they must stay here until Gundulf gives his blessing. I cannot allow otherwise.'

'You are forgetting Gundulf's protectorate. *To obey my wishes, in all matters concerning them.* Is that not what Gundulf's wise words said?'

'The wishes of yourself *and* Thomas Chulkhurst,' replied Avicia. 'I will heed this instruction when I hear these words from Thomas himself.'

'Did he not tell you I was to decide on any matters after his departure? His wishes were clear and you cannot disobey a protectorate signed by the Bishop and read out in your own chapter house.' Gudrun's heartbeat grew loud in her ears and she forced herself to maintain a measured tone. 'I need detain you no more with this discussion, Mother Avicia. Please call for our guide and his ox wagon. We leave at first light on the morrow.'

'Thomas did not mean for you to devise such a heinous plan. He left you to administer the details of the journey. Not to rule on the fate of the Maids themselves.'

'You are not privy to the mind of my husband, nor the additional duties with which he charged me when we were alone. I will take responsibility for my decision when I inform Thomas upon my arrival in Biddenden. You need not concern yourself with matters between man and wife.'

'I will pray that God forgives you,' Avicia said, and left without waiting for a reply.

AVICIA'S MIND WAS SPINNING. She was certain that this turn of events would never have been in Gundulf's contemplation when he drafted the protectorate. If Gudrun should depart in the morning and deposit the Maids with the lepers, then even if she were found to be at fault the Maids would never be allowed to leave for fear they would have become infected.

Avicia needed to act fast. She caught up with Alard as he was saddling his horse.

'Alard, I need you to take an urgent report to Bishop Gundulf. Tell him that Gudrun, wife of Thomas Chulkhurst, has acted upon receipt of his protectorate to declare the Maids will spend the rest of their days at the leper colony in Chatham and has used the authority of his protectorate to insist she be obeyed. If these are not Gundulf's wishes, he must intervene before she departs. Once the Maids enter the colony, their fate will be sealed.'

Alard's brow furrowed. 'I do not claim to know the mind of my master,' he said. 'But I feel he will be vexed by this news. Delay her departure for as long as you are able. I must leave now. There is no time to waste.' He threw a leg over the saddle and dug in his spurs, and Avicia stood there until the clatter of hooves receded as the cobbles turned to hard earth.

As Alard sped away, Gudrun approached, and by the time she reached Avicia the emissary was already in the distance. She looked at Avicia, all pretence of civility now vanished.

'I would have wished to present my thanks and good wishes to Alard for delivering Gundulf's protectorate, had you told me of his departure. I hope he will not think ill of me.'

Avicia remained silent.

'No matter,' Gudrun said, looking around the forecourt. 'Will you assist me in locating an ox cart and driver? If not, I will walk to the village and find one for myself.'

'You should ask for Umfrey the farmer,' Avicia said, reluctantly. 'He is a strong man, and virtuous. I tell you his name to spare you from any misfortune. Your plan for the Maids is a wicked one, but it would be uncharitable not to protect you from harm.'

'It is for the best. But I sense from your words that I will not have your co-operation. No matter, I will find Umfrey and strike a bargain for him to take me to Chatham and on to Biddenden. You can arrange for the Maids to be prepared for their journey. There is no need to tell them of this change of plan. They will be less obstructive if they remain in innocence of their destination. Please obey me on this.'

Avicia turned and walked away, seething with anger. It would be a fast gallop indeed that would allow Alard to ride to Rochester, seek an audience with Gundulf and return to Malling with his response before Gudrun departed. Umfrey was her only hope. He was a stout man, strong in his youth, who drank until he dropped every night at the Malling Inn. It took him until mid-morning to shake of the excesses of the night before and to be up and about on his business. That might buy Avicia the time she needed.

Sister Agnes gasped with horror when Avicia told her of Gudrun's plan.

'It is a fate beyond cruelty for two innocent souls to have to bear,' she cried, spinning in anguish as she pushed her fists into the sides of her head. She clutched her crucifix so hard her knuckles turned white. 'We must have no part of this devilish plan.'

Avicia felt her shoulders slump. 'We have made a vow of obedience and Gundulf's protectorate commanded that Gudrun and her husband should be obeyed on all matters to do with the Maids. Gudrun *and* her husband, mind – but she has her own interpretation of the text and certainly none beyond her husband Thomas or Gundulf himself have the power to deny her instructions. Alard has departed with all haste to tell Gundulf the news.'

'I pray that your plea for help arrives in time,' Sister Agnes said. 'Gudrun is right, to the extent that we cannot ignore a protectorate that instructs us to obey her, if that is indeed its intent.' She whimpered softly for a moment, then relaxed her grip on the crucifix. 'I will prepare the Maids for their journey come what may. Whether it is to salvation or damnation is in the hands of the Lord. We must hope that Alard rides hard.'

'We must also pray for how Gundulf will respond. He is a godly man, but a pragmatic one. The Maids are a problem for his diocese – an unwelcome distraction from the great work that will stand as his eternal legacy on earth. Gudrun's plan, wicked as it is, may absolve him of any responsibility, notwithstanding his best intentions. Even a short delay instructing Alard as to his reply would mean it would not be heard before the Maids enter the leper colony. Once the Maids are inside its doors, Gundulf's problem is solved.'

Sister Agnes pushed the crucifix into her chest. It seemed to fill her with strength and she stood tall and straight.

'We must do more than trust to Divine Providence,' she said.

Sister Agnes held a finger to her lips. Avicia asked no more questions. Whatever the sister was planning, it had to work.

MATINS WOULD BE HELD well before dawn as usual – a groggy affair that tested many a nun's faith. All were grateful to sleep for a few hours before Lauds at daybreak and Prime an hour later. But Sister Agnes did not head back to bed; instead, she slipped quietly out of the abbey. She stumbled through the dark to Malling, the familiar path now a snare of tree roots, a maze of wrong turnings. There was no moon, and a late star lingered between the clouds.

She headed straight for Umfrey's sunken hut, pausing to marvel at the thunderous, ale-soaked snores emanating from within. The first hints of red appeared on the horizon as she unlatched the gate to the paddock where Umfrey's two oxen slept. She picked up a tree branch and struck one of the beasts on its boney rump. It gave a low bellow as it rose to its feet, and its companion followed.

There was a moment of silence and Sister Agnes froze, then relaxed as Umfrey's snores continued.

'Whish-che! Whish-*che!*' she said, as loudly as she dared, and used the branch to guide the beasts towards the gate.

Once through, they lumbered down the main track through the village, softly, like footfalls upon wool, Sister Agnes cajoling them along. Once beyond the village, the oxen stopped in their tracks, reluctant to move further from home. A strike with her branch was met by a disgruntled bellow, so she dared not risk going further. She stood off to the side, cajoling them with her voice, her arms making wide circles, and the great brutes turned and plodded away from the track, disappearing into a thick stand of trees. That would have to do. She headed back to the abbey to be the first at Lauds, where she prayed for forgiveness even more resolutely than usual.

Gudrun joined the nuns for Prime prayers.

'I am ready to depart, Mother Avicia. As soon as Umfrey the farmer arrives with his ox cart, I will fetch the Maids and we will be on our way. It is but a short journey to Chatham – there is no need for Sister Agnes to accompany us. From there I will travel on to Biddenden and will spend the night at a coldharbour on the way. Farmer Umfrey will be arriving shortly and we will be gone before noon.'

Gudrun became more and more agitated as time went by and Umfrey failed to appear.

'Curse the soaken oaf,' she said, as the bell rang for noon Sext prayers. 'His promises are as worthless as alchemist's gold. He will make our journey a late one with his drunken ways.'

'Umfrey is not one I would rely on to rise with the cock's crow,' said Avicia. 'But even by his lamentable standards this is a late rise. Come. Let us celebrate Sext prayers together. It will give us one more chance to pray for the Maids' salvation.'

Gudrun ignored the barb, but joined the nuns in prayer. Avicia kept glancing at Sister Agnes, and the nun could tell that the prioress was trying to connect her with Umfrey's late arrival.

As noon passed and the afternoon wore on, Gudrun became more and more agitated. Finally, in mid-afternoon, there was a ring of the bell at the abbey gate. It was Umfrey.

'My idiot son did not secure the beasts before nightfall,' he complained to all who would listen. 'They wandered off and I have given hours to finding them.' He snorted. 'Much time has been wasted. Let us make haste with our departure.'

There was a commotion at the Abbey gates. It was Alard. He dismounted, steam rising from his horse's flanks. He walked up to the assembled nuns, his expression grim, and without ceremony he addressed Gudrun.

'Gudrun Chulkhurst, I have ridden through the night and endured a rough camp to bring to you this directive from Bishop Gundulf himself. His protectorate was to ensure the safety of the Maids, either here in Malling or at your home in Biddenden. He believes you have wilfully misinterpreted the terms of the document to mean that you can change the fate of the Maids without consultation, and in so doing you have disrespected the agreement into which you, your husband and the Bishop knowingly entered. You are to make a solemn vow before God that you will take the Maids to Biddenden, and further that you will do no harm to them once there. Any reneging of these vows will lead to your excommunication from the Church and Thomas Chulkhurst's obligation to provide for the Maids solely by himself. Will you swear these vows in front of these witnesses here and now?'

Gudrun looked helplessly around her. Avicia and Sister Agnes composed their faces into expressions of pious impassiveness. Umfrey slipped discreetly into the background. Gudrun's voice quavered, her body trembled.

'I do so swear, emissary. I meant no ill to the Maids. I learnt only of the sanctuary of Chatham during my stay here, after Bishop Gundulf had left. I believed a life away from prying eyes, where the Maids could earn their place in Heaven by providing care and succour for the victims of the scourge who reside there, was something of which all would approve. If this belief was ill-founded, then I will humbly follow the good Bishop's instruction.'

Alard made her repeat this with her hand on a Bible, then took his leave. Gudrun looked physically broken by this turn of events, her shoulders slumped and her eyes glazed and distant.

Avicia seized her chance to press home the advantage.

'I can forgive you your words and actions, Mistress Chulkhurst, and take them to be the deeds of someone overcome by fear and trepidation of the responsibilities forced upon you, rather than the actions of someone with a malevolent heart. But the safety of the Maids is paramount to me, and your husband needs to be aware of what transpired here, in case such temptation should ever enter your mind again. Alard's admonition from the Bishop needs to be repeated to him.'

'No. No! He should be … spared the pain,' Gudrun said, a look of terror on her face.

Avicia gave a conciliatory smile. 'If you do not want this known to him, there is one more promise you need to make. Sister Agnes must not only travel with you to Biddenden, she must also stay on there, for as long as she feels is necessary, to ensure the Maids' place in both your home and the community. I do not believe you to be a bad person, Gudrun Chulkhurst, but you have shown by your actions these last few days that you are prepared to render the Maids' position perilous to suit your own ends. Let Sister Agnes be guardian to the Maids. Then we will never speak of this day again.'

Avicia waited, and Gudrun finally mumbled 'Yes', and bowed her head. Avicia performed a blessing and then rose, taking Gudrun's hand as she did so. Neither woman spoke as they left the chapter house.

Chapter 9
Mary

Today! We're going to Biddenden today!

    Mother Avicia came to see us and told us we are leaving straight away. Straight away! I am so excited. We are going to travel in a special box that we have to stay in, wrapped in a blanket, until we get there.

That sounds exciting.

Biddenden! Even the name is magical. It will be a happy place, full of kind and generous people. Mother Avicia tells me Father's farm has one hundred and sixty acres, which is how you measure how big something is. One hundred is the biggest number I know, so the farm *must* be big. I wonder if it stretches all the way to the edge of the world?

Father must be rich and powerful, as well as kind and generous.

Mother hasn't visited since she came and prayed with us that one time after Father left. She must be very busy, making all the arrangements. I can't wait to play with the village children who haven't been splitted yet. Once Eliza and I are separate, I will work hard every day to repay Mother and Father's kindness. Mother will love me even more and I will find a handsome man to be my husband and when God gives us children, we will look after them from the day they are born, not wait until they are old enough for the splitting.

I'm getting too excited. I know I am, but it is so difficult to stop myself. My insides are moving all the time. Eliza says hers are the same. Sister Agnes is coming with us, but her face looks pale, nearly white, like she's ill. I hope she will be well enough to travel. I tell Eliza that when Sister Agnes sees our new home, she will fall in love with it and want to stay with us forever, but Eliza tells me not to be silly, nuns don't live on a farm, God needs them to stay in the abbey and do Good Deeds.

She hits me for upsetting her, but not too hard.

We leave The Room a few hours before Nones prayers, when the sun is still high in the sky. I wonder why we have not left early in the morning, but don't say anything in case we have to stay another day. It's strange to see how busy the abbey is, full of nuns dashing about, running their errands. And we can walk wherever we want! But it all gets too much for us. In the end, we sit with Sister Agnes in the undercroft. I hold Eliza's hand as we wait.

Her hand is always warm. She says mine is always cold.

Mother Avicia comes to fetch us in a short while.

'Farmer Umfrey is ready to depart,' she says to Sister Agnes. 'Come, bring your charges with you.' She turns to Eliza and me. 'You are about to embark on a great adventure, young Maids of Biddenden. Be brave and strong, and remember God is always looking after you. Come and say farewell to the sisters of Malling.'

We step outside, and the nuns are lined up, all in a row, staring at us without smiling. As we start walking, it is hard to breathe. I feel so lightheaded I think I am going to faint.

I grab Eliza's waist, like I always do when I'm afraid.

'Please, Mother Avicia, let us stay here with you,' I cry out. 'I don't want to go.'

Sister Agnes takes my arm and guides Eliza and me along the line of nuns. I feel Eliza shaking too, but it's me that does all the crying.

I know deep down she's just as scared as I am.

Farmer Umfrey is a big, fat man, with red cheeks and hair that comes out of his ears.

'I've seen worse sights than this in my time,' he says to Mother Avicia, struggling to pull back a big metal bolt on the back of a box fixed on top of two big wheels. 'Come, get them inside. We can still make Maidstone by nightfall.'

In front of the box is the biggest animal I have ever seen. Horns stick out of its two heads, it has two huge bellies, two hairy tails flicking from side to side. It turns its big brown eyes to me. They look kind, but a little stupid.

I decide I like it.

It hasn't been splitted yet either, from what I can see. It is joined at the shoulder, higher up than where Eliza and I fit together. I haven't seen any people or creatures that haven't been splitted before and I want to have a look at how others manage, but farmer Umfrey stands in my way and I can't get a better look.

Eliza starts jumping up and down, causing me to shake.

'Mother, Mother, over here!' she shouts. I'm annoyed she has spotted Mother before me. She always does things first. I look over at Mother and she stands there, not moving and not smiling either.

Trust Eliza to annoy her.

Sister Agnes comes over to help Eliza climb into the box. Farmer Umfrey puts his hand under my armpit to lift me up. His nose is big and red and he is very smelly. I'll make sure he helps Eliza next time. I look around to see what is inside. Some hay on the floor and a small window at the front. When they close the door, it will be very dark inside.

'Mistress Chulkhurst, please come forth, it is time to depart,' I hear Sister Agnes say. Mother says something I can't hear, then I hear Sister Agnes again. 'We have a long journey and they are already anxious about what lies ahead. A moment of your time will do wonders to comfort them.'

Mother comes over and flicks her hand in front of her face, as if to get rid of a bad smell.

'We have many miles to travel and I want to hear no noise from either of you,' she says, turning to Sister Agnes for agreement. Sister Agnes gives a half-nod, but looks sad. Mother bends over and picks up the cloth bundle that contains all our things and throws it into the box beside us. 'Here are your belongings,' she says. 'Look after them.'

The bundle falls open, revealing our dolls. With one movement we both lean forward and grab our own. I clutch Maud to my chest, Eliza does the same with Edith. Mother sees this and smiles for the first time. She looks so beautiful when she smiles. She speaks again, more gently this time.

'Come my little children, make yourself comfortable.'

Then she spoils everything by crying.

Sister Agnes climbs in and gives us both a hug. 'I will be walking outside with your mother. Farmer Umfrey will lead the oxen and we should be at our coldharbour before nightfall.' She drops her voice to a whisper. 'Keep wrapped in your blanket and do not make a commotion, just as your mother has said. Shout an alarm if you get into a predicament. If it can wait, make no trouble until we break the journey. It will be a rough track until we reach Week Street at Maidstone. Lie still and it will soon be over.'

We tumble about as the box begins to move. We try to get comfortable, and find the best way is to sit under the little window at the front. Sometimes we reach a level bit of road and if that lasts for more than a minute, we stand up and look out to see what is ahead. Eliza always says she has to see first, but I am in such a good mood and so excited I don't mind. Mostly it is trees, but once there are some men carrying dead rabbits all tied together. Sister Agnes walks at the front with farmer Umfrey, Mother next to them, looking very dignified, her back so straight. Farmer Umfrey and Sister Agnes are talking all the time, but Mother never joins in.

It's nice that she's shy like me.

We have some bread and cheese for lunch, and we are allowed to go outside to do our business but afterwards Sister Agnes tells us we have to sit inside the box until everyone finishes eating. At one point we hear voices and farmer Umfrey quickly closes the door until they pass. Sister Agnes tells us there are many robbers in the woods and they will take us away and kill us if they know we are there, so we keep very quiet until the door is opened again. I'll be glad when we get to a safe place.

Although I'm excited, I'm also frightened.

As the birds begin singing in the evening, we stop moving and I hear farmer Umfrey's voice through the window.

'This will be the coldharbour for tonight. I don't dare venture on to the inn at Maidstone. Here we'll be safe from prying eyes.' Mother says something in a whiny voice and farmer Umfrey shouts at her to be quiet. I decide I don't like him very much. He's rude as well as smelly. I push against Eliza to show it is my turn to look out the window, but she pushes back.

I start crying.

'See?' It is farmer Umfrey's voice again. 'You think you can keep that thing quiet all night? We stay here. It might be a rough dwelling, but that suits me fine. It is less than a league from the town. No traveller will want to crowd in here with us, if the warm fires of Maidstone beckon.'

I don't know what a coldharbour is so when farmer Umfrey opens the door, I ask Sister Agnes. It is a roadside shelter for travellers, she tells me. Nobody lives there all the time, so there are no meals or comfortable beds, just a simple fireplace and a roof to protect against the weather. We are to stay locked up all night in the box and the others are to stay in the shelter.

As it gets dark we hear all sorts of strange noises around us, and we both cry and cry, even when farmer Umfrey shouts at us to stop.

Then the bolt on the door slides open, and we both scream, expecting a monster to be there, come to eat us alive, but it is only Sister Agnes.

'Dear, dear,' she says to us. 'I am ashamed at my thoughtlessness. You should not be left alone on your first night outside the abbey.' And with that, she climbs up inside the box.

Farmer Umfrey appears, staggering a little, looking even bigger in the pale moonlight.

'As you wish,' he mumbles to Sister Agnes, closing the door and locking all three of us inside. His breath is even worse than usual, and the strangest sound comes from his chest, or his throat, as he stumbles away.

The box is almost completely dark, with just the faintest glow of moonlight through the small window.

'Try to get some sleep, young ones,' whispers Sister Agnes. 'We have another long day ahead of us on the morrow.'

It is nice, all of us in the box, and a calm comes over Eliza and passes into me. On the morrow, we will arrive at Biddenden. Maybe Mother and Father will sleep with us that night.

I can't believe it the next morning. When Farmer Umfrey opens the door of the box, there is already bright sunlight! It must be after Lauds prayers, maybe even after Prime! I have never woken up to bright sunlight before, and my eyes hurt. I rub them over and over again. Sister Agnes sits up and brushes herself down, then helps us out to do our morning toilet.

There is some of yestermorn's bread left, so we chew on that while farmer Umfrey gets ready. Now that I can see more clearly, I notice his animal isn't joined together like Eliza and me. It is two separate big cows with some wooden thing on their shoulders that holds them together. I feel disappointed, I don't know why.

Eliza doesn't seem to notice, so I don't tell her.

I am hoping Sister Agnes will stay in the box with us, but we are locked in by ourselves again as we rock about on the road to Maidstone. After about an hour, I hear lots of noises. The road is better now, and we are able to stand up and look out the window without the swaying knocking us over. It is amazing! Men shouting about things for sale, dogs barking, squealing pigs, hissing geese, cart horses clopping by. This must be Maidstone.

There are so many things to see, I think my head will explode.

Then I realise. There are women with babies everywhere. I count four, five, six in as many minutes. There are groups of children running and shouting, some following our cart, yelling at farmer Umfrey to tell them what is inside.

None are joined together.

Eliza pushes me aside again, and I don't protest. My chest tightens. I know what I have seen. I think I know what it means. But I don't want to believe it.

Eliza is looking out the window, her eyes bright and glossy, taking in everything around her. She has her hand over her heart and her face is flushed with excitement. Seeing, but not seeing. For a moment, I wonder if I should leave her like that. I am feeling sick now. My heart is shrinking inside me.

I can't keep my discovery to myself a moment longer.

'Eliza, do you see?' I stammer the words out, the tears pouring down my face. 'Do you see the village children?'

'Some, just a moment ago. Now I hear them shouting behind us.' Her voice sounds so excited. 'No, look, here's some more coming to join them. It's wonderful, Eliza. So many of them.' She laughs. 'Farmer Umfrey is waving a stick at them, telling them to go away.' There is a bang on the door. 'Oh, now he's getting angry. The children are trying to open the door.'

'Do you not see, Eliza?' I repeat. 'Look at them, look at them! What do you see?'

'See what? What is ailing you, Mary? This is the happiest day of our lives.'

'It is the worst day, Eliza. The worst day. Look at them all. How many are joined? How many children are younger than us, and are attached to each other? Tell me you see one, Eliza. At least one. Tell me there is somebody else like us in all these people.'

'None,' she replies, shrinking back as she speaks. 'Not a single one … What does it mean, Mary? Where are all the ones like us?'

'There are none like us.'

Suddenly, everything makes sense.

'That is why we are kept hidden in a room, why everyone cries when they meet us. We are the only joined maids on God's earth. And we will never be splitted.'

I expect Eliza to start crying, but instead she is silent. The box gives a sudden jolt which causes us to fall over and we lie on our backs on the floor, staring at the ceiling. There are a few more shouts, the sound of something heavy hitting the box, but the sounds fade into the distance as we leave Maidstone behind.

Sister Agnes told us the Romans built Week Street and it was a very good road. The box stops swaying and rocking, and all we can hear is the crunch of stones under the wheels.

Sister Agnes shouts that we will be on this good road all the way to Biddenden. But I don't care about living in Biddenden anymore, or even having Mother love me.

I don't care about anything. Nothing matters anymore.

Chapter 10

The Maids' dull torpor cast a deathly pall over the rest of journey. As dusk fell, Sister Agnes ached to know whether they would reach the Chulkhurst longhouse by nightfall as planned. No-one had spoken since they had passed through Maidstone. She glanced again at Farmer Umfrey, hoping to gain some clue as to their progress from his grim expression. Nothing. Only the fact they had passed another coldharbour an hour before, without a pause as the shadows lengthened, gave her hope that their journey would soon be at an end.

They arrived at the Chulkhurst longhouse suddenly and without ceremony. 'Lord be praised!' Gudrun exclaimed when she saw its outline appear out of the evening gloom, and quickly looked at Sister Agnes as though embarrassed at displaying even this small demonstration of relief.

The light of a lantern appeared, swaying wildly, as a figure ran towards them. A voice called out, 'Gudrun, is that you?' and this was followed by the sound of a stumble and a curse. Gudrun's response was a wordless, feral cry of anguish and relief, followed by uncontrolled sobbing.

'Oh, my good wife!' said Thomas Chulkhurst as he ran towards them. When he reached the cart, the light of the lantern showed the relief on his face. Sister Agnes and Farmer Umfrey maintained a respectful distance as the couple hugged each other. Eventually Thomas peeled himself away.

'Pray tell, how was the journey?' he asked.

'Most stressful,' Gudrun replied. 'The Maids fell into rapture on our departure and were most unruly on the road. Farmer Umfrey feared their shouts would excite curiosity when we arrived upon Maidstone, and it so transpired. A crowd pursued us the length of Week Street, demanding to know what it was that was inside the cart that had to be hidden from view. I feared for our lives if the Maids had been revealed. We—'

'They were but children, Master Chulkhurst,' said Farmer Umfrey, 'intent on no more than childish mischief. A few words and the smack of my rod and they soon dispersed. No-one under my care need ever fear for their safety.' He glared at Gudrun. 'And from that moment onwards, the Maids were as docile as lambs.'

Thomas turned to Sister Agnes. 'There is no sound from the Maids. Has the journey made them unwell?'

'I do not know what troubles them, Master Chulkhurst. They were filled with excitement when we set off, but as we left Maidstone, their manner changed. They have uttered not a sound and show no interest in their arrival. I cannot judge the reason.' She knelt on the ground and closed her eyes in prayer.

Farmer Umfrey spoke, loud and impatient. 'There is a good hour remaining in the day before the last light is gone. Take charge of my cargo and let me be on my way. I have had my fill of this venture.'

'Bela, our handmaiden, has prepared some fine victuals,' Thomas replied. 'Surely you will accept a night's hospitality after your long journey?'

Farmer Umfrey shook his head. 'The company of my beasts and the bleak surroundings of a coldharbour are more enticing than any of the comforts you could offer me here. Begging your pardon, Master Chulkhurst, I mean no disrespect, but every moment I spend on this Devil's errand is a moment in Hell. Give me my recompense and I will be on my way.'

Thomas's gaze flitted between Gudrun and Sister Agnes, but it was Sister Agnes over whom he held his lantern, taking in a deep breath as he loomed above her. 'What transpired on this journey? What evil spell has been cast? Eliza and Mary are silent, when I would expect to hear their cries for release. What fate has befallen all of you?'

Gudrun grabbed her husband's arm, her eyes blazing with anger. 'It is your wife from whom you should seek answers,' she said. 'There has been no calamity. We are but tired from the ordeals of our journey. The Maids are silent because they are in a mood of abject melancholy. They have seen for the first time the sights of the outside world, and have come to realise the wretchedness of their existence.'

Thomas looked over at the cart. 'But they have survived? And there has been no discovery of their existence? For that at least, we should give thanks.'

'Give thanks all you want, but I must depart,' Farmer Umfrey insisted. 'I have fulfilled my part of the bargain, and want to be detained not a moment longer. Take these things into your possession and let me be gone.'

Thomas bristled. 'They are not "things", Farmer Umfrey, but two of God's children that He put on this earth. No matter, their accommodation has been prepared for them. Follow my light and I will discharge you of your duties. I have ten rabbits in a game bag for you, and a haunch of smoked venison as an extra bounty. I hope you consider that a fair price for your travels.' Without waiting for a reply, he turned to Sister Agnes. 'You are most welcome to bide here until you feel restored from your journey.'

'That would be a blessing,' she said, deciding to say no more about staying on until the commotion of their arrival had subdued. Thomas beckoned his wife to join him and they went ahead of the cart, down a rough track off the main path to the longhouse. Dark trees bent together, whispering secrets to each other. They came to a roughly built byre with a gate secured by a large iron bolt. Thomas pulled back the bolt to reveal the interior.

'Sister Agnes, say a benediction of welcome to bless the Maids' abode.' He glanced away, shuffling his feet and clearing his throat as he waited for her to respond.

Sister Agnes squinted in confusion. 'This is merely a steading, in which to pen beasts in the winter, is it not? No human being, especially a child of frail disposition, can live in these conditions.'

Thomas swallowed hard before he spoke. 'Before I left Malling Abbey, my wife and I discussed how best to prepare for the Maids' arrival …'

Gudrun stepped over and squeezed his hand. Thomas patted her arm before continuing.

'I have put this arrangement in place until the time is right, to avoid any chance discovery. They are to stay there at night, and at all times when they are not being directly supervised.'

Sister Agnes ducked through the entrance of the byre and looked inside. A mat of straw lay on the hard clay floor. Gaps between the wooden joists were filled with wattle and daub and there was a wooden bucket in the corner, half-filled with water and a ladle next to it. It was even more austere than their room at the abbey. She clambered back out and tried to put on a brave face. 'As long as there is love and Christian charity shown to the Maids, their material world will matter not. The weather tonight is fair. I will spend this first night here with the poor souls. They will be mightily afraid to be left alone in such a rough abode.'

Gudrun jumped in to speak. 'What a kind heart you have, Sister Agnes. Come, let us clear the cart so Farmer Umfrey can be on his way. Thomas, why don't you settle your business with the good farmer, while Sister Agnes and I prepare the room for the Maids?'

Thomas closed his eyes for a moment, then started nodding vigorously. 'A fair plan, Gudrun. Time is our enemy tonight. Ensure Eliza and Mary are settled quickly while I deal with Farmer Umfrey's despatch. Once Sister Agnes is made good to bide here, we can adjourn to the longhouse and you can tell me all that is pressing from your journey.'

The men lit another lantern and headed off. Gudrun turned to Sister Agnes. 'Let us deal with the Maids quickly,' she whispered. 'The more time they have to become aware of their new surroundings, the more trouble they will be.' Without waiting for a reply, she headed over to where the oxen had been tethered and slid back the door of the cart.

The Maids cowered in the darkness at the back.

'We are here at last,' Gudrun said quickly. 'Climb down and Sister Agnes and I will show you where you will sleep. It is late of hour and she will be with you tonight. On the morrow, Master Chulkhurst will greet you and tell you what will be expected of you here.'

The two girls pushed further up against the far side of the cart. Sister Agnes said gently, 'Come Eliza, come Mary. This is the beginning of a new life for you. Let us all sleep soundly together, and all will become clear in the morning. Your mother and father have prepared a bed for you tonight. It is a simple arrangement, but a cosy one. Farmer Umfrey will be returning for his cart in a few minutes. You don't want him to leave with you still in it, do you?'

The two girls looked at each other. Eliza shifted forward an inch.

'That's it, good girl. Come, I see a lantern approaching. Be brave, my dear children. Give me your hands and let me help you out of the cart. You will enjoy the firm ground under your feet and the fresh air in your lungs after so long a journey.'

As the girls slowly clambered down from the cart, Sister Agnes motioned for Gudrun to step away. She took Eliza by the hand and shepherded the Maids into the steading. Sister Agnes laid the lantern on the floor and watched as the girls looked around the cramped room, frowning and blinking rapidly.

Thomas and the farmer were standing in the doorway.

'Say goodbye to Farmer Umfrey, and thank him for bring-ing you here,' Sister Agnes told them. The Maids shrank into the corner, shaking their heads. 'Then I will speak for all of us. Thank you, kind sir, and God speed for your return to Malling.' Tears welled as she spoke. Farmer Umfrey returned to his oxen, untethered them and slapped them with his whip to get them moving. As they lumbered off, pulling the now-empty cart, he turned and looked back.

'A pitiful sight to behold,' he muttered, half to himself. He stood tall and addressed Sister Agnes. 'Tell no-one of my involvement in this diabolical escapade. Farewell, servant of God. I fear neither you nor your charges are welcome here, or anywhere else in God's kingdom. May you one day find solace and comfort from this ordeal you have undertaken. My peace will only come when I am far away from this place. I want never to be reminded of this dark day.'

As Thomas closed the gate to the pen, Sister Agnes felt as if a prison door was closing on her, that she was being punished for the crime of caring about the Maids. Thomas had not yet been informed that Gudrun had agreed to her staying on in Biddenden – the price of the nuns' silence for her attempt to have the Maids sent to the leper colony. There was still time to release Gudrun from her promise. Vague thoughts of returning to Malling streamed shapelessly through Sister Agnes's mind, like the long sad vapours of the moonlit sky. The Maids burst into an outbreak of sobbing as yet another wave of despair washed over them. Sister Agnes scolded herself for her lapse into weakness.

She settled the Maids on the straw mattress and lay beside them, twisting and turning, trying to get comfortable on the hard clay floor, the weeping of the Maids only adding to her despair. There will be a servant of God in this parish, she told herself, and he would help her out of this abyss. She prayed for that to be true.

A single candle flickered in the darkness and Eliza and Mary started whispering to each other. Sister Agnes could hear each one trying to goad the other to speak out.

'If you have something to ask of me, ask it,' the nun said, moving the candle closer to them. 'I know there is something troubling you, my dears. Let me share the burden with you.'

Eliza finally spoke. 'It's the splitting, Sister Agnes. It's not real, is it? It doesn't happen to other children, so they become grown up when they come apart. No-one in this world has been born joined, save Mary and me. And that means we are doomed to spend all our days together.'

Sister Agnes held up her Bible in front of her, like a shield of protection. 'I have heard you talk of this splitting on many an occasion. It is a thought I have never tried to force into your minds. I considered it a fanciful notion you entertained to give you hope in your predicament, and could not bring myself to be the one who dashed your precious hopes for salvation. I left your mistake uncorrected, not out of malice or deceit, but out of kindness and love. Yes, it is true, my dear maidkins. There is no place on God's earth where it is known how to split apart those whom God has joined together. Make peace with that news, and live your days accepting of your fate.'

Their cries went deep into the night, until exhaustion overtook them and sleep released them from their torment.

Chapter 11

Sister Agnes woke early and slipped out to find Thomas and Gudrun sitting at the longhouse table, finishing off their breakfast of bread and ale. A young girl was sitting cross-legged on the floor, chopping vegetables and mutton for that day's potage.

She took a deep breath and went over to them.

'The Maids are at slumber,' she said. 'Seeing the outside world for the first time on their journey made them realise the peculiarity of their predicament. It has vexed them deeply, and that was the reason for their melancholy on arrival.'

'Poor dears,' replied Gudrun, without lifting her eyes from her plate.

Sister Agnes ignored her. She said to Thomas, 'I did not mention this in the commotion of last night's arrival, but before we left Malling I petitioned Gudrun to allow me to stay and be a guardian to the Maids, at least until we know them to have no further need of special care and knowledge. Mother Avicia has given her blessing. Gudrun has graciously agreed to my request. Will you do the same?'

Thomas looked surprised. 'This a most generous offer, Sister Agnes, and one that shows your kind heart.' He turned to Gudrun. 'But why did you not tell me of this plan? The provision we have made for Eliza and Mary's upbringing takes no account of someone sharing what little accommodation we have found to spare for them.' He nodded to the young girl and said to Sister Agnes, 'Bela sleeps at the far end of the room from Gudrun and me, but a nun should not share the sleeping place of a married couple.' He scratched the back of his neck before continuing. 'There is scarce enough room to accommodate Eliza and Mary in the housing we have arranged. Surely Bela could provide the assistance you need?'

Bela's mouth fell open at the idea, fingers touching her parted lips.

Gudrun said, 'You are a girl of good courage. You will not be in terror of the sight of those poor creatures.'

Bela blanched and began chopping the vegetables more fiercely. After a moment, she spoke, her voice quavering.

'Is it true what Master Chulkhurst said? They are two young maids, joined together in the one body?' Her gaze darted back and forth between Sister Agnes and Thomas.

'It is true,' Sister Agnes replied, 'and I will not deny the revulsion aroused in some on first beholding them. All are struck with much distress and there will be no shame if that happens to you. I was no different when I first laid my eyes on them. But I have come to love and admire them, as I would any of God's children. In time, I am sure you will feel the same.'

Bela smiled at that, and her brow softened. 'I will try to follow your example, Servant of God. The Chulkhursts have provided a home for me, ever since I became an orphan. I will care for the Maids, as my master and mistress have cared for me.'

'What I saw of the Maids' accommodation last night did alert me to the hardships Sister Agnes would endure in providing this help,' Gudrun said. It seemed to Sister Agnes that she chose her words carefully. 'In truth, I wanted to give her a chance to absolve herself of the obligations to which she has committed. I had planned to discreetly enquire if she were still of the same mind, lest I embarrass her by praising her generosity and kindness in the event she had had a change of heart.' She spoke more confidently now. 'So, Sister Agnes, you have seen the Maids' living arrangements, which you would have to share. Do you find them agreeable?'

'Surely where you have placed the Maids is but a temporary arrangement?' Sister Agnes replied. 'They will succumb to the grippe within days if they live in such damp conditions; brain fever if their toilet festers on the floor. That place is a danger to their health and yours.'

Thomas swept an arm around the room. 'This is a working longhouse, Sister Agnes. People come and go here as they please, and the doors remain unlocked during the day. It would not be possible to keep Eliza and Mary in this dwelling without them wandering off and exposing themselves to harm. They could easily be struck down by some passing stranger or by a superstitious villager who accidentally encounters them when stopping by on some errand. Gudrun pointed out these truths to me before I left the abbey and bade me chose a dwelling that could be secured to stop them roaming too far afield. It may not be ideal, but it is in their best interests.'

Sister Agnes was unable to conceal her shock. 'You would have your children live in a filthy pen suitable only for the beasts of the field? That is not the arrangement Gundulf would have sanctioned when he granted his protectorate.'

Thomas stood up, his knuckles cracking as he clenched his fists. 'You forget yourself, Sister Agnes. You arrive here uninvited and seek to interfere in the arrangements we make in our own homestead. I think it best if you make haste to return to your abbey and pray to God to forgive you for your incivility.'

Sister Agnes bowed her head in humility. 'Forgive me, Master Chulkhurst, Mistress Chulkhurst, I meant no disrespect. My concerns for the Maids made me speak words that are not becoming of a servant of God. Your fears for their safety, were they to encounter a hot-headed visitor whose hand went to the hilt of his dagger before his brain offered counsel, are wise and well-founded.' But a quiver of resistance ran through her, giving her the courage to speak more. 'Surely, though, it is within the bounds of Christian charity to keep the Maids safe and also in accommodation that will give them vigour in both mind and body? It would not take many days to construct a lean-to to your fine dwelling that would be both secure and comfortable. For my part, I am happy to endure these conditions in the meantime, to ensure no ailments befall the Maids while it is prepared for them.'

Thomas looked at Gudrun for her reaction. With none forthcoming, he turned to Sister Agnes. 'Yes, a simple task, but one fraught with difficulties,' he said, glancing at Gudrun again. 'I have yet to inform the village elders of Eliza and Mary's presence, and such news needs to be handled with great delicacy. I would need two strong men to help me build even the most humble of rooms for the Maids, and it would be impossible to keep their presence secret while they worked here. They might suspect something was afoot or, worse, catch a premature glimpse of the Maids before I had the blessing of the village elders. That could do our cause more harm than good.'

'Then pray share this news,' said Sister Agnes, 'before the day is out. There is no merit in waiting. Be strong and let your heart take courage, for it is the Lord your God who goes with you. He will not leave you or forsake you.'

Thomas lowered his head. 'But it is not from any lack of sprit that I have not yet sought an audience to bring news of Eliza and Mary's arrival. A description of what has become familiar to us could strike fear into the hearts of those who have to imagine the horror, so I thought it best to wait for their arrival. But you are right – I should tarry no longer. I will ride to the village now and inform the elders of our news.'

Gudrun squeezed Thomas's hand. 'Tell only Father Drogo in the first instance. Summon him here to see the Maids and to provide wise council. It is right that a man of God should be the first to give you guidance on how the Maids should spend their lives.' She turned to Sister Agnes. 'I trust that meets with your approval?'

'Of … of course,' said Sister Agnes. 'Forgive me twicefold. I meant no disrespect with my comments. And you are right. A man of God will guide us to do the right thing.'

Gudrun patted her husband's arm. 'Then hurry forth, Thomas, and send a message to Father Drogo that we require his urgent ministrations. I will try to make the Maids' quarters more comfortable as we await his arrival. I am sure his words will guide us as to the best path.'

THE PRIEST WAS a small man, a fact accentuated by the voluminous nature of his robes. Sister Agnes was wary of him from the start. He exuded a bloodless reluctance, as if every moment spent in another's company was an unnecessary distraction from some higher cause. He greeted the Chulkhursts with an icy indifference, seemed to regard Sister Agnes as an inconsequential inferior, and made it clear this journey to discuss accepting the Maids into his congregation was an affront to his dignity.

'I heard strange tales of the coming of your daughters into the world when I arrived in this parish,' he told Thomas Chulkhurst. 'I never deigned concern myself with the prittle-prattle of village peasants and their stories of cacodemons in their midst. But now you tell me that two strange beings were indeed brought into the world under your roof, and have been cared for and nurtured in secret by the nuns of Malling Abbey all these years.' Drogo sighed and pulled up the cuffs of his robe. 'And you have seen fit to bring them back to whence they came, and call upon me to give a blessing to their return. I cannot see why you burden me with such an undertaking. I know not the nature of their deformity, but there are many in this world who have afflictions that they must bear with fortitude.'

'I want my daughters to walk freely,' Thomas replied, 'and your benediction would reassure the good people of this village there is nothing to fear from their presence. I have a protectorate from Bishop Gundulf himself, stating no harm should come to them. I would like you to inspect this and beg most humbly that you assign your authority to it also.'

Drogo's shrug displayed a blank absence of interest or empathy. 'Let them look the other way if they are offended by your daughters' presence. I am too busy to be bothered by such whimsical demands. What could be so repugnant as to require my blessing?'

'Sister Agnes knows them best. Let her tell you of their affliction.'

The nun shrunk back in her chair. 'It is better you put it in words, Master Chulkhurst.'

Drogo rose to his feet in a portentous rage. 'I shall waste no more time on these childish games. There is no deformity in this kingdom that needs a priest's blessing to allow common folk to see it without descending into madness. Next time you call upon me, Thomas Chulkhurst, be sure it is a matter of some importance.'

Thomas beckoned him to sit down. 'It is no ordinary deformity, Father. My daughters were joined in the womb and can never be separated. They are two souls, but with one body between them, sharing every moment of life together.'

'I will not hear such blasphemy,' Drogo raged. 'What you speak of is witchcraft and sorcery. I will not be party to it. Let me be on my way.'

'Bring Eliza and Mary to us, Sister Agnes,' Thomas said softly. He put a hand on Drogo's shoulder. 'Spare me a moment more, good priest. You can see with your own eyes.'

Drogo fingered the cross around his neck, but did not rise to leave.

Sister Agnes left without waiting for a reply, and returned a few minutes later with her charges. Despite his attempts to feign indifference, Father Drogo craned his neck to try to see what was behind her in the doorway.

'I'd like to present my daughters, Eliza and Mary,' Thomas said with cold formality. He turned to the Maids. 'Enter, Eliza and Mary, and allow yourselves to be seen.'

'What trickery is this?' Drogo exclaimed, holding his cross in front of him. 'Do not tempt my patience, Chulkhurst. Keep up this pretence no longer.'

'It is no pretence,' Thomas replied. He strode over, and with a quick movement pulled up the Maids' smock, exposing the join at their hips. The Maids screamed in horror at the indignity and pulled away, causing Thomas to lose hold of them. They huddled in the corner, crying inconsolably.

Drogo threw himself prostrate on the ground. 'Be gone with them, be gone!' he yelled. He jumped up and headed out the door, running as fast as he could.

Thomas disappeared in pursuit. Sister Agnes went over to the Maids, smoothed down their smock and tried to calm their crying. Once their sobs had reduced to quiet whimpers, she took them to the steading and they said a prayer together. As they finished, she heard the door of the longhouse open and close.

'Rest for a while,' Sister Agnes said to the Maids. 'You may play with your dolls until I return.' Without waiting for a response, she headed back to the longhouse.

Thomas was pouring himself a cup of ale. 'I fear we may have made an enemy, not a friend,' he said with a heavy sigh. 'The priest ran off like the hounds of hell were chasing him, screaming curses like a man possessed. I will walk into Biddenden on the morrow and talk to him once he has calmed after the events of today. He has not yet perused Gundulf's protectorate and when he does so, he will surely see the need for his authority to be added to it. If I can persuade him to return, we can arrange for him to see Eliza and Mary at play and try to warm his heart to them.'

The following morning, Thomas kissed Gudrun goodbye and headed off to the village. Gudrun stared after him, then turned to Sister Agnes, running a jerky hand through her hair. 'All depends now on how well Thomas can bend the will of the men of Biddenden to his cause. We must be prepared to honour the outcome of the debate, whatever it may be.'

Gudrun was right, Sister Agnes realised. The fate of the Maids depended on gaining the village's support.

Now it was up to Thomas to achieve it.

Chapter 12

Thomas walked the one-hour distance from his longhouse to Biddenden to find Father Drogo was already presiding over a session of the Hundred Court, sitting in a large chair next to the village cross and communal bread oven, where important meetings took place. A crowd of twenty to thirty men had gathered around him, the heads of every longhouse and sunken hut in the village, each jostling for position to get close to where the discussions were taking place. Thomas was shocked. The Hundred Court met once in every month and was where important matters of village life were debated. According to tradition, the court made its rulings based on collective decisions, but in practice a rich nobleman was the chairman and dominated proceedings. He knew that only in cases of great urgency would the court be summoned between regular sessions, and in such event, in the absence of someone of high enough rank, the senior clergyman of the village would preside. Thomas could not remember the last time Drogo had run the court.

Standing next to Father Drogo was Hamond, the village dean. He would have authorised the calling of this special court and put Drogo in the chair. Deorwin, the reeve or village headman, the most senior of the village elders, was addressing the crowd as Thomas arrived. The fact that his friend was speaking gave Thomas some small comfort.

Deorwin broke off when he spotted him.

'We do not have to pass judgement on our good neighbour, Thomas Chulkhurst,' Deorwin told the other elders. 'Look, he has come amongst us. Let us have him tell his own truth of what Drogo says he has witnessed.' He turned to Thomas. 'Drogo has told us you summoned him to witness a sight of such great horror that it was only his strong character and devotion to the Lord that prevented him from turning to madness as a result. He petitioned Dean Hamond to call this meeting of the Hundred Court without delay, with a view to organising a posse of village men to drive out the cacodemon from our midst. What lies behind these claims?'

Thomas gasped and his legs weakened beneath him.

'I came to Biddenden today,' he said, 'to inform the village elders of the return of my daughters to my home after many years in the care of the good sisters of Malling Abbey. They were born with a most tragic deformity, and many thought they would not be long for this world. But they have triumphed over adversity, and now deserve to return to the bosom of their family. I met with Gundulf, Bishop of Rochester, and overseer of Malling Abbey, to discuss their safe return and he issued a protectorate, in his own hand, to ensure they can live amongst us, safe from retribution. I have it with me.'

Drogo jumped up from his chair. 'Tell them of this deformity. Let our elders judge whether you bring a horror into our midst.'

Thomas tried to keep his voice calm and measured. 'My dear Juliana, whom many of you will remember with love and sadness, died giving birth to twin girls. They were born joined together at their hips so they will live side by side, bound together until the end of their days. They are not demons, but two innocent children who have to suffer this most monstrous affliction. Do not make their suffering worse by turning against them.'

There was a collective gasp.

'You see?' Drogo spat out the words. 'Thomas has from his own mouth confirmed the terrible sight I described to you. Let us act now and rid ourselves of this evil in our midst.'

'You say you have with you Gundulf's protectorate?' Deorwin asked Thomas. 'If so, show it to the court.'

Thomas unravelled the goatskin document and handed it to Father Drogo. 'You may read it to the court,' he said.

Drogo studied the document for a few moments and read it aloud. Despite the fact that most of the elders – and indeed Thomas himself – could understand only a little Latin, the solemnity and reverential tone of the protectorate made it sound like a prescription that had to be obeyed.

Drogo spoke again, almost dismissively. 'It says only that Thomas and Gudrun Chulkhurst should be allowed to have their daughters live with them in their house.'

He handed the protectorate back to Thomas and addressed the crowd. 'That can be their choice. But let us demand of Thomas Chulkhurst that this monstrous apparition remain locked up and hidden from view, so no-one else should ever have to suffer the sight my eyes have witnessed. And let us pray its days are not long on this Earth.'

A murmur of alarm and fear swept over the crowd, and Thomas knew the reason well enough. Drogo was a firm and authoritarian priest, who frequently struck fear into the heart of his congregation by his condemnation of the evil sins committed by those around him. As far as this gathering were concerned, for their priest to be so horrified by what he had seen meant that whatever was at Thomas's house must be dreadful in the extreme.

'Let us petition Gundulf to rid us of this evil,' shouted one of the villagers. 'Send them back whence they came.'

'Aye, aye,' was the murmured response.

Drogo's eyes gleamed with triumph. 'Let it be known that that is the will of this court!' he shouted. 'That this Chulkhurst evil should be banished from our midst.'

Thomas looked around helplessly. 'They are but innocent children, strong of mind and body. They will do no-one any harm. Why can they not stay with me?'

'How do we know this protectorate was written in Gundulf's hand?' someone called out from the crowd. 'Thomas Chulkhurst could already be under the demon's spell and trying to deceive us. We need protection from this evil.'

Drogo nodded sagely but did not reply. A few more outbursts from the crowd and the groundswell of opposition to the Maids would become unstoppable.

Thomas called for quiet. 'Let me put my hand on the pyx,' he said, 'and swear that these words are truly Gundulf's. I also swear that the Maids were cared for by the nuns of Malling who called on Gundulf to decide on their fate. One of the nuns of the abbey journeyed with them to look after them here. She has cared for them for many years and shows much affection towards them. Believe me, elders of Biddenden, they can do us no harm.'

Drogo's expression was one of false pity. 'It is indeed a double calamity you have suffered, Thomas Chulkhurst. Your first wife was taken from you in childbirth and this most hideous deformity was brought into the world, which has defied God's natural order by remaining on earth to torment those who encounter it. If you wish to remain in this torment, so be it. But do not inflict a similar anguish on your friends and neighbours. Your malformed offspring, by the grace of Gundulf, shall be cared for at your abode. But they are never to step outside the walls of your property and you must shield them from visitors to your farm and from any passing strangers who know not what lies inside. This is my judgment, which I humbly petition Deorwin, reeve of Biddenden, to ask the village elders to agree to.'

Deorwin gave Thomas an anxious glance. Thomas nodded in return, his body slumped in defeat. Deorwin took a deep breath and walked over to the other elders, standing together.

A woman's voice called out, 'Have you no pity for these unfortunate souls? How can you judge what you have not seen?'

It was Ada, the village alewife. She pushed her way through to stand next to Thomas, and turned to address the crowd. 'Do our elders believe us to be a village of faint-hearted cowards, who need to be protected from sights that could cause us distress? Can two young maids really strike such fear into the heart of the stout people of Biddenden that we must be protected from ever catching a glimpse of them? I think we are made of stronger stuff. If they do no harm, let them live amongst us.'

'Be quiet, shameless harridan,' shouted Drogo. 'You have no locus to speak here.'

Thomas knew this to be true. Women were not allowed to testify at Hundred Courts, but strong-willed individuals like Ada often spoke their minds. She would not be silenced. She pointed to a man at the back of the crowd.

'Poor Baldric was struck down by some accursed ailment that ate away half his face. Yet he is always welcome at my alehouse and I see many of you here who carouse with him. Are we now to shun those whose appearance displeases us? If that were the case, many a bedraggled ruffian would find themselves barred from my inn, and the nights would be less boisterous as a result. I say again, how can you judge what you have not seen? Appraise others by their character, not the fineness of their features. And if these maids are upright and noble, and blameless for their condition, let us welcome them into our hearts.'

A few of the elders gave shamefaced nods. Deorwin seized his chance. 'Let us assure ourselves that the children of Thomas Chulkhurst present no threat. I propose that Thomas here permits me to meet these children, to examine them and present my conclusions to the next Hundred Court. If they can do us no harm, they should be free to walk amongst us.'

One of the other elders spoke next. 'I have young children that were born at the time of Juliana Chulkhurst's untimely departure from us. If, as Father Drogo says, the presence of these young maids is a sight too abhorrent to behold, I need to know if my children should be spared from such distress. Let all such elders as share my concern be included in the party that decides on their fate.'

This compromise satisfied the villagers. Enough of the elders would be involved in the decision to make sure the

Maids would not be forced upon the village. Drogo, sensing the mood turning against him, decided to acquiesce.

'Those of the elders,' said the priest, 'who wish to journey to Chulkhurst Farm, let them be known to me. We will consider their appraisal when we next meet. Is that the decision of us all?'

It was agreed and people started to disperse. Ada slipped away to avoid further rebuke from Drogo.

Deorwin came over to talk to Thomas.

'There was no time to reach you when Drogo petitioned Dean Hamond to convene a summary assembly of the Hundred Court,' he said, shaking his head. 'I am sorry. It was good providence you arrived in time to temper the judgment Drogo was seeking to hand down. Maurice, the elder who spoke out, is a good man and will be fair in his deliberations. Nigel and Osbert are two of the other elders I saw informing Drogo they wish to be included. With Hamond and myself, that makes five elders who will decide. We should go straight away, before Drogo attempts to plant more seeds of doubt in their minds.'

'I must inform my wife of these events before you arrive,' replied Thomas. 'Let me return home and announce your visit. Make your arrival when the sun is over High Tilt Hill. We will be waiting for you.'

THOMAS RETURNED to his farm and told Gudrun and Sister Agnes about the events of the day.

'A group of elders will be arriving before the day is out. Let us prepare Eliza and Mary for their visit.'

It was Sister Agnes who sounded a note of caution. 'As with all things to do with the Maids, we should move slowly and with caution. Let them be presented to the elders, but let the audience be a brief one.'

'But they return to the steading once the elders depart, yes?' said Gudrun. 'Your plan to keep a lock on their movement is a wise one, good husband. They would bring themselves to harm if they were allowed to roam freely.'

Thomas hesitated. 'For the moment they should live secure in the steading. But if this audience with the elders goes well, I will seek the labour to build more permanent accommodation for them with all due haste. And for you too, Sister Agnes, if your mind is made up to stay here. Not only will we benefit from your support, but also I fear I may have made an enemy of our priest by standing up to him today. Your knowledge of the Scriptures may well be important in rebutting any further attempts by him to use God's words to harm Eliza and Mary.'

SISTER AGNES SPENT the next hour with the Maids, coaxing them out of their melancholy.

'Your joining is something no-one else on Earth has had to suffer,' she told them. 'Now you know the truth and must make the best of it. Your father has returned from the village where all were told your story. The most important men of Biddenden are to journey here to meet you, so you can be welcomed into their lives. Show them how special you are, just as you showed Bishop Gundulf when you met him.'

'I don't want to be special. I want to be like everyone else,' Eliza said. 'Why can't we be normal, Sister Agnes? It's not fair.'

The nun smiled sympathetically. 'Our time on this Earth should be spent in proving our faith in the Lord Jesus Christ. God gives you these burdens so you can overcome them. That makes you stronger and better as you grow up. Show that you will not let your affliction stop you leading a full life. Then a full life you will be allowed to live.'

For the first time, there was a glimmer of brightness in Eliza's eyes. 'A full life? Climb a tree? Swim in a river? Play with the village children? Is that what they will let us do?'

'Perhaps,' replied Sister Agnes, trying to hide the doubt in her voice. 'But only if they see you are courteous and obedient maidkins, born of a respectable family, who bring joy to those that meet with you.' She tried to look severe for a moment. 'And for that, you have to be on your best behaviour. And you, Mary ...' she said, as Mary tried to cower behind Eliza. 'There must be no sulking. Will you both promise me to be the good girls I know you are?'

'But the priest did not think we were nice,' Eliza replied. 'He screamed and ran away, even though we did nothing wrong. Won't these other people do the same?'

'Father Drogo was surprised, that's all. Like when you see a mouse. You scream, don't you? Even though you know it will do you no harm. Your visitors today will not be surprised when they see you. You will not be a mouse and frighten them away.'

Mary ventured a small smile. 'That's silly. People aren't mice.'

'Exactly,' Sister Agnes replied, clapping her hands. 'So, they won't be scared, will they?' She clasped her crucifix to find the strength to sound positive. 'Come, the day is moving on. Let us prepare for their arrival.'

～✗～

THE ELDERS ARRIVED late afternoon and Thomas presented the Maids to them. It was a more subdued affair than the meeting with Gundulf at Malling Abbey, but Sister Agnes's words had worked well at lifting the Maids' mood a little. Eliza recited the Lord's Prayer, but couldn't be coaxed into saying it in Latin. Mary shouted 'God save King Henry!' before burying her head in Sister Agnes's cassock. But it was still an impressive show.

The elders stepped outside and Deorwin addressed them, while Thomas listened intently.

'These are the innocent children of Thomas Chulkhurst, whose virtuous family have lived amongst us since the arrival of William of Normandy. I see no reason why their presence could cause any ill.' He drew himself up. 'Are there any who find cause to contradict me? Speak now, or forever stay silent.'

There was a long pause, crackling with tension. The elders looked at each other, each waiting for another to speak. It was Maurice, the elder who first voiced concerns at the Hundred Court, who was the one to say something.

'If they are to be safeguarded by Gundulf's protectorate, let Gundulf be held accountable for any disorder they may cause. If he agrees to be their protector, he must be responsible for the consequences.'

Deorwin nodded. 'As your reeve, allow me to inform Gundulf of the consensus of the elders – and the responsibility we ask him to bear. Then the Maids can live freely amongst us.'

They went back inside to tell the women of their decision.

Sister Agnes hugged the Maids so hard they squealed in discomfort. Thomas patted Gudrun's hand in a more subdued gesture of gratitude. Gudrun stiffened as he did so, but managed a weak smile. Thomas poured each of the elders an ale.

They downed in one gulp and left.

GERBERT AND GASTON arrived two days after the Hundred to start work on the Maids' new home, a lean-to extension to the Chulkhurst longhouse.

Thomas had chosen them because they were quiet men who got on with their work, and hopefully not the sort who would spend their time trying to catch glimpses of the Maids to regale the customers at Ada's alehouse with stories of what astonishing sights they had seen. As well as having similar-sounding names, as was common with brothers, they looked the same too. Each had a mop of thick, unruly black hair and a rugged build that marked them out as men who earned their living using their strength rather than their intelligence. Thomas knew them well. They had married at fourteen and fifteen, to two sisters the same age, and all had lived the last ten years in the same cotter house, seven paces long, five paces wide. They had never ventured more than a half day's walk from Biddenden their entire lives.

Thomas explained to the men that the lean-to was to have a roof of thin stone tiles and to be built of cob. He described the correct proportions of sand, stones, clay and straw, but the brothers' attention kept wandering. Even to those who never troubled themselves with the world around them, the intrigue of the Maids clearly proved irresistible.

Thomas shook his head. 'You know the story of those for whom this dwelling is being prepared. My daughters are weak from their journey and have already had to face the elders of the Hundred Court. They will not recover until their new dwelling is ready for them. It will take forever if all of your energy is spent trying to catch a glimpse of them.'

The two brothers blushed and muttered a feeble denial. A few minutes later, Thomas spotted Gaston wandering around the outside of the house rather than getting down to work. His patience snapped. 'I see it is best to satisfy your curiosity and be done with it. Let me introduce you to my daughters. The nun who cares for them is with them in the longhouse. Once you have feasted your eyes, I expect you to fix all your attention on your labours.'

Without another word, Thomas headed off to the longhouse, Gerbert and Gaston following behind. As Thomas stooped to enter the dwelling, he glimpsed one of them surreptitiously making the sign of the cross.

Thomas paused to allow his visitors' eyes to adjust. He took a certain pride in his home. It was a substantial building, as befit a successful farmer. The oak plank walls were joined edge-to-edge and footed in a heavy sill-beam. There were no windows, with only the slight gaps between the oak planks letting in any light. The earth floor was covered in reeds from the banks of the nearby River Beult. In the middle of the single room, a square of stones surrounded the hearth, and above the flame a pot of bones for soup hung from a tripod.

The heat always made the walls expand and contract, softly creaking. It was the sound of a home at peace, resting.

At the one end was a manger, with two young calves lying beside it. And beside the hearth were Eliza and Mary, watched over by Sister Agnes, playing with their dolls. After they had met with the elders, their mood had calmed. Bela was next to them, grinding some corn, relaxed in their presence. It was a scene of domestic normality, not at all what the brothers had expected.

They squinted into the gloom. The two girls had their backs to them, and were engrossed in making up a story together, using their dolls as characters, moving them around the floor as they enacted what their words described.

'I want to climb a tree today,' Eliza's doll said.

'I will come with you,' Mary's replied. The two girls started moving their dolls up the iron tripod from where the cooking pots hung.

Sister Agnes gave a laugh full of genuine warmth, then looked up at the visitors.

'Look, Eliza. Mary, look! Here are the men I told you about who have come to build our special house. Say thank you to them for coming here today.'

Eliza and Mary turned towards them, like flowers to the sun.

'Thank you,' they said in unison.

SISTER AGNES STOOD behind the Maids, a hand on each of their shoulders. A smile flashed over her face, but inside, her stomach was churning. Since the elders left, these would be the first villagers to catch sight of the Maids, and she knew their reaction would be critical. Sister Agnes had foreseen that the brothers would have to see Maids before they could start working on the lean-to, and had spent the morning schooling the Maids to be on their best behaviour. She had spent the last half-hour playing their favourite game with them. This first encounter had to be as undramatic as possible.

'This is Maud,' said Eliza, holding up her doll. Mary was supposed to do the same, but instead squirmed with embarrassment.

'Thank you, Eliza,' Sister Agnes said quickly. 'If Mary doesn't want to tell the name of her doll, let's not force her. Remember we all agreed to be on our best behaviour today.'

Sister Agnes addressed the brothers. 'I hope it pleases you that your work here will bring joy and contentment to these two deserving souls. Let us not detain you, I know you are busy men.'

Gerbert and Gaston stood stock-still, their staring eyes betraying a bewildering labyrinth of emotions – incredulity and amazement, shock and confoundment. They stammered an incoherent acknowledgement, then reeled and swayed out the door, Thomas following behind.

Sister Agnes considered their reactions. Shock, perhaps, but neither fear nor rage. A good sign.

OUTSIDE, THOMAS MOTIONED the brothers close and said, 'Would you like a drop of ale?'

Gerbert nodded mutely; Gaston gazed into the middle distance.

Thomas produced two wooden cups of ale and the men took them with trembling hands and drank them in an instant. Finally, Gerbert spoke.

'The village was abuzz with rumours after the Hundred Court was convened with no nobleman in attendance, and the word was that two ungodly children had come to live amongst us.' He drank another draught of ale and belched loudly. That lifted his mood. 'Many are waiting to hear tales of what we have seen today. I do not think my simple words will be able to do justice to what I have witnessed.'

'The plan is for Eliza and Mary to spend their lives here in peace and solitude,' Thomas replied wearily. 'They have lived all their lives in the abbey at Malling and are little experienced in the ways of the outside world. I do not want them to become the focus of any attention from the village. Eliza and Mary were revealed to you today so that you would go about your work and not spend all your time trying to sneak a glimpse of them. Filling the alehouse with stories of what you have seen today will lead to a procession of intemperate troublemakers heading to our home on the morrow. I respectfully ask – no, I demand – that you respect my wishes and stay silent.'

Gerbert fiddled with the sleeve of his tunic. He cleared his throat before answering. 'Forgive me, Master Chulkhurst, but it would be foolish to believe something such as this could live amongst us without attracting curiosity and prying eyes. There are already stories being told to those who were not at the elders' meeting, that a woman with two heads or a half-human creature has been brought to live at your farm. You will spend all your days fighting off meddlers and busybodies bent on finding the truth and having a tale to tell about their encounter with what they find here. It would be far better for you to be the master of these confrontations. The Maids should be introduced to the village, shown openly to all that want to see, and you should answer any questions God-fearing folk may have about them. Better that than constant gossip and tittle-tattle amongst those with idle hands and loose tongues. Then there will be some small hope they will be left in peace.'

Thomas thought about this for a moment. 'I have a protectorate from Bishop Gundulf which, contrary to the impression conveyed by Father Drogo earlier, specifically guarantees the safety of my daughters. Maybe we could organise a welcoming fayre to introduce them to the villagers. The protectorate could be read out to introduce them, and I will pay for the day's food and drink. The promise of free victuals should ensure the crowd is well disposed and the bishop's strong words should curb the passion of any hot-headed agitators who might seek to do mischief.' Thomas gave a crisp nod. 'Your idea is a good one, Gerbert. I will speak to Deorwin about it this very day. With his blessing, we will hold the welcome fayre on this moon's quarter day.'

Gerbert grinned widely. 'And for our part, Gaston and I will speak no words of what we have seen today, no matter how many attempts are made to loosen our tongues in the alehouse tonight. It is four days until the quarter day. The secret can be kept until then, but I would not delay further. The fishwives were already chattering as we left this morning.'

Thomas left Gerbert and Gaston to begin work on the lean-to and headed to Biddenden to speak to Deorwin. The reeve had just returned from the port at Tenterden. The sea channel out to Rye Bay and the English Channel meant it was an important landing point for goods from France and Deorwin was sorting through a consignment of fine linen that was destined for the seamstresses at Yalding. He greeted Thomas with a hearty handshake.

'Well met, good friend Thomas.' He looked around. 'I would take care as you wander in these parts. Our friend the priest is still sore from his humiliation at the Hundred Court and has not given up on doing you ill. The village is buzzing with stories of strange demons residing at your home.'

'I know this well,' replied Thomas. 'My two workmen arrived this morning, the brothers Gerbert and Gaston, and I made sure they saw my dear daughters soon after their arrival. They witnessed them at play, and our handmaiden at ease in their presence. Their reaction gave me great hope; it was one of wonderment and awe rather than fear and panic. Gerbert is a solid fellow, with much wisdom for one who earns his living only by the fruits of his hard labour. He bid me arrange a welcome fayre on the next quarter day, to show Eliza and Mary openly and without shame or fear. By demonstrating there is no horror hidden from sight in my home, I hope others in the village will also respond with Christian charity rather than the crazed rantings of fearful zealots. And there will be a whole roast hog to feast on, and twenty barrels of ale, all paid for by my own purse. That should ease the acceptance of my daughters' presence amongst the people here.'

Deorwin put down the bundle of cloth and considered Thomas's words.

'A brave plan, Thomas. It has much to commend it. I would struggle to find the courage to take such a bold step, but I admire your strength of will to see no harm comes to your unfortunate kin.' He put his hand on Thomas's shoulder. 'Biddenden will be a merry place that day on account of your generosity. Richard of Canterbury, who deals with the secular matters of Anselm, Archbishop of Canterbury, is arriving on the morrow to purchase some of these linens I have secured. He is a fellow with an adventurous spirit who has the ear of his lord. Why don't I bid him stay a day to be guest of honour at the feast? He is a man of commerce more than a man of religion. You have the Church's blessing with Gundulf's protectorate. Some secular patronage would further secure your position.'

Thomas nodded. 'Were such a noble man to give my family his blessing, it would indeed confer great status on my household. Eliza and Mary's presence at the fayre will be brief; they are unaccustomed to crowds and I do not wish it to be too much of an ordeal for them. If Richard would be satisfied with but a fleeting glimpse of them, your plan is a good one.'

Deorwin slapped Thomas on the back. 'Till the quarter day fayre, then. It will be an occasion Biddenden will remember for many years to come.'

Thomas smiled, but he wondered whether he had detected an uncertainty in Deorwin's voice.

Chapter 13
Mary

I'm scared.

Eliza's not, she thinks this is a great day. Biddenden is having a 'Grand Fayre' to welcome us to the village. Everyone will be there, and they will be there to see *us*. That's because we are the only two people joined together in the whole world, Sister Agnes told us. That means we're special.

She says everyone likes to look at special things.

Father is organising the feast at the fayre and Mother keeps going into the village to make sure things are ready. Everyone is excited apart from me. An important man called Richard of Canterbury is going to be there. Canterbury is where Anselm, the Archbishop of Canterbury, lives and Richard speaks to him every day. An archbishop is even more important than a bishop. Last year the King said Anselm could rule Kent for him because he was too busy ruling the rest of England.

That's how important he is.

But I like to listen, to learn things, not talk and show off. That's why I'm scared. Sister Agnes has told me that when we meet new people I must, must, *must* say something. Eliza is always showing off, and now that we are to be introduced to all the people of Biddenden she will get to show off to more people than she's ever shown off to in her entire life. She's practising saying the Lord's Prayer in Latin, like she did for Father at the abbey, and she is even learning a song Sister Agnes is teaching her called 'The Song of Roland', about a big battle that happened over in France, where the Normans come from. Sister Agnes says she has a beautiful voice.

I think it's loud and ugly.

Eliza has been bouncing about all the time, getting far too excited, and has been annoying me even more than usual. I don't want to go to the fayre. I told Sister Agnes and she got annoyed with me, before God told her to be kind again. She said Eliza can say the Lord's Prayer and sing her stupid song, but all I have to do is say, 'Long live King Henry, long live Archbishop Anselm,' really loud.

That's twice as much as I said to the elders.

Gerbert and Gaston finished our new house today and so we will sleep in it tonight with Sister Agnes, instead of that smelly damp room we've been living in since we arrived. I like Gerbert and Gaston. They're brothers just like Eliza and me are sisters, but not joined. They are big and strong and kind, and Gerbert gave us both a kiss on the top of our heads when he said goodbye and wished us good fortune at the fayre. Eliza says she's fallen in love with Gaston and when we grow up, she's going to marry him and I'll have to marry Gerbert.

I tell her not to be silly but she just laughs.

And I like Bela too. She's older than us, but only a little bit. God took her mother and father to Heaven and she came to live in our house. God only took our first mother to Heaven and left Father behind to look after us, so she must be twice as sad as we are. But she doesn't show it. She talks to us every day, and even plays with us sometimes, if she's not too busy. She says we are both lucky to have a sister, even one joined to us, as she doesn't have a sister or a brother or a mother or a father.

I didn't know other people can be sad too.

When the time comes, it feels so good to be in our new room, with fresh reeds on the floor, that we sleep until after the sun has risen in the morning. Sister Agnes wakes us and tells us she has been up since Lauds, praying to Jesus and the Virgin Mary that all will be well today.

That's good. Everything is going to be alright.

It is a lovely sunny day. Mother and Father are rushing about getting everything ready and my stomach keeps whizzing around inside me. Eliza is excited and happy and I can feel her happy blood coming into me and I can't stop it making me excited too. When the sun is high in the sky, Deorwin's ox cart arrives and when we climb on, I go to hide under the blanket.

'Drape it over your shoulders, dear maidkins,' I hear Sister Agnes say. 'And see all there is to see as we journey to Biddenden. Today you travel openly in the world for the first time. Rejoice in the day!'

I clap my hands, then Eliza does too.

Sister Agnes looks pleased but Mother is sulky and grumpy. She must be nervous too. Maybe if she claps her hands and rejoices she'll feel better. As the cart lumbers along towards the village, Deorwin is leading the way, with Mother and Father and Sister Agnes walking beside us. I keep looking at all the things I can see and ask Sister Agnes the name of everything. She tells me the names of the trees and the birds and the plants, but then said she's tired and asks me to stop. I try, but I can't. My mind is like a big, big piece of cloth; it soaks up everything it gets told, but it never gets so wet that anything drips out. Everything I learn stays there forever.

I want to know everything.

As we get nearer to Biddenden, some small boys spot us and shout, 'The Maids! The Maids!' and soon we are surrounded by a crowd of people, all jostling to see us. Father waves a stick to try to chase them away, but more and more keep coming. Soon we reach the village and see the fayre is already under way. At first everyone is cheering and singing, but as our cart goes along the main street the people cease cheering and, one by one, fall silent.

Eyes, eyes. Everywhere.

I am scared again. Eliza is the same. She puts her arm around me and squeezes me very, very tight. We grab the blanket and wrap it around ourselves. I feel I am about to cry, then I see Gerbert and Gaston up ahead, and they give us a cheery wave.

It feels wonderful, like a sudden burst of sunshine on a cloudy day.

Deorwin stops the cart next to a small platform made out of wood. A man is there, dressed in fine robes. Deorwin speaks.

'In the presence of you all I, Deorwin, reeve of Biddenden, call on Richard of Canterbury, advocate of His Excellency, Archbishop Anselm, to read a protectorate written in the hand of Bishop Gundulf of Rochester.'

My tingles are getting stronger now.

The other man climbs up onto the platform holding a piece of goatskin. Eliza squeezes me so tightly under the blanket that it hurts. The man speaks in Latin. There is silence when he finishes.

'I repeat these words in the common tongue,' he says, even louder. "*Let these baptised children, Eliza and Mary Chulkhurst, pass freely and live safely amongst you. Obey the wishes of their parents, Thomas and Gudrun Chulkhurst, in all matters concerning them.*"'

I am so proud to hear him speak my name.

There is a murmur from the crowd. Everyone is staring at Eliza and me. Deorwin speaks again. 'Thomas Chulkhurst, bring your charges onto this platform, so all may know to whom Gundulf has granted his protection.'

The good feelings go away.

Father steps down from the platform and bids us stand up. We do so, still holding onto the blanket.

'Do not trouble to bring your blanket, my dears,' Father says. But it is too scary. We shuffle off the cart and up to the platform. Father's face has a flash of annoyance, but when he looks straight at us, I can see he isn't really angry.

'Let it fall,' he whispers.

But we can't. Father gently tugs the blanket and it slips through our fingers.

They can see us.

There is a gasp from the crowd, shouts of, 'No! No!' and a lot of pushing and shoving as people try to come closer. Eliza and I hug Father, turning our back to the crowd. As I bury my head into Father's tunic, Deorwin addresses the crowd.

'I will not allow the day to descend into disorder. The Maids have Bishop Gundulf's blessing and our adherence to the terms of the protectorate is observed today by Richard of Canterbury.'

Eyes, eyes. Nothing but eyes.

I hear Richard's voice. 'I have travelled far to spread the word of God, and have made pilgrimage to the Holy Lands in the East, but never in my days have I seen a sight such as this. Let us have tolerance and mercy for what we see before us.'

I want to be invisible, like the wind, and blow away.

'Come, Eliza, turn and say the Lord's Prayer,' Father whispers. Eliza shakes her head. Father's gaze darts to me. 'Mary, will you speak?'

I shake my head too.

Father pulls himself up and speaks again, his voice loud and strong.

'Good people of Biddenden, I wish you to meet Eliza and Mary, the offspring of myself and my late wife, Juliana, who many of you will remember fondly. They have been cared for by the nuns of Malling Abbey since they were born six summers ago, and have now returned to be with us. There is nothing to fear from them. They are of sound mind and will live out their days in pious devotion to God. Enjoy the feasting and drinking today, and welcome them to our community. We are indeed blessed to have such marvels living in our midst.'

There are no cheers. Just the sound of women sobbing, of one or two men calling out.

Deorwin says quietly to Father, 'Allow them to leave now, Thomas. The shock has been great indeed. Return to your home and let me take the measure of the crowd throughout the day. Tarry here and the Maids will become distressed, and that might inflame the mood still further.'

Please, please, yes. Do as he says.

Father does not reply, but climbs down from the platform. Eliza and I keep our heads buried into his tunic. I grab Sister Agnes's hand and Eliza and I climb with some difficulty onto the cart. Some of the crowd are close to us now, yelling, unfamiliar hands touching and prodding us.

Both of us scream with all our heart.

Richard of Canterbury's voice rings out. 'Leave them be! For pity's sake, do not harm these defenceless creatures. We have all seen today something that will remain with us for the rest of our days. Let us end the Maids' ordeal of public display. They should be allowed to live their life in quiet seclusion, untroubled by further torment and suffering. They have much to bear in their lives as it is.'

Our screams turn to wails as Deorwin starts to move the ox cart through the crowd.

'Where Is Gudrun, Sister Agnes?', Father says. 'I left her here with you.'

I peek out from under the blanket and see Sister Agnes looking panicked. That makes me even more scared.

'She told me she went to seek Drogo the priest,' she told Father. 'I do not know where they are to be found.'

Where is Mother?

Father glares around the crowd. 'I do not want to delay our departure a moment longer than is necessary.' He calls to Gerbert: 'If you or your brother catch sight of Mistress Chulkhurst, tell her we have already departed. I dare not test the mood of this throng a moment longer. Tell her to make haste to return.'

The ox cart rumbles forward as Deorwin leads the oxen out of the village. A large number from the crowd follow us in silence. There is no more shouting. When we are a few hundred yards from the village, Father turns to address them.

'Eliza and Mary are tired from their ordeal and are in much distress. Please let us return to our home in peace. It may have been somewhat foolhardy to bring them here today, to put on a show for all to see, when they have spent their life hidden away from the world. Dismiss now, and I promise I will return on the morrow, and hold forth at the market cross to address your concerns and answer your questions as well as I am able. That is my vow to you. Now please, give us all some peace.'

Please, please.

Father must be very important, because that's exactly what they do, except for a few really annoying people who follow us all the way to the gates of our house.

'Be gone, will you!' Father shouts as Deorwin pulls the oxen to a halt. 'There is no more to see today. Disperse now or you will not be made welcome at the parlay I will hold on the morrow.'

Yes, yes, go away.

We hurry down from the cart and into our special house. Sister Agnes slides the door lock shut, lights a candle and hugs Eliza and me tightly.

'You did well today, my dears,' she says, and that makes me feel more cheerful. 'I am proud of you. We will visit Biddenden again, when composure returns to the village. Now let us bring some peace and tranquillity to our own souls by resting a while.'

But I never want to go to that nasty village ever again.

Chapter 14

I t was dark by the time Gudrun returned from the village. 'Apologies, dear husband,' she said to Thomas. 'I sought out Father Drogo to see if his mood towards the Maids had improved. I thought I would be gone an instant, but my search for him was long. When I returned to the fayre you had already departed, so I waited for Gerbert to bring me here. Much ale had been drunk and I dared not travel alone.'

'You are safe and that is all that matters,'Thomas replied. He sighed. 'It was a mistake to parade Eliza and Mary in front of the villagers so soon. The protectorate should have been read, nothing more. With every moment they were on view, the crowd were becoming more and more unruly. We were lucky they did not become truly belligerent.'

'There will never be normality when the Maids are out in public,' Gudrun said. 'There will always be a risk that their appearance will lead to mayhem, fear and chaos. This is what Drogo told me. Disorder will follow them everywhere and they will remain a source of morbid curiosity for the rest of their days. Our farm will be like a prison for them.'

'I do not trust that priest to have Eliza and Mary's well-being at heart,' Thomas replied. 'The words of Gundulf's protectorate were much stronger when spoken by Richard

of Canterbury than in Drogo's version. He is an enemy of
the Maids, not a friend.'

'Nevertheless, you told me of his displeasure at the
outcome of the elders' meeting and I wanted to try to win
his support. He wants no disorder in his parish.'

'That is what we all desire. I promised I would return
on the morrow to answer any questions and concerns the
villagers may have. But I am fearful that I will not know the
answer to all that will be asked. There is much about Eliza
and Mary's condition that is a mystery to me.'

'Then ask Sister Agnes to accompany you. No-one knows
the Maids better than she. I can care for them while you
are gone.'

Thomas's face lit up with relief. 'If anyone can convince
the villagers that there will be no ill to come from Eliza and
Mary living within us, it is Sister Agnes. I will not disturb
her now; she is at sleep with the Maids. We will tell her of
this plan on the morrow.'

SISTER AGNES MADE no objection to Thomas's plan that she
accompany him, and convinced herself that it would be good
for Gudrun to spend some time alone with the Maids, to be
solely responsible for them for the first time. She made sure
the Maids were settled in Gudrun's charge, then she and
Thomas set off for Biddenden. By the time they arrived at
the village, a sizeable crowd was already milling about the
market cross. The questions started immediately.

'There was trickery in what we saw yesterday! Will you
confess it?'

'Are they joined together for all eternity?'

'Do they have two souls?'

'Can we hear them speak?'

'Have they had a Christian baptism?'

Thomas raised his hand.

'Let us conduct these discussions in an orderly manner. I will do my best to answer your questions, but much is mysterious about their condition. They are truly unique beings in this world.'

It was Sister Agnes who ended up answering every question.

'Eliza and Mary were born joined together and will remain so for all their days,' she told the crowd. 'I have cared for them since they were babes in arms. There is a closeness between them that is wonderful to behold. Not only do they share every moment together; the one feels everything the other does. If one eats, the other feels full. But the connection is only a physical one. They cannot read the other's minds and they often desire to do different things at the same time. But they cannot. Every action, every movement is something they have to perform together.'

'I cannot imagine a life of such torturous constraints.' That was Ada, the alewife. Others reflected on this thought and a murmur of sympathy passed through the crowd.

'The last few days have been especially taxing for the children,' Sister Agnes went on. She tried to keep her voice calm and reassuring. 'Joined is the way it has always been for them, it's all they have ever known. Hidden away in Malling Abbey, they formed a view that their condition was commonplace and those of us they were permitted to see had started our days in a similar way, joined together. To my shame, I did not disabuse them of this notion. It was only when they left the abbey and saw the outside world for the first time they realised the truth. They are still children, and cannot yet grasp the enormity of what they have to deal with. May God forgive me for my deception.'

Ada spoke up. 'It is we whom God must forgive, for our unruly behaviour yestermorn. Let us make amends today, promise we shall do them no ill and allow them to visit freely amongst us. Their uniqueness brings us honour, not shame.'

Richard of Canterbury was present but had stayed back, observing. When people started to disperse, he and Deorwin approached Thomas to discuss the outcome.

'You acquitted yourself well, Thomas Chulkhurst,' Richard said. 'And you, Sister Agnes. You demonstrated that anyone whose heart is good and true has nothing to fear from the company of the Maids. Yes, there are a few of superstitious bent who are fearful of anything that is new and strange, but the words that were spoken rang true.' He smiled. 'The tongue of an alewife is well used to calming an unruly mob. Once the fervour surrounding the return of the Maids to Biddenden has died down, there should be no fear for their safety living here.'

'I would have been more reassured,' replied Thomas, 'if Drogo the priest had been in attendance and the villagers had heard his concerns tested in open debate. I fear he will stay in the shadows, seeking every opportunity to undermine acceptance of the Maids into the community.'

'He dare not contradict Gundulf's protectorate,' Richard replied. 'And you can add the weight of my support to their cause. The Maids will have to suffer constant curiosity about their condition, which I fear will be overwhelming at times, but that is a nuisance that can be managed. I admit, I too marvel at witnessing such a rare phenomenon. I will inform Archbishop Anselm on my return to Canterbury of all that has transpired here. To that end, may I be permitted to meet with the Maids once more, so that I may best represent them to His Excellency?'

Thomas agreed, and he and Sister Agnes departed Biddenden with Deorwin and Richard.

❧

GUDRUN WAS TENDING to a mutton stew that was gently simmering in the longhouse cauldron. She started on seeing two such august visitors arrive unannounced.

'Thomas, you should have sent a messenger to tell me men of such high degree were accompanying you to our home,' she said, blood burning her cheeks like the breath of a hot wind. 'I am not dressed for visitors and have no victuals ready to offer.'

'Fear not, good lady,' said Richard. 'It is I who have been presumptuous, entreating your good husband to grant us an audience with the Maids. I still cannot free my mind of what I witnessed yesterday.'

'The first sight will haunt you always, like the memory of some distant sadness,' Gudrun replied, nodding her head in sympathetic understanding. Then she noticed how Richard's features were quite at ease, and realised it was wonderment that lay behind his words, not horror and revulsion. Deorwin also displayed a certain calmness of spirit; and indeed, Thomas and Sister Agnes had a more relaxed air about them than when they had set off for Biddenden. The meeting had obviously gone in the Maids' favour.

Gudrun rallied herself. 'Bela, our handmaiden, has only just taken the Maids to their room to settle them for the night. Do you want me to fetch them for the audience you desire?'

'If settled, it is best they are not disturbed,' Richard said. 'I can return on the morrow.'

'It is early for the Maids to be at rest,' Sister Agnes replied. 'Perhaps it is not too late to disturb them. I will check.' Without waiting for a reply, she went outside.

AS SISTER AGNES SUSPECTED, the Maids were still awake and playing with their dolls, Bela patiently embroidering in the corner. Sister Agnes spoke to the Maids softly, but with quiet insistence.

'Two important men have come to visit you,' she told them. 'Deorwin, the reeve of Biddenden, and Richard from the city of Canterbury. They were most disappointed not to hear you sing yesterday, Eliza, and wondered if you could do so tonight. And Mary, would you say, "Long live King Henry" to them? They will be most happy if you do so.'

'No,' said Mary, hugging her doll.

'You never do anything,' Eliza said to her. 'You're boring, boring, boring.'

Mary's chin trembled, and Sister Agnes bent down to console her.

'Hush, hush. Mary, if you don't want to say anything, then of course you need not do so. But be nice and let your sister sing. You want to be nice, don't you?'

Mary didn't reply, but Sister Agnes stood up as if all had been settled. 'Come, dear maidkins, and let us greet Deorwin and Richard. I too look forward to hearing Eliza sing.'

Sister Agnes allowed herself a smile as they left the lean-to. Eliza would no doubt also have refused, but Mary's scolding had given her little choice but to perform. Once in the longhouse, she said the Lord's Prayer in Latin, and when everyone broke into foot stamping applause, Mary gained the confidence to speak out.

'Long live King Henry. Long live Archbishop Anselm,' she said, in a clear and confident voice. More foot stamping followed and when Eliza sang 'The Song of Roland', Richard was moved to tears.

'Archbishop Anselm will hear of this moment,' he said when Eliza had finished. 'These two young girls are a wonder to behold.'

'It is not the Archbishop of Canterbury I need to consider my daughters favourably,' Thomas replied. 'Even though that would be a great honour indeed. Father Drogo still harbours fear and resentment towards the Maids. I revealed them to him upon their arrival, but he fled at the sight and convened the hearing of the Hundred Court to have them banished from the village, or worse. Had not Deorwin pushed for a gathering of the elders to visit our home to see the miracle of the Maids for themselves, I do not know what summary justice might have been meted out.'

Richard frowned. 'The priest had read Gundulf's protectorate and still sought to do them harm? Then I will have Anselm inform Gundulf of his insolence. The bishop will not take kindly to a lowly village priest disregarding his words.'

To the evident surprise of the men, Gudrun interrupted their discussion. 'Father Drogo is a man of good intentions. Had he not alerted the Hundred Court to the presence of the Maids, their discovery would have caused even greater disorder than we saw when they were revealed to the villagers. He forgives others for their sins. Do not ask that Gundulf punish him for doing what he believed to be right.'

Thomas's mouth fell open. 'You should not interrupt our discussions, good wife. Especially if it be in support of one who wishes harm to the Maids.' He suddenly recalled Gudrun's absence when they departed the fayre. 'But you spoke to Drogo at the Maids' welcoming fayre. Do tell what he said. Have his views softened since he first set eyes on my daughters?'

Gudrun blushed crimson and averted her gaze. 'Forgive me, husband, for my lapse of decorum. My emotions got the better of me and I spoke without thinking. I ask all of you to pardon my lack of respect.'

Thomas gave a grim-faced nod and Gudrun continued. 'It is true that I have visited Drogo often since my return from Malling, as I sought his forgiveness for my failings as a wife and a mother when I first set eyes upon the Maids. He has absolved me of the sins of selfishness and cravenness I displayed at that time. He says that only God knows if the Maids are a blessing or a curse and that He will ultimately pass judgment on them, in this life and the next.'

'That is a view to which none can object,' Thomas said hurriedly. He appeared anxious to bring the discussion to a close. He glanced at Deorwin and raised his eyebrows, inviting him to talk.

'It is decided, then,' Deorwin said. 'I give thanks to you, Richard of Canterbury, for your words of support, and we can take reassurance that the presence of the Maids will be tolerated by both village and Church. Let us conclude our discussions on that note.'

Deorwin and Richard excused themselves and Thomas poured himself a large tankard of ale which he drank in one draught. As he poured himself another, he let out a long sigh.

'The worst of the Maids' ordeal is over,' he said to Gudrun. 'Now we can get on with our lives.'

Gudrun did not reply.

Chapter 15

Gudrun's mood seemed to have improved the next morning. 'It is fine weather these days,' she said to Thomas, 'and it is time Eliza and Mary saw some more of the world, but without the distress we saw at the Biddenden fayre. I will take them for a walk through the wood, to bring some strength to their bodies. Sister Agnes, you always spend your mornings teaching the Maids the ways of the world, and your devotion shames me. You must have a day of rest. It will be an adventure for both the Maids and myself.'

The nun thought for a moment before replying. 'That is truly a generous offer and one which I'm sure will find much favour with Eliza and Mary,' she said. 'But it would be no ordeal for me to accompany you on your wanders. The woods can be a perilous place to visit, and there is no telling who you might meet and what their reaction might be.'

Gudrun laughed. 'Come, come, good nun. We are not talking of going on a crusade. I will venture only into the edges of the wood, based on your good counsel. But it is time the Maids got to know me as a mother. For that bond to be forged, it is best to journey just the three of us.'

Sister Agnes gave a hesitant nod. 'I am sure the Maids will enjoy the day. Let us tell them of the adventure ahead.'

Eliza and Mary were excited at the thought of going for a walk with Gudrun, the most excited they had been since they had arrived at the Chulkhurst farm. At the sound of their eager chattering, Sister Agnes knelt down in a prayer of supplication. It was right and proper that a mother should want to spend time with her children, and she was displaying the sins of jealousy and envy. The danger that some could rise up and try to have the Maids banished from the village, or do them harm out of fear and superstition, seemed to have passed. The meeting with the villagers had been the first small step towards their new life. And that new life would only come fully to fruition when her role as the Maids' guardian was no longer required.

When they returned from their hour-long walk, the Maids were as merry as bees in clover. They regaled Sister Agnes with stories of what they had seen – frogs hopping through the grass by the stream; woodlice scurrying away when Gudrun tore some bark off a fallen tree; centipedes hiding under stones. Joy rioted in their eyes. The trip had been a success.

Sister Agnes listened with mixed emotions. Now that Gudrun was becoming a true mother to the Maids, she was a guest who was in danger outstaying her welcome. The Maids' needs were not burdensome. Bela could provide all the help that was needed and she was becoming like another sister to the girls.

Sister Agnes's thoughts turned to returning to Malling.

EARLY NEXT MORNING, Sister Agnes awoke to groans and whimpers coming from the Maids' end of the room. She rose up, bleary-eyed, the morning light still not strong enough to see clearly. As her eyes adjusted, she was shocked by what she saw. The Maids' skin was red, sweat was pouring from their brows, and they were shaking uncontrollably. She felt Eliza's cheek. Burning hot. The two girls were barely conscious, their groans sounding more and more desperate and severe.

She ran to raise the alarm, but when she reached the entrance to Thomas's longhouse, she stopped herself from entering. It must be the sweating sickness, she realised. If someone was strong and in good health it was possible to recover from it, but the very young, the very old and those who were infirm usually succumbed to its deadly embrace. She had spent much of the night huddled up against the Maids, just as their symptoms were developing. She should not go inside.

'Thomas. Gudrun. Awake!' she called. 'The Maids are unwell.'

A scuffling sound behind the door signalled she had been heard, so she headed back to the Maids' room. She waited with them, mopping their fevered brows. Thomas was the first to arrive.

'Wait for a moment,' said Sister Agnes. 'The Maids have a fever and I fear they are coming down with the sweating sickness. You would be best to keep apart from them, and from me. No doubt I will also suffer from the night I have spent with them.' As she spoke, she could feel a stab of heat piercing her like a knife. She wiped the sides of her eyes. The fever was building.

'Thomas! We must do as she says!' Gudrun said from behind them. 'We must isolate the Maids and Sister Agnes too. I will prepare some rue leaves to purge the yellow bile from their bodies. Let us pray it will restore them to good humour.'

Gudrun departed.

'Have any others been struck down?' Sister Agnes asked Thomas.

'None that I know, thank God. Bela is well and is already at work. Only you and the Maids seem afflicted.'

'And Gudrun is well?' Sister Agnes asked, concerned. 'The sweating sickness strikes quickly, so the Maids must have encountered the disease on their walk.'

'She is quite well,' replied Thomas. 'Wherever this bad humour came from, she has been spared.'

The fever was taking hold of Sister Agnes, but she forced herself to keep her mind clear. 'There is something in the woods that caused the fever to reach the Maids. You must find out what it is, and warn everyone to avoid it at all costs.'

GUDRUN WAS WAITING by the door of the longhouse when Thomas returned a few hours later.

'Biddenden is free of fever,' Thomas said, 'but there is a group of horse catchers living in the forest and one of them visited the village yestereven. Some of their number are said to have the sweats. A woman had died and one of the herdsmen asked Drogo the priest for a burial. He was given rue leaves and told to stay away, at their camp, until it was clear that no-one else was afflicted.'

'Then it must have been their camp that we encountered. The sickness must have lingered there.' Gudrun put the palm of her hand to her open mouth. 'I remember now. The Maids were weary from their walk and we chanced upon some blankets abandoned in a clearing, and a circle of stones where a fire had been. I bade the Maids rest on the blankets and they fell into slumber from their exertions. I sat apart, so as not to disturb their sleep.' She pressed the palm of her hand to her heart. 'That must be how I was spared the sweating sickness working its evil curse on me.'

'One small blessing to come out of this misfortune,' Thomas replied. 'Let me take them some more rue leaves and tell Sister Agnes of this news. Then we must leave them to their suffering. We will have to remain strong if we are to help them fight this scourge and take no risk that we too are stuck down. We can only pray that their fever breaks before it is too late.'

AS THOMAS AND GUDRUN sat alone that evening, despondently sipping the last of the day's mutton soup, there came a knock on the door. Gudrun looked at Thomas in some surprise, given the hour, and went to see who it was.

There were a dozen or more villagers from Biddenden, led by Ada the alewife. She was the one who spoke.

'Word had reached us, Mistress Chulkhurst, of your husband's enquiries today and that the Maids and the Malling nun are ill. We have come bearing food and drink to try to sustain them and you through this dark hour. Please let us be of assistance.'

'You must not stay here,' protested Gudrun. 'The Maids and Sister Agnes are indeed hot with fever, and the air around them is full of their malady. Your words are kindly spoken, but be fearful of your own ill health and stay away from us. We will care for each other as best as we are able.'

'Let that risk be shared by all that care about them,' Ada replied. 'The Maids are a wonder of the age and it is a great honour that they live amongst us. It would be a tragedy if they were to perish. If each of us spends but a little time with you we will not give the bad humour of the sweats time to affect us. They need to drink fresh ale and eat plenty of meat to fight off this scourge. We have bought such provisions with us.'

Despite the risks, there was no shortage of volunteers willing to visit Sister Agnes and the Maids with fresh provisions in the days that followed, and Gudrun and Thomas were in awe of their kindness. Ada was the most frequent, and when her duties at the alehouse meant she couldn't spare the time, there was always some other eager villager to help out. Most reported that they were greeted with a fleeting glimpse of the Maids on their visits, and a mumbled 'Thank you'. It seemed to have become a mark of status in the village if you had a story to tell about visiting the Chulkhurst Farm.

Each evening, as Gudrun waved goodbye to that day's helper, she blushed in shame at how it had taken others to show her that the Maids could be loved. As for her darker thoughts, she pushed them further and further from her mind.

SISTER AGNES'S HEALTH slowly improved, until she was able to assist in caring for the Maids. She prepared a brew of basil leaves cooked in wine and laced with honey, the same healing drink she prepared, as the abbey infirmarian, to treat any fevers that struck down the nuns. Within a week, both girls were able to get through the day without assistance. But with the threat of sweating sickness receding, the number of visitors became greater, not fewer. It wasn't just concern that made people want to help the Maids; it was also an insatiable curiosity that had grown up around them. The few villagers who feared the Maids or were disgusted by them were learning more and more to keep their thoughts to themselves.

Sister Agnes had a growing pride that the Maids were becoming accepted by the villagers, and the change in their circumstances served as confirmation that her decision – to leave as soon as she was able – was the right one. It was *their* community and their family who should guide them through their life. She was an outsider, and one who had pledged her life to serving God by living the life of a nun – not providing care for two children, no matter how deserving. Her time with the Maids was drawing to a close.

After waiting a few days more to make sure her fever did not return, Sister Agnes left the Maids playing with their dolls to tell Thomas and Gudrun of her decision.

'I need accept no more of your boundless hospitality,' she said to them. 'The Maids are well and have become settled in your home. God has tested their resolve by bringing forth the sweating sickness, and it has turned out to be a blessing, not a curse. Their frailty has brought out the best in the hearts of the villagers and we have seen the girls welcomed into the community, with many of the common folk beating a path to your door to provide succour and assistance. They no longer need a nun to care for them; indeed, they will grow stronger and more independent when I depart. It is time for me to return to Malling.'

Thomas could not conceal his shock. 'I am saddened by your decision, good Sister Agnes. The Maids do indeed seem to have won the hearts of the villagers, but there will still be many trials and tribulations ahead. It will be a struggle to overcome them without your help and guidance.'

'Your knowledge and wisdom will continue to grow, do not fear,' replied Sister Agnes. 'I should not stand in the way of children growing up bonded to their mother and father in the union of the family. That is the bond the Church tells is the one most good and true.' She looked at Gudrun as she spoke. 'It is time for the Maids to discover that.'

'And we likewise,' replied Gudrun, her voice rich with emotion. 'They will be heartbroken at first, but it will be for the best in the end.'

'NO. NO! PLEASE don't leave us!'

Sister Agnes had waited until the morning of her departure before telling the Maids. They blocked the door of the lean-to in a vain attempt to stop her.

The nun smiled at them, shaking her head in feigned annoyance. 'Now Eliza, Mary. You cannot stand in that door forever. Why are you so cruel, making the sad moment of my departure take longer than it need? You are two fine young maids. You have seen how many from the village have come to care for you in your time of need. Upon my departure, you will have a place in the longhouse to live with your mother and father as a family, rather than stay in this room with me. Rejoice at your new life; think no more of your old.'

'But you can't go, Sister Agnes. I don't want you to,' protested Eliza. 'You have always cared for us, no-one else can.'

'You dishonour your parents with these words, Eliza. There is nothing I can do that your mother cannot. Is there, now? Tell me, if you can.'

Eliza sobbed. It was Mary who consoled her. 'I want to love Mother, Eliza, just like I love Sister Agnes. Let us do so together.'

'We have to do everything together,' Eliza replied. 'You cannot love Mother on your own.'

'Then love together,' Sister Agnes said with a flourish, as if Eliza's protestations had been addressed. 'Now, I am travelling alone, and need to reach Maidstone by nightfall. Your last duty is to assist my departure.'

There wasn't much the Maids could really do, but getting them involved in the preparations for leaving helped soften their resistance. As Eliza and Mary stood alongside Gudrun and Thomas, with Bela in the background, there were both tears and smiles as they bade her farewell.

SISTER AGNES WALKED ALONE, trusting her memory to get her to Maidstone and from there on to the main road to Malling. The track was straight, following the old Roman road heading north, and she thought she would have no problem finding the way. But it became indistinct, and she had walked some miles to the east before the position of the setting sun told her she was heading in the wrong direction. Reluctantly, she retraced her steps, but taking the wrong path had lost her several hours. As night fell, she had got only as far as the coldharbour they had passed on her outward journey, four weeks earlier.

Darkness oozed out from between the trees and the presence of a group of tethered colts alerted her to the fact that some horse catchers had stopped at the shelter. She hoped that this did not foretell an unruly night. She went inside, and was pleased to find they were a group of two families, and had brought no ale. Sister Agnes joined them around the meagre fire in the middle of the room. The conversation was that of all travellers – where they had been and where they were going. She told them she had travelled from Biddenden.

'Biddenden! The name is cursed to me,' the leader of the group exclaimed. 'My good wife, Muriel, succumbed to the sweats in the east marshes and we headed to the village to secure some healing plants to drive out the scourge from her. But by the time we reached the Biddenden woods, our journey was in vain. She breathed her last nary an arrow shot from the village.'

Sister Agnes offered her condolences, but a second man brushed them away. 'Save us your pious sympathy, nun. My brother Ailwin is too good a man to let his feelings be truly known, but he feels that God deserted him at that dark time. Your priest at first refused to lay her soul to rest and made Ailwin perform an unholy ritual before he would perform the simplest of burial ceremonies.'

Sister Agnes frowned. 'Is it Father Drogo of whom you speak? He is a good man, committed to do God's work and would countenance no act of heresy being performed in his name. Indeed, he pursues what he sees as blasphemous behaviour with the utmost vigour.' She permitted herself a grim smile. 'What was this unholy ritual you speak of?'

Ailwin looked at the floor as he spoke. 'The sweats is a cruel affliction, causing great indignity to those it captures in its claws. The blanket my wife was wrapped in was saturated in her flux, the pus and sweat from this cruel disease. When she was dressed in her shroud for burial, I should have taken the blanket and ensured that every thread was burned in a purifying fire, but Drogo said this would give energy to the evil spirit and release it into the air to spread further misery. He made me fold the soiled cloth and place it under the roots of an alder tree in the forest. There he said the evil spirit would decay into the soil below and sink down to Hell itself.'

'Have you ever heard of such blasphemy?' Ailwin's brother asked Sister Agnes. 'I am not a learned man, but I know this is not the teaching of the Church in this matter. Your priest is contradicting the word of God, not following it.'

'He is not my priest, I was but a visitor to Biddenden,' Sister Agnes said. Her mind was racing, searching for answers to explain Drogo's behaviour. And then it came to her. Gudrun's frequent meetings with the priest. Her walk with the Maids into the woods. Their chancing on some blankets upon which Gudrun allowed the girls to lie, and to rest. The Maids contracting sweating sickness, but not Gudrun ...

Sister Agnes tossed fitfully during the night, trying to decide what to do next. Drogo was a zealot, who believed the Maids were the Devil's children and would stop at nothing to see them perish, but was prevented from doing so by Gundulf's protectorate. If they were to die, it had to look like disease or accident. Gudrun had been his accomplice. Sister Agnes had been too eager to believe that Gudrun now had only the best of intentions for the Maids. She would stop at nothing to have a life free of responsibility for their care.

And if she failed once, Sister Agnes realised, then she could try again.

The next morning, Sister Agnes ascertained that her fellow travellers were heading for the horse market at Cranbrook, where they would be staying until they sold their new steeds. That would give her the time she needed. She raced back to Biddenden as fast as she could. The track was familiar now, and she arrived just after noon. She decided first to seek out Deorwin and inform him of what she had discovered. Thomas might baulk at confronting his wife with so heinous an accusation.

Sister Agnes spotted Deorwin negotiating with some wool traders and told him her news. He shook with rage as she detailed her suspicions. After dismissing the traders, he banged his fist into the palm of his other hand. 'Drogo knew he had to act quickly,' he said, 'before Gundulf heard of his opposition to the Maids and issued a second protectorate. And Gudrun is too easily swayed by those who promise her a better life. It is clear that she sees the Maids as a burden, not a privilege. The generosity of the villagers may have opened her eyes to the fact that the Chulkhursts will not be the outcasts she fears. But it would have been too late in the absence of the villagers' help in the Maids' recovery, and had you not possessed the skill to treat them with your own remedies.' He frowned. 'But I cannot take action on such serious a charge unless I hear the words from the horse catcher himself.'

Deorwin tightened his fists. 'It is but a half-day's ride to Cranbrook. I will send word to Thomas that he has to join me in a posse on the morrow, on the pretext of chasing down a passing thief who has fled the village. He must have no clue as to our real intentions, so that he does not alert Gudrun. You should stay at my dwelling tonight and remain out of sight. My wife will attend to your needs. You will have to travel with us to Maidstone to identify the horse catcher. Are you comfortable in the saddle?'

'I rode in my youth, before I was called to God,' Sister Agnes replied. 'I will ride as hard as is seemly, if that is what is required to see justice done.'

Deorwin nodded his approval and they set off for his home.

THOMAS ARRIVED at the market cross at sunrise the next day. There should have been five other horsemen, maybe more, for a posse, the usual number of strong men who could be summoned by the reeve to hunt down any fugitive who had committed a crime. Instead, there was only Deorwin.

'Has the posse been cancelled?' Thomas asked, trying to hide his irritation. 'I rose early to be at your command, and have many pressing matters at my farm to have wasted my time on a fruitless journey.'

Deorwin laid a hand on his shoulder. 'The pretence of the posse was a necessary one, to get you here at this hour and for you to be abroad from your farm today. Come to my longhouse and all will be explained.'

At Deorwin's longhouse, Thomas gave an incredulous stare when he saw Sister Agnes, and he listened in horror as she recounted her story.

'I cannot believe my wife would stoop to such depravity,' he said. His eyes were glazed, uncomprehending. 'But … if she was so determined the Maids should die, why did she not arrange for them to be felled by an assassin in the woods?'

'Because it would be clear a crime had been committed and a hunt would have been launched for the killer. She could not take the risk of their being caught, and her crime exposed.'

Thomas fixed Sister Agnes with a stare and slowly shook his head. 'Had any other than you told me this story, I would have smit them down for vilifying my wife so. Let us ride to Cranbrook and hear what story this horse catcher has to tell.'

'He has no knowledge of the consequences of his actions, so for my part I took his words to be in good faith,' Sister Agnes replied. 'But it's right that you should judge for yourself.'

They set off, the sight of a nun on horseback attracting shouts of astonishment as they passed the occasional farm on the way. When they reached Cranbrook, Sister Agnes dismounted quickly to restore her dignity. Deorwin took her mount and they headed to the horse fair.

Sister Agnes pointed out Ailwin and Thomas, and Deorwin asked him to repeat the story he had told her. Ailwin glanced at the reeve's pendant around Deorwin's neck, then looked at Sister Agnes. 'Of what crime do you accuse me, servant of God?' he asked, and bounded to his feet as if contemplating whether to flee. 'I have done no harm to you and neither have my kin.'

'I have accused you of nothing, and you should not fear being in the presence of the reeve of Biddenden,' the nun replied. 'The sad tale you told me of your wife succumbing to the sweats contained some intelligence which will help uncover the sinful actions of others. Tell the tale you told me, nothing more, and then be thanked for your assistance.'

Ailwin gulped back a sudden sob. 'My wife was struck down at the last full moon. Her skin was on fire, yet she was shaking with the cold. I wrapped her in our sleeping blanket and I cared for her day and night, but it was to no avail. She passed from this world after three days of the most terrible torment. I came into Biddenden, which I believed to be a virtuous place, to ask your priest to bless her passing and lay her body to rest. He did so, but demanded a strange condition. I was to take the blankets my wife had lain in these three days and fold them into a bundle to be left in the Biddenden woods. Then we were to leave the woods immediately.' He looked anxiously at Deorwin and Thomas. 'Tell me, good sirs, what mischief have I been party to? I sought only for my wife to have a Christian burial, no matter how peculiar the demands that were made to obtain it.'

'We do not come here to accuse you of any crime, horse catcher,' Deorwin reassured him. 'Merely to ascertain the details of this strange account. Tell me, where in the woods were you to place this bundle?'

'In the roots of an alder tree, on the banks of the Claybridge stream, in a clearing flanked by birch trees. The priest was very specific.'

'I know this place,' said Thomas. 'It is in the woodland pasture where my pigs graze in the autumn and winter. It is an arrow shot, maybe two, from my farm. Gudrun would know it well.'

'Then you have told us all we need to know, horse catcher, said Deorwin. 'May you have good trade at the fair and we will detain you no more.' Deorwin gave him a strong handshake and turned to Thomas and Sister Agnes. 'This good fellow has given us enough. Let us make haste, back to Biddenden.'

WHEN THEY ARRIVED at Thomas's longhouse, Deorwin and Sister Agnes stayed out of sight while Thomas arranged for Bela to go to and play with the Maids. He returned to the longhouse to be greeted by Gudrun.

'How was the posse, my dear?' she asked. 'Has the thief been bound in the stocks?'

Thomas did not reply, but beckoned Deorwin and Sister Agnes to enter. Gudrun stared at the nun, her eyes wide. 'Sister Agnes, what has befallen you on your journey that you have returned so soon?'

Deorwin stepped forward, the flames from the longhouse fire casting his shadow over Gudrun. 'Sister Agnes has returned because she has learnt of the treacherous plot you and Drogo had hatched to harm the Maids. How your visit to the woods with them was to cast the sweats upon them, to end their days on this earth.' He went on to tell the rest of what had been discovered, his voice growing louder and sterner with every sentence.

'How can you accuse me of such a crime?' Gudrun cried when he had finished. 'Would you take the word of a horse catcher over that of your loving wife? He and his kind are no more than itinerant vagabonds, quick to turn any misfortune into an opportunity to acquire coin, with no thought of the righteousness of their actions. You should have him flogged for spreading such lies.'

'If you deny your involvement, then on the morrow I will take the Maids to the Claybridge clearing, and ask them if this was the spot where you came across the blanket and told them to lie in it. If they say yes, you will stand condemned by the mouths of innocents and it will be all the worse for you. For the last time, tell me if the words of the horse catcher are true.'

Gudrun pulled at her hair and avoided eye contact with Deorwin. 'I did not have so evil a plan,' she said between sobs. She took a deep breath before continuing. 'I had sought council from Drogo regarding my fear that caring for the Maids would destroy our lives, and he told me that he had tried to have them cast out of the village but was prevented by Gundulf's protectorate. As a man of God, he said he could not lift his hand against them, but when he heard of the horse catcher's death from sweating sickness, he saw an opportunity to test if they really did have God's protection. If the Maids were given the cloth of someone who had succumbed to the disease, it would be God's will whether they lived or died. He promised me that if the Maids should perish, God in His mercy would replace our loss – that I would soon be with child if I joined him in this test. I followed his orders in good faith, trusting that God was guiding his actions.'

Thomas stepped past Deorwin, grabbing Gudrun by the shoulders and shaking her violently. 'You will hang for this treachery, and Drogo next to you.'

Gudrun turned to Sister Agnes, and went down on her knees. 'Help me, Sister Agnes, help me, please. I thought

Gundulf had taken advantage of Thomas's good nature by expecting that he should nurture and protect the Maids. I thought we would be outcasts for having such a vile sight in our midst. But I see now that the people of Biddenden have good hearts and are not troubled by the Maids' appearance. I see the evil of my deeds. I have been shamed by how the villagers have cared for – indeed, cherished – the Maids through their illness and have chastised myself every day since their recovery for having once wished them harm. I beg you, plead with my husband to give me a second chance and I will be a good mother to them, caring for them with all my heart for the rest of my days.'

Thomas towered over her. 'You care nothing for my daughters. You are trying to save your neck from being stretched.'

Sister Agnes spoke next. 'Master Chulkhurst, what we have heard today is shocking indeed. But it is the wellbeing of the Maids that should guide our decisions. They need a mother, especially at this time when they are at their most fragile, having arrived in this strange new place. I can stay and care for them a while longer, but as they grow more worldly they will need someone other than a nun to guide them.'

With newfound conviction, Sister Agnes added: 'I would say, give Gudrun another chance, and have Drogo go on a pilgrimage to reflect on his sins. The Maids know nothing of the plot against them and dearly want Gudrun to love them, as they love her. Spare her from punishment and trust that she will make good on her repentance by caring for them – perhaps more than any other would do. For my part, I promise to stay and care for the Maids until there is no doubt that Gudrun is sincere, and has mended her ways.'

Deorwin thought for a moment. 'These are wise words for you to consider, Thomas. Perhaps Gudrun will indeed be a dutiful mother if she is spared.'

Thomas was racked with indecision. 'Maybe it is I,' he said, 'who have been too forceful, expected too much. Caring for the Maids is a duty that should be not taken lightly, yet it was I who insisted we do so. Gudrun, if I pardon you for your sins, do you promise you will never again try to harm Eliza and Mary?'

'Harm them? I promise much more than that, dear husband. I will devote myself to their wellbeing, their education. I will give them everything they desire. When I saw the numbers who turned up at our door to wish them well, many of them strangers to me, I felt a deep shame at what I had done, and would have given anything to undo the actions I was party to. I make this pledge not out fear of your wrath, but because I see now the error of my ways.'

Thomas took Gudrun's hands and helped her stand up. They embraced, Thomas a little awkwardly, Gudrun holding him so tight she almost squeezed the breath out of him.

'Now we have the priest Drogo to attend to,' Deorwin said, ignoring the display of affection and forgiveness. 'Even a priest can hang should his crimes be sufficiently heinous, but as you say, it is not the only option. His fear of the Maids is great and deep-rooted and they will never be safe while he still has the opportunity to do them harm. I will confront him with our knowledge of his deeds and have him journey to some far-flung place of pilgrimage as soon as possible. Come, let us inform him of his fate.'

It was dark now, and Thomas lit a stave of wood and headed off with Deorwin. They found Drogo alone in the priest house and he listened impassively as Deorwin outlined the charges against him. He took in a long, pained breath and closed his eyes.

'I was tricked into this subterfuge by Gudrun Chulkhurst,' he said, speaking slowly, stretching out the words. 'She was the one to come to me with this devilish plan to have the Maids fall ill. She has ambitions far beyond her upbringing as the daughter of humble cotter and feared that they would be thwarted by the drain the Maids would make on the Chulkhurst purse. Let me confront her with her greed and avarice in front of the elders and have her punished for her sins. Then God will be satisfied that justice has been done.'

'What matters most is what is right for the Maids,' Deorwin replied. 'And Gudrun, despite her sins, is best placed to care for and to nurture them as they grow and prosper. She may have wished them ill, but if she is spared retribution we are satisfied she will be moved to devote her life to the Maids. If this is to be possible, however, the story of your dark deeds, and hers, must remain forever secret.'

Drogo saw his chance. 'If you decide to spare her, I vow to never speak of these events. Just as my lips are sealed on what confessions are made to me, so I will stay forever silent on Gudrun's sins. Now let us join in prayer for wellbeing of the Maids and put this sorry tale behind us.'

'Your own sins cannot be washed away by prayer alone,' Deorwin replied. 'A priest who would have had the blood of innocent children on his hands cannot live amongst us. You must leave forthwith, wrap your belongings and make a pious pilgrimage to Rome. Only a blessing from the Pope can wash away your sins. The long journey will afford you ample time to reflect on your actions.'

'A cotter's daughter is welcomed back into a longhouse, while a priest must endure an arduous journey of years?' Drogo wailed in despair. 'That is not justice. Only a meeting of the Hundred Court can hand down such a sentence.'

'Then have your justice there. The sickness of the Maids brought out a wave of love and care from the people of this village. When they hear of your crime it will not be banishment that is called for. Priest or no priest, you will be burned at the stake and your body buried without Christian ceremony. It is only to protect the Maids from one day hearing of your terrible deeds that I do not myself insist on a trial. It is your choice. Leave this village with all praising you for your sacrifice and devotion in making a long and arduous pilgrimage – or face the wrath of the villagers and the flames of eternal damnation.'

Drogo's face was as pale as wax. 'I promise I will speak no more of this. On my word as a man of God.'

'There is no way to know,' said Deorwin, 'whether you might conspire again to do harm to the Maids. They are fragile and vulnerable and it would take only the subtlest action against them to cause them much hurt. The only way to protect them is for you to be gone.' Deorwin's lip curled a fraction. 'And be gone quickly. Were a malady to strike the Maids while you are still present, I would hold you accountable, and have this sorry story told to the elders.'

FATHER DROGO ANNOUNCED his pilgrimage at that Sunday's Mass. Gudrun watched him leave a few days later, cheered by the unsuspecting villagers, but with his back already bowed by the thought of the many miles ahead of him. She praised her good fortune and looked over at Eliza and Mary, the smiles on their faces like sunshine on a flower.

Her daughters.

1117

~

Chapter 16
Eliza

Father stands by the empty stockade, fists on hips, elbows wide. He gives a deep, satisfied sigh as a farmer pulls on the rope around the heifer's neck and heads off with his purchase. We have sold the last of this year's stock and Father slips the six silver pennies into his leather purse. He crinkles his forehead as he looks at Mary and me, a twinkle in his eye as he runs his hand through my hair, then Mary's.

'I doubt if any farmer in the Lathe of Scraye has yet sold six yearling cattle, and our skeins of wool are traded at the best price I can remember. Change out of your welcoming smocks, my dear daughters. Your job is done.'

Mother started making us pretty dresses a few years ago, when Father realised the reason why so many traders went out of their way to purchase his wares was so they could catch a glimpse of Mary and me. We still get a few shouts of 'Monster!' and 'Cacodemon!' from some of the locals, especially after a day's drinking, and an unwary traveller's face still drains of blood when they see us for the first time; but now we are a source of pride for the village, not shame. We are introduced to any visitor to our home who asks for us. And Father's farm is flourishing.

Mother is happy too. For a long time, she was quiet and sad, but she cheered up when the villagers started coming to the farm to buy cattle from Father. We now have six farmhands working our fields and have been able to afford to make our house bigger, with thicker oak plank walls and a stone floor covered in fresh reeds every week from the river instead of hard-packed earth. The house is now big enough for Mary and I to have our own bed, so no more uncomfortable nights lying on a layer of reeds on the floor. Fine woollen robes hang from the wooden pegs on the walls of Mother and Father's bedchamber, and we eat meat every evening. Mother and Father started making noises more often during the night, which Bela said were blissful sounds, but when I asked why, she laughed and didn't answer.

But it was the lord of the manor's planned sojourn to Biddenden that had Mother at her most excited. Even Father was cheered beyond measure. William de Ashford was our new lord, after Robert de Montfort went on a pilgrimage to Jerusalem and left the lands of the Lathe of Scraye to King Henry. The gossip in the village was that Robert had upset the king and had to choose between exile and death. In any event, the king gave de Montfort's lands to William, one of his favourite courtiers. William took the name of Ashford, where the manor house was situated. It was a half-day's march away and this was his first visit to our village.

The elders had decided we should be presented to William, and to be announced as the marvel of his land. Mary said she didn't want to be a marvel, but I didn't mind. Everyone stared at us all the time anyway. Father said it was a great honour and would make Mother happy, so Mary agreed we should do it.

When the day of the lord's visit came, we walked into Biddenden late in the afternoon to meet him. By the time we were halfway there we could already hear the sound of the gathering crowd. We arrived to see each generation of villagers engaged in their own entertainment. Young boys and girls were throwing stones at a tethered hog, laughing with delight when a well-aimed strike brought a torrent of anguished yelps; the younger men were engaged in a lively drinking contest, egged on by their female counterparts; a passing jongleur, who made his living moving from town to town and entertaining with feats of juggling, acrobatics and music, was leading a slightly older group in the chorus of a song about knights and magicians from foreign lands; and a huddle of old men were playing a game of nine-man's Morris, oblivious to the suggestions of onlookers. Elsewhere there were little family gatherings playing tunes on bells, drums and pipes. A butcher was selling snacks of hot sheep's feet, cooked over a log fire. The rich smoke drifted over the crowd. I had never seen the village so lively.

Bela introduced us to some village girls. They tried to pretend there was nothing different about us and talked of everyday things. We chatted about the weather, and whether it was true what they said about Robert de Montfort. But the pity in their eyes gave voice to the deepest of truths – they could not imagine, even for a moment, what it was like to be us. I think the ones who touched us, poked us, giggled amongst themselves when they thought we did not notice – these were the ones who were the most honest. We were unlike everyone else, as different as a cat from a dog.

Then we joined Mother and Father. Father was chatting to Gerbert and Gaston, arranging for them to do some more work for him. They helped out at busy times like harvest and, with the farm expanding all the time, there was always some more work for them to do the rest of the year. They were the first villagers ever to meet us, the first outsiders not to be terrified at the sight of us, and for that reason we seemed to have a special bond with them. They saw us for who we were, not what we were.

The market cross was decorated with flowers, and two high chairs had been set up in the village cross for the lord and lady of the manor. It was late in the day when they arrived. I was a little surprised – I expected the lord to be the tallest, most handsome man I had ever seen, but instead he was short and bald, with a huge belly. The lady was pretty, but not as beautiful as Mother. I tried not to look disappointed as Mother handed Mary and me the posies we had made that morning.

'William de Ashford, Constance de Ashford, allow me to present Eliza and Mary Chulkhurst, the Maids of Biddenden, two souls forever joined together,' said Deorwin.

We stepped forward and handed the posies to Constance, just as we'd been instructed.

'God bless William de Ashford, Lord Ashford, Baron of the Lathe of Scraye,' I said, and the crowd cheered. Mary remained silent and I gave her a squeeze. She was supposed to say the same to Lady Constance.

William didn't seem to mind. 'Well met, Eliza and Mary!' he boomed, his voice deep and throaty. 'I have travelled far on crusades, but a sight such as this is the most wondrous in Christendom.' He turned to Father. 'Well met, Thomas Chulkhurst! Tell me more about these Maids. How many years do they have?'

I become annoyed when people ask Father about us when we're standing there and can speak for ourselves, but Father was so roused by the occasion he didn't seem to notice.

'This mid-summer, Eliza and Mary will be seventeen years old. That is something we will celebrate, and celebrate well. I am going to organise a special birthday fayre in their honour. It will be a day of merrymaking, for the Maids are well loved by all who know them.'

Mother nodded her agreement.

'A great day, indeed,' replied William. 'I had heard that the shire of Kent had much to recommend it. Now I can see that is true. It would do me great honour were you to allow me to host your jubilee. Come, stay at Ashford Manor and let the Maids be introduced to my fine friends, who will be most curious to make their acquaintance.'

I felt a little scared, and Mary in turn must have felt my fear, because even though she will have been even more frightened than I, she sent feelings to make me less nervous. It's something we do all the time, sending silent, secret messages to each other through the vessels of our bodies. We bowed our heads together, but said nothing.

Mother's voice trilled with pleasure. 'Come, come, Eliza, Mary. You will have a nice smock made specially for the occasion by Goody Webb, the finest seamstress in all of Kent. You will find you have many admirers, looking so fair.'

My heart fluttered at that, and my excitement went tingling into Mary, making her give a little grin. Mother clapped her hands. Father smiled, pleased our anxiety had passed.

'Then it is decided. William de Ashford, you do us great honour with your generosity.'

Mother skipped gaily home at the end of the feast. That night the blissful noises went on even longer than usual.

A WEEK LATER, Mother brought us our morning milk instead of Bela, her eyes sparkling and gleaming. Father stood behind her.

'My dears, your father has some news for you. Wonderous news. Tell them, Thomas.'

Father put his hands on our shoulders. 'You should not talk of this until it is made public,' he said. 'It is best not to tempt fate by celebrating our good fortune prematurely. But as your mother has shown fit to be so impetuous, I will share the secret with you. William of Ashford will send a messenger to Ralph d'Escures, the Archbishop of Canterbury himself, to be the guest of honour at your birthday fayre. William would like you, Mary, to write a plea for his attendance in your own fair hand to show the talents you possess. But we are to say nothing of this until we know his intentions.'

My head was spinning with excitement. Having Archbishop Ralph attend would be an unimaginable honour. The Archbishop of Canterbury was the most important cleric in the land. He had the ear of King Henry himself, and was even in contact with the Pope. A lord of the manor would not expect him to grace his table at a celebration as of right; for him to join in celebrating two lowly country girls was an honour beyond belief.

Mary prepared a piece of goatskin to write out the invitation. She is always studying, having learnt to read and write, although many say it is not seemly for a young woman to know such skills. I try hard not to mind, but the things she wants to do are so boring. The only useful thing was that she studied the ways of farming, so she could best advise Father on what actions he should take. As a result, our crops have been ripening early, our livestock quickly fatten and our sheep rarely succumb to foot rot.

All I like to learn about is music. I got a flute for my eighth birthday and I practised it when Mary was studying. I could play jigs and reels and Mother liked me to accompany her singing when we made social calls.

Mary scratched a simple message with her oak gall ink and Father gave it to a messenger to take to Canterbury. As the messenger rode off, I marvelled at the fact the words she had written in Biddenden could travel across the land and be read by the Archbishop in Canterbury within the day. I couldn't wait to hear his response.

WILLIAM'S MESSENGER visited us two weeks later. Archbishop Ralph had said yes! The messenger announced that William would bestow the most generous of birthday gifts upon us. We could have a present of whatever we desired.

I knew what I wanted. A lyre. I'd seen a jongleur play one once, and it was the most beautiful musical instrument. The jongleur told me angels play them in heaven and he let me strum its strings. If William gave me one, I would practise every day and give Mary my flute so she could become a musician too. I would write music for flute and lyre and we would become jongleurs ourselves.

Mary said no. Typical. She wanted to be allowed to make a physic garden, like the one the nuns had in Malling, and to use the plants to treat anyone in Biddenden who fell ill. I didn't see the point of it, but Mary insisted. I'd have to spend a lot of time in a cold garden so Mary could use her gift, but Mary would get to sit by a warm fire while I practised my lyre. That wasn't fair.

It surprises everyone we are so different. People expect us to think the same, do the same, be the same, but they forget our heads and our minds are our own. For me, life should be bountiful, happy and gay. I cannot run wild and free, but I would never let the burden of my condition stop me from enjoying the magic of music, the joy of laughter. Mary is ever quiet, serious, and studies all the time. She faces her burden by becoming stronger to overcome obstacles, by being ambitious to achieve all she can. She wants to learn more about everything and complains that the noise and my arms moving as I play on my flute are distracting when she is trying to study.

But Mother is like me; she thinks it important not just to work hard but to enjoy life. Mother likes to have fun and so do I. Sometimes it feels as though Mother and I are joined in mind, and Father and Mary too. I wish I was joined to Mother, not to Mary.

I RECEIVED MY LYRE a few weeks before the party. The lyre-maker showed me how to tune it to my flute and taught me a melody to play – 'Tertasimon', a tune from ancient times. But it was so difficult when I tried myself. I started off using a single finger and plucked the strings slowly; but to play properly I had to use all my fingers on both hands. Mary became really impatient and started to fidget when I practised, which made it even more difficult. It was impossible to practise the lyre when all she wanted to do was explore the meadows in search of herbs, and tend the physic garden.

We had to reach an agreement.

'You want to tend your garden and I want to play my lyre,' I said to Mary. 'Let us divide the day between us. You will have the time until the sun is at the highest to work in the garden, and I will have the time until the sun passes High Tilt Hill to play my lyre. As the shadows lengthen, we need to restore our strength to begin afresh on the morrow. From that time until nightfall, we shall be together as a family. This will be a fair and just division of our time.'

Mary said yes to this and I had a secret thrill of delight. There was always some event in the morning that needed immediate attention and it would be Mary's time that would be spent dealing with it. And when we were together with Mother and Father in the evening, Mother would always ask me to entertain us all. I had been very clever.

William has given Mary half an acre of land close to our farm for her physic garden, a strip of meadow on the edge of the outskirts of Biddenden which is part of his demesne, the land on his manor reserved for his own use. Father decided to build a wall for shelter, so Mary could grow some plants that needed special care. Gerbert and Gaston were asked to do it and said it would take them two se'nnights to complete it, fourteen days, as they had little free time with the demands of harvesting. That meant I could practise in the mornings as well, unless Mary could think of something she could do then, before the garden was ready. Sometimes she met with the old men of the village to ask what ancient cures they knew of, and what healing herbs should be planted in the garden. But these conversations were not every day and usually lasted only a short time. For the rest of morning, as well as in the afternoon, I could practise and practise. By the time the birthday feast came along, I could perform a simple rendition of 'Tertasimon'.

I couldn't wait to play it.

OUR OX CART RUMBLED up the path to Ashford Manor and Father gave a grunt of satisfaction.

'The sun is high in the sky,' he said. 'We have made good time. Let us hope our hosts are ready for us.'

I had enjoyed the journey. When we arrived in Biddenden all those years ago, we were made to hide, as though we were some shameful secret that the world should not be allowed to discover. Now Mary and I sat proudly at the front of the cart. Some strangers stopped to exchange a few words with Father, and had the usual look of shock when they noticed our joining. A mother pulled her children away from staring at us, telling them in panic to avert their eyes; other than that, it was the usual surreptitious glances of curiosity from those who had heard of us, but were seeing us for the first time. One young boy ran ahead, shouting, 'Come look, come look!' over and over again, and Father whacked him on the ear and told him to be off. I caught the boy's eye as Father did so. He gave me a big grin that made me blush.

One of William's servants took the oxen from Father and led them into a pen, another gave us a jug of ale which we drank quickly after travelling for so long. Ashford Manor wasn't just one building as I had thought. It was several: a chapel; some storage areas; accommodation for visitors and, furthest from the others, the kitchen, built completely from stone. Kitchens were always catching fire, so it made sense to have them well away from everything else. And there was one building much bigger than the rest – the main hall, where the feast would be held.

We were taken to a sunken hut near the manor house where we were to stay for the night. Once inside, Mother fussed after us, combing our hair, adjusting our clothes, as a guard went to tell William of our arrival.

'Now be calm, be calm,' she said. 'Think of this as a normal day. Try not to get too excited.' She dropped her antler comb and picked it up, fumbling it in her fingers. 'Be calm, be calm,' she repeated. 'Just a normal day.' I giggled and the wiggles from my body made Mary do the same. We were the ones calm. I had never seen Mother like this.

'My great and worshipful lord,' Mother whispered, *'my divinely favoured lady, blessed be your household. May you continue in good health and good spirits. We render you our grati-tude for this honour you have bestowed on us.'* Mary nodded impatiently for the both of us. We had practised these words over and over again for the last few days; there was no need to be reminded.

A guard arrived to tell us that William was ready to greet us. We walked over to the manor hall, crossing an earthen bridge that spanned a deep ditch dug all around the house – to deter, the guard told us, any unwelcome visitors. The guard nodded to another standing at the gate to let us through.

I had not realised how huge was the manor hall until we stepped inside. The room was easily fifteen paces wide and thirty long, with a steep roof rising to the height of three men. There was a fireplace in the middle, red embers burning on some raised flagstones, and the rest of the floor was made of wood. It felt so strange to walk on something so smooth. I looked around, drinking in every detail I could see. The walls were plastered white and painted, moon and stars on one side, butterflies and flowers on the other. Huge candles were impaled on metal spikes along the length of the room, not yet required in the afternoon light. I stared up to the ceiling at the jumble of wooden beams criss-crossing each other like a latticework veil to the heavens. Everything about the room was big, so big. It took my breath away.

I felt pulled along by Mary, which annoyed me until I realised I'd been distracted by the grandeur around us and was ignoring William and Constance, sitting on a raised dais, waiting for us to greet them. William sat on a large seat, a silk canopy hanging over him, the rich red fabric hanging down behind. Constance sat on a smaller seat by his side. Gone was the unassuming figure I had seen at the Biddenden fayre. The reflected glow of the afternoon sun on the red silk made William de Ashford look like a god.

Mother gave us a signal and we said our greeting together, curtseyed and handed over our posies. We don't like doing things together, we like to show we're different. But we'd promised Mother and Father, and we did it perfectly. I patted Mary's hand to show how proud I was of her.

'It will be a full hour before the sun begins to set,' said William. 'The first guests will be arriving shortly. Archbishop Ralph arrived this afternoon and he is at prayer in the chapel. He has said he will grant the Maids an audience before the feast. Thomas, Gudrun, I hope your hut is to your satisfaction. Make yourselves comfortable until the Maids return from their audience.'

Mother and Father stiffened slightly – trying, I think, not to show their disappointment. William took us to his private chapel, situated at the back of the fenced enclosure. We entered to see a figure kneeling at the altar, his back to us. William spoke, his loud voice now softer and more reverential. 'My most venerable and divinely favoured archbishop, I recommend to you Eliza and Mary Chulkhurst, the Maids of Biddenden, for whose festivities you have chosen to grace us with your presence.'

Archbishop Ralph rose and turned to face us. My heart leapt. He was as strong as a tree trunk, a purple cape draped over his barrel chest, and easily six feet tall. Sometimes even the bravest and stoutest of men have a moment of fear flash across their eyes when they see us for the first time, but with him there was just a kindly twinkle as he looked upon us.

'You were known to my predecessor, Anselm of Canterbury,' he said softly, 'and Gundulf spoke of you many times. But still my mind tells my eyes they are deceiving me when I look upon you. Come, young maids, join me in prayer.'

I was sad hearing Gundulf's name. I remembered him from when he visited us in Malling Abbey. When he died some years later, Mary and I cried for days at the passing of the man who had reunited us with Father and given us our new life together in Biddenden.

'Did you know Bishop Gundulf?' I asked.

Archbishop Ralph blinked, as though annoyed at the interruption.

'He nominated me to succeed him as Bishop of Rochester shortly before he passed to the Lord. I was there at his death-bed. But our conversation can wait until my liturgies are completed. Kneel next to me.'

It was a command rather than a request. The twinkle had disappeared.

Archbishop Ralph finished his sacrament a few minutes later and led us to the benches in the chapel. He addressed me first. 'Tell me your name,' he said.

'Eliza Chulkhurst,' I replied. I pointed to Mary. 'This is—'

Mary nudged me in the ribs.

Archbishop Ralph noticed. 'So, you must be Mary Chulkhurst,' he said to her. 'Do you always have to keep your sister out of trouble?'

I quivered with embarrassment, and Mary looked confused. 'No,' was all she could manage.

The Archbishop nodded. 'And now we are all gathering here today to celebrate your seventeen years on this earth. I hear you have received two fine gifts. Tell me of their meaning.'

'Many have been good to us, and we in turn want to do good by them,' I replied, a little hesitantly now. 'I have a lyre to create joy through music and have already been given the chance to practise it. Mary will ... I will let Mary tell of her gift.'

Mary blushed. There was an awkward silence. Finally, she said, 'I was given the use of some of William's demesne for a physic garden, which I will use to grow plants and herbs to treat the villagers of Biddenden.'

'A fine ambition,' said the Archbishop. 'And yours too,' he said to me as an afterthought. 'As long as you make music to bring joy to others and help bring them closer to God, not for the sin of vanity. A young woman should be modest in displaying her talents.'

I squirmed, certain that the Archbishop could see right through me. I had put in hours and hours of practice in the last few days, and Mother and Father had said my playing of the tune was very fine indeed.

The Archbishop turned again to Mary. 'Do I need to caution you, young Mary, on the dangers of producing a physic garden without an understanding of how the body functions? What do you know of such things?'

Mary looked pleased and I knew why. Her initial plan was to copy the garden at Malling and to grow the best six or seven plants for treating common and obvious maladies. She had sent a messenger to Malling to ask what plants these should be. When Sister Agnes had learnt of her plans, she had sent Malling's current infirmarian to teach Mary the science behind the treatments. Sister Agnes was now Mother Agnes, having taken over as abbess when Mother Avicia died a few years ago. Avicia had herself been promoted to abbess on Gundulf's death. Mother Agnes couldn't spare the time to visit herself, but Mary had still learnt a lot from the infirmarian's visit.

'A healthy body is balanced in its humours,' Mary said to the Archbishop. 'And medicinal plants have four properties – hot, cold, dry and moist – which can bring the body back into balance. I would grow sage, betony, hyssop, rue, camomile, dill and comfrey, to purge the body of venom and pestilence.'

Archbishop Ralph's bushy eyebrows leapt to the ceiling. 'You know much for one not formally schooled in the ways of healing. How did you come by this knowledge?'

'The abbey where we lived at first had a fine physic garden and I was visited by its infirmarian last year. She told me much, which I have written on goat skins to make sure I make no mistakes in my treatment.'

'You write? And read too, I imagine.' Mary nodded. 'You have much to commend you, Mary Chulkhurst. And you, Eliza, do you share your sister's talent?'

'I too can read and write,' I replied. Well, at least the first was true. 'My time is spent learning the stories of the great sagas and poems from passing jongleurs, so I can best recount these tales to all that want to hear.'

'Very impressive,' said Archbishop Ralph, half to himself. I could see he was about to say something else, but instead he gave a little shake of his head. 'Come, the guests will be arriving and you should be there to greet them. This will be a night to remember.'

Dinner was announced by a chamberlain blowing a horn and everyone proceeded to the hall. Father led, with Gudrun; Mary and I followed behind. The great hall had been transformed. The smouldering embers of the afternoon had been fanned into a roaring fire, with every corner of the room touched by its comforting warmth. William and Charlotte sat with Archbishop Ralph on the raised dais at one end. Only they sat on chairs; the rest of us sat on benches. Long tables had been set around the walls and everyone was settling into their places. There must have been six score and more present. The floor was spread with straw and herbs to keep out pests and provide a little fragrance. I breathed in the scent to calm my racing blood.

I had never seen so many together in the one room. William's barony comprised sixteen hundreds, each an area of land big enough to support a hundred families. All the reeves were there, along with the haywards, who were in charge of maintaining fences and enclosures. Everyone seemed to know each other and the noise of conversation, laughter and shouts of greetings was deafening. We stepped into the light of the candles. Every eye was upon us.

Deorwin spotted us and came over. 'A great sight, is it not?' he said, gesturing to the crowd. A low buzz of conversation started up. 'Come, take your seats. Archbishop Ralph will soon be giving his blessing for the meal.'

He found us a place as near to the top table as was seemly. The Archbishop gave his blessing and the meal began. The meat had been boiled in a large cauldron until tender. Just as at home, we cut up our food with a knife and used our fingers to eat; but here, servants were on hand with fresh bowls of water and towels. I was surprised to see that the dishes were served for two people, with one person cutting the food and breaking the bread of the other. Father explained the tradition that the more important person had their food cut by the other, and so Mother would have to cut his food.

'Which of us should it be to cut?' I asked Father, panicking that he might say Mary.

'A difficult decision. How can I choose?' he said. 'Mary is a little taller than you; shall we make that the reason? Take no offence from my choice.'

I tried to think of another way to choose, but Mary spoke first. 'Eliza will be playing her lyre, so today she is the first of us. Let me break you some bread, dear sister.' She took the trencher of bread and broke it in two. I did not have to say anything. Mary would feel that my skin glowed in gratitude.

Bowls of peas and beans, parsnips and burdock were passed along from table to table. Jugs of ale were constantly filled. Mary doesn't like ale so normally I like to drink a lot for the fun of seeing Mary becoming drunken from my blood, but she had been so kind, I only took a few small sips. That was probably just as well, as I was so nervous.

After the dessert of cheese and apples, William rose to his feet, the chamberlain blowing his horn again to silence the crowd.

'Welcome, friends. The harvest has been good to us this year, and we celebrate its plenty at this feast. It is a great honour that Archbishop Ralph has graced us with his presence, and we thank you, Your Excellency, for that fine blessing.' The archbishop nodded an acknowledgement. William took a sip of ale, then continued. 'This is my first year as your lord and already I have seen many wonders in this lush and bountiful corner of England. But none greater than my guests of honour tonight, Eliza and Mary Chulkhurst, who have travelled here from Biddenden to be with us on the occasion of their seventeenth birthday. As you will know, none of their like is known in any other part of England. And they have agreed to share their talents with us this evening. Good Maids of Biddenden, please entertain us.'

The buzz of conversation that had greeted our entrance was stronger now, having a sharp edge of amazement at this news. I have never understood quite why people should be surprised we can do certain things – or anything, for that matter. Even to see us do the simplest of tasks usually brings gasps of surprise.

Father fetched my lyre and Mary and I shuffled to the front of the room, to the side of William's high table. I gave a strum of the lyre's strings to settle my nerves, and began to play. 'Tertasimon' was a simple tune to play and although I made one or two mistakes, I could tell even Mary didn't notice. When I finished, everyone banged their knives and bowls on the table in appreciation. William congratulated me on my playing and the tables were cleared away. So many of William's guests wanted get a closer look at us that a crush developed, and Mary and I backed ourselves up against the wall. There was introduction after introduction – my head whirled with all the names. There were polite questions about our health and other matters, but nobody really knew what to say.

After agreeing yet again that the food had been delicious and the weather was not too cold, Mary nudged me that we should leave. I had thought I would want to stay all night, perhaps even play my lyre again, but now I was finding it overwhelming. I whispered to Father that we were tired and wanted to go to bed, and saw the look of relief in his eyes. He was obviously feeling the same way.

As we were saying our goodbyes, I thought nothing else could happen that could make the day even more special. Then Archbishop Ralph came over to speak to Mother and Father.

'Your children have very special gifts,' he told them. 'Eliza has a beautiful touch on the lyre for one who has only begun to master the instrument. But it is Mary's talent that I would like to nurture. Care of the sick is an important instrument of good work and many have devoted their lives to restoring healthy balance in the bodies of the deserving poor. But it is a calling that has fallen out of fashion in these recent times. I would like Mary to come to Canterbury, to study the medical texts that we hold there, so that she can enrich her knowledge to treat those who most need her help. Would that be acceptable to you?'

It took Father a few moments to reply, such was his shock. Every one was an age.

'But of course, Your Excellency. It would be the greatest of honours. But I am burdened with the responsibilities of managing my farm. Could such a pilgrimage wait until after the harvest season?'

'I would like to oversee this arrangement personally, but I have pressing matters of state to deal with.' There was an edge to the Archbishop's voice. 'The Archbishop of York has proclaimed he will not profess obedience to Canterbury, and is resisting even the entreaties of King Henry to do so. He has the support of Pope Paschall. I must journey to Rome, to seek an interview with the Holy Father and explain to him the disputes that are distracting his Church in England from doing good deeds. Surely these matters are more pressing than the turnips in your fields?'

Father bowed his head. 'My mind is in a whirl at the magnitude of what you have told me. Forgive me, Your Excellency. I am a humble countryman and have no comprehension of worldly affairs. My daughters will journey to Canterbury as soon as you tell me all is in readiness for their arrival. If I am detained at Biddenden, my wife will accompany them.'

The Archbishop nodded. He turned to Mary. 'And Mary. Are you prepared to devote yourself to studying these ancient texts?'

'It will be a great honour,' she replied.

I was irritated at all the attention she was getting, but Mary spoke again: 'Will there be opportunity for Eliza to learn new skills with her lyre? There are only so many hours in a day that I can usefully devote to study. It would be only fair that when I am resting my mind from this learning, she can take advantage of the opportunity.'

Archbishop Ralph looked bemused. 'I have not yet adjusted my mind to the peculiarities of your condition. As the two of you will be visiting my great city, so the two of you should benefit from the learning that you can receive there. There will be a short time set aside for lessons in music from my palace troubadour. May you both prosper as a result.'

The talk was of nothing else on the journey home. A commoner family from Biddenden was to journey to one of the great cities of England, at the personal invitation of the Archbishop of Canterbury himself.

I couldn't wait for that day to arrive.

Chapter 17
Mary

Mother, Eliza and I arrived at Canterbury's Worthgate just as the city gate was closing for the night. Normally it would be a good two-day's march from Biddenden to Canterbury, but as Father could not spare the time to travel with us, he had not wanted us to stay in dwellings on the way. We had set off very early and Eliza and I sat in a cart pulled by a stout pony, with young Harry from the village as our guide. His father delivered animal skins to the tanners who produced the hides for the many leatherworkers in the city to make the belts, saddles, gloves and breeches that were sold all over Kent and Sussex. This was the first time Harry had made the journey on his own, but he knew the path well.

'We are the Chulkhursts of Biddenden,' Mother informed the gate's watchman. 'We have journeyed here for an audience with Archbishop Ralph, at his bidding. We have lodgings at St Sepulchre's Nunnery. Pray inform us of its whereabouts.'

The watchman pointed to his right. 'The nunnery is outside these walls, on the Dover road. Make your way round to the next entrance, Ridingate, and carry on five hundred paces past the gate. Men are not allowed to stay the night in the nunnery, so your guide would be best to proceed on to St Gregory's Priory, on the far side of these walls ...'

While they talked, Eliza and walked a little way back and tried to take in all there was to see from outside the city walls. A castle towered above us, a tower in each corner, each built of stone. There were a few stone houses in Biddenden, but none as huge as this. Even William de Ashford's great hall looked small by comparison.

I wondered if you could reach Heaven from the top, or touch the sun and moon.

Mother hurried back to us, scolding us for having walked away from the gate, but her annoyance could not hide her excitement at arriving at this great city where we were to be received as guests of honour. Despite the lateness of the hour, she too lingered a few moments, taking in the sight that lay ahead of us. The clang of the city gate closing snapped her out of her thoughts.

'Let us hurry to the nunnery before Compline, as the nuns will retire for the night after the service,' she said. 'Harry, be sure to return for us at first light, won't you? We will let the Archbishop know of our arrival as soon as he has risen.'

St Sepulchre's Nunnery was smaller than the abbey at Malling, and surrounded by a wooden fence with a round church in the furthest corner. Mother rang the bell next to the entrance, and a nun left the church and came running towards us.

'Who rings the bell at so late an hour?' she demanded. 'We receive visitors no later than the Vesper service. Now we are at supper and Compline prayers will begin shortly. Come back and announce yourself in the morning.'

'I am Gudrun Chulkhurst and these are my charges, Eliza and Mary Chulkhurst, here for an audience with Archbishop Ralph. We have travelled from Biddenden in one long day to avoid undue scrutiny of our persons. If you have been told to expect our arrival, you will also know the reason for our discretion. Can you not find it in your heart to admit us at this hour?'

I couldn't help smiling to myself. Announcing our identity and giving the Archbishop's name would be enough to ensure our immediate entry. The nun's eyes widened and she strained to get a better look at Eliza and myself. Over the years we had become cleverer and cleverer at making clothes that disguised our joining, and unless someone looked carefully, they would think we were simply two young women standing close together. It was only when we moved that the pretence could be discovered, and even then we had developed a gait that would, at first glance, give the appearance of one of us supporting the other in their walking. Many a stranger had encountered us and moved on without realising our true nature.

But this nun obviously had her own notion of what to expect. She opened the door and stepped out, looking anxiously in all directions. 'Begging your pardon, Mistress Chulkhurst, I was not informed you would be arriving today. Hurry in, I will inform Mother Abigail of your arrival.' She caught my eye and I tried to give a smile of reassurance, but she was already flapping about, flustered and nervous in equal measure. 'Quick, quick, enter,' she repeated.

Eliza gave a laugh. 'Good sister, worry not,' she said, her voice soothing and composed. 'We have journeyed since daybreak and have caused no commotion on the road from

Biddenden because of our uncommon condition. Do not be perturbed by our arrival.'

The nun gave some indecipherable reply and we entered the nunnery grounds. I could feel Eliza mischievously walking deliberately slowly, as if to tease the poor woman for her nervousness.

'Stop it, Eliza,' I hissed at her. 'Be kind for once.'

The other nuns, around ten in all, had now left the refectory and were walking towards us, a formidable-looking woman at their front.

'God save you,' she said to Mother. 'I am Mother Abigail.'

Mother tried to hide her pride, replying rather formally: 'God save you also, Mother Abigail. I must apologise for the lateness of the hour. The road from Biddenden is long, and we did not want to coldharbour overnight.'

Mother Abigail brushed away the apology. 'Your chamber is already prepared, since the Archbishop told us you would be arriving before the next full moon.' She turned to young Harry. 'You can go on to the priory. The sisters will take care of the bags you carry for the Chulkhursts.'

Harry was on the cusp of manhood. Two of the younger sisters stepped forward to volunteer as porters, but Mother Abigail shushed them away and had a more portly nun take the bags. Despite our tiredness, Eliza's giggles rippled through to me and I had to supress a desire to laugh. Mother had warned us we must behave with decorum throughout our stay.

It was strange to be in a nunnery again, and long-forgotten memories were stirred as we settled down for the night: the smell of incense wafting through the night air; the muffled sound of the nuns rising from their sleep in the middle of the night for Matins; the flickering of torch flames guiding them to the church. The next morning we joined the nuns for Prime prayers and broke our fast with a simple meal of bread soaked in milk.

None of us was hungry for anything more.

Harry was waiting for us when we got to the nunnery gate. All of us were excited. Even Mother could not hide her impatience to see the marvels that lay inside the city walls. The guards at the Ridingate waved us through and told Harry to turn right at the second crossroads he came to. That road would lead straight to the archbishop's palace.

We stepped inside.

To shock, then disappointment.

I had always thought Biddenden was an untidy and unkempt village, but Canterbury was disgusting. The houses looked the same – small huts made of wood, mud and thatch. But they were jammed together, like they were fighting each other for every piece of ground. Every inch of space was used for something. If the townsfolk couldn't fit in another house, they fitted in a stall selling bread or ale. If it was too small for a market stall, they'd squeeze in a pigsty. If too small for that, they'd find the space for a water barrel.

And the stink!

Everyone has their smell, but with so many people close together it was overpowering. I thought I was going to faint for lack of fresh air. The road on which we walked on was a sea of mud and turds, animal and human. Rubbish was everywhere and we had to keep lifting our feet carefully, so our wooden clogs didn't fall off. Someone emptied a bucket of putrid water into the street and a wall of stench hit us. I'd always imagined Canterbury would be like a paradise on

Earth, more beautiful and fragrant than any Kentish dale. A large brown rat ran across our path in front of us and Eliza and I screamed in unison.

'Hush, girls. Don't attract attention,' said Mother.

I almost laughed at how silly that was. I'd never heard anywhere so noisy. The clamour from the workshops; the shouts from hawkers trying to sell us something; the dogs everywhere setting each other off on barking frenzies. And on top of it all, people, so many people; all shouting at the top of their voices to be heard over the din.

'Is it always like this?' I asked young Harry, as my foot got stuck in the mud yet again.

He helped me pull it out. 'No, of course not,' he replied. He grinned. 'If you want to see real mud, come here after a storm. And when the sun is strong, the smell is worse than one of old Geoffrey's farts.'

Mother cuffed young Harry on the back of his head for his language. As we walked on, I held mine high to maintain a ladylike decorum, and was pleased to see Eliza copy me. When we turned right at the crossroads, I noticed some terraced stone seats, arranged in a semi-circle. They looked ancient and had already crumbled in places. Eliza asked Harry what they were. 'A theatre,' he replied. 'It was built by the Romans, who conquered us before William the Bastard. See that flat stone?' He pointed to a large boulder, long and flat. 'People stood on it and entertained all the people sitting on the seats. It must have been a grand sight.'

Eliza gasped, excitement spread across her face. 'That must have been a wondrous spectacle. I wonder if the Archbishop will permit such magnificent things again?'

She had stopped to gaze in wonder and I became irritated. Eliza's head is always full of ideas about music and dancing. I could think of nothing worse than standing on that stone and having everybody stare at us. I glanced down to the left, and saw the royal castle at the Worthgate entrance, where we'd first arrived the night before. The large stone tower could be seen more clearly now and it was my turn to stand and stare in astonishment at all these new marvels. Almost every house in Biddenden that tried to have a second floor ended up falling over eventually.

How could men be so clever as to make heavy stone rise up into the sky?

A slap from Mother shook these thoughts out of me. 'I said we must not linger once inside the city walls,' she hissed at us. 'Every moment we delay reaching the Archbishop puts you in danger of being noticed before we are under his protection. Hurry, and don't stop again. And Harry, do not fill Eliza's head with nonsense about theatres and Romans. She does not need to know about such fancies.'

My ear was still stinging from the slap. It was unfair. Eliza had been the one to stop first, but as usual I received the punishment for the two of us. I made Eliza walk fast, which she hates. She is a little smaller than me, so when I take big steps she struggles to keep up.

Serves her right.

As we got nearer the palace the streets became wider and the houses bigger, with the upper floors sticking out above the street. Most of these belonged to craftsmen or traders, with their shops and stores on the ground floor and living quarters above. The smell got less rank and the jostling crowds subsided, but that was not all good news. It meant that it was now easier for the townsfolk to get a good look at us.

Luckily, we reached the gate to the palace before anyone shouted out about us, and once we gave our names we hurriedly passed through the gate. We all breathed a sigh of relief as it closed behind us. A man came over and introduced himself as Waleran, Archbishop Ralph's emissary, and told us the Archbishop would see us immediately after Sext prayers. I was pleased for the delay. It gave us all a chance to compose ourselves after the stress of our journey through the city.

When the bell tolled announcing the prayers were over, we were ushered into the chancel of the church and sat waiting in the quire, where the congregation sat on wooden benches during services. When the Archbishop came in, I scarcely recognised him from our meeting in Ashford. Then, he was dressed in a brown felt cloak – fine quality but the same as any prosperous trader would wear. Now he was clothed in his official vestments: a white gown, embroidered around the cuffs and neck, with a wrap across his shoulders that formed into a hood similarly embroidered. I had never seen someone dressed in white before, and wondered how it was kept so clean and didn't turn yellow. The gown was kept closed by a cincture, a knotted cord with tasselled ends around his waist, and a crimson stole around his neck was evidence of his place in the hierarchy of the Church.

He was like an angel of the Lord.

After we had exchanged pleasantries, Archbishop Ralph went over to the sanctuary, the secure part of the church that housed the tomb of a saint. From a locked chest he produced a manuscript, which he brought over.

'This is a copy of *Summarium Heinrici*, an encyclopaedia of healing written by the monks of Germany. Do you know where Germany is?'

'Not exactly,' I said.

'It is a country over the sea, further east than France. I have arranged for a tutor to explain the contents of the book, as I would not expect a country maid – even as learned as you, Mary – to know all the Latin it contains. It will tell you all that is known about the healing powers of the plants, and how best to treat those who suffer from the most common maladies.'

I examined the book, which was written on vellum, with the first letter of each chapter illustrated in bold, vivid colours. Every word had been painstakingly inscribed in beautiful, flowing letters, each page a perfect square. I had never seen anything like it. All the documents at Malling and in Biddenden were scratched on simple goat hides, tiny words squeezed into every corner, from its stretched-out legs to its soft wide belly. I could read about half of what I saw at a glance, though some was in strange words that did not even look like Latin.

'That would be a great honour, Your Excellency. I will be a conscientious student.'

Eliza squirmed. I ignored her.

Archbishop Ralph must have noticed, because he turned to Eliza next.

'And you, fair Eliza, will have to be patient while your sister learns these important skills. You must promise to help in any way she desires of you.'

Eliza stared at the floor.

The Archbishop laughed. 'Try not to look as though you have been given a penance. You will also profit from your visit to this great city. I have arranged for my troubadour to give you instructions on the playing of the lyre before you leave, and on the morrow's eve there will be a welcoming feast in honour of you both. Your fame will spread across the city before the moon has waned. You will be a secret of the village of Biddenden no more. You will be able to travel freely throughout my diocese, blessed with the protection of the Church for the rest of your days, and may they be long indeed.'

Eliza's happiness rumbled through me like thunder. We returned to the convent, dizzy with excitement; and the next day Eliza and I spent all our time bathing, washing the dirt out of our clothes and preparing as much as possible for the big event.

Mother went for a walk in the countryside beyond the town gates and came back with her trug full of wildflowers. Before we set off back to the city, she wove two garlands of flowers through our hair. She stepped back to look at us.

'You look like two princesses', she said.

I cried with joy at the pride in her voice.

That evening, we reached the Archbishop's palace without incident, and waited in an anteroom while the guests assembled in the main courtyard. One of the Archbishop's assistants came to get the three of us, and when we stepped into view there was a gasp from everyone. The Archbishop made an agreeable speech, describing how God moves in mysterious ways, and how no-one was to judge ill of us because of our predicament. Mother made a thank-you speech on our behalf.

I was even brave enough to say, 'God bless Archbishop Ralph, God bless King Henry,' without being asked, and everyone cheered. I blushed.

Eliza took her lyre and played 'Tertasimon' to even louder cheers and applause.

I didn't mind.

The rest of the evening was full of festivities. Mother sat next to Eliza. Archbishop Ralph sat next to me, but he spent most of the evening talking to Waleran and the other men. Some local musicians played tunes with wooden pipes, and everyone clapped along. A *chanson* was recited, a long, long poem about French knights and magicians which I found a little boring. A jester told jokes about farting which were very rude and I blushed to the tips of my ears. He finished off by making a tune with his farts, at which point Archbishop Ralph stood up and shouted at him to leave and then apologised to Mother, Mary and me. Mother said thank you with a serious face and, when Archbishop Ralph wasn't looking, she winked at Mary and me.

It was the best time ever.

THE NEXT MORNING, we returned to the Archbishop's palace and met Ymbert the Wise, the monk who was to be my tutor. After introducing us, the Archbishop told us he must return to his other home, Southwark Cathedral near London, to prepare for his trip to Rome. He entreated me to study hard, wished us good fortune and left.

Ymbert talked very slowly as he explained how to regulate the humours of the body by the use of different medicinal plants and roots.

'When God created the world, all the elements served mankind, and knowing that man lived, they busied themselves aiding his life in every way.' His voice was a drone. 'The earth's vital energy, its power, can be consumed by man, if he knows how to harness it. He must know which plants to choose, and how they should be prepared so they have the greatest effect.'

Despite the sleep-inducing tones, what Ymbert said was fascinating. But not to Eliza. She became more and more restless as time went on, and her twists and turns made it very difficult for me to concentrate. We took a short break for lunch; I hoped she would be calmer in the afternoon.

She got worse.

Ymbert was explaining the difference between plants that grow from air and those that grow from wind. 'The air plants are gentle on the digestion and produce happiness in anyone who eats them,' he told me. 'They are like a person's hair, always light and airy. Wind plants are dry and heavy and make you sad. They are like the dry sweat on skin. Let us chant the list of air and wind plants so they stay in your mind. We will repeat each name until you know the nature and property of each plant in full. Recite after me ...'

Ymbert started intoning the names of plants, their category and properties. Beans were hot, and cured indigestion; millet was cold, and strengthened the blood; horsemint was hot, and killed parasites of the skin. On and on and on – and after finishing his long list, he started again, saying the plant name and expecting me to respond with its nature and properties. I got so many wrong. The list was too long, with over fifty names. *'Malum, malum,'* Ymbert would say after each of my mistakes. 'We repeat again, until you name and ascribe each plant correctly. Only by constant repetition will these words stay in your brain.'

I was a little better the second time, but on the third round I forgot ones I'd got right the first time.

Eliza was exasperated. 'Concentrate, Mary,' she shouted at me. 'I remembered that one. Ymbert, can I say the answer, if I know Mary's wrong?'

'No, you may not,' replied Ymbert. 'Archbishop Ralph has chosen Mary Chulkhurst to be tutored. You have to be silent.'

Eliza kept quiet until I'd completed the list four more times, then she complained again. 'It's silly for me to stay silent. I have to be here while she learns and I'll be with her when she treats the sick. Mary got half the list wrong again. We'll never be done unless I help her.'

Ymbert raised his voice. 'The rules for teaching *Summarium Heinrici* have been written down by the monks of Nursia and are not to be tampered with. The master speaks the words and the pupil repeats them until they are recalled correctly. Recital is a daily discipline, so that none of this great knowledge is ever forgotten. You are not the pupil, Eliza, and have no authority to speak on these matters. Now we will start the list again, and I will not tolerate any more interruptions.'

Eliza became more and more impatient and bored as the day wore on. After the twentieth recital, she could stand it no longer.

'I weary of this. I need to do something also. Give me some relief from this torture!' She jumped up and down in irritation. Ymbert put his hand on her shoulder to settle her and she pushed it away. 'Leave me alone. I was blessed by Archbishop Ralph, and only he can instruct me. Unhand me at once.'

Ymbert turned on her like a thundercloud. 'I will not be addressed so discourteously. Ymbert the Wise is the foremost

scholar of the medical arts and only the most senior obedientiaries in the land are accorded the honour of receiving
the wisdom of my words. Go forth, you uncommon maids.
This lesson is at an end.'

His words pierced me like thorns. I didn't yell at Eliza after
Ymbert left, which made her feel more sorry for her actions
than if I'd got really angry. From being the centre of attention the night before, we were now alone and friendless in a
strange place. Ymbert was supposed to take us to Eliza's troubadour after his lesson was finished, so that she could receive
her training on the lyre. Now that Ymbert had gone, we had
no way of knowing how to find him. We sat and waited
for someone to come to us, but time went on and nobody
appeared. Eliza was sobbing now, and I was sad her dreams
had gone along with mine. Eventually, Harry appeared to
take us back to the nunnery at his appointed time.

Shameful, abject disaster.

We headed back with a silence between us. Eliza made me
promise not to tell Mother what had transpired and we spent
the evening listening to Mother's stories of her walks around
Canterbury, her descriptions of the hogs being butchered,
the ring of the smith's hammer working the iron. Twice she
was recognised from the feast and she told me the whole
city was abuzz with the news of our presence. She was so
thrilled, it helped take my mind off the calamity of the day.

The next morning, as we prepared to leave to see if Ymbert
would return for my tutoring, I pleaded with Eliza to be
better behaved. All I could get out of her was a mumbled
promise that she would try. She insisted on bringing her
lyre. 'Ymbert said he did not want me to speak in his lesson,'

she told me. 'But the strumming of my lyre will not be an interruption.'

Ymbert appeared, but he was still in a black mood and made Eliza take a vow of silence before deigning to continue my lessons. At the first break in my recital, Eliza took up her lyre and strummed gently. When Ymbert returned, I pleaded with him to allow her to play softly as we practised our learning by rote, and he reluctantly agreed. But I found it impossible to concentrate, worried all the while that there would come a point when Ymbert decided Eliza's playing was disturbing the lesson. When we started the second recital, I was getting more responses wrong than even the first time I had tried the day before.

Ymbert threw his hands in the air and told Eliza he would not permit her to play anymore. She burst into tears and yelled and cried that everyone was so unfair to her. Ymbert's patience snapped. He announced he was returning to his ministry on the morrow.

'The Archbishop shall be told of your behaviour,' he said to us, 'and I, Ymbert the Wise, will not be responsible for the consequences.'

As he stormed out of the room, I couldn't contain my anger anymore. 'Eliza,' I said, 'See what you have done! We had so many opportunities here to learn so many great things and to meet so many wonderful people and you've spoilt it for both of us.'

She tried to reassure me. 'Don't worry. Archbishop Ralph has arranged a reception for us, and Ymbert would not dare disobey him by leaving our instruction incomplete. Let him take some of his own remedies to cool down his blood. He will be here when we return on the morrow.'

She was wrong.

When we returned the next day, we were told that Ymbert had already left. The *Summarium Heinrici* had been locked away in its chest and there was no-one else in Canterbury who was authorised to teach from it. We returned to the nunnery and told Mother the news.

'You stupid, spoilt, girl,' she yelled at Eliza. 'How could you ruin everything with your selfishness? Now we have to leave Canterbury in disgrace, spurned by one of the most learned men in the land. Your father will hear of this, and I would not be surprised if he breaks your fine lyre over your head and uses it for firewood. It is what you deserve.'

As we prepared to leave Canterbury in disgrace, Eliza was distraught.

'Let us promise ourselves,' she said, 'never again to obstruct each other's wishes, never again to allow quarrels to prevent us from working in harmony. We shall speak with one voice, be of one mind, and agree the one thing we are doing next.'

I tried my best to give her a hug. We had made a solemn pact. This would never happen again.

Chapter 18
Eliza

Ashamed of my selfish behaviour in Canterbury, I was pleased when, some months later, it was I who came up with an idea that would increase Mary's knowledge of the healing powers of herbs.

'When you requested the help of Malling Abbey to set up your physic garden, Mother Agnes sent her infirmarian to Biddenden to provide you with assistance,' I reminded her. 'You learnt a lot from her in the few days she was here. Why do we not journey to the abbey ourselves, so we can learn more fully the skills she possesses? After all, Mother Agnes was the infirmarian when we were children there. Now she is the abbess, surely she might be gracious with her time and share with us her lifetime of learning of the healing arts? I am sure we would be welcomed if we were to return.'

Mary thought it was a wonderful idea but Mother could not be persuaded to return to Malling with us.

'I have too many dark memories from my visit there,' she told us. 'I do not want to be reminded of the person I was when I first learnt you would be returning to Biddenden to live with your father and me. Let me secure young Harry to be your guide. You can travel to Malling without me.'

I tried to tell Mother that Mary and I bore her no ill will for being at first anxious about looking after us, but she would not listen. 'My fears were more than a few doubts and worries,' she told us. 'Your father has forgiven me, but I still feel shame at my behaviour. I feel God has punished me by not blessing me with a child and bringing you a brother or sister, despite all of the measures I have tried to be fertile. It is a great sadness, but let us not dwell on such sorrow. You are both a blessing to this household, and to all you touch with your gifts. But I am not ready to return to the place of these dark days from my past.'

Mother could not be persuaded, so we prepared to journey without her. Father arranged for young Harry to be our guide, Fordwin the village priest our chaperone. It would not be too difficult a route; we would travel north to Headcorn, where we would follow the River Beult until it joined with the Medway. A few miles further north and we would reach Malling.

We set off a few days later and when we arrived at the abbey gate, our hearts leapt at the sight of our home from all those years ago. We both cried with happiness as a familiar figure approached us, her bustling gait slower, but still recognisable. Mother Agnes called out when she was a few paces away.

'Eliza! Mary! Is that you?' She laughed at the ridiculousness of the question. 'My mind is in a whirl, could there be others like you in this land?' She had reached us now, and looked us over, her eyes sparkling with a motherly pride. 'My, how you have grown. When I received your request for assistance with your physic garden, I was tempted to travel myself to provide the learning you requested, but an abbess should never leave her abbey unattended. It pained me to send Sister Beatrice, but she gave me a full account when she returned of the wonders you have achieved. That pleased me greatly. Come, tell me – why have you travelled here to be with us again?'

Mary told her about how Archbishop Ralph had blessed her physic garden and wanted her to have the advantage of the great knowledge stored at Canterbury Cathedral; how he had departed and left Ymbert the Wise to be our teacher; and how Ymbert had dismissed us when we showed him disrespect. A flush crept across my cheeks as Mary told the story, and my stomach hardened as I prepared myself for Mother Agnes's rebuke for my foolhardy ways.

Instead, she waved away my fears.

'Many say Ymbert the Wise is not a good teacher. But I should not get involved in such gossip. You are welcome to stay and learn all that I can teach you. Sister Beatrice can show you new ways to care for the plants. Come, let us meet her and the other nuns. Some will remember you from when they were oblates and you were infants. But all will have heard the story of the Biddenden Maids. You will find a warm welcome from all.'

We met in the chapter house each afternoon and Mother Agnes explained to Mary how the human body worked.

'There are four elements that hold the world together,' she told her. 'Fire, air, water and earth. Their distribution and function constantly sustain us, just as they are spread throughout the rest of the world and have their effects in nature. These four elements are in all of us – from fire we have the warmth of our bodies; from air we have our breath; from water we have our blood; from earth we have our muscles and bones.'

Mary wrote everything down on the sheaf of goat skins she brought with her.

Mother Agnes's speech was always unhurried, her posture relaxed, as she shared more learning as to how the four elements rule our lives.

'Fire gives us sight, air gives us hearing, water gives our body movement, and earth gives us the ability to walk. Just as nature keeps these elements in balance, and there are storms, plague and pestilence when they are not, so the body needs to be kept in balance. If the body's balance is out of kilter, the person can become sick and even die. To bring the humours of the body back into balance, you must add heat or cold, dryness or moistness, or some combination of them all. Only then can an illness be cured.'

All this, Mary laboriously wrote on her goatskins. Sister Beatrice gave Mary a plan to expand the garden to encompass all the plants necessary for bringing the humours into balance: galingale and zedoary for heat, psyllium and goatsbeard for cold, tithymal and chervil for dry, kale and dandelions for moist. Many of the farmers' crops such as oats, wheat and barley also had medicinal properties, so they could also be used for cures without taking space in our gardens, and there were wild plants growing in the forests and the meadows that also had their uses.

Who could have thought there was so much in nature to cure so many ills?

When we returned to Biddenden, I did everything I could to help Mary to expand her physic garden. As farmer's daughters, we knew a good garden had to be sheltered, able to receive the blessing of the sun, fecund, green and not too dry. I soon became as enthusiastic as Mary about our project and we worked on the garden night and day. Although I found it exhausting, I never complained. I was her servant in this endeavour – a worthy penance for my ill-considered ways in Canterbury. I would allow her to devote all our time to her passion, without complaint or resistance, until she released me from my obligation. I was as excited as Mary for the garden to flourish, so we could begin our healing, but there came a time when all we could do was wait for the plants to grow.

Finally, Mary needed to spend less time establishing the garden, and I had the chance to practise my lyre. I could still use only one finger, and was only able to slowly tease out a simple tune. There were seven strings on the lyre, and soon I was able to use extra fingers to play faster and better. 'Tertasimon', the one song I knew, could just about be played with one string, but sounded so much better when I used all seven. I started on the more complex ancient Greek tunes of 'Exasimon' and 'Dodekasimon'. Soon, I mastered those as well.

Mary loved to hear me play and never complained about my clumsy attempts to improve. But no matter how much I tried to persuade her, she had no interest in learning herself. We were observers of each other's world and it was wonderful these worlds were different. God ordained that our bodies were bound together, but not our minds. Our minds soared off in different ways, giving us a degree freedom from each other.

The autumn harvest days were when the work on the physic garden became intense again, as the plants had to be picked and stored and preserved in such a way to keep their properties intact until the next growing season was completed. Some were dried, some preserved in tinctures, and we were kept busy every day extracting the vital essences of the healing plants and incorporating them in balms and ointments. By the time the dark days of winter arrived, the shelves of my infirmarian sibling were stocked with a range of potions of which the greatest monasteries in the land would be proud.

I marvelled at how many of Mary's cures involved elements from outside the physic garden. A stonemason visited with a defect of the chest, evidenced by breathlessness and a constant wheezing, which Mary treated by having him inhale yew tree smoke to dissolve the bad humours out of the body. A ploughman's wife put jasper stones in her mouth until they were warm and moist and then placed the stones on her belly to calm her stomach pain. Many of those who were cured hailed their recovery as a miracle and called Mary a saint. That made me happy. I felt as though God had forgiven me for my trespasses in Canterbury.

Mary was the one who had all the attention, so when a messenger arrived at our longhouse one short winter's day, I was surprised that it was me he had come to talk to.

'I bring a message from Robert de Crevecoeur, Baron of Chatham, lord of the manor of the Lathe of Aylford,' he said to Father. Aylford was the lathe to the west of Scraye and stretched all the way from the River Thames to the marches of Sussex. 'Baron de Crevecoeur has heard news of the feast at Ashford, where Eliza, your daughter, performed on the lyre. He requests she perform at his Christ's Mass feast, where your lord, William de Ashford, will be a guest. He would wish that she play her tunes and accompany his jongleur as he tells tales of great deeds and heroism. The better men from all four lathes of Kent will be in attendance and you will be paid five silver pennies for her performance.'

The messenger turned and bowed to me, before addressing further my astonished mother and father.

'And Baron de Crevecoeur extends his hospitality to you, Thomas and Gudrun Chulkhurst. Although you will not, of course, dine in the main hall on the night of the feast, you will be most welcome to attend the festivities afterwards.'

Father explained who Robert de Crevecoeur was. 'The de Crevecoeurs came from Lisieux in France and own great swathes of land in our county,' he told us. 'It is said over two thousand sulungs are in their possession. There is no finer family in the south of England.'

Two thousand sulungs! How could one man own so much land? One sulung is the land a farmer needed to support his family for a year. My mind spun like a child's toy at the thought. I looked at Father. What would he reply? My first reaction on hearing the news was horror that I might embarrass myself, but already a certain excitement was creeping through me.

Father said to the messenger, 'I have raised my daughters to speak their own minds. It is Eliza who should give you the answer, not I. Speak, Eliza. Do you wish to agree to this undertaking?'

'My sister Mary would have to give her consent,' I replied. 'Her work here in Biddenden matters greatly, tending her physic garden and treating all those deserving souls who suffer from the imbalance of their humours. I can do nothing that would interfere with work of such importance.'

I did not need to say this. I could already sense Mary's support, her excitement at the great honour offered me. But others didn't know about that. I wanted Mary to speak, so they knew I had her blessing.

'Eliza has spent many long hours assisting me in the garden,' Mary said. 'The new season's potions are prepared and the ground will now lie fallow until the first shoots of spring. I give my blessing fully and freely to this wondrous invitation.'

As Father discussed the arrangements with Robert de Crevecoeur's messenger, Mary whispered in my ear. 'Sister, you have earned my full forgiveness and I am humble with gratitude for how much you have sacrificed to bring my dream of a garden to reality. We are equals again, and I am to do your bidding as much as you do mine. From the morrow, you must pick up your lyre – I look forward to these noble families hearing its pleasing sound.'

I practised constantly. There was to be a reading of *Beowulf* at the feast and I was to provide music to accompany it, as well as other songs of heroic deeds. I would also play unaccompanied: 'Exasimon', 'Dodekasimon' and, of course, 'Tertasimon'. I sat the lyre on my knee and practised until my fingers bled. I found I could play longer than anyone else, because when my left hand, with which I held the lyre, became tired, Mary could take over and hold it for a few minutes while I rested.

Mother laughed with delight the first time she saw Mary do this.

'The lyre is a fine instrument for two that are joined to play,' she said. 'Mary must hold it thus when you are performing.' I protested that my arm only ached after long practice and would not tire when playing just three songs, but Mother insisted. 'It will provide much fascination from the audience. And what else is there for Mary to do, when all eyes are on you both while you play?'

Mary said she didn't mind, so I reluctantly agreed. But I felt uncomfortable that our joining should be used for entertainment.

We set off from Biddenden a few days before the Baron's feast. Father had worried that the village elders would take offence none had been invited to join us, but Deorwin laughed off his concerns.

'It is a great day, when our humble village is honoured at a feast given by one of the great families of the land,' he told Father. 'I will await your return to hear stirring tales of what magnificence you have beheld. Eliza, Mary – go forth and do your village proud!'

I blushed at his generosity of spirit.

We set off to the cheers of the villagers who had come to see us off, Mother riding a palfrey whose docility and kindly nature were famous; Father a courser of such spirited carriage and demeanour that he made anyone who rode him look like a nobleman. Our cart was pulled by two ponies, so we were a grand sight as we headed off to Ashford, where we were to join William de Ashford's party before going on to Chatham in company. From Ashford we were a party of twelve, with William's guards and servants walking alongside us, and as we passed through small villages on the way, crowds came out to greet us and gasp at Mary and me. The crowds became larger at each village.

'My tenants know well their cheers will benefit them when it comes time to set the rent on quarter days,' William told Father. 'I do not persuade myself these displays of allegiance are anything other than to protect their interests. But on this occasion, word of our journey has preceded us and the wonder of the Maids far outweighs any veneration they may have for me. The crowds are here for the Chulkhursts today, not the Ashfords.' He slapped Father on the back, a little too heartily, and he winced.

When we arrived at Robert de Crevecoeur's manor house, we were shown to our quarters and Father was summoned for an audience with the Baron. When he returned, his face was flushed with excitement.

'News of our journey has come to Chatham before us,' he announced. 'And every nobleman arrived for the feast has congratulated Robert de Crevecoeur on his discovery of the Maids. Your mother and I are not to be treated as the attendants and guardians of tonight's entertainment as expected. We will join the feast, sitting at the same tables as the most noble families of Kent. There is no greater honour to be had.'

Mother was ecstatic and I was pleased to see them both so happy. It had been decided I should play my tunes at the beginning of the festivities, as all eyes would be on us, and no other performer would be able to survive the distraction of our attendance, while everyone took in every aspect of our appearance. Blushing with modesty, I played my three Greek tunes, then accompanied the invited jongleur, Masci, who, after telling jokes and juggling, performed the epic poem *Beowulf*. Masci was the most renowned performer in all England and my skin prickled at the intensity of his reading. As I weaved my music around his words, it was as though the two of us were performing a dance, invisible to the audience. I would never have the experience of moving unencumbered to the music at a village fayre, but as Masci and I performed *Beowulf* together I felt free of Mary's body for the first time. Instead, I became joined in mind to Masci, staring into the forget-me-not blueness of his eyes, each glance and nod he gave me creating that same oneness I thought that only Mary and I could share.

After our performance was over, Robert de Crevecoeur came over to talk to us.

'That was a fine performance, Eliza. Was it not, Masci? Did I not tell you that even a man of your travels would experience here a wonder beyond belief?'

'Truly remarkable,' agreed Masci. He turned to me. 'I felt your emotions stirring as I told of Beowulf's slaying of the monster. I heard correct, did I not?'

A tingle swept up the back of my neck and across my face. I felt my stomach harden, that all the secret intimacy I had felt had been revealed. My throat tightened and I did not trust myself to speak, for fear of further revealing my discomfort.

Luckily, at that point William de Ashford joined us.

'Did I not tell you of the wonders that reside in my manor?' he said to Robert. 'Is there anything in the Lathe of Aylford that can match the Biddenden Maids?'

'There is nothing in my lands that can match this curiosity, that is true,' replied Robert. The merriment had left his eyes, leaving them cold as winter sky at sunset. 'I fear I will have to match you in other ways, good neighbour. By good fortune, my lands are prosperous and I am well favoured by King Henry. I will have to satisfy myself with these small comforts.' These last words were spoken like a blade sent home to its scabbard.

My embarrassment at Masci's comments was replaced by a growing unease. There was a tenseness in the air, William and Robert behaving like two wary dogs circling each other, each waiting for the first strike. William looked away, giving a chuckle to show he considered being the first to break the gaze between them to be of no consequence.

'Eliza, your playing has improved magnificently since you graced us with your lyre playing at Ashford,' William said to me. Without waiting for a response, he turned back to Robert. 'It was I who gave Eliza the gift of the lyre, so she might learn the instrument and entertain us at my harvest feast, where even Ralph d'Escures, Archbishop of Canterbury, was in attendance.' He looked around. 'I see no such great dignitary has made the journey to your Christ's Mass feast, Robert. No doubt the winter roads make travel more difficult.'

Mary tugged at me, and I did wonder if it would be prudent to avoid further witness to this duel of words. But Robert gave a roar of laughter, and slapped William on the back. 'You do me kind to permit such an excuse,' he said, exaggerating his attempt to bring his laughter under control. 'But any who have not journeyed here today have been spared the risk of encountering the King's displeasure. Have you not heard Henry considers the lyre to be an instrument of rebellion? It is used to play music of sedition by those who oppose Norman rule. It is already no longer heard at court and there is talk of it being banned throughout the land.' He turned to Masci. 'Tell me, Masci, you regularly perform at court. Is what I hear true?'

'God has bestowed on us the magic of music,' Masci replied diplomatically. 'It has the power to do good or evil, to help cure people of maladies of the mind, soul or body as well as to conjure up spirits that would be of help or to do your bidding against enemies. Music is all these things and more. Whether it is a voice, a lyre or any other instrument, music can do good or it can do harm. The intention is in the mind of the performer, not in the form of the instrument.'

It was a clever response, but Robert's news had filled me with dread. William de Ashford had honoured me by choosing me to exercise his right of entitlement to be entertained by his subjects. Would he ever risk the lyre being played in his presence again? Surely this news would soon spread to every village and town in the land … All my hours of practice would be wasted.

Robert decided to leave while he had the upper hand.

'Well said, Masci the jongleur. None can doubt that when you perform, it is only the glory of King Henry you have in mind. Fill your jug with ale, so you are refreshed for your second performance.' Robert paused to give his final words the most impact. 'But no more lyre playing, eh?' He wagged his finger, his grin splitting his face in two. 'I do not want to find myself on a pilgrimage like William de Ashford's predecessor.' He bowed to all around him and strode off.

Father had the sense to usher us away before William could think of something to say.

Why, oh why, did I have to ask for a lyre?

I didn't want to stay for the rest of the feast, but to leave early would have been too great an affront to our host and it would be impossible for Mary and I to leave without being noticed. But in the end, I was glad I stayed. When Masci returned for his second performance after the feast was over, he produced a musical instrument I'd never seen or heard of. He called it a *'vielle'*.

'It is quite new,' he told the audience. He took a long rod of wood with a string of cat gut pegged to it, and slid it across the five gut strings of the instrument. He looked over to Robert. 'And is now played at all Norman courts.'

Robert smiled and gave a gracious nod. I dared to glance at William. His face was as dark as thunder.

But all my fears and worries of the evening vanished as Masci started playing. The vielle was the sound of heaven, the melody rising tenderly and lingering in the air, like the haunting perfume of newly-pressed flowers. After he finished, I wanted to know more about it and persuaded Mary we should talk to him. When I said I'd never seen anything so amazing, he burst out laughing.

'It is I who does not believe my eyes,' he told me. 'I had been told the two of you were joined together forever, but could not in my mind imagine such a thing. And to find you have such talent as a musician is a curiosity I will remember for the rest of my days. Are the two of you really of one body?'

I was shocked at his directness. Only those we knew really well spoke to us of our joining – a stranger had never dared ask us such questions. But I reasoned he was a man who lived a different life from the one lived by everyday people, an adventurer who travelled the world making his living by entertaining the most noble in our land. I was still in the clouds from our playing together. I could tell him anything.

'We are two minds and two bodies. Only our blood flows between us and we feel each other's movements as if they were our own. Other than that, we are as much two separate people as any others in the land.' I could feel Mary squirming with embarrassment next to me, but decided to go on. 'And we know every heartbeat of each other's life. Every memory, every experience is shared. We never have a private moment.'

There was a strange look in his eyes. He took my hand. '*Every* moment? Do you not avert your eyes when the other is performing the most personal of tasks? Surely you must find a way.'

He had gone too far. 'Sire, you ask the most impertinent of questions. Yes, there are many moments when we would wish to be alone. But we cannot. That is God's will and we have to endure it.'

Masci looked around, noticing that, as usual, all eyes in the room were upon us.

'You are right, I must apologise for my curiosity. My life is a footloose one, and I revel in each new spectacle, each new experience, that every day does bring. So you like my vielle? Let me show you a little of its workings. But not here – I may court attention but I do not like being so … observed. Come, follow me. I know a place.'

We went over to speak to Father. 'The jongleur is going to show me how to play his new instrument,' I told him. 'It is too noisy to talk here. May we go outside?'

Father broke off from his merriment. 'Do what is best,' he said. 'It would be a fine skill to acquire.' The men he was with gave a little cheer, and we hurried away from the clamour of the room.

We stepped out into the night air with Masci. A cool breeze strayed through the gardens, refreshing me with the tang of its touch. In the far distance, a wolf howled. For the first time in the evening, I could relax, away from every eye that stared.

Mary was calming down also, and she tenderly stoked my arm.

'It's so nice to escape the attention for a moment,' she said to both of us. 'I don't think I could have taken much more of being on display.'

'You should not blame everyone,' Masci replied. 'It was a wondrous sight to behold, the two of you.' He looked straight at me, his gaze intense. 'Your playing of the lyre was exquisite, Eliza, as delightful to the ear as cool well-water to thirsty lips. I will remember this night forever.'

I blushed and changed the subject. 'Your vielle is as much a marvel,' I said. 'How do you contrive to make such beautiful music with it?'

I expected him to put the vielle to his shoulder to show me, but instead he placed it gently on the ground. 'The music can wait for the moment. My curiosity knows no limits. Are you able to live a full life, despite your condition?' He looked straight at me, his eyes full of kindness. I felt a little flutter inside.

'We do not talk of such things,' Mary replied, spoiling the mood. I turned to glower at her and she tugged at me to go back inside.

I stood my ground. 'We do everything two sisters can do, more even. Some see our burden as a curse, but we see it differently. We have to be stronger to overcome it, helping and caring for each other so we can do the things that we each desire. Mary is my constant companion, there to help, to advise, to discuss every moment of every day of my life. We are each other's teachers, and that has made us more skilled and learned than many others. It is the one blessing of our condition.'

It sounded boastful, but I did not want to be the object of his pity. Masci looked impressed. 'You are one with everything? Even love?' he asked, with a strange little smile.

'Yes, I love Mary very much,' I replied defensively, unsure what he meant.

'No. I mean this sort of love.' And with that, he leant forward and kissed me.

We jumped back in shock together. 'No!' I yelled, although I felt my heart was going to burst.

'No?' he replied, much quieter this time. 'Are you sure?' He kissed me again; stronger but also more gently. It was no more than a moment, but it seemed to go on forever.

My mind was in a whirl, my body full of the strangest sensations. My shout had been an involuntary reaction, caused by sheer astonishment. But it had been my secret dream, one I'd not even shared with Mary. Now, after this second kiss, I wanted more.

Mary pulled on me again, stronger this time. 'Eliza, we must go. Now.'

I had no choice. I let her start to lead us back inside, but Masci spun round and blocked our way.

'I'm sorry,' he said, his expression confident, controlled. 'I thought you would enjoy it. I promise not to touch you again. Can we talk further?'

'If you want to talk, we can do so in the hall,' Mary replied. 'It is already scandalous enough we are alone with you outside.'

As we rushed back into the hall, the hubbub of chatter dimmed, as it always does when we enter a room. I glanced back to the entrance, but Masci had the sense not to follow immediately after us. We did a little curtsey to acknowledge the attention and went to find Mother.

Mary spoke for us.

'We are becoming tired after all this excitement, Mother. Would it be possible to retire to our room?'

The evening's entertainment had finished, so it was now permissible to depart. But a flash of annoyance still played across Mother's face. She obviously had no wish to leave.

'Certainly,' she said, making sure she was heard by those around her. She was smiling, but at the same time clenching and unclenching her fists. 'Come, let me escort you to the quarters Robert has prepared for us. I will see you settled and leave you to your sleep. You have done well tonight. I'm sure this will not be the last of the invitations to such a grand occasion.' She turned to the group of people to whom she had been talking. 'Please excuse me for a few moments, nothing more. A mother should always attend to the wishes of her children.'

As we settled into our bed after Mother hurried back to the hall, my mind was still buzzing from the kiss. There was nothing secret about our existence now, and Masci had not been repelled by our appearance. Could I lie, one day, with Masci, the way Mother lay with Father? Usually, we discussed everything together, but the shock of what had happened had made both of us untypically quiet.

'Masci kissed me,' I said eventually, my voice no more than a hoarse whisper.

Mary's body stiffened. 'God does not let a man lie with two women. Do not talk of this again,' she replied.

I decided not to say any more. But as I lay in the darkness, my mind danced with dreams of seeing Masci again.

1118

~

Chapter 19
Mary

When spring arrived, I headed into the woods and fields around our farm every morning to collect wild plants and take cuttings from shrubs to build up the pharmacy. Father had allowed me to build a small stone steading to store everything. It was cool and dry to keep things well preserved and securely locked, safe from rats and other vermin.

I was so busy. My time was taken up gathering and cultivating the plants for treatments but I constantly had to stop what I was doing to attend to anyone who needed my remedies.

Things became chaotic and I needed a system, so I began working on the garden in the mornings and only receiving visitors in the afternoon. For those suffering from the most serious illnesses, where the imbalance was deep within the body, I would visit the home of the poor soul afflicted in the evening and administer my cures to them there. Sometimes there was nothing that could be done; a person's dull eyes would tell me their soul was departing and they were shortly to be visited by death. But for many that I treated, their bodies returned to health.

I blushed with pride when I saw their rude recovery.

Eliza hardly picked up her lyre after we returned from Chatham, even to play it in the privacy of our own home. She was depressed, not just about the rumours there would be a ban on playing the lyre in public, but also because she still entertained thoughts of Masci the jongleur. I prayed it would not be too long before memory of him dimmed.

My prayers went unheeded.

We were doing our morning weeding and dividing up some of the herbs when we heard someone approach.

'Hail Eliza, hail Mary,' a call came, as casually as if from a regular visitor.

It was Masci.

'I worried I would not be able to find your home in Biddenden, but I should not have been concerned,' he said. 'When I arrived at the alehouse last night, every person there knew the whereabouts of the Maids of Biddenden. I did not realise you were so famous.' He pulled a leaf from a sage plant in the garden and rubbed it between his fingers, sniffing the aromatic oil on his fingertips. Then he let the crushed leaf fall to the ground, and looked around with a vaguely interested gaze. 'This must be the healing garden everyone talks of. Splendid.'

If anything, Eliza was more astonished than I was.

'Masci, what are you doing here?' she asked. 'Surely you did not come all this way only to seek us?' I could feel her heart racing.

He laughed. 'I did. And I brought my vielle with me to give you a lesson on how to play it – to save you from being tried for treason with all the other lyre players in the land.' He laughed. 'You left so suddenly I did not get a chance to make my offer the last time we met.'

I needed to protect my sister's honour. 'You subjected my sister to unwelcome attention, sire,' I said. 'Please be gone. We have no need of your assistance.'

Masci turned to me and gave me a level stare.

'I apologise for my indiscretion.' He bowed. 'To you both. I was overcome with the heady thrill of seeing such an uncommon sight as the two of you and could not help but imagine what it would be like to lie with you. It was foolhardy, I see that now. Such things are for one man and woman only. It was wrong of me to embarrass you both.'

Eliza spoke quickly before I could reply. 'What brings you to Biddenden then, Masci the jongleur?'

'The hope of hearing your fair voice again,' he replied. 'And to bring a proposal for you to consider.'

I did not like the way this was going. I willed Eliza to dismiss the jongleur, but instead I felt her body soften with the joy of his presence.

'Pray tell,' she said to him.

'I have been a jongleur since I was a small boy, and my father before me. But never have I seen a reaction such as the one I witnessed at your appearance at Robert de Crevecoeur's Christ's Mass feast. You are a fine player of the lyre, so you provide an evening's merry entertainment.' He smiled. 'For as long as King Henry permits it to be played, that is. But more than that, you are both a marvel for all to observe.' He glanced over to me again, warily this time. 'Were we to perform together, we could travel the length of the kingdom, choosing to entertain at only the most noble feasts. Maybe even perform for the King himself. I come to offer you to join with me, for us to be travelling jongleurs together. I saw how much you enjoyed giving your lyre recital. Imagine a life of performance and applause, and receiving much coin for your endeavours. What do you say?'

I could stay silent no longer. 'Women do not take the life of a jongleur. Any one who did would be thought no more than a harlot, plying her trade wherever she went. We are respectable maids of this community. Not two whores you can exhibit to those seeking lascivious thrills at some drunken bacchanalia.'

Masci pulled himself up to his full height and puffed out his chest. 'You should know that I am no itinerant gleeman who plies his trade in unruly houses of disrepute. I am Masci, jongleur to the nobility. Your virtue would be unquestioned.'

Then Eliza spoke, a sadness in her voice. 'Your offer is a generous one, dear Masci, and performing for Robert de Crevecoeur was a joyous occasion. But the two of us have made a solemn oath that we will support each other in all we do. Mary's life is here, tending her physic garden and healing the sick. In turn, her ears have to suffer my playing of the lyre every moment we have free. I cannot ask her to abandon her vocation, purely to indulge my journeying throughout the land.'

I blushed with pride at her reply, but at the same time felt wracked with guilt at my selfishness.

'It is not my desire to thwart my sister's passion,' I said. 'But my work is needed here, and many souls are dependent on my ministrations to keep their humours in balance. And we made this oath not only to each other, but to God. There are many who believed our joining would mean we would not be long for this earth. We are now almost eighteen years and in good health. Every day we thank God for this miracle. It is only fitting we honour His name in return.'

Masci shook his head. 'You can celebrate God's good grace by making His world more beautiful with your music.'

Eliza's face had been changing with every turn of the conversation, like a field of barley under a summer breeze. I could tell she was tempted by Masci's offer, and wondered what game he was playing. She looked over to me, her eyes wide with expectation. I gave the smallest shake of my head. Tears welled up in her eyes. That melted my heart and I ached to give her what she desired.

But I did not trust Masci.

I said, 'I see my sister longs to grant you this request, Masci the jongleur. But many would say a maid should be modest and shun attention, not flaunt herself in front of all and sundry. Let us seek my father's counsel on this. But only if you promise to abide by his decision and be on your way if he desires that do so.'

He agreed. Too easily.

We took Masci to meet Father and he listened as the jongleur outlined his proposal. When he had finished, Father tapped his fingers for a moment.

'I do not understand,' he said, 'why you have made so much effort to have my daughter perform with you. You spend your days at the table of some of the greatest noblemen in the land. Why do you feel the need to travel to our humble home to have Eliza play beside you? She is an able lyrist to be sure, but there are many more suitable musicians who could join you on your travels.'

'I marvel at what your daughters have achieved, Master Chulkhurst. I ask only that others see these wonders for themselves. And yes, an opportunity to see the Maids of Biddenden is one that no person in this land, no matter how high their station, would want to miss, to see with their own eyes how they deport themselves. I could ask for many times the coin I receive for my own modest talents were Eliza to accompany me.'

Masci ran his hands through his hair and leant forward to give his words more intensity. 'I see you are undecided. Then grant me one wish. It has been a long walk to travel here to meet with you all. Join me at your village alehouse tonight. Let Eliza accompany me while I tell some stirring tales to the good people of Biddenden. The ban on the lyre is still just London talk and we will avoid any songs that could stir rebellious thoughts. Let your neighbours hear a recital that is more commonly the preserve of lords and nobles. It will be an enjoyment that will stay with them for many a day to come and you can judge whether Eliza playing her lyre with me is a fitting endeavour for a young maid to pursue. What I am proposing would make your daughters wealthier than they could ever achieve tending their garden. They would become the talk of the land.'

Mother could contain herself no longer. 'Husband, there would be no hint of impropriety if we were to accompany them, were they to travel with the jongleur. Think of the many fine merriments we would be able to enjoy.'

Father shook his head. 'Life is more than the riches of the purse. It should be lived in devout obedience. Music should be performed for the glory of God, not merely to make our hearts glad. You are proposing we live a life of enjoying one feast after another, savouring so much frivolity that we become sated with lust and jaded about the simple things in life, rather than gratefully accept the modest rewards of honest toil and labour. We are unworldly country-folk. Your life is not for us, Masci.'

Masci was not ready to give up. 'Let us at least have this performance in your village. All the coin we receive, we will give to your priest, to hand out as alms to those he feels deserve charity. And if you feel our entertainment is both decent and worthy, then let Eliza display her talents without compromising Mary's good works here. I am no gardener, but even I know there are long winter months when the physic garden would need next to no tending and care. In this season, let me secure engagements that are within easy reach of your home. Eliza can develop her talents, honour our Creator, and the physic garden will not be harmed by both your daughters fulfilling their destinies. What do you say?'

I could feel that Eliza was aching for Father to say yes. Against my better judgement, I decided to speak.

'Father, Eliza and I are locked together,' I said. 'We live in each other, through each other, by each other. We *are* each other. But we are also two separate minds, two separate people, who will always be together. We have learnt the only way we can share this life together is by being equal in what we give each other. Eliza has given me her everything to enable me to create my physic garden and achieve my dream of becoming a healer. I must do the same for her. Let her play her lyre with Masci, and let her music be heard by all. I can make sure my garden does not suffer when she is fulfilling her dreams.'

Eliza was astonished. I had never spoken like this before, and I would never normally dare tell Father what he should do, especially in front of others. But he showed no hint of anger.

'A daughter should not instruct her father in the ways of the world,' he said. 'But let the jongleur put on this performance. If I see it does not bring our family into disrepute, I will grant his wish for you to travel with him to whatever gatherings I feel are appropriate for respectable young women to attend. Masci, if you wish to put on a show in our village, speak first to Deorwin, the reeve. If he grants permission, make yourself known to Ada, the village alewife.'

Masci bowed his thanks and headed off to make the arrangements.

He soon returned. 'There was much excitement at the news and Ada is brewing as much ale as can be obtained for the day after next. That will be May Day, a fine day for a celebration. I will recite *Beowulf*, and we shall have a dance that I will teach your good neighbours – the *carole*. It is a simple pursuit, but one which will promote great happiness. Those who want to dance hold hands and form a great circle and those whose modesty forbids can sing the music of the dance. It will be as gay an evening as any your village has ever enjoyed.'

MASCI DID NOT EXAGGERATE. His reading of *Beowulf* brought gasps from the crowd, for most had never heard the words before and many small children had to be carried out crying as Beowulf battled impossible odds against demons and beasts. By the time he began organising the carole, Masci was already the hero of the village. He formed the dancers in a circle, men and women by turns, then explained the moves, which were a step to the left, then to the right, and then to swap with the partner to the left of you. After a few rehearsals, which collapsed with much hilarity, they were ready to begin.

Masci sang a ballad, with the rest of us singing the chorus, 'Bow-down, bow-down,' which was the signal for the swap to take place. We sang one song, then another. I had never seen such joy on people's faces. By the end of the evening, I knew this was what I wanted to do forever.

Masci promised to return later in the autumn with news of feasts at which our appearance would be welcome. They were everywhere. From Rye to Romney, Cranbrook to Canterbury, and of course at William de Ashford's manor house, every noble family in the land wanted to meet with us and hear Eliza perform. The carole was always the highlight of our performance and it gave me so much joy watching Mother and Father join in the fun. I did sometimes look at everyone enjoying themselves, swapping partners at every chorus, and think how wonderful that would be for Eliza and me, but I told myself not to be so silly.

I would never dance the carole. But I could do other things.

Eliza had used the time until Masci's return to prac- tise her lyre every evening until her fingers ached. Some of our hosts were nervous at her playing the instrument, but Masci reassured them that although it was now never played at court, it would not incur Henry's wrath to know that ancient tunes were played upon it – only if his subjects dared sing songs of rebellion. And even to my unmusical ears, her playing sounded like the voice of angels. She had begun to compose her own melodies, the beauty of which brought tears to my eyes.

I was nervous at these gatherings, because now I did more than just hold Eliza's lyre. Eliza had convinced me that standing next to her doing nothing looked a little strange, so one of the village boys had made me a timbrel, a simple drum, by stretching a goat skin across a wooden hoop. When I hit the centre of the skin it gave a loud, deep sound. At first I would hit it randomly, but I soon got a feel of the music and used it to mark out the tempo of Eliza's playing. Even though I didn't have a musical bone in my body, I could pass myself off as accompanying her.

But there was another reason I was nervous. The kiss. We had never talked about it after Canterbury and I didn't know what Eliza's reaction would be if Masci were to try again. I promised myself I'd always make sure Mother was around so he would never have the chance.

WE DID SIX PERFORMANCES over the winter. It gave me great joy to see how much Eliza enjoyed performing, especially when it was the melodies she wrote herself that got the best reaction. Mother and Father were always invited to sit at the host's table, an honour that was great indeed, even for a prosperous country farmer. Mother persuaded Father to buy her a long silk dress, and she was always the most beautiful woman in the room. As we lay in our sleeping room after one performance, she whispered into the darkness, 'I am prouder of you than any mother can be of her children. You are an honour to your family, and are loved by all whose lives you touch. Nothing I could dream of could give me more joy than to be here with you.'

Then she cried a little, which was strange.

It was the happiest time of our lives, and when we came to the last performance of the winter, even I was sad the season for entertaining was almost over. We had travelled to Maidstone, to perform at a feast to celebrate the arrival of the new year, when Father fell ill in the morning. Soon, he had a fever and was vomiting. Eliza agreed to cancel her rehearsal with Masci so I could melt some honey into warm wine and make Father take some small sips of the healing draft. His condition improved only slowly. Mother decided that she needed to stay with him in the evening, to mop his brow and tend to his needs.

Eliza was nervous at not having properly prepared for her performance, but she and Masci were so accustomed to playing together by now that they could communicate by nods and glances. When she accompanied him to *Beowulf*, she strummed the lyre harder than I had ever heard her do before, throwing her head back at the end of each passage, swinging her hair as she played. When we finished, I could feel her buzzing with excitement.

Normally we were allowed to stay after our performance to meet the guests, but Father had agreed the concert could proceed only if Masci escorted us back to our quarters immediately after we finished. As the door of the dining hall closed behind us, Eliza was bouncing up and down in excitement.

As we passed into a side corridor, they began kissing immediately. I turned away, too embarrassed to look, but could not block out Eliza's little gasps of pleasure. I felt an awakening inside myself, and my body twitched to new and unfamiliar sensations.

As the feelings became more intense, my body started aching to be kissed, to feel Masci's hands upon me. I turned and looked at them for the first time, and that made me feel the desire even more. I dug my nails into the ball of my hand, trying to prevent myself from reaching out to have Masci bring his attention to me. Just when I could stand it no more, there was the sound of a door banging shut and loud voices coming towards us. Masci and Eliza disentangled from each other and smoothed down their clothing.

I had to act quickly.

'We must go to Mother and Father with all haste,' I said. 'If you desire these intimacies, they must wait until there is no chance of discovery. If you had been observed in these last few moments, our reputation would never have recovered from the scandal.'

I pulled on Eliza and she looked at Masci and then at me.

'You are right, sister,' she said. 'Let us not tarry a moment longer. She gave Masci a last peck on the lips. 'Please, dear Masci. Take us to our parents.'

The feelings inside me faded and we walked outside to the small house in which we were to stay for our visit. The moonlight caught on our breath as we hurried along in the cold night air. At the entrance to the house, Masci hugged Eliza again but did not kiss her.

'Good night, fair Eliza,' he whispered to her. 'Good night, Mary,' he said to me, with a little bow.

Father had made good improvement and did not think he would be any impediment to our heading back to Biddenden the next day. I could tell Eliza was disappointed – she was hoping to be around Masci for longer. As we settled down in our bed in a small back room away from our parents, we started a whispered conversation.

'I am in love with Masci,' Eliza told me. 'I cannot bear to think it will be many months until I see him again.'

'You and I cannot be in love,' I replied. 'Not in the way you mean. You would never have a private moment together as man and wife. I would be party to your every word, your every action. When he lies with you, it would be as if he was lying with me also. All decent people would be offended by the very thought of this.'

'We have been in the same room as Mother and Father when he mounted her. And any who stay in a coldharbour are used to the activities of the night going on around them. Were you to lie next to us, it would not be a sin.'

'I would consider it one.' I thought about how my body ached as Eliza's hot blood had flowed into me. 'I cannot help but be a part of any lovemaking. That is different from the activities of the family room and the coldharbour, as you know well. You need to give up your love for Masci.'

Eliza was adamant. 'You treat me wrongly, sister. Let me ask Masci to come with us to Biddenden. I will take confession with Fordwin the priest and see if he would bless our marriage. Fordwin is a wise man, and speaks to God. Surely, if he were to give his blessing, you would not be so immovable in your opposition?'

I knew Eliza was deceiving herself if she thought any priest would sanction such an unholy matrimony. But at least if she told her desires to Fordwin during confession, he would not speak of what she confided in him. Her secret would be safe, a scandal avoided. And when Fordwin denied her, as deny her he must, it would create no ill will between us.

Then a pang of conscience stabbed me.

Eliza would be humiliated by being refused and that would cause her much distress. The thought soon passed as I realised that only by experiencing that pain would she be able to put this idea behind her.

'Very well,' I said. 'As always, I do your bidding dear Eliza, as you would do mine.'

'Masci can follow us to Biddenden, so he is on hand to hear Fordwin's decision,' said Eliza. In her excitement she spoke a little too loudly. I heard Mother stir in her sleep.

'Hush,' I said. 'Let us speak no more on this tonight. On the morrow, we shall find Masci and you can tell him of your plan.'

❧

THERE WAS MUCH COMMOTION the next morning as we prepared for our journey home. Eliza looked anxiously around to make sure she found Masci before we left. Finally, she spotted him saddling his pony and asked Father if she could go to say her goodbyes. We ran over, something we rarely did, but Eliza's face was a picture of excitement and there was no slowing her.

As we came closer, I saw the look of alarm on Masci's face.

'Masci, my love,' Eliza said, in a loud voice with no thought of who might hear. 'Come with us to Biddenden and meet with our priest. We shall tell him of our love, and he will bless us so that we do not have to ever be parted again.'

Masci backed off a step or two. 'Our love? A priest? Eliza, I know not what you mean by this.'

Panic was written all over Masci's face but Eliza was too ecstatic to notice.

'I mean, to be married. When you kissed me last night, it was like angels had lifted me and carried me to Heaven. Mary has given her consent, and will not intrude on us when we are man and wife. We can have a future together.'

Masci recovered his composure and gave a nervous laugh. 'You have mistaken me, Mistress Chulkhurst. Last night was some sport, nothing more. I am a man of unbridled curiosity and after a few glasses of ale my mind was whirling, thinking about how matchless an experience it would be for me to bed you. My mind rested on that thought, as butterflies might rest on a flower. It would be a tale I would tell only on the rarest of occasions.' He reached beneath the saddle flap and pulled the girth tighter. 'I am a man of the road,' he said. 'Never one to settle on one place or one person. I take my pleasure where I find it.' He laughed again, more sympathetically this time. 'Eliza, I thought you would know our time together could only be fleeting. I hope I did not deceive you.'

Eliza burst into tears and let out a scream. As usual all eyes had been on us, so there was an immediate gasp from those nearby.

'Hush, sister, hush,' I said, in as firm a tone as I could muster. I fixed Masci a stare. 'You, sir, are a rogue to treat my sister so harshly. You should suffer a penance for your actions.'

Masci looked at me and then back to Eliza. 'You didn't think ... you couldn't have ... Oh my God, Eliza! I could not marry you. No-one could. You should take snatched moments of intimacy where you find them and enjoy them as you did with me. There will be many who would be interested and enthralled to partake of forbidden fruit, especially fruit so exotic.'

'We will never meet again,' Eliza said through her tears. 'Good day to you, sir.'

She spun around so quickly I lost my balance. We stumbled to the ground, standing up slowly to recover some dignity.

Masci put his hand on Eliza's shoulder. 'No, no, my pretty. Do not desert me. We have many fine performances ahead of us, and I know you will enjoy all the coin we can earn between us. Do not let a simple misunderstanding ruin everything.'

Father had reached us by now, drawn by Eliza's scream. He paused to collect his breath as his ailments caught up with him.

'What is going on here?'

'Nothing of any consequence,' I said quickly. 'It is always a moment of emotion when saying goodbyes.'

'A trivial matter, sir, I assure you,' said Masci, shuffling his feet.

Father looked at Eliza. 'Is all well with you, my dear?' He shot Masci an accusatory glance.

'Quite well,' Eliza replied, pulling herself together. 'If you have settled the matter of the coin with Masci, it is time we began our journey. Farewell, Masci the jongleur. I must leave to help my sister tend her physic garden.'

Masci bowed, and we hurried off without a backward glance. Father left us alone to complete the leaving arrangements.

Eliza held herself together until Father was out of earshot. Then she started sobbing again. 'I gave my heart to Masci,' she said. 'He took it and used it to play a game with my feelings, to use me to open doors to perform in the greatest halls in the land, and no doubt to have some sport with me afterwards. But he does not want to love me, to cherish me or to honour me.' She sobbed still harder. 'I feel ... destroyed. To be no part of his life is to be nothing.'

'Forget Masci,' I replied. 'He is not worthy of your anguish. Forget pain, remember only how great and gifted a woman you are. Forget this dark day and think only about the joys that lie ahead.'

'I have been a fool to think any man would take me for his wife,' Eliza said. 'And I disrespected you by my wanton behaviour. I cannot lose what I never possessed, but that does not make this agony more bearable. I will love Masci only in my dreams, for in my dreams he will love no-one but me.' She took a deep breath. 'Let us fulfil our lives through your healing, Mary, and let me write great songs that will be sung across the land. That is the way we can find true happiness. Let us leave the bedchamber for others.'

I put my hand on her arm. 'You did not disrespect me, dear sister. Let us leave these nobles' halls behind until my garden falls fallow again. We have much to do in Biddenden.'

Father called. We set out for home.

1119

~

Chapter 20
Eliza

I had made a fool of myself with Masci, but it was to good purpose. With the spring growing season upon us, Mary needed to spend long days in her physic garden, expanding the number of plants she tended and preparing tinctures and portions to heal the sick. I didn't mind. Working in the garden took my mind away from Masci and it was good to be doing something worthwhile. Mary's fame as a healer was spreading and people were travelling from far and wide.

When we finally had an evening free, I picked up my lyre again and started to sing.

What is love? Jongleur, thou woundest,
Thou woundest, mine heart.
Oh, I know not whither thou art,
Or whyfor thou tearest me apart.
If ever thou beest mine, yeve me a sign.
What is love? Jongleur, thou woundest,
Thou woundest, mine heart.

Mary clapped her hands. 'That is so beautiful, Eliza,' she cried. 'When did you write this?'

'J … just now,' I said. 'I was playing the strings with both hands and found a pleasing melody. As I repeated it again and again, my thoughts went to Masci and the words seem to fit. What do you think, Mary? Do you like it?'

Mary frowned. 'Very much. But they are sad words. Should you not sing of something else?'

I shook my head. 'Something else? Like heroic deeds of battle, or the vanquishing of foes? Leave these to the male bards to sing, along with their bawdy tales of young maids losing their virtue. Let me sing of the joy of love and passion, of the anguish of betrayal and loss. If you and I are denied the world of love with our bodies, let us live it with our minds.'

I wrote another song the next day and, a few weeks later, an epic tale of a wife awaiting her husband's return from a crusade, only to discover in the end he was slain on the field of battle. They were private follies, to ease my painful thoughts of Masci, but Mary tried to convince me otherwise.

'It is May festival at the next full moon,' she reminded me, 'and there will be much merriment during the day. In the evening, Ada's tavern will be full to listen to Geoffrey's farting jokes and stories of copulation, which are disgusting and have been heard many times before. Let us provide a little decorum to the proceedings. Play your lyre and sing your new songs. They will be treasured indeed.'

I was reluctant, but when Mother heard of the plan she would countenance none of my protests. 'When you go abroad it is you who are praised for your musical skills,' she told me. 'But here in Biddenden, you sit in your sister's shadow as her good deeds in the physic garden receive all the acclaim. You both should be celebrated here, and I speak for many when I say that hearing words and music of beauty instead of Geoffrey's farts will be much appreciated. If you will not do this for your own delight, please do it for mine.'

I laughed at the crudeness of Mother's argument. I had never heard her use such language before. 'If you tell me my contribution will be welcomed, I bow to your wishes,' I said. 'Tell Ada the alewife of this plan, so she may advertise it to the villagers. My performance will be short, but hopefully kind to the ear.'

In the end, I sang and played for over an hour, and Geoffrey became agitated at having to hold in his farts for so long before his show. He distracted himself by getting better acquainted with Ada's fresh ale, so by the time he came to perform he was even more crude and incoherent than usual. As we left at the end of the evening, I heard muttered praise, and someone saying that it would be my services that would be called for at village gatherings in future. I hoped Geoffrey would not be too offended.

FROM THAT NIGHT ON, whenever it was a fine evening around the full moon, I would draw a crowd around me and entertain them with my songs. After a mid-summer's evening performance, a tall man, a stranger from outside the village, came over to introduce himself. He looked familiar and when I heard his voice, I immediately recalled who it was. Waleran of Canterbury, the Archbishop's emissary.

'Thank you for a most pleasant evening,' he said to me. He turned to Mary. 'And Mary, I hear your physic garden has grown from strength to strength. Archbishop Ralph has returned from Rome and requests your presence to discuss some plans he is considering. Can you make the journey soon?'

'Of course, good sir,' Mary blurted out without thinking. 'Is his enquiry so urgent? It will take some days to ready my garden to remain fertile while I am gone. Do you know what he wishes to discuss with me?'

Waleran gave a small shake of his head. 'The Archbishop is not used to waiting when he requests an audience.' His face lightened. 'But I know how pressing the good work is that you do here.' He turned to look at me. 'And you, dear lady, are also blessed with a great talent. The songs you played were known to me. Many a troubadour has visited our city in the last few months and included new songs in their performance. I had not realised their origin until now, but I should not be surprised. They are not the tales with which troubadours usually entertain us. They are words that only the sensitive soul of a woman could have written.'

I blushed. 'You are most kind, Waleran the emissary. I'm glad you liked them.' I could not believe what I had heard. My songs, performed by others? I was so proud and excited. Had Masci heard them? Would I ever know?

Waleran sought an audience with Father, who reluctantly gave permission for us to travel to Canterbury. It was his busiest time and he would be unable to travel with us. Waleran offered to be responsible for our safety, but Mother insisted she would be happy to travel with us. She tried to persuade Waleran that a concert should be held during our stay and that she should be invited, despite her husband being at home, but he rejected such a scandalous proposal. Despite a slight illness of temper, she agreed to accompany us.

IT HAD BEEN TWO YEARS since we last visited Canterbury and I was amazed at how much had changed. There were now thirty large stone houses in the town, double the number from before. Mother Abigail at St Sepulchre's told us the monks who lived at the Cathedral Priory were making plans to pipe water to the priory and abbey, so they would be able to have a bath every week if they wanted to. How can man be capable of such cleverness?

But when we met with Archbishop Ralph, I was shocked by his appearance. A huge ulcer disfigured his face. The archbishop saw us stare.

'It was a long road I travelled to meet the Pope in Rome,' he told us. 'And God tested me with many hardships on the journey.'

Mary looked more closely at the Archbishop's face. 'Your ailment is worrying to me, Your Excellency. It must be treated with the flour of broad bean without delay. Blend a pennyweight with water, prepare it into a cake and dry it by the fire. Each day, place a cake over your affliction to draw out your pain and you will be cured.'

I was shocked by Mary's impudence, but the Archbishop merely gave a weary sigh. 'You know your treatments well, Mary Chulkhurst, but my malady is too deep to be treated in this way. My personal physician has already performed this treatment, but to no avail.'

'Then there is a stronger remedy which I have only just perfected,' Mary replied. She stared at the ulcer. 'Take some chervil; three times as much female fern; five times as much elfwort, and cook in water. Squeeze out the water through a cloth and fry the herbs in fresh pork fat with some sulphur. Anoint your wound with this thick paste for five days and take a bath each day to remove the humours and stench. This will bring your body into balance, no matter how deep the poison has penetrated.'

Archbishop Ralph doubled over with a rasping cough that sounded like it would never stop. Finally, he was able to speak. 'This remedy is unknown to my physician. Have you performed it before?'

Mary nodded. 'We travelled much over the winter so that Eliza could perform at feasts throughout the Lathe of Scraye, and at these feasts I have met many travellers and healers who have told me what cures are practised in other lands. When we are at Biddenden, there are ten, maybe twenty visitors a day to my physic garden. I have learnt through subtle adjustments to produce the most effective remedies.'

Archbishop Ralph absentmindedly stroked his face. 'This conversation has further convinced me of the righteousness of what I summoned you here to discuss. Since my return from Rome, I have given great thought to my legacy here on Earth when I am called to God. Archbishop Gundulf, my predecessor at Rochester, is renowned as Gundulf the Builder, the man responsible for some of the greatest constructions in the land. Word reached me of your good works. People are battling against their infirmity to travel from neighbouring villages to receive your tinctures and remedies.'

The archbishop began coughing again, each rasping bark making him weaker and weaker. He took a cup of water before continuing. 'Even though your heart is full of charity, you cannot tend to all of the poor who would benefit from your services, because many cannot make the journey to your place of healing. But the Church could fund the cost of a physic garden in every village. Rather than create great cathedrals and statues of gold to honour God, I want to honour Him by creating a land where everyone in need, from the noblest lord to the poorest vassal, receives treatment for their ailments. And we start here in Kent. I would like you to find someone in every town and village across the county to plant a garden such as yours and prepare the remedies and cures you dispense in Biddenden. Train them in your arts, and instruct them how to set up physic gardens to be run under your supervision.'

He went into another coughing fit, and we waited for him to bring it under control. 'I want every soul under my care who suffers an unfortunate affliction to know there is help close at hand to aid them in their recovery, if that is God's will. No-one in any of the five lathes of Kent should be more than a half-day's walk from a garden, and treatment, and no-one should be turned away if they lack the means to pay for their cure. What say you, Mary? Will you perform this duty for me?'

I could feel Mary trembling all the way through me. She turned and looked at me and I nodded my agreement. 'With all humility I will,' she replied. 'Such a plan would greatly honour God. To do such good works in His name would be indeed an honour. Tell me what I need to do.'

'Let us discuss more in the morning. I am weary and need to rest. I will have Waleran source the plants you described and you can prepare the cure and anoint me with it. I bid you farewell until the morrow.'

I was quite subdued as we travelled back to the nunnery. I did not begrudge Mary the honour that had been bestowed on her, but it would mean that I could never travel to the great halls of Kent to perform again. If Mary were to be responsible for so many physic gardens, and for teaching the ways of healing to those who tended them, it would be a full-time occupation, all year round. I would have to deny myself what I most enjoyed.

Mary spent the evening planning how she would build up a chain of physic gardens. Mother raised the practical concerns that would need to be addressed. 'We cannot fund this from our own purse,' she told Mary. 'The Archbishop needs to provide a stipend for your use. We should discuss the practicalities with the Archbishop and return to Biddenden to seek your father's approval.'

Mary agreed, and we went bed with our heads still spinning all the events of the day.

We rose at dawn to celebrate Prime prayers with the nuns. When we entered the chapel, we found everyone distraught. Mother approached Mother Abigail, who was sobbing. 'What calamity has befallen you all?' she asked.

Mother Abigail couldn't answer at first, then managed to control her tears sufficiently to reply.

'Archbishop Ralph has been struck with apoplexy. It came as he was removing his vestments after celebrating mass last night. He cannot move, nor is he able to speak. His doctors say he will never recover.'

'Alas!' Mary cried. 'Apoplexy is the most serious and deepest imbalance of the humours. A thick and dense humour in the vessels of the brain blocks the passage of the animal spirit in a man, and I know of no treatment that can dissolve a blockage so deep. I fear he cannot be saved from this most monstrous affliction.'

'Can your anointment of herbs and sulphur not be tried?'
I asked her. 'Archbishop Ralph said himself such a treatment
was not known to his physicians.'

'It is to treat ulcers on the skin. I have not heard of it being
effective as a treatment for apoplexy. It will not penetrate far
enough into the body to reach the thick humour of the brain.'

I persevered. 'His physicians should know of this remedy
in any case. They will want to do everything they can to
save him.'

We set off for the Archbishop's palace, but when we
arrived at the gateway we were barred from entering. Mother
insisted the guards call for Waleran the emissary. After a
long delay, he arrived to greet us. He had aged twenty years
overnight.

'You know of Mary's talents as a healer and how
Archbishop Ralph believed in her skills,' Mother said. 'Let
her come to his bedside now to tend to his needs. It is God's
will that she should have been on hand when he was struck
down. You must persuade his guards to let her pass.'

'No-one is allowed to see the Archbishop, save his
personal physician,' Waleran replied. 'If he remains too
infirm to perform his duties, there are many people who
seek a share of his power who would want to take advantage
of that sorrowful situation, rather than pray for his recovery.
He must remain protected, and that means he must receive
no visitors.'

'But Mary is a great healer. The Archbishop himself called
for her to be here at this time. Could not an exception be
made for her?'

Waleran gave a darting glance towards the palace guards.
'No-one would dare make such a suggestion. Indeed, there are

some who say the Biddenden Maids may not be the devout and caring sisters they seem to be, but are the Devil's children in disguise, who caused Archbishop Ralph to be struck down with this malady. It is best you leave with all haste, lest there becomes a threat to your safety. I will send word if the Archbishop makes a recovery and can see you again.'

Mother went to argue, but Mary stopped her. 'Waleran is a good man, and we must heed his words,' she said to Mother. 'Come, let us return to St Sepulchre's Nunnery and say our farewells. We must not add to the disorder in the city. That is how best we can aid Archbishop Ralph's recovery.'

We trudged back to Biddenden, despondent and forlorn.

WEEKS PASSED, and there was no word from Waleran. A leatherworker from Canterbury passed through Biddenden and told Deorwin that Archbishop Ralph was still involved in some decision-making inside the church, but was unable to speak clearly and did not officiate at mass or any other ceremonies. His face had dropped on one side, the left of his mouth drooping lower than the right; his speech was slurred and garbled and he had difficulty understanding what people were saying to him. It was clear he would never again be able to champion grand schemes such as the establishment of the church physic gardens.

'The dream of a place of healing in every Kentish village is over,' Mary said when she heard the news. She became listless, picking at her food, and people began to voice concerns about her gaunt appearance. I had to practically starve myself to give her the motivation to eat and soon I lacked the energy to do even the simplest of tasks.

I had to help her pull herself out of her malaise.

'If a great dream is dashed, then achieve a hundred small dreams instead,' I told her as she wearily tended her garden one autumn afternoon. 'How many people have you made well since you first planted your garden? Their numbers are too great to count. You are the greatest healer in the Lathe of Scraye and you dishonour those you have helped by dwelling on the thoughts of what might have been.'

A woman approached, holding her child, the infant making a high-pitched cough as it gasped for air. 'See?' I said to Mary. 'This mother will have walked far to have you treat her child for chincough. Once you give it a few sips of your water mint tincture, it's distress will be lessened and the mother have much relief from her fear and worry. Every day you perform miracles of healing. But unless you can renew your energy, soon your supplies of potions will be exhausted and you will have to turn away those who seek your help.'

'It is not I who perform such miracles,' Mary replied, 'but those who came before me who uncovered the secret properties of nature all around us – they are the ones who should be praised.' She went off to attend to the baby. After just a few sips of her potion, the cough had already begun to improve. Mary smiled, the first time in weeks. 'You are right as always, dear sister. Archbishop Ralph's apoplexy has indeed been a cruel blow. I would do anything to see his dream of the Kent physic gardens become a reality, but I shame myself in my self-indulgence, in allowing myself to wallow in despair.' She smiled again, more brightly this time. 'Come, Eliza. Let me put these dark thoughts behind me and ask that tonight you play me a cheerful melody on your lyre. It is a time to look forward, not behind.'

She started raking the ground with renewed vigour.

AS THE NIGHTS grew longer and the growing season came to an end, my thoughts turned to performing again. Over the summer, when time permitted, I had sung my songs at harvest fayres in nearby Bethersden and Cranbrook and had been much gratified by the acclamation I received. I longed to perform in the great halls of Kent again. But with no Masci to organise these engagements, it would mean long journeys to their estates to offer my services, and more journeying to turn up at the time of our performance. Small, neighbourhood fayres would have to suffice.

Then Mary surprised me by suggesting we travel all the way to Chatham to meet with Robert de Crevecoeur again.

'Robert has great wealth and harbours ambitions of achieving fame and immortality,' she said. 'He is a neighbour of William de Ashford, but they are rivals to be favourites of the King. Let us visit his hall to propose that you perform for him again. And when we have his ear, I can put Archbishop Ralph's idea of village physic gardens to him and ask for his blessing and sponsorship. Giving up a few acres of land will be of little consequence to him, given how vast are his holdings. Once the gardens are established, a small payment every quarter day from his exchequer would provide all the funds required to provide charity for those too poor to pay. He could become the champion of this noble project instead of Archbishop Ralph. It would guarantee him a place in history, as well as much affection from the people of Kent in his lifetime.'

I was impressed by Mary's astuteness. Robert's aides would not readily permit a commoner to seek an audience with the lord of the manor to make such a proposal, far less a woman. But for me to seek an audience to propose an evening of entertainment was a more trivial matter, and a request that might be granted without great formality. For once, our joining was a blessing. Mary would be present too, and she could speak out and press her case.

Then I realised the flaw in her plan. 'Our allegiance is to William de Ashford,' I said, 'our feudal lord. Biddenden is part of his dominion, the Lathe of Scraye, and it is to him that we should make such a proposal, not a nobleman in a neighbouring lathe. Were he to hear of our subterfuge, we would bear the brunt of his wrath. Should we not first proposition William to be overlord of the physic gardens?'

Mary shook her head. 'William has not long been granted these lands and does not yet have the resources to fund such a scheme. It is to Robert that we should turn for support. The Lathe of Aylford is barely a morning's march away from Biddenden. If the physic gardens were for his lands, it is only right he should be the overlord.'

I was troubled. Mary was always the sensible one, forever reining in my flights of fancy. Now it was her who was having a rush of blood to the head. But I could not argue with her logic. Robert de Crevecoeur was not only a man of great wealth, but he was also known to be vain and proud. Were we to present our plan to William de Ashford and be refused, Robert would not take kindly to a plan that had already been turned down.

We set off to Chatham, with young Harry as our guide again. His behaviour had been impeccable on the previous trips to Canterbury, so it was judged acceptable that we travel without a chaperone this time. The route was familiar from our journey there almost two years before. When we crossed the ford at Headcorn and passed into the Crevecoeur lands, I could not help but feel uneasy. This was a bold proposition, and there could be repercussions if it were to go wrong.

We passed through Maidstone and stopped at the cold-harbour at Boxley, a half day's march from Chatham. We wanted to arrive early and fresh the next day. Our presence attracted the usual interest, but knowledge of our existence had spread widely by now, so it was excitable curiosity that greeted us, not fear and suspicion. We set off early the next morning. Before the sun was at its highest in the sky, we arrived at the Crevecoeur estate.

Robert's steward met us at the entrance. I remembered him from our performance on our previous visit. I told him I had come to offer my services as an entertainer and he ushered us into the manor house while he went off to see if his master would receive us. It was so strange seeing the place again, and memories of Masci kept rushing through my head. Luckily, there was not too long to wait. The steward returned and said Robert and his bride-to-be, Rohaise de Kent, would see us straight away.

We were shown into the great hall, where Robert sat, Rohaise next to him. That was a good sign. I was sure such a cultured lady would appreciate my songs rather than the uncouth fare of the typical travelling troubadour. I told Robert I had been performing in the villages around

Biddenden on fair summer evenings and would relish the opportunity to put on a winter performance for him.

Robert nodded. 'Rohaise has been by my side for many a year and she has blessed me with a strong son, Elias. I have promised her that when circumstances permit I will make her my wife, so there can be no dispute that he is heir to my estates. That time is now, and our marriage contract will be proclaimed from the pulpit on the next holy day. Your songs of love would be most fitting at the celebrations afterwards. Do you agree, dear Rohaise?'

Rohaise smiled her assent. I could not believe my good fortune. My timing had been perfect.

I could feel that Mary, too, was caught up in the excitement. She would want to know whether fate might also shine favourably on her proposal.

'If I may trouble you, my lord, to hear another petition,' she said, her voice shaking.

The Baron's steward tensed and stepped forward. 'You forget your place, young lady. Baron de Crevecoeur should not be formally addressed unless I have sanctioned it first. You are admitted to this audience solely because it would be impossible for you to be excluded. Do not take advantage of this unique circumstance to proposition the Baron without permission.'

Robert waved away the objection, but the thunder on the steward's face made me concerned. Mary had made an enemy, but she was so caught up in the moment she did not notice.

'I had the honour to be summoned by Ralph d'Escures, Archbishop of Canterbury, on his return from Rome,' she told Robert, 'and had an audience with him the day he was struck down with apoplexy. He told me of plans he had been developing on his long journey home. I have shared them with no-one up to now. I—'

'God protect him,' Robert said. The steward came forward, more forcibly this time, but again Robert beckoned him to stay back. His eyes burned with curiosity as to what Mary would tell him.

Mary proceeded cautiously. 'Before leaving for Rome, Archbishop Ralph arranged for me to be schooled in the arts of healing and how to use the medicinal properties of the plants and artefacts of nature to restore the body to good health, should its humours become out of balance. I planted a modest physic garden in Biddenden and treat any who need my help. The Archbishop heard of my success on his return and proposed a grand scheme, that gardens like Biddenden's should be set up in every village in his diocese, with himself as patron. To my astonishment but great honour, he asked me to be the one to assist in this ambitious plan.' Mary paused and took a deep breath. 'But he was struck down before his proposal could be put in motion. I have thought every day about how saintly an idea it was, and how cruel that it should be denied because of the calamity that befell the Archbishop. I seek another patron for this grand scheme, and you, sir, are one of the wealthiest and, if I may say so, most munificent men in Kent. Would you consider using your great fortune to realise the Archbishop's dream?'

'The overlord of such a scheme would be much revered,' said Robert. He held his hands out, as though weighing the air. 'But I must say no. I have commissioned the building of a grand castle, in Leeds, a short distance from Maidstone. It will provide a defence against any Norman incursions and bring peace and stability throughout the Lathe of Aylford and beyond. Such a venture makes a high demand on the coffers of my estate. There is no scope for any other great plan.'

The steward could contain himself no longer. 'My lord, you should not humble yourself by explaining the treasury of your barony to a mere farmer's daughter.' He turned to Mary. 'You have tricked your way into the Baron's presence to make a proposal to him without any regard to due protocol and procedure. You should be thrown into the stocks for your impertinence. What say you, Robert? Shall I arrange for this malapert to be chastised?'

'Let her be,' replied Robert. He turned to Mary. 'Your tender age and good intentions will save you from punishment for your impudent behaviour. But it is true – the Baron of Chatham should not have to explain himself to a commoner.' He squared his shoulders and lifted his chin a fraction. 'I think it best you leave forthwith.' He spoke with an angry authority, as the full extent of Mary's subterfuge dawned on him. 'I was going to add, and never venture here again, but I do not know where that leaves us with the festivities we agreed with your sister.' He rubbed his nose. 'What say you, Rohaise, to hearing an evening of song from Eliza Chulkhurst?'

I dreaded to hear what was coming next.

'I have never heard of a nobleman being so gracious after suffering such embarrassment from a commoner,' she replied. 'But I cannot witness such shameful scenes and be equally forgiving. No matter how sweet are the songs of Eliza, she must perform them with Mary at her side, and her sister's presence would be a reminder of this shameful day, and a blight on the merriness of the evening. Let us find another troubadour for our betrothal.'

And with that, we were ungraciously ushered out of their presence. Mary was beside herself with remorse. 'I forgot my station and pressed Baron Robert too hard for his support. And you have been punished as a consequence. This was an audience to discuss the playing of your music. It was selfish of me to use it for my own ends.'

'It is a bitter blow, that is true,' I replied. 'But it is no more bitter than I inflicted on you, when Ymbert the Wise was teaching you the ways of the physic garden. Today, a burden has been lifted from me. We have now each suffered from the other's behaviour when following our dreams. Let us learn from it, and be of even greater support to each other in the future. I have forgotten already. Let us speak no more of this.'

I nodded. 'Maybe fate has had a hand in this. Our lord is rightly William de Ashford and our fealty should be to him. Let us visit him with your proposal, and ask for his patronage for a physic garden in Sittingbourne, Faversham, Tenterden, Appledore – all the major villages in his lathe. That is a more modest proposal, and one more fitting for you to champion. Let others observe the good work you will do, and see fit to emulate it. You should not take on more than you could prudently manage.'

Mary brightened at that. 'You are right, dear sister. My reason became clouded by ambition, I strived to achieve too much, too soon. Let us visit William de Ashford after we have returned to Biddenden, but first make our proposal to Deorwin. Our village reeve should take it to William's steward, so that this time we follow due process.' She sighed. 'I have learnt a lesson today, that a farmer's daughter needs to practise humility and not be so forceful in trying to bend great nobles to her will.'

WE RETURNED TO Biddenden and met with Deorwin.

'You know Waleran the emissary summoned us to an audience with Archbishop Ralph,' I said to him, 'and that when we met him, the Archbishop outlined a great plan for physic gardens throughout the land, starting here in Kent, with my sister charged to oversee their formation based on her own garden here in Biddenden.'

Deorwin smiled and nodded. 'A great honour, Mary the Healer.'

'Great indeed,' Mary replied. 'And one that would bring renown to our village. But calamity struck, and Archbishop Ralph was stricken by apoplexy before any actions could be taken. Now he is being nursed in sickness and will never recover enough to see through this grand scheme.'

'Calamity indeed. And so now you are looking to William de Ashford to take on this obligation? I think you overestimate the size of his exchequer. What you propose would be a formidable undertaking, with no sure reward in sight for the sacrifices he would have to make.'

'My proposal would be a more modest one, limited to the villages of the Lathe of Scraye. This is a time of great progress in the art of healing and it is not considered blasphemy to claim that a skilfull apothecary can cheat death and return the sick to health. Some say my garden in Biddenden is a place of miracles, but it is no more that the diligent application of a knowledge that grows every day. These learnings should be shared more widely, so that every village can be blessed as Biddenden is blessed. Were William de Ashford to be the champion of such an endeavour, his name would be revered throughout the lands of Kent and beyond. Though only a newly appointed baron, he would have fame and reputation equal to any in the land.'

Deorwin smiled. 'Your words would soften even the stoniest of hearts, Mary Chulkhurst. And none can doubt the great service your physic garden has provided. But would that not suffer, if you embarked on such a plan of such adventurous daring? I would be failing in my duty to do the best for our village if our healer were gone, never to be seen again.'

'My own physic garden will always be the one closest to my heart,' Mary replied. 'I make you a promise here and now that I will never fail the people of Biddenden while pursuing these grand ideas. If I make you that vow, will you make representations of this plan to William, so that he gives them due consideration?'

Mary saw from the smile on Deorwin's face that she had succeeded.

DEORWIN WENT to Ashford ten days later and when he returned, his demeanour had changed.

'I have been made to look a fool,' he told Mary. 'William's steward was already aware of your scheme, for he had met with Robert de Crevecoeur's steward on estate business a few days before. He was told of your impudent demands of him when he had graciously agreed to receive Eliza to discuss a simple proposal to make a merry winter feast. William de

Ashford is furious that a vassal from his estate should petition another nobleman without seeking his permission, and is further enraged that you should seek him out as a second choice for an endeavour de Crevecoeur has already refused.' He gave Mary a glassy stare. 'I had to use all my powers of persuasion to convince him you meant no disrespect to him, or to Richard de Crevecoeur, and that your behaviour was only that of someone young of years, who had become overzealous after having their head filled with false ideas by our ailing Archbishop. Be grateful he has not summoned you for a chiding. But my advice is to keep yourself limited to humbler activities, the physic garden at Biddenden and no more, and be grateful your reckless behaviour has not had direr consequences. And do not involve me in your fanciful schemes again.' He stalked off without waiting for a response.

Mary's hopes had been dashed and our brief time of glory had come to an end. Biddenden would be our world from now on.

1120

Chapter 21
Mary

There were no more invitations for Eliza to perform at Chatham or Ashford. No grand patrons presented themselves for a scheme to have physic gardens throughout Kent to provide care and treatment to those who needed it. Our ambitions were shattered into fragments. But we adapted. Eliza continued to write her songs and poems and they were well received when she performed on village quarter days; I tended my physic garden so I could provide any cure that was demanded of me. When we were children we had dreamt of being the same as everyone else. As we got older, we dreamt of being special. Now we simply wanted live out our days in harmony with those around us.

We were happy. Until the *White Ship* disaster.

It was at the end of November when the news reached us. The *White Ship* had sunk in the English Channel off the French coast. Only one survived out of three hundred souls on board. The cream of English nobility drowned, included William Adelin, the only legitimate son and heir of King Henry. The King was distraught, and there was great unrest as to who would become the next King of England. Norman interlopers eyed the English throne and Robert de Crevecoeur was speeding up the building of his castle at Leeds. Tension cracked in the air.

The village elders decided to hold a requiem mass for the safe passage to Heaven of all the souls who died, and for the King to recover from his grief and produce a new son and heir. Eliza said she would write a poem about the disaster, and would in due course set it to music, and was given the great honour of being allowed to read it at the church service. She worked day and night to finish it on time and by the day of the service she had it ready.

She was excited. I was worried.

Fordwin the priest finished his sermon and beckoned Eliza to come forward. We walked to the front of the congregation, and Eliza recited her poem from memory in a loud, clear voice.

> *On a November night a shouting rent the wintry sky,*
> *It leapt o'er the deep – the grievous cry*
> *Of three hundred living that now must die.*
>
> *An instant shriek that sprang to the shock*
> *As the ship's keel met the sunken rock.*
> *The ship was eager and sucked athirst*
> *As a swimming bladder fills when pierc'd;*
> *And like the moil round a sinking cup,*
> *The waters against her crowded up.*
>
> *It turned as a bucket turns in a well,*
> *And nothing was there but the surge and the swell.*
> *The Prince that was and the King to come,*
> *There in an instant did succumb,*

When told, King Henry lay as dead;
Speechless still he stared from his bed
And despite his rule, his pride, his reign.
Good King Henry ne'er will smile again.

There was a stunned silence from the congregation. Service was always conducted in Latin; English was considered by some to be offensive, almost blasphemous. And for English to be the language of the words spoken about a King was clearly thought disrespectful in the extreme. Eliza had told me of her plan; she said she wanted her words to be understood by as many people as possible and had sworn me to secrecy. I had doubted the wisdom of it then, and from the looks on everyone's faces, I regretted it even more now.

When the service was over Father pulled us outside, his face a mask of fury.

'Eliza, how could you treat God and King with such contempt?' He turned to me. 'And Mary, I always thought you were the sensible one. How could you let your sister do such a thing?'

'It was a secret,' I replied. 'Our solemn promise to each other is that we never betray something the other does not want to be known. I pleaded with Eliza not to do this, and I desperately wanted to tell you of her intentions, but I could no more betray my vows to her than I could strike her down with my hand. I am sorry, Father.'

Eliza twisted her body into a position that was especially uncomfortable for me. I cried out in pain.

'Stop that, Eliza!' Father shouted. 'Do not punish your sister for having the sense to see the folly of what you have done, and out of a misguided sense of duty not act to stop the madness of your actions. I feel there will be repercussions indeed for the foolhardiness you have shown today.'

Eliza looked shocked at his anger. 'I have done no wrong,' she protested. My stomach tightened as Eliza's racing heartbeat sent her anxiety through me. 'Our village is grieving, with every God-fearing loyal subject of the King lamenting the loss of William Adelin and the other poor souls who perished. I thought my words would give some comfort, but only if they were known. The rituals of mass are familiar to all since childhood; they do not have to be in the common tongue to be comprehended. But my words had not been heard before. Even the few who are conversant with Latin would lack the quickness of mind to understand the words if I spoke them in the language of the Church.'

Father shook his head in disgust. 'I should never have allowed you to experience the adulation of an audience when you performed with lyre and voice. You seek out attention, even when it is not seemly to do so. You have brought shame on your family with your display of conceit today. The name of Chulkhurst will be darkened by your disrespect.' He wrung his hands, as if washing away a sin. 'Do not expect the elders to look favourably on your actions.'

He was right. A few vociferous zealots in the village called for Eliza to be banished from the Church, even penalised for her blasphemy, but they were drowned out by others, many of whom I had healed, who pointed out that I would necessarily be punished by such actions as much as Eliza. In the end it was agreed that Eliza should be chided for her actions, her punishment being that from that day on, her songs would remain unsung and her poems unspoken.

A passing troubadour told of the festivities for Robert de Crevecoeur's marriage to Rohaise and regaled the people of the village with stories of the great celebrations on the wedding day itself. The songs of Masci were the most talked about feature of the entertainment. Masci himself had passed but a short distance from Biddenden on his journey to the wedding, the troubadour told them.

'My songs have given me great joy and satisfaction, but also deep despair,' Eliza told me as we worked in the garden after the troubadour left. 'My heart is not strong enough to suffer more pain on their account. Let me pledge my time to your endeavours from now on, Mary the Healer. We shall be as one in treating those with bad humours.'

Eliza was banned from entertaining and I had fallen out of favour with the lord of the manor. Our fall from grace was complete.

~ 1121 ~

AT THE START of the new year, the news that King Henry had married Adeliza of Louvain was greeted with joy throughout the land. Adeliza would be expected to produce a son. Henry's first wife, Matilda, had died two years before the *White Ship* disaster, and it was unthinkable that his only surviving child, also called Matilda, would one day rule as queen.

Eliza was enthralled by the news. Every time we went into the village she would ask Ada what the latest gossip in the alehouse was about the royal marriage.

'Some say that it is ill-timed,' Ada told us, 'so soon after the death of William Adelin, others that it is the best of timing. But in truth, the marriage was arranged long before the tragic events at sea. Its purpose was to bring some comfort and distraction to the King following the death of Matilda. And it is a fair match. Adeliza's father owns size-able territories in France and Germany and her mother is a descendant of the great Emperor Charlemagne. And so renowned is Adeliza's beauty that she is known as The Fair Maid of Brabant. I do not think Henry will need much encouragement to play his part in producing an heir.'

Ada laughed at that, but Eliza replied in a dreamy voice, 'I imagine her as beautiful as a pearl, her skin white and glow-ing, her hair flowing down her back like a golden waterfall. The most beautiful vision ever to walk on earth.'

'Well, the King must indeed be smitten,' Ada said, 'for he has granted Adeliza not only the vast lands of her prede-cessor but extra estates in Bedfordshire, Devon, Essex, Gloucestershire, Hertfordshire and Middlesex. Not that she will be spending much time there, by all accounts. She and Henry will spend not one night apart until she is with child. And Henry may be as old as Geoffrey the Flatulent, but he has the vigour of a man barely out of youth. Adeliza will find a day in the saddle tough to bear after performing her queenly duties all night long.'

A crowd had gathered to listen to our conversation, and they roared with laughter at this last observation. I stayed silent and blushed. It was unbecoming of a woman who was not married to be party to talk of the events of the bed chamber. But Eliza found this aspect of the story the most enthralling of all.

'It is said the King has already bedded all the ladies of the royal court at Windsor,' she said, her eyes wide, 'and picks the fairest wench at every home he visits to spend the night with him. The number of sons he has sired out of wedlock could provide a second army, if Amaury de Montfort were ever to invade.'

Ada agreed. 'Yet only a single son and daughter born in wedlock, and now that son lies at the bottom of the sea. That is God's punishment for spreading his seed so widely. But there will be no more courtesans until a new heir is produced. Given what is said about Henry's manhood, I don't know whether to envy Adeliza or to pity her.'

Ada cackled with laughter, and even Eliza joined in. I decided to bring this uncouth conversation to an end and announced that I had evening watering of the physic garden that should be attended to. Reluctantly, Eliza agreed we should head back home.

'I would dearly like to write a song in praise of Adeliza and another to celebrate when we hear news of her confinement,' Eliza said as we walked back to the garden. 'Do you think when we are greeted with such happy news, the village elders would relent on their ban on my performing again, and let my voice be heard telling of the joy of a new life bringing salvation to England and saving us from the perils of anarchy? Tell me that will be true, Mary.'

Perhaps Eliza was right, that a time of rejoicing could mean that past sins would be forgotten. But soon the happiness that spread through the land in expectation of Henry's child was brought to an end by the return of the sweating sickness. I treated strong fevers with cinquefoil, a weed that grew in meadows. Cinquefoil was very hot, and the fluids drove out the heat of fevers. I would pound it and mix it with flour and water to make a little cake, which I would spread on hempen cloth warmed by boiling water and tie around the belly of the person affected. They would heat the cloth by the fire when it cooled down, and the hot cinquefoil chased away the fevers and made them vomit. Then they would be well again.

But this fever was stronger than the usual ones, and soon more and more villagers were arriving, their bodies burning from the disease. Old Godwin the blacksmith became so hot his life was extinguished and stories were reaching us of many more deaths in other villages. The elders met to discuss the crisis and many of the villagers gathered to hear what they had to say. Eliza and I stood at the back of the crowd, along with Mother and Father. I felt shame that my cinquefoil cakes had failed to stop old Godwin's death, and thought that many would blame me for it. Eliza told me not to be silly.

She did not know the pain a healer feels when their remedy fails.

Deorwin spent the early part of the meeting trying to find out what was true and what was rumour about the disease. It had started on the north coast, at Whitstable, he established, and had spread to Canterbury. Then it had crossed into our lathe at Ashford and people were falling sick in nearby Bethersden. With the death of old Godwin, it had reached our doors.

One of the elders was arguing this was all part of God's punishment for the sinfulness that was spreading through the land, following on from His vengeance in sinking the *White Ship*.

'Word has reached me from Canterbury,' he said, 'that there have been a score of deaths in this last moon alone. Archbishop Ralph remains incapacitated by his apoplexy, and the senior clerics are worried that we are being punished for the sins of the King. His taking a new wife, less than two months after his son's death, is seen by many as hasty. They worry God's retribution can only increase.'

'I cannot believe this,' Deorwin replied. 'King Henry is a good king, and he has done much to glorify God during his long reign. It is his kingly duty to act swiftly to secure a new heir to the throne.' He took a stick and scratched an outline of the Kent coast in the earth, putting crosses to mark Whitstable, Ashford and Bethersden, then drawing a circle to show where Biddenden was located. There was a gasp from the crowd. The sickness was moving in a straight line towards us.

'You see?' he said to the other elders. 'This is not God's vengeance, striking down from the Heavens. Fever is spread through a miasma, a dense cloud of affected air. This has been known since Roman times. We can no more stop its progress than we can command the wind to change direction. It is now almost upon us, and we can only pray it passes onwards with all speed.'

'And there is no way to stop it?' another elder asked. 'Then we are doomed!'

A cacophony of voices rose from the crowd, and a group of women began wailing hysterically. A man shouted that it was the Jews' fault – that they were poisoning our wells.

Deorwin banged his stick on the village calling-bell and appealed for order. 'We must keep calm heads and face down this threat. I see Mary the Healer is amongst us. Tell us Mary, is there no other remedy for this terrible affliction?'

My mouth dropped open, and the gasp from the crowd was even greater than when Deorwin drew his map. Women were not allowed to speak at elder meetings, although that never stopped Ada making her views known. But never in living memory had a woman actually been invited to speak.

The crowd parted in front of me and I had no choice but to respond. 'I consulted my goatskins, looking for ideas,' I said, my voice shaking. 'Hazelwort is another plant whose heat can drive out fever. Celandine is cold and moist and if cooked in wine might cool the temperature. But so far, none seem to be having any effect.'

The elder, Maurice, interjected and I breathed a sigh of relief that I had been spared from having to say more. 'My father has told me the stories of a great pestilence that swept through the land in times before the Conqueror,' he said. 'I worry it might be visiting us again.'

Maurice was known as the wisest and most erudite of the elders. His comments were always measured and based on a thoughtful appraisal of the situation. If he said all was lost, no-one would argue against him. A deadening silence fell over the crowd.

Unbidden, like a seed on fallow ground, a plan sprouted in my mind. I took a deep breath and summoned up all my courage to speak again.

'There is a power that we possess,' I said. All eyes were on me now. 'Others in the village are sick, but none are yet as bad as old Godwin became before he passed. They are all from the same families, and most are those living close together by the market cross. The farmers remote from the village seem so far unaffected by the sweats, but they breathe the same air as us. Could this miasma not stick to the flesh of the body, and then move to another who passes into its cloud? Were we to cover our skin in goose fat, and shroud our bodies in cloth, staying at home and not mingling with each other, then the miasma would find nothing to grip with its evil touch. It would disappear on the wind, sparing us from its cruelties.' I took another deep breath. 'I would like to try such a remedy.'

Deorwin clasped his hands together, as though he were offering a prayer. His gaze darted to Maurice, who nodded mutely.

'None would doubt your skills as a healer,' Deorwin said. 'You have my blessing to try.'

'For this to work, it is not just the sick who must pay heed. The whole village will need to take part. All of us, no matter of what status or calling, will need to cover all of our skin for the winds to carry this airy evil spirit away. The elders will have to command all to comply.'

Osbert was the first to protest. He was a shepherd and his pregnant ewes would soon need to be attended to. 'It is the sick who need your services, not the healthy. No elder could subscribe to behaving as you suggest when there are trades to be done, and fields to be tilled. You have spoken thrice at an elder meeting, Mary Chulkhurst. Let that be enough.'

Fordwin the priest spoke up in my defence. 'I have seen many in this village visit Mary's physic garden and receive treatments that cure the imbalance of humours. The Archbishop of Canterbury, Ralph d'Escures, is a great admirer of Mary's talents, although even her powers cannot enable him to recover from his apoplexy. If our humble village has such a great healer in its midst, it would be a foolish vanity to ignore the advice she gives. We should be as one in fighting this disease. Jesus tells us the body is not one member, but many. Let us all make sacrifice together to defeat this enemy, and not expect the sick to assume the burden alone. That would be God's way.'

I had never heard Fordwin speak on such secular matters before, and neither had the rest of the village, so his words had a great impact. No-one dared speak against him and be seen as contradicting the Word of God. Deorwin announced that the fight against the miasma would begin on the morrow. I laid out a plan as to what must be done, and asked that everyone pass it on to their neighbours. The meeting broke up and everyone hurried off to make their preparations.

I was nervous. But excited.

THE OPERATION began at dawn. Geese were slaughtered and each household was responsible for procuring a bowl of goose fat to cover their skin. The women baked loaves of horsebread, made with all kinds of grain – rye, barley and oats – along with dried peas and beans. The ingredients were plentiful, and the bread was hard and tasteless, but it would last for weeks. Moistened with weak ale, it would provide all the sustenance the villagers needed. The following day, guards were posted at a makeshift coldharbour on the road to the village, turning away any who came to visit. Everyone was to remain in their homes, covered in goose fat and swaddling to prevent the spirit from reaching the skin.

Then it was a matter of waiting. And praying for wind – better yet, a full-blown storm – sufficient to carry the miasma over the village and away.

As we waited, the dismal march of death strode ever forward. Other poor unfortunates started developing symptoms and had to suffer alone or with their families. I was desperate to treat them, but worried that by doing so I would move the spirit through the village.

Each day I looked upwards, willing the grey early spring skies to fill with energy and rid us of the fever. But the mornings were foggy, the afternoons dull and dismal under gloomy, leaden clouds. I began to worry that the dreary monotony would lead to stirrings of rebellion against the tedious existence the villagers were forced to endure. Then, on the third day, a cool chill was in the air. I felt the wind freshen on my face, saw the clouds roll up into tall columns as they sucked in the energy of the heavens. The birds went quiet, the cattle settled down in the fields. This was it. The moment of truth had arrived.

A few heavy raindrops splattered on the ground, releasing a musky scent into the air, the smell of rebirth, of renewal. There was a pause of just a few moments, as if a monstrous goliath was summoning his strength before unleashing his powers upon the Earth. Then the storm began in earnest – roaring wind, angry and incessant rain. Usually we would huddle together when we heard the elements lash the roof and walls, Father poised to respond to any calamity to befall the farm, the rest of us silently praying for the storm to pass. But this storm was different. It was a saviour, not a destroyer, and we willed its strength to grow and grow.

It subsided suddenly, in the dead of the night, and as the sky cleared the stars seemed to glow with renewed vigour. I had never felt the air so fresh and clean. It truly felt as though the miasma had been blown away.

And it had. After the storm, with each day that passed there were fewer and fewer victims of the sweats. After ten days, we had not one new sufferer. A meeting of elders was convened to decide what to do next. Once again, I was invited to attend.

'It seems our village has been spared,' Deorwin said to me. 'And for this you have our gratitude, Mary the Healer. We have loosened the grip of the airy spirit which inhabited our village and the strong winds have driven it from our doors. Let us send word that we welcome our neighbours back into our lives – and let us feast tonight! I, for one, am mightily sick of horsebread.'

There was a chuckle from the other elders. 'And you, Mary the Healer, will be guest of honour,' one cried. There were mutterings of agreement.

The experience of the last meeting gave me pause, but I couldn't stop myself from speaking. 'That is two great honours you bestow. First to invite me, a woman, to this gathering, and then to honour me thus. May I say more?'

The tone of the mutterings turned to disapproval. 'We discuss serious matters of the village here,' one elder said. 'Women's minds are too easily swayed by emotion to take part in these debates.'

I bit my tongue. Once again, I had gone too far.

Deorwin fixed me with a piercing glare. 'Women are skilled in the ways of the body and know how to care for others. You are exemplary in your talent at these womanly skills but do not confuse them with how best to govern others.'

Father interceded on my behalf. 'Mary was but caught up in the passion of the moment,' he said, 'which shows the wisdom of your words, Deorwin. Can I confer with my daughter, to find out what it is that troubles her enough to disrupt your deliberations? If I judge it to be of merit, let me speak on her behalf to the council.'

I explained to Father my concern, that the spirit would be present in neighbouring villages and would be passed to us again were the villagers to visit with the miasma present on their bodies. 'We need to keep the guards posted on the road to the village until all around are cleared of this disease and not let any pass into our village, no matter what their station or how hale and hearty they appear. Let commerce take place at the village boundary, with six paces between those of our village and any that come to trade. Otherwise the airy spirit will return and we will have a life of goose fat and horsebread again.'

Father relayed my words, and eventually the elders agreed. For the next few weeks, Biddenden gained the reputation of being a forbidden village, but it was worth it. Multitudes died all over Kent before the sweats passed, but Biddenden was spared. Every villager who passed me in the street tugged their forelock in respect.

Finally, as a full moon rose over the village marking a month since my proposal was accepted, Deorwin announced to a large crowd by the village cross that the sweating sickness had passed. Cries went up that I should be rewarded for my services.

'Tell us a wish I can grant, Mary the Healer,' said Deorwin. 'Something that will demonstrate to you the gratitude we feel for your wisdom and council.'

The last few weeks had been uncomfortable for me, fighting my natural shyness to lead the fight against the disease. But there was one last pronouncement I had to make, before I could slip into the shadows again. 'If you truly desire to give thanks for this blessing we have had, there is one gift you could afford me. Let my sister's voice be heard and her music played, whenever we join together in celebration and remembrance. That would give me more joy than any gift of coin or land.'

Deorwin smiled, realising he had brought about the lifting of Eliza's ban by his own hand. 'I was thinking more of a material gift, but no matter. Unless any voice be raised in protest, I declare that Eliza Chulkhurst is free to take up her lyre again and make merry at any village gathering.'

There was a hush as everyone waited to hear if anyone would speak out. A few moments later, the silence was broken by a huge cheer. Eliza's sobs of gratitude shook through my body and my spirit soared like the highest eagle in the sky.

Our lives were complete again.

1122

~

Chapter 22
Eliza

The decision of the first elders' council of the new year was a surprise. A celebration was to be held in spring, the anniversary of the sweating sickness being banished from our village. Mary and I were summoned to hear the proclamation announced at the conclusion of the meeting. Deorwin made us stand in front of the other villagers while he delivered the news.

'Mary Chulkhurst. Assisted by your good sister Eliza, you saved the village of Biddenden from catastrophe. While all around us an airy spirit took the lives of good and true people from all over Kent, here the spirit could not bring its evil curse because of the wisdom of your actions. Any of us who in the past questioned your learnedness in the ways of healing, now beg your humble forgiveness. To show our gratitude, and to celebrate our delivery from this evil pestilence, we shall have a village holiday, and you shall be guests of honour. From this next Lady Day and onwards, there will be a celebration to give thanks, and a ceremony to honour the part you played. May God bless you both.'

My heart froze, then pounded, and I heard Mary's short breaths next to me. How could we be so honoured?

The village baker made some horsebread cakes of the kind we had all eaten while we hid from the miasma, shaped into our likeness, which many villagers kept as mementos of the day we saved the village. There was talk of establishing a tradition of making these each Lady Day, so their part in combatting the disease would never be forgotten.

'We will be remembered forever,' I told Mary, 'We can ask no more than that. Let us remain humble with that thought for the rest of our days.'

Finally, we had found peace and contentment. We slept deeply that night.

SADNESS REVISITED Biddenden in the late summer, when word reached the village that Archbishop Ralph had finally succumbed to his illness. There was to be a great memorial service to be held at Canterbury Cathedral, and Deorwin was invited to attend, along with all the other reeves of the Kent villages. He announced that the Chulkhurst family would be the other village representatives at the ceremony, as Mary and I had been known to the Archbishop.

We set off the day before the ceremony, camped outside the city at nightfall and the next day headed into Canterbury. Mary and I wore the cloak that best disguised our join-ing from the crowd, and we managed to observe the entire, and entirely beautiful, service without our presence being discovered.

Except by Waleran. The Archbishop's emissary recog-nised us and asked us to visit him before our departure. We returned the next day and Deorwin took us to the narthex, an entrance at the west end of the cathedral, opposite the altar. It was the part of the church where secular discussions could be held. Deorwin bowed to Waleran and stepped outside. We felt so inconsequential, Mary and I, in this huge chamber, in the presence of someone of such great authority that even Deorwin had felt humbled in his presence. My mouth felt dry and my every sense was heightened. The heady scent of incense hung in the air; a beam of light from a high window sliced down to the ground, almost solid in its intensity. At the far end of the church a door creaked open and the sound echoed around the vast walls.

Waleran smiled to put us at our ease.

'It is good to see you both so well,' he said in introduction, 'even if the occasion is one of sorrow. Word has reached me of the miracle of Biddenden when you saved your villagers from the horrors of the sweats. You will find a place in Heaven as a result of your endeavours.'

We both blushed and I felt I should say something to show humble modesty.

'It was all Mary's doing, Waleran the emissary. I only followed her commands.'

'Ah, Eliza. You also have achieved much since we last met. I have heard your song lamenting the tragedy of the *White Ship*.'

Suddenly my face and neck were impossibly hot. 'I … I meant no disrespect, I swear,' I said. 'Please find it in your heart to forgive me.'

To my surprise, Waleran laughed. 'You do not need forgiveness, Eliza Chulkhurst, you need praise. Your words and music have travelled far, and have given the common people much solace at this time of tragedy. I have heard it performed within the very walls of this city and it has even travelled as far as London. It is because of that, I wished to speak with you.'

Was he serious? A mixture of pride, confusion and anxiety swept through me.

Mary spoke for me. 'Master Waleran, my sister is overwhelmed by your words.' She squeezed my hand in encouragement and I fought hard not to burst into tears.

'You are right to be overawed by all you have done,' Waleran replied. 'Your words have been heard by The Fair Maid of Brabant herself, Adeliza of Louvain, Queen of England. She was moved by them and has asked me to convey her appreciation of your heartfelt tribute.'

I collapsed onto the floor, so suddenly that I caught Mary unawares. For the first time in years, we rolled over in an ungainly tumble.

'She did?' I said, as we stumbled to sit upright, my voice strangled by the tightness of my throat. 'You met her? What did she say?'

'What I have told you. That your words were pleasing. She said the King flew into a rage when he first heard them but now finds solace in their recital, though only a new male heir will truly lift his melancholy.' He paused for effect. 'And when I told her of the curiosity of your condition, she bade me make arrangements to receive you here in Kent. She travels with Henry soon, to inspect the progress on the building of the castle at Leeds. The King would have been expected to stay a few nights at Robert de Crevecoeur's manor house and enjoy some hunting, but he was persuaded by Adeliza to journey on to William de Ashford's abode and hunt in his forest, which will be named King's Wood in his honour.

You will be aware of the ... rivalry between the two men. The arrangements have caused Robert great consternation and William is delighted to be so openly seen to be in the King's favour. You will be made warmly welcome at Ashford Manor when you go there to meet with the Queen. It is on the first full moon after the autumn equinox that she will grant you an audience. Be sure to attend.'

I picked myself up with as much dignity as I could muster. 'This is indeed a great honour. But Mary and I are simple country maids, we know nothing of how to address a queen. I fear I may offend her, and were I to do so, my shame would be unbearable.'

'The Queen does not stand on ceremony and indeed will enjoy a moment away from the formality of Henry's court, and to be spared the raucous revelry of the King's hunting party,' Waleran replied. 'She will meet you in secret, once the King and his noblemen have departed, and will want to put you at your ease. But I instruct you to tell no-one, save your parents. Knowledge of the Queen's whereabouts is a dangerous secret that should not be shared.'

Having made our promise, we hurried off to tell Mother and Father. We found them waiting for us by the palace gates.

'What news of your meeting with Waleran?' Father asked. 'Is there to be some other ceremony of thanksgiving you have been asked to attend?'

'Waleran is still Waleran the Archbishop's emissary,' I replied. 'But now he brings missives from the court of King Henry. We are to meet with Adeliza, Queen of England, during her trip to Kent, at the time of the autumn equinox, in the hall of William de Ashford. She wants to meet the composer of "The *White Ship* Lament".'

Mother almost fainted and it took a moment for her to recover. Father did not know whether to attend to Mother or to press me for more details.

'Bring some water,' he shouted to one of the guards. As the guard ran off, he turned to me. 'Are you to be punished for disrespecting King Henry? Why did you write such foolhardy words anyway?'

Mother was recovering now and looked at me with a slow, disbelieving shake of the head. 'Queen Adeliza has summoned you to her presence?' she said, her voice full of wonder. 'Tell me this is no jest on your part.'

'No jest, Mother. And, Father, no punishment either. Adeliza approves of my words and says they have brought some small comfort to the King. Our meeting is to be a joyous one.'

The guard arrived with a cup of water, which Mother waved away.

'Then this will be a day to remember forever,' she said. 'Thomas, you can have Deorwin announce this great honour on our return. The villagers of Biddenden should know they have a queen's favourite in their midst.'

'No, Mother, the visit is to be a secret,' I replied. 'In these troubled times there should be no intelligence abroad regarding the King and Queen's whereabouts.'

Mother crinkled her brow in faux annoyance. 'There are no agents of Norman aggressors hiding in Biddenden. And any we tell will be sworn to secrecy.'

'You will speak to no-one of this,' Father said, in a sharp tone I had never heard him use towards Mother before. 'Eliza courted disaster with these words once before, and we will not risk dishonour to our family a second time. Vow to me now that no mention of this great honour will pass your lips until we are granted leave to do so.'

Suitably chastened, Mother promised. But she still couldn't hide the excitement in her eyes.

THE DAYS PASSED in stately procession, and soon it was time to set off for our meeting.

We took the road to Ashford, and arrived at the manor house as night was falling. William greeted us cordially, our earlier snub of his patronage forgotten. We were told we would be staying in an adjacent longhouse which provided good views of the manor entrance, and were to stay out of sight until the King's party had gone hunting for the day. Messengers had arrived to say that the royal party would arrive the day after next.

How could we contain our excitement till then?

The day of the royal arrival came and we stayed in our room until we heard the commotion of the advance guards arriving. We could not resist peering through the window to try to catch sight of King Henry and England's new queen. I thought it would be impossible, with many nobles and their fine ladies coming and going, to know who was the King. But then I saw a huge horse approaching, as wide as an ox cart. Father said he had heard of such beasts, *'destriers'* he called them, the largest of the war horses, bred in France and imported into England at enormous expense. Its ears were back and its nostrils flared, as if it was angered by its smaller relatives skittering about its hooves. It walked with a slow, deliberate pace. As its enormous hooves pounded on the earth, it was as if the ground was shaking beneath it.

Sitting astride it was King Henry. It had to be him. He was old, much older than Father, but looked immensely strong. Thick grey hair flowed down over the collar of a velvet cape of a blue with an intensity I'd never seen before. The collar and cuffs were made from ermine and it was lined with a vibrant yellow silk. There was something incongruous about such a bear of a man cloaked in such beautiful colours. As he passed the longhouse, he looked straight ahead, his back as straight as the trunk of a pine tree. Even when he moved out of sight, his presence hung in the air.

I had barely recovered when I spied Adeliza. I gasped again, but in surprise this time, not in awe as I had with the King. She was riding a pure white palfrey, its coat so groomed that it shone like silk, a white fur bridle on its head. But she was so young! I stared at this slender, graceful vision, as delicate as a poppy in bloom, unable to believe my eyes. When I had imagined her, my mind conjured up images of a wise and beautiful woman, kind and gentle to all she met. Instead, I saw a young girl, graceful and demure, but younger even than Mary and me.

The palfrey ambled past, its smooth gait making Adeliza look as graceful as a swan. Now that she was closer, I could see that not only was she beautiful, she had a luminescence that shone out from her as though she was bathed in the light of an eternal golden sunset. Once she was safely out of sight, Mary and I finally released our breath.

'Have you ever seen such perfection?' Mother said. Her eyes had the look of flinty ambition she had when she would harangue Father to dress her in noble finery. 'And to think that on the morrow, she will meet with the Chulkhursts of Biddenden, at her request, to become acquainted with the singer of 'The *White Ship* Lament'. Oh, if only William had requested that you perform tonight, Eliza, to entertain the King of England. What a story that would be to tell.'

Having me perform for the King had been the first thing she had made Father enquire of William when we arrived in Ashford, and I was relieved when he was told no. The welcoming feast was of great importance to William, having so long been in the shadow of Robert de Crevecoeur. With the building of Leeds Castle, Robert had become the King's favourite and William had thought his chances of receiving a royal visit gone forever. Now Henry was here, but at the insistence of his queen, not from his own choosing. William was taking no chances that the evening would be anything other than a huge success. An unpredictable country maid, singing a lament about the King's dead son, and playing an instrument that he was seeking to ban, was altogether too risky a proposition. William had told Father in no uncertain terms that Mary and I were to stay out of sight until after the King's hunting party had left. Only then would we be permitted to be presented to Adeliza.

Mother, however, had not given up hope.

'Promise me you will petition Adeliza to perform for the King before his departure,' she implored me. 'Maybe he would grant an honour to our family if he were so pleased. You cannot let such an opportunity pass.'

There was a time when I would have done anything to please Mother. But not now. 'We have been summoned for an audience with the Queen at her request,' I replied. 'And it has been made clear that we are to meet with her, and her alone. I do not believe that King Henry is even aware of our existence. I will speak only when spoken to by Adeliza, and only to answer any questions she may address to me.'

Mother looked shocked at my stubbornness and turned to Father for support. 'Hear how your child addresses me, after we have made this long journey to give her our support. Speak to her, Thomas, and tell her to do your bidding.'

Father looked around helplessly. 'Eliza and Mary have been forthright in their actions in the past, and have caused much disorder as a result,' he told Mother. 'It is one matter to incur the wrath of a baron, it is another to cause offence to a king. Let us proceed cautiously on this occasion. But, Eliza, if Adeliza were to offer you an opportunity to perform for the King, promise you will accept it.'

'Of course, dear Father, I will obey your wishes,' I replied. I smiled to myself. I had already said I would do the Queen's bidding, but now Father had shown it as a concession on my part.

'It is agreed,' he said, giving a single clap to celebrate the deal. 'It will be a momentous day on the morrow.'

THE KING'S HUNTING PARTY rode off at dawn. A short while later, William de Ashford's steward came to fetch us. 'The Queen will receive all four of you, but her audience is to be only with the author of "The *White Ship* Lament".' He paused. 'That is her wish,' he said, in a tone that brooked no argument.

Mary's laughter rippled through me. I kept my face as solemn as I could. 'By your leave, good steward,' I replied, 'if you can find a way for my sister to depart for my audience, we will both be most grateful.'

I cursed myself for my impertinence having promised myself to behave, but the steward just laughed.

'The steward of Ashford should not be challenged by a woman, but in any case I am at a loss as to how to deny you the same audience as your sister. Come, let us meet the Queen.'

The incident had lightened the atmosphere, and we entered the manor house more relaxed than I had anticipated. A red cloth had been draped over a chair and incense filled the air. Bowls of flowers had been placed everywhere. It looked so different from when we had last visited, four years before. We had entered a place of enchantment.

The four of us stood together in a group while the steward left to fetch Adeliza. I could feel Mary's blood getting hotter, and I tried to breathe slowly. Nobody spoke.

Adeliza appeared, two maids-in-waiting accompanying her. She seemed to float rather than walk and I couldn't help but glance at her feet, to make sure that she did indeed move like the rest of us. She was so light and graceful, it was as if a gust of wind would have her dance through the air like a dandelion seed in a meadow. I stood and stared. And stared and stared.

Mary snapped me out of my reverie. '*Diex vos sait*, Your Majesty,' she said, and we curtsied together before her. I had been in a dream these last few moments, when I should have been making the greeting. Father bowed and Mother, too, gave a curtsey.

'God bless you, Eliza Chulkhurst,' Adeliza said in reply. 'It is rare I am greeted in the words of my homeland outside of the royal court. How did you learn the Norman tongue?'

I couldn't believe how badly this was going. Adeliza would expect that the first to greet her would be the one she had summoned for an audience. And to make matters worse, I didn't know French as Mary did, so I had no choice but to speak in English.

'God bless you, Queen Adeliza,' I said, my words stuttering as I tried to get them out. 'It is I that am Eliza Chulkhurst. This is my sister, Mary, who has been forced to speak on my behalf while my mind was spinning at your arrival. Please forgive my discourtesy.' I felt like bursting into tears. To fail to address a lord correctly was the most unpardonable and disrespectful thing you could do, and many an honest man had been banished from a nobleman's presence for such a disrespectful breach of etiquette. To offend a queen was surely an even greater crime.

To my amazement, Adeliza laughed and turned to her maids. 'You see? I said this would be a most singular meeting. Already they are playing games, trying to hide their identities. Watch carefully, they will be swapping to the other's side next.'

The young girls giggled. I stood motionless, not sure whether I was supposed to join in with the laughter. Adeliza went over to the chair covered in the red cloth. A maid-in-waiting quickly brushed it with a horse-hair brush and Adeliza sat down, as gently as autumn leaves floating from a tree.

She addressed Mother and Father. 'You must be the parents of these remarkable women. Thank you for escorting them to me. You may go.' She smiled her dismissal.

The sudden change was startling. In an instant, she had gone from a frivolous little girl to a queen to be obeyed.

Mother and Father bowed their heads, shuffling backwards as they left the room.

Adeliza settled back in her seat and relaxed again. Now her look was of a puppy, eagerly awaiting its favourite treat. 'Let us talk as equals. When I heard the words of "The *White Ship* Lament" at a feast honouring those who died, I thought it a magnificent work, although it threw the King into a great rage. The jongleur who performed it was lucky not to spend the night in the *oubliette*. All present presumed he had written the poem, but when the King reacted so, he cried out that he had not. When I discovered these words had been written by a farmer's daughter, I was intrigued to find out more. We have female troubadours, the *trobairitz*, in Occitania in the south of France, but I have never heard of a woman performer in this land. And when the jongleur told me your astonishing secret, I knew then that I must set eyes on you to see this wonder for myself.'

'The jongleur was Masci, was he not?' I asked. Saying his name was like a winter ache in a wound. 'I have played with him in this very hall.'

'You are as full of surprises as your sister,' Adeliza replied. 'Yes, it was indeed Masci the jongleur, who had gambled all on being appointed the King's bard by his performance. Instead, the King has forbidden his name to be spoken again at court, which is why we meet so secretly today. The King has been travelling energetically through his realm this last year and he bids me always to be at his side. When he spoke of visiting Kent after our pause at Windsor, I lobbied his trusty courtiers to speak highly of the hunting grounds of William de Ashford, so we could have these few moments together. We may not have a chance again. If he returns early from a day in the saddle with only a meagre bag to show for it, my ruse will be exposed and we will be heading back to Westminster as soon as we break our fast on the morrow.'

'I am saddened that King Henry did not find solace in my poem,' I said. 'I should vow never to utter these words again.'

'I fear there are no words ever written that could shake off the malaise that has overwhelmed the King since William Adelin perished. He wishes for his daughter, Matilda, to be his heir, but many English lords say they will not be subservient to a woman.' She sighed. I could see now why Henry wanted her constantly by her side.

Adeliza's mood brightened again. 'I must not dwell on these matters,' she said, 'especially as our time together is so precious.' She turned to Mary. 'Your sister is a poet and entertainer, but you seem to be equally remarkable. You know the formal greeting that is spoken to a person of nobility in France. How do you come to be so well informed? Do you also have remarkable talents to display?'

Mary blushed so hard my own cheeks reddened as her blood flowed into me. Finally, she spoke. 'Eliza is the talented one. Take no account of me.'

I said quickly, 'Mary does herself a disservice, Your Majesty. She is most learned in the ways of healing. She tends a physic garden in Biddenden which is famed throughout Kent. My endeavours may please the ear, but it is Mary who is the gifted one. Her talent saves lives.'

'Most remarkable,' Adeliza replied. 'You were made special by your birth, and have achieved yet more distinction with your lives.' She called over to her attendants. 'Bring a stout bench for these two good maids to sit on. I venture we will be conversing for a while longer.'

The maids-in-waiting scuttled off and returned with a seat for us. Mary and I settled ourselves on it.

'I have not yet touched on what is most distinctive about you. Permit me to ask about the circumstances of your joining. Have you ever known of others like you?'

'There are none in all of Christendom, to the knowledge of any who know of us. Why God chose this form for us is a mystery to which only He knows the answer.'

'But you are able to endure it? Does it cause you much suffering?' There was genuine concern in Adeliza's voice.

'It's annoying, but it's never really painful,' I confessed. 'It's all we have ever known. We are meant to be together. If we separate, we'll die.'

'Have you tried? Do you not want to find if there is any physician in the land who could make the cut to free you of each other?'

I gave a rueful smile. Most people couldn't help but think that question, but only Adeliza had ever asked at a first meeting.

'No surgeon could perform such a task. We can never be alone. I've never had a moment that only I have known. But I know Mary's gestures as if they were mine, I feel every movement of her through my muscle and bone. No-one can ever understand the quiet connection that flows between us. For me, that is a blessing rather than a curse.'

I could feel that Mary wanted to speak. I nodded to her.

'When Eliza plays her lyre, I don't just hear her singing, I feel it coming through my body,' she said. 'Everyone else hears the beauty, but only I am able to feel it. That is a special gift God has given me.'

Tears welled up in Adeliza's eyes. 'A queen is privy to many extraordinary sights and stories,' she said. 'But none have ever compared to that which I have seen and heard today. I admit to having an unseemly curiosity that excited me to discover more about your curious condition, but I was also moved by the fine words of your lament, Eliza. *Ayant dit cela*, it is your work, Mary, that may benefit most from our meeting.'

At that moment a cloud must have shifted in the sky outside. A beam of low winter sunlight penetrated the room, turning Adeliza's hair into a golden halo. She looked like a painting of a rapt saint, lost in heavenly musing.

'The previous Queen, Matilda of Scotland, was much engaged in politics and the affairs of state,' Adeliza told us. 'These intrigues do not interest me much and I wish to be known as a royal patroness of the arts, but also institutions that can do good among the people. I am to establish a lepers' hospital in Wiltshire, in honour of the late Queen, and I would like to become sponsor of your good works here in Kent.' Her eyes sparkled. 'I heard that such a scheme was considered by Archbishop Ralph before he was struck down. Maybe I can ensure the plan comes to fruition. There is talk of King Henry travelling to Normandy next year, to meet with Count Fulk of Anjou on the matter of their alliance, and so I will be passing this way again. I will talk to the King in the meantime and gain permission to visit your garden in Biddenden, and to announce that more should follow your example. If that is pleasing to you?' She said this last sentence with a girlish grin on her face, knowing the delight it would give to Mary.

She was not wrong. Mary fanned herself with her hand and bounced on her tip-toes. I forgave her the discomfort. 'Pleasing indeed,' she replied, her voice trembling.

Adeliza turned to me. 'I would dearly like to hear you perform, Eliza,' she told me. 'But I cannot risk the wrath of the King should he learn that I have listened to a lyre being played. He is minded to ban its playing in public, so only Norman songs are heard that stir the blood. I would counsel you to learn another instrument to honour your voice, Eliza, if you want your singing to be heard *à l'avenir.*'

'But my songs are songs of love and honour lost,' I protested. 'The gentle strumming of a lyre is no threat to order.'

Adeliza shook her head. 'That may be a topic we return to at some future meeting. In the meantime, sing strongly, dear Eliza, but put down your lyre. May your words always bring joy and comfort to those who hear them.' She stood up. 'And now I must bid you farewell. My King will be returning soon. But I shall give you a gift, to remind you both of this special day.'

She beckoned to a maid of honour. 'Here is my offering to you,' she said, addressing us both. 'A *mirour* from France.'

It was a case made of two round bronze discs, small enough to fit in the palm of my hand. I opened it and gasped at what I saw: a flat shiny surface like the ice on a pond, as bright as a fallen fragment of the sky. I gazed in astonishment at my reflection, turning it in different directions to see how the image changed with each movement. I showed it to Mary and she cried out in disbelief. 'Look!' she cried. 'Look, Eliza!'

I stared at its glimmering surface. There, in the mirour, I could see all of the other side of Mary's face. We looked straight at each other for the first time in our lives, laughing and crying, oblivious to all around us, even Queen Adeliza.

I could see Mary's face. All of Mary's face. I devoured every inch, every angle of a countenance so familiar, but never before seen in its entirety.

It was a miracle.

1123

~

Chapter 23

Mary

We opened Adeliza's mirour every day to gaze at each other. I turned it to see every detail of Eliza's face and was vain enough to gaze at my own reflection, over and over again. Eliza said if she was rich and powerful like a queen, she would have a palace with mirours on every wall, the height of a man, so we could see all of each other whenever we wanted to. I said I'd make a hole in every wall, so I could sit on one side and Eliza on the other and we could be alone in a room when we wished.

The mirour showed us that we looked very much alike. We had always tried to be different from each other and hated when people treated us as if we were just one person. We never finished each other's sentences or spoke in unison when replying, even when we could have done so. But now we saw how similar we were, we decided we liked that. Our interests became closer; Eliza learnt to read and write and I became more interested in the poems and songs she performed. Poetry became my new passion. I wrote down the words of the epic poems of the day on goatskin hides, and spent time reading them, transported to the worlds they described. For these precious moments, I was alone in these imagined places; I didn't need a magical palace of mirours or walls with privacy holes.

King Henry's ban on lyre playing in public had finally been made law, so Eliza now had few opportunities to play her music. She could only strum her lyre at home, and the sound had a sadness about it. The only public entertainment permitted was juggling and acrobatics, and sometimes the reciting of some plainsong verse. Eliza took up painting and sketching instead, and we spent many a rewarding night together, me scribing the words to a new poem of heroic deeds I had heard, Eliza creating a likeness of Mother and Father in oak gall ink. We worked on embroidery, the two of us, creating a shield of two entwined flowers. Mother said it would make a fine Chulkhurst family crest.

Life flowed along its accustomed stream. Father's farm was doing well, and whenever someone from a wealthy family needed their humours to be put into balance, I would be generously rewarded. We had plenty of food on the table and ample time to enjoy doing the things that pleased us. I was always saddened when some unfortunate made an arduous journey from another village to seek me out, and my cures were not able to save their life. Eliza wished Henry's ban on the lyre would be lifted, so she could perform again. But these were burdens we learnt to bear.

IT WAS IN FEBRUARY, almost a year since we had met with Adeliza, that Waleran the emissary arrived in Biddenden, with William de Ashford's steward, Adam, at his side. Waleran said he had a proclamation to read, from the court of King Henry, no less, and Deorwin assembled the villagers to hear it. He had sent word to Father we must attend, so it was with a mixture of fear and trepidation that we stood in the crowd, waiting to hear Waleran's words.

"*Let it be known, that Adeliza of Louvain, Fair Maid of Brabant, Queen of England, has today bestowed great honour on Eliza and Mary Chulkhurst of the village of Biddenden,*" he read, his voice booming out across the crowd.

There was a gasp of astonishment. Mother had told all who would listen that she had journeyed to Ashford with us so we could have an audience with the Queen, but few had believed her. The villagers were on edge, waiting to hear more.

"*Eliza Chulkhurst has been named Royal Trobairitz, chaunter of songs, bard of poems, and is granted seal of approval to perform and entertain in the name of Adeliza of Louvain. Let no man deny her this right. And to recognise this honour, Queen Adeliza has bestowed upon Eliza Chulkhurst this gift, and has commanded that I present it to her.*"

Waleran produced a vielle. I had only ever seen Masci play this instrument, and he had guarded his carefully. I smiled at Adeliza's wisdom. There had been much grumbling that music was no longer played at fayres and celebrations with the banning of the lyre.

Eliza would be in great demand. She turned and looked at me, biting down a smile, her eyes glowing with an inner light.

But Waleran had not finished. "*And let it further be known that Mary Chulkhurst has been granted a royal warrant to examine the subtleties of plant and animal to heal the sick and weak in her physic garden in Biddenden and to plant further physic gardens in the towns of Tenterden and Appledore. Adeliza of Louvain has entreated William, Baron of Ashford, Lord of*

*the Lathe of Scraye, to provide two acres of land in each of these
towns, to which he has graciously agreed.'"*

Little jumps of excitement moved inside me; I felt the
hairs on my arms crackle with energy. I swallowed a shout
of glee to prevent it showing my excitement.

Waleran concluded his proclamation. *"Let us hope these
physic gardens flourish and provide salvation from many ills.'"*

The crowd cheered. Eliza was lost for words and I certainly
could not find the composure to speak. All we had dreamt
of when we had met with Archbishop Ralph had come true.

Eliza wanted to spend time examining her vielle, but I
had urgent matters to attend to. I approached Adam the
steward before he left. 'It is most generous of His Lordship
to grant me these acres of land,' I told him. 'I shall be forever
in his debt.'

Adam laughed. 'It is William who should be thanking
you, Mary the Healer,' he said. He saw the look of confusion on my face and took me aside, out of Waleran's hearing.
'He has been much troubled that he is thought of as of no
consequence to the King, with Robert de Crevecoeur's bold
design of Leeds Castle bringing much favour. And now,
for the price of a few acres of land, he has found a way to
please Adeliza of Louvain, and, through her, to be in the
King's good graces. He cheers the day when Robert refused
you the wish that Adeliza has now granted, and will be sure
news of Robert's denial will find its way to the Queen's
ear. Once you prove the physic gardens in the south of the
lathe are bringing great benefits, William has entreated
me to establish others in the north, at Sittingbourne and
Faversham, so no-one in the Lathe of Scraye is more than
a day's journey from assistance.' He laughed again. 'Who

would have thought so much influence could be bought for such little coin?'

I smiled as sweet a smile as I could muster.

'I devote my life to this endeavour as a means of doing good works, not as a calculation of how much I can profit from the misfortunes of others.' I dared say no more in case I caused offence. 'But no matter what his reasons, William of Ashford's plans are indeed welcome. When can I see the land he has set aside for me?'

'We can journey on the morrow, if you so desire. I would counsel you to act speedily. The word from court is that King Henry intends to travel to France, to do battle with Amaury de Montfort, the Norman lord who has risen up against him. Adeliza will travel with him, and will wish to tour your physic gardens on their way to Dover. Be sure to impress her. William will make his play of establishing the northern gardens if you succeed.'

Father accompanied us, along with Adam, to Tenterden and Appledore, where the land for the physic gardens was already marked out. In Tenterden it would be near the marshland to the south of the town, in Appledore close to the ferry to the Isle of Oxney. Both were waste land, never farmed before, a particular of which Father was quick to make Adam aware.

'This is good, fertile land your lord has granted us,' Father told the steward. 'But it will need to be ploughed and harrowed. That will have to be done soon, before the spring planting. Do you have the coin to provide for this?'

Adam shrugged. 'William spoke of the land, nothing more. Cannot you do this yourselves?'

Father looked annoyed. 'It will need four strong men and a team of oxen to have this ready by Lady Day. William will have his villiens in these towns. You will have to impose this burden upon them.'

Adam commanded four such men in Tenterden, and the same in Appledore, to prepare the land without delay. The men glared at Father and Adam, but dared not refuse. Tenant farmers were entirely dependent on the lord of the manor, and had to pay dues and services in return for land. Father explained what work needed to be done and said we would return after Lady Day to check on its progress.

I should have been pleased that things were underway, but instead I had a sick feeling in my stomach.

'I fear we have not endeared ourselves to the good people of these towns,' I told Adam, 'by having their neighbours pressed into working for us because they are tied to doing their lord's bidding. And I will need one of these villiens to till the soil and then fetch and plant the herbs that will grow. The garden will not succeed if those who work on it are filled with resentment.'

Adam looked thoughtful. 'There is more to this undertaking than meets the eye, it seems. These gardens are not something you can organise for yourself from the coin of those you treat?'

'We receive some coin from gratitude in Biddenden, that is true. But many who need my services can provide no more than a rabbit for the pot to show their thanks. For William's gardens to be a success, he will need to provide coin, as well as land. We cannot command a villien to do all that is required solely from their fealty to their lord.'

Adam promised to pass these words on to William and departed.

He returned a week later with William's reply. 'William de Ashford will make a grant of three English pounds a year to provide for the maintenance of his gardens, two pounds for Tenterden and one for Appledore. He awaits news that all has been prepared for the royal visit and trusts there will be no further demands on his good charity.' He said these last words with a hint of menace in his voice.

Three English pounds would mean someone could work on the gardens and dispense the treatments, and the gardens would need no other income. Any donations could be used to expand and grow what had been already planted. I thanked Adam the steward and, immediately after he departed, pressed Father to travel with me to Tenterden and Appledore to tell the good news.

'I will be able to reward the villien I judge the most worthy,' I said, 'with a labour that will give them great standing in their town, and with an income equal to that they could make from their fields. Hopefully, it will clear away any ill will.' I sighed with relief. 'The patronage of a queen can indeed cause miracles to occur.'

Father did not share my enthusiasm, and when we reached Tenterden I found out the reason why. Taking instruction from a maid was too humiliating an idea for the villiens to contemplate. In both Tenterden and Appledore, I could find no-one knowledgeable in the ways of the land who would be happy to be instructed by me as to how to become, in effect, the town apothecary.

I returned with Father to Biddenden disheartened and fearful. Having pushed William to be more generous, I would now fail in my promises to him.

'We cannot travel to three different villages to tend their physic gardens and maintain all in a fit state,' I said to Eliza. 'And if William de Ashford exercises his feudal authority and orders a villien to care for the garden, they will do so only with resentment. Such a person will not make any effort to prescribe the best treatment for an imbalance of the humours. It will be a healing garden in name only.'

'Surely there must be someone in the village who would welcome the appointment as village apothecary?' Eliza replied. 'If not a villien, someone else. They would have the gratitude of all who visited and would be rewarded in coin for their efforts.'

'I need someone knowledgeable in the skills of growing plants. But every farm hand is already pressed to make preparations for the coming year. They would have little time to spare for something new, even with the reward of coin.' I sighed. 'I have been more than foolhardy in agreeing to Queen Adeliza's wishes. I cannot face telling her of my failure.'

In the evening, Eliza was reading her goatskin poetry when she had an idea. 'It occurs to me,' she said, 'that the words on this goatskin will be there forever. And in Canterbury there is the *Summarium Heinrici*, which contains all that is known about treatment of the balance of the humours. But that is a sacred document, written on parchment by the most devout of scribes and kept locked in the cathedral vaults. Only the Archbishop and Ymbert the Wise have the key. But why not make your own book of knowledge, scratched out on goatskin, with instructions that show someone not skilled in the ways of plants to ensure their thriving? Some simple drawings, perhaps, that would be clear to one who was not familiar with letters? It could tell what should be planted and when, and what should be prepared and applied to treat the most common imbalances of humour.'

'Would it not be blasphemy make a copy of sacred words? Ymbert the Wise guards the *Summarium Heinrici* jealously.'

Eliza shook her head. 'It would be no copy. You have your own knowledge, handed down to you by Mother Agnes and nurtured by your experience and investigations. There can be no crime against God for using that information to spread good works in His name.'

She was right. 'It could indeed be a plan,' I said. 'My words of knowledge and advice would not disappear in the air; they could survive forever and help guide those with good intentions. Alice, the ferryman's daughter, could tend the garden in Appledore. I treated her last year and found her to be bright and earnest maid. Her duties at the ferry are light, and her father promised me any favour for bringing his daughter back to health. And the widow Haunild in Tenterden is honest and hardworking. She could manage the garden there.'

Eliza became enthused by the plan. 'You could also instruct Bela to become the gardener, rather than our handmaiden, in Biddenden. This would give you time to meet with Alice and Haunild to instruct them on matters the goatskins do not describe. The village apothecary could become a woman's work, like that of an alewife. Ale will have its alewife, healing will have its healing wife.'

'And once all is in readiness,' I said, 'you would have time to master the vielle. Come, let us share this plan with Mother and Father. If we receive their blessing, then we can meet with those who would become our healing wives. We may yet be able to honour Adeliza's wishes.'

Father agreed, and Bela told us many a young maid from the village would be honoured to become our new hand-maiden. I spent the next two weeks writing out instructions for Bela while Father met with village families, looking for a replacement handmaiden. By the time he agreed that Hilda, the daughter of Nigel, one of the village elders, would be a suitable replacement, I was ready to begin schooling Bela in the ways of the physic garden.

It was a good test of how the plan would work. Bela had often listened to my ideas for perfecting my cures and so was already familiar with the treatment of many imbalances. Still, it was laborious work. I started with the rose, making a symbol to represent it and pressing a petal next to it to remind Bela of its meaning, along with a symbol for sage, next to a sage leaf, and so on. Then I explained their respec-tive subtleties.

'Rose is cold,' I told her, 'and this coldness contains moderation – which is useful. Someone with small ulcers on his body should place rose petals over them. This draws the mucus. Rose, and half as much sage, may be cooked in water with fresh, melted lard, and an ointment made from this. The place where a person is troubled by a cramp or paralysis should be rubbed with it, and they will be better.' I showed the sketch I had made of the rose symbol pointing to an arm with marks on it, and then the one with two rose symbols and one sage symbol pointing to a stick figure's stomach. 'Study these drawings and on the morrow I will test whether you remember the cures they describe.'

Bela nodded, a little nervously, but I could see she under-stood what I was telling her.

I smile. 'All will become easier with practice. Now, let us consider the four healing pathways and the elixirs to treat them ...'

And so it went on, day after day, for the next two weeks. We made slow progress at first. Bela had never before been taught so much all at once – her life had been spent learning simple practical tasks around the home. I tried to employ the method that Ymbert the Wise had used to school me in the learnings from the *Summarium Heinrici*, repeating each fact over and over until Bela had it memorised; but it proved impossible. Bela burst into tears as she failed yet again to remember something she had managed to recall just the time before.

'There is too much to know to be a healing wife,' she said between sobs. 'Let me return to changing the reeds on the floor and lighting the morning fire. I have failed you, mistress Mary.'

I realised what I must do: instruct her on a treatment and then ask her questions about it, until it was as familiar to her as the household tasks she had been learning since childhood. After that we made progress, and it helped me prepare to teach Alice and Haunild how to run their gardens. Schooling them would be more difficult. Bela and I had grown up together; she was already familiar with the garden and I would often be around to answer any questions she might have. Alice and Haunild were almost strangers to me, and I would pay them only a brief visit twice in a moon.

I met with Alice first. She was a young woman, recently married to the son of a village elder. Her new husband had died of a sudden apoplexy, a cruel blow for one so young. It had destroyed the spirit inside her and she had taken to wandering the saltwater marshes and wildflower meadows on the Isle of Oxney, taking her father's ferry to that wild part of the Lathe of Scraye. She was gaining notoriety amongst the Appledore villagers, some saying she was touched, stricken; others saying that she had gone mad. Many waited for the day when she would not be at the ferry point for the last crossing from the island, the marshes having claimed her, releasing her from her torment. When I told her father of my plans, he begged me to appoint her.

But I needed someone of sound mind to work the garden, someone I could trust to be reliable when I left them to return to Biddenden. I waited at the Appledore crossing for her to return on the evening ferry, so I could ask her about her lonely walks.

Alice's appearance was gaunt and haggard, but I saw she once would have had the bloom and ruddy complexion of a wholesome country maid. 'It is the solitude that I crave,' she told me. 'The sight of husband and wife, mother and father, fills me with despair.'

I looked into the sadness of her eyes and realised that my joining to Eliza was not the greatest burden to endure in life.

'The best way to honour the memory of your husband is to help cure others of their ills,' I told her.

Eliza told her the words of one of her songs: '"Look to the sun, and nary a shadow ye shall see."'

Alice nodded at that, and I could see that the work she would do for me would bring great benefit to her, as well as helping others. But it was Eliza who finally convinced her.

'If you live your life in defeat, then you will be defeated,' she told Alice. 'God has treated Mary and me harshly, and I have complained in my heart that many of life's pleasures are denied us. But if much has been denied, much has also been given. I cannot do the work that a normal maid would do, so I have time to focus on words and music. Mary longed to perform great and noble deeds, but instead performs simple deeds that are great and noble in their consequences. Throw off the shackles of your despair and join her in this great endeavour.'

A walk through the meadows convinced me that Alice already understood the subtleties of nature. She was familiar with many of the flowers and herbs I used in my potions and even told me much about their growth I didn't know. When she saw the great sheaf of goatskins I had prepared to train her in the ways of a healing wife, she found a purpose to her life again. A new spirit rose from the shackles of her despair, like a bird soaring free from an outgrown cage.

Haunild was also a widow, but one who had lived a long life and was stoic about the loss of her husband. She traded wool with the wool-staplers, but struggled to put enough food on her table because they would not give her the same price they would a man. William's stipend was what attracted her to be a healing wife, but she was a doughty woman, honest and true, so I did not fear that she would shirk in her duties. At first, I was embarrassed at having to instruct some-one who was more my father's age than mine, but Haunild soon put me at my ease. She lacked Alice's natural inquisi-tiveness, but she was a conscientious student, making her own marks in oak gall ink on the goatskin drawings I had made for her, to help her remember my instructions. Despite her age, she was as strong as a man, able to move the stones in the garden as easily as a child spins a hoop.

By the end of the second moon I had two trained healing wives, three if you counted Bela. I was satisfied that they had learnt the basic knowledge they would need to treat any in their village who was struck down with maladies. Tenterden and Appledore would join Biddenden in having their own physic gardens and a healing wife to tend them.

Maybe the first three of many.

Chapter 24
Eliza

Mary tried to visit the Tenterden and Appledore gardens every ten days or so, taking with her the latest goatskin drawings to teach Alice and Haunild new remedies and to answer any questions they had. Each visit took a full day, then there was a day's travel, and she also had to work on her latest drawings; so there was little opportunity for me to practise the vielle, and I even felt somewhat guilty taking what little time there was. Mary's work was much more important, and with every visit, the esteem in which she was held in these other villages grew higher.

Now that he could use us to court favour with Adeliza, Mary and I had come back into favour with William de Ashford, and I received an invitation to play the vielle and sing my songs at his Christ's Mass feast. Adam the steward promised that this time we would stay in the manor house itself. Mother persuaded Father to let her have a new gown for the occasion. Father said we must have one too, and that added even more excitement to the coming event.

As winter approached, the physic gardens lay fallow, which gave me more time to practise the vielle before the great feast. It had proven to be a difficult instrument to master, as I had to hold down three of the strings with my left hand while sliding the bow across them with my right. I tried tucking it under my chin to play it, but Mary was in the way. Finally, I came up with a solution, bracing the lower end against my chest and with a strap around my neck to hold it in place. After that, I soon learnt to play the *chansons de gestes*, songs of heroic deeds which had become very popular in France. But my favourite song was one I had written myself, a homage to Adeliza called 'The Fair Maid of Brabant'. I would play a gentle melody at the start of the song, and then put down my bow and sing my words of praise.

Would, one day, Adeliza herself hear these words?

THE GREAT HALL of Ashford Manor had been festively decorated for the Christ's Mass feast. A huge Yule log was to be kept burning throughout the twelve days of the Christ's Mass celebrations; the walls were decorated with holly wreaths, their dark green leaves and red berries warding off evil spirits; sprigs of mistletoe, the bringer of fertility and protector of crops, were everywhere. Like all the other guests, we had fasted since the day before, so the huge trestle table, groaning under a carcass of beef and assorted fowls, partridges, geese and suckling pigs, was making our stomachs turn somersaults of delight. A richly decorated boar's head was the centrepiece and flagons of mulled braggot, an extra-strong ale with honey and cinnamon and spiked with brandy, was being served to guests as they arrived. Mary and I wisely declined and watched with amusement its effect on those who drank copiously on an empty stomach.

The Lord of Misrule directed the boisterous festivities. His word was law, and we watched in fascinated horror as he directed a game of Hot Cockles, where blindfold victims had to guess who slapped them from behind. If they guessed right, the slapper became the victim. Luckily Mother and Father were not chosen, and our participation was carefully avoided.

A bean was hidden in a loaf of bread and the person who found it became king of the feast. To our delight, it was Deorwin who discovered it, and so he had the task of introducing me when it came time for me to perform at the end of the meal. The audience was hushed as we stepped into the centre of the room, some out of astonishment at the sight of Mary and me, and some out of exhaustion after the exertions of the day. I was pleased by that. The lyre was an instrument you could hide behind, but holding only the vielle in my hand, I felt cruelly exposed. It was the first time I had performed at such an important feast since I had played with Masci. Now I was on my own.

Nervous as a cornered rabbit, I started to play. I shouldn't have worried, though. The vielle was a new instrument to most of the crowd, and the novelty of the sound disguised any failings in my playing. I sang songs and played melodies, every time receiving the warmest of applause. At the end of the evening, I steadied myself to perform 'The Fair Maid of Brabant'.

'I hope you have enjoyed my playing tonight,' I said to the audience. 'And hearing the sound of the vielle, which causes no displeasure to our great King Henry. It is a new instrument in these lands, and I have only recently discovered its mysteries. Thank you for being kind enough to excuse my mistakes.'

A ripple of laughter gave me courage to continue.

'Some of you might not know that this vielle was a gift to me, from Queen Adeliza herself.'

Another ripple, this time of surprise from those who had been unaware of this fact.

'I have composed a song to her, to show my appreciation for her kindness and generosity to Mary and me.' And with that, I started singing.

High above all, a cloth of state was spread,
And a rich throne, as bright as sunny day,
On which there sat most brave embellished,
With royal robes and gorgeous array,
A maiden queen, who shone as Titan's ray,

In glistening gold, and peerless precious stone,
Yet her bright blazing beauty did assay,
To dim the brightness of her glorious throne,
As envying herself, that too exceeding shone.

The song went on for six stanzas more, my voice getting stronger with every line I sang. When I finished, the entire crowd stood and cheered. It was the greatest moment of my life.

MARY AND I MET with William de Ashford again before we departed with Mother and Father back to Biddenden.

'Your performance was most pleasing,' he told me. 'Since the banning of the lyre it has been many moons since the sound of music filled these halls. And you have an uncommon gift to write your own songs, rather than just recite the words of others. Will you visit again, and sing to all a tale of my heroic deeds?'

Coldness hit me in the stomach. I could hear Mary breathing hard next to me. For a moment, I panicked. I had a question and I didn't know how to ask it without causing offence. For what heroic deeds was William known?

Mary came to my rescue. 'Your deeds are many and varied, Baron William. Which ones would you have Eliza make the subject of her song?'

William puffed his chest in pride. 'You are right, we should not tire the ear with too many tales at once. Sing of my good deeds in creating the physic gardens of Kent. Eight English pounds a year to provide for their care and provision, and for that I turn the head of the Queen of England so Henry favours me over Robert de Crevecoeur, even with his fine castle at Leeds. What a favour you have done for me, Maids of Biddenden!' He laughed heartily, poured himself a tankard of ale and downed it in a single gulp.

I knew Mary hated that he only cared about the physic gardens because of the influence they bought him, so I was surprised at her reply.

'Gardens require the delicate nurturing of nature, they are not as resilient as a castle made of stone and wood. I have two good women running my gardens in Tenterden and Appledore, but there is much work for me to do when I inspect them.'

She went on, 'Queen Adeliza will pass through Kent when she journeys to Normandy with King Henry next year, and may wish to visit the places of healing set up in her name. May I help in ensuring the sight of these northern gardens is pleasing to her? I can visit in the spring and make sure all is in order for the growing season. When she hears of your even greater endeavours, your currency at court will rise as a result.'

William glared at Mary. Clearly, he felt that her comments could be construed as criticism that his gardens would not flourish without her help. 'I have chosen Colin and Savaric, two of my most loyal lieutenants, to oversee the gardens. They need to rest their bones after a lifetime of service. They are good men and true.'

'And they know the properties of the plants and the subtleties of how to grow them – and treat ailments with them?'

William frowned and I wondered if this question had ever occurred to him. 'I am sure they do. And if not, there must surely be someone in the town who can provide good counsel, or they could travel to Minster Abbey on the Isle of Sheppey and seek help from the monks there.' He nodded, as if to convince himself. 'Yes. Good men and true,' he repeated, a little less certain this time. Adam was standing nearby. William glanced at him and received a supportive nod.

Whatever his words, Mary had surely planted some doubt in William's mind.

'There would be no harm,' he conceded, 'in your paying a visit to see for yourself how they prepare for the new season. I will arrange for my steward to accompany you to the gardens once the festivities of Lady Day are over.'

Mary bowed in gratitude, but she looked troubled. If there were things to be improved, proud warriors would not take kindly to being told so from a maid.

~ 1124 ~

MARY MADE TWO copies of her goatskin instructions over the winter and we travelled to the new gardens as soon as the first buds of spring appeared. Her worst fears were realised. Colin's garden was disorganised, with herbs planted randomly. Savaric's planning was non-existent. Neither of them had any idea of how to administer even the most basic of treatments. They obviously regarded their appointment as town healers as a sinecure for a life of service to William, and had shown little enthusiasm for making their gardens a success. Both men bristled at the suggestions Mary made, and only reluctantly accepted her goatskins outlining what was needed to treat imbalances of the humour using the gardens' herbs and wildflowers, many of which were in any case lacking.

'William de Ashford,' Mary said with despair, 'is boasting to everyone that he is the patron of the Lathe of Scraye physic gardens. But he cares little about helping the sick and is putting men in charge to reward them for their service to him, not because they are – or would ever care to become – knowledgeable apothecaries. I can teach Bela, Alice and Haunild about the healing properties of plants because the gardens of Tenterden and Appledore are within easy reach of our home. But Sittingbourne and Faversham are more than a day's journey. And even if I did travel to them frequently, Colin and Slavic will not allow themselves to be seen receiving instructions from a country maid. Most who seek out their services will be disappointed with the care they receive, and the spread of rumour about their ineffectiveness will tarnish the reputation of the gardens I can manage.' A rare anger flashed across her eyes. 'Curse William for his conceit, I can see no good coming from this.'

'And I have to find the words praising his munificence ...' I replied. 'William de Ashford cares nothing about others and only wishes to better William de Ashford.'

Mary remained thoughtful once we returned to Biddenden, worrying about the physic gardens to the north. After a few days, her mood lightened.

'Colin and Savaric are proud men,' she said. 'They would want to do good, but lack the knowledge to do so and will not accept instructions from a woman. My goatskin drawings may be a little help, but they are simple instructions and need me on hand to explain them more fully. The parchment scrolls in the possession of the Archbishop of Canterbury are much more detailed and would tell them all they needed to know, but they are kept under lock and key. But what if there were to be copies, on simple goatskin, written with ink from the oak gall? They would not constitute as beautiful a document as the scrolls of learning transcribed by the monks of Canterbury, but they would suffice to act as an alternative *Physica* to aid those who wish to learn the craft of healing. If I were to make such a document, Colin and Savaric could consult with a man of words in their village the priest or any other who can understand the written word. They would become learned in the ways of healing without having me teach them.' She became more and more enthused by the idea. 'There is a new Archbishop enthroned in Canterbury, William de Corbeil. Let us entreat him to open the Canterbury scrolls to me, so I may begin such a task. I could provide my *Physica* for every new physic garden that needs one.'

I tried to look positive about the idea, but Mary spotted my dismay. 'What distresses you, dear sister? We have no secrets from each other.'

I hesitated. 'I feel so selfish saying these words. But writing out the commands of the Canterbury scrolls is an arduous task indeed. And you have also learnt much over the years which is not in the scrolls. It will mean many long days sitting at a table while you complete your work. And if I spend the time practising my vielle, my movements will frustrate your efforts to write with a steady hand. I would have to sacrifice all, for you to do this. It is my noble duty to support you in this saintly endeavour, but my heart is weary at the price I will have to pay.'

'You are right, my dear sister. Even with someone to work the garden at Biddenden, the writing of my *Physica* on top of visiting the gardens in Tenterden and Appledore would take up far more time than is fair. I will have to choose between having three physic gardens to deal with, or writing my *Physica*. I cannot do both.'

'Curse this joining!' I said. 'And curse the ambitions that our fame has placed in our minds. Every action is a compromise, every decision a conflict. Why should I be so selfish as to prevent you achieving your dreams of having physic gardens throughout the Lathe of Scraye? It is far better that you help the sick and weary than that I entertain them with a pretty tune. If William de Corbeil does you the honour of giving you access to the Canterbury scrolls, then I will sit alongside you and dutifully help to copy these words of healing. One day the task will be completed; then we can revisit my dreams.'

I felt a sickening as I said these words. I knew it was the right thing to do, and I would be rewarded in Heaven for my sacrifices. But as I played my vielle that evening, I savoured every note I played, every word I sang. Soon I would be consigned to a time of drudgery, mindlessly copying out words that only Mary fully understood.

THE VISIT OF ADELIZA to Biddenden was the biggest event in the village's history.

Preparations had been going on for two weeks, once we heard she would visit when Henry travelled through Kent on his way to Dover. Colourful cloth was tied to every post and tree and the village bull stood tethered by the market cross, eying proceedings with a wary disdain. It had been draped with a caparison decorated with the royal arms and hung with bells. All the village elders' wives were trying to outdo each other in their finery. As everyone waited for the Queen's arrival, even Deorwin looked nervous. Finally, there was a shout from one of the village lads, perched at the top of a giant oak tree. The royal party had been spotted and would soon be arriving at the village. A nervous hush descended on the waiting crowd.

Adeliza arrived, riding her pure white palfrey, two stewards flanking her, the royal banner flying from the top of the poles they were carrying. A retinue of ladies-in-waiting, manservants and royal guards brought up the rear.

'Good people of Biddenden, welcome your queen, Adeliza of Louvain,' announced one of her stewards. The crowd cheered in response.

The village bull swung on his rope from side to side at the noise, and let out a loud bellow. The steward eyed him nervously.

Adeliza dismounted and walked towards the elders. Deorwin let himself be known by stepping forward.

'Adeliza of Louvain, Queen of England, I am Deorwin, reeve of Biddenden. Our village humbly welcomes you and gives great thanks for the honour of your visit.' He paused and looked over to us, catching Mary's eye. She nodded and he took a deep breath before continuing. *'Diex vos sait,* Your Majesty,' he said, stumbling over the unfamiliar tongue.

Adeliza burst out laughing, breaking the spell of royal awe and showing her to be the young woman she was.

'The county of Kent appears to have many fine French speakers,' she replied. 'I have heard these words only once outside of the royal court and they were spoken by someone from this very village.' She looked over at Mary and me. 'And there I see the author of the greeting,' she said, beaming us a great smile.

Mary shot a worried glance at Deorwin, to see if his pride had been wounded by Adeliza's jest, but his face remained impassive. Adeliza went to walk over to us, but a discreet cough from one of the royal stewards reminded her of the protocol.

She turned back to Deorwin. 'Thank you, good sir, for this most generous welcome,' she said, looking at the village bull as it tried to maintain its dignity while covered in colourful cloths and jangling bells. *'Ma parole!* I have never seen such a magnificent animal so handsomely caparisoned. Now. Please introduce me to the elders of the village.'

After Adeliza was introduced to each of the elders in turn, she startled everyone by asking to be introduced to their wives. Caught unawares by such an unconventional request, the welcoming ceremony descended into chaos for a few minutes until eventually order was restored. I could hardly contain my frustration. It was Mary and me that Adeliza had come to see, and it was taking far too long for her to reach us.

Finally, the welcome ceremony was complete and we could be formally introduced.

'Queen Adeliza, you have honoured us today in visiting our humble village,' Deorwin said. 'But all of us know it is the Maids of Biddenden you have come to see, Eliza and Mary Chulkhurst. Before we celebrate your presence with the greatest feast this village has ever held, the Maids wish to give thanks for the kindness and generosity you have shown them.'

Mary spoke first. 'Adeliza of Louvain, Queen of England, William de Ashford has generously bestowed physic gardens in your name in the villages of Tenterden and Appledore, ably tended by your servants Alice of Appledore and Haunild of Tenterden.'

Alice and Haunild stood forward and curtseyed to Adeliza. Adeliza nodded in acknowledgement.

Then I spoke. 'Adeliza of Louvain, Queen of England, you kindly bestowed upon me this vielle, such that every part of Kent, from manor hall to marketplace, can rejoice in the sound of music again. I wish to sing a song to celebrate your greatness, I hope you find it pleasing.' And with that I sang 'The Fair Maid of Brabant'.

Adeliza laughed as I sang of her beauty, cried as I described her homeland of Brabant, which I had imagined as a glorious, heavenly place. When I finished, she clapped her hands in joy.

'You have done me great service, Eliza Chulkhurst. I am flattered by these words and they have brought me much delight. I hope to hear them again soon.'

I presented Adeliza with a goatskin copy of the song, relieved it had been so well received. Now it was time for the feast to begin. Adeliza's party were chaperoned over to where a hog was roasting on a spit. Large chunks of meat were carved out for the royal party, broad leaves used as dinner plates. Adeliza wished only the smallest piece, and after it was cut into even smaller pieces by one of her manservants, proceeded to eat it daintily from a silver plate, spiking each piece on a slender knife. All around her, the villagers tore at the meat with their hands.

After all had finished eating, Adeliza called over to her steward. He received a whispered instruction and went over to speak to Deorwin.

Deorwin looked a little disappointed, but nodded and stood up to address the crowd.

'My friends, we must leave Queen Adeliza to her audience with Eliza and Mary Chulkhurst.' There was a groan of disappointment from the crowd, and I was both embarrassed and proud. 'The Queen has deviated from King Henry's party to make this visit and wishes to be reunited with him by nightfall. Come, let us give the Chulkhursts the opportunity to conduct their discussions in private.'

The crowd slowly dispersed; the two stewards marked out a square of ten by ten paces and stationed a guard at each corner. Three chairs were produced from the royal carriage and Mary and I sat down across from Adeliza. Her steward stood off to the side.

'Tell me of your happenings since we last met,' Adeliza said. 'Eliza, how do you find the vielle? I see you have mastered it well.'

'In a manner,' I replied. 'A few simple tunes to entertain those who are kind enough to listen.' That wasn't true. The instrument had been a delight for me, and my playing was much in demand, but modesty prevented me from saying so.

'And you, Mary? I look forward to seeing your physic garden here in Biddenden. And what of Appledore and Tenterden? Do the gardens flourish there without your constant presence?'

'Thriving, Your Majesty. You have seen my two good healing wives there, Alice and Haunild, whom I am teaching in the ways of extracting the subtleties from the plants to treat the common ailments of their townsfolk. William de Ashford has been most generous in providing all we need.' Adeliza hadn't asked about William, but Mary was astute enough to sing his praises anyway.

I decided to honour him also. 'William de Ashford has done much more than you asked of him, Queen Adeliza. Not only has he supported Mary with the gardens under her care, but he has initiated his own gardens at Sittingbourne and Faversham in the north of the Lathe of Scraye. All who live in his barony have but a short journey to receive the help they need.'

'Joyous news,' Adeliza said, her excited voice sounding like a lark's message to the morning dawn. Her brow furrowed and she turned to Mary. 'But that would be a long march for you to be in attendance. How do these gardens fare?'

I cursed my stupidity. Why had I put my sister in such an impossible position? She now had a choice: to expose William's plan as the struggle it was, or tell a falsehood to Adeliza that all was well. Mary squirmed her body in a way she knew was painful to me. I deserved it.

She took a deep breath before replying: 'I paid a brief visit to each, at William's request. Once his apothecaries become learned in the ways of the healing plants, they will be fine physic gardens, to equal the ones we have here.'

'But they are not now at their best. Is that what you tell me?' Adeliza had sensed the hesitancy in her voice.

'Not yet, Your Majesty. But they will be in time. Would you like to see what we have done here in Biddenden?'

To our relief, Adeliza accepted the offer and I prayed the topic of the other physic gardens had been forgotten. But later, as Adeliza made ready to leave, she returned to the subject.

'These northern physic gardens trouble me. How can we ensure that all the knowledge you have here can be shared with those who need it?'

Mary looked lost for a reply, so I decided to try to help again. 'My sister has plans to write a *Physica*, a great manual containing all that is known about healing and the humours of the body. When it is complete, any who are conscientious in wanting to do good deeds will be able to do so by consulting its words. William's gardeners are good men, with caring hearts. Once they are supplied with knowledge, their gardens will flourish.'

'As will any others who receive this *Physica*,' Adeliza replied. 'God speed for its completion, Mary Chulkhurst. A copy should be in the possession of every town in England.'

Adeliza turned to her steward. 'How many towns are there in Henry's domain? I desire a copy of this book to be in every village in the land.'

The steward coughed. 'There has been no count since the Domesday Book, Your Majesty. But I would venture a guess at five hundred, maybe more.'

Adeliza's face clouded. '*Bien sûr*, this will be too great a task for the Biddenden Maids to complete on their own.' A ray of sunlight broke through. 'No matter. My counsellors will find a way around this problem if I instruct them to do so. Mary, you need only produce one *Physica*. I will command others to make copies.' She gave a smile of satisfaction that showed she thought all problems could so easily be wished away.

Now it was Mary's turn to come to my aid. 'The burden will be great not just for me, but for Eliza,' she said. 'Already she must demonstrate much patience when I partake of my pursuits. The only time she has for herself is in the evening, when she is free to play her vielle. Were I to try to write my *Physica*, it would deny Eliza her greatest pleasure. Our life has to be an accommodation of each other. I cannot always be the one directing our behaviour, no matter how worthy the reason.'

The lady-in-waiting standing behind Adeliza gasped, and it was only then that I realised the gravity of what Mary had done. To challenge the decision of the Queen of England was a serious offence. Mary could be in a lot of trouble.

'Mary did not mean to offend, Your Majesty,' I said quickly. 'It will be my great honour to remain still while she writes her *Physica*.' We were making things more difficult for each other by the minute.

Adeliza looked at us, her face a mixture of concern and surprise. Then she stood up and walked around all four sides of the guarded area in which we sat. The guards eyed her intensely, as if poised for a command that would see us carried off to the stocks for Mary's impudence. Mary and I remained silent.

Eventually, Adeliza spoke. 'A queen does not expect to see her commands debated by those who receive them,' she said. For the first time there was a serious look on her young face, as though she was struggling with some weighty issue. 'But when I command one Biddenden Maid to do something, I have to realise that two are affected. I have a solution to this dilemma which might prove to be an elegant way to resolve the predicament in which you find yourselves. Eliza, were the words of your song written in your own hand?'

'Yes,' I replied. 'Mary learnt these skills first and taught them to me. I am not as proficient as she, but have mastered enough to transcribe "The Fair Maid of Brabant".'

Adeliza's face lit up at that, and her gay girlish manner returned. 'Then it is solved, this conundrum in which we find ourselves. I shall commission both of you to write me a treatise. Mary, you shall produce me the *Physica*, which can be used to spread knowledge of healing throughout the land. Eliza, you have shown of your talent in the words of "The Fair Maid of Brabant". Now you shall do the same for King Henry. You shall write an account of his reign – let us call it *The Romance of King Henry* – which will tell of all the great deeds which my husband has achieved. His life has been beset by tragedy and a gift such as this from me will greatly lift his spirits. What do you say, Maids of Biddenden? Will you both become scribes to please your Queen?'

Adeliza's steward stepped forward before I could reply. 'The writing of such an account would be a matter of great sensitivity, my Queen. Especially if it has a royal sponsor. The King's advisers would need to select a suitable author and he would have to be well briefed as to what message such a ballad would convey. It is not a decision that should be made lightly.'

'Tish-tosh! This is a loving gift from a wife to her husband, nothing more. It does not need hours of debate, however worthy the counsel.' She turned to Eliza and spoke in a mock whisper behind the back of her hand. 'The King's counsellors have instructed my steward to remain at my side when I am outside the King's presence, for fear I may cause havoc with my requests. When I was first crowned, I did cause some disruption when I ennobled those of my servants who pleased me, but I am less carefree now. Still, it appears I still need a chaperone to save me from my own foolishness.' She turned and glowered at the steward. 'But this is not such an occasion, and I will not be told I cannot praise my husband.' She turned back to Eliza and me. 'Will you perform these duties, as I request?'

'Of course, Your Majesty' we said together. I agreed to have *The Romance of King Henry* ready for when she returned to England. Next year, she told us, maybe later. Mary would write up all she knew in her *Physica*, so that copies could be made for every town in England.

Adeliza had her official scribe draw up an ad hoc declaration on the spot, instructing William de Corbeil to give Mary access to the scrolls locked in the Canterbury vaults. Our heads were spinning with excitement. Rather than be punished for insulting the Queen, we had ended up being rewarded for it.

When the declaration was completed, all that remained was to say our goodbyes to Adeliza. We curtsied deeply before her and pledged our eternal loyalty. Before she left, I had one final task to perform. 'Queen Adeliza, when last we met, you presented to us a most wondrous gift, a mirour to allow us to see each other full of face. We were abashed that we had nothing to give you in return, so please accept this small token today.' And with that, I handed her a Biddenden cake, from the annual thanksgiving service that had been held the past Lady Day. 'These are fashioned by the people of Biddenden in our likeness to give thanks for the sweats passing from our village. This is the last from this year's ceremony. It would be a great honour if you would agree to receive it.'

Adeliza bowed her acceptance and we stood for a moment, glowing with pride in the presence of our Queen.

And wondering when we would meet again.

Chapter 25
Mary

S t Sepulchre's Nunnery was familiar to us now, and we didn't ask Harry to wait when he dropped us off at the gate. Mother had stayed back in Biddenden. William de Corbeil, the new Archbishop of Canterbury, had a reputation as an extremely devout man who had no time for social gatherings.

When we arrived at the Archbishop's palace the next day to present our letter of introduction from Queen Adeliza, we could see that much had changed. Waleran, Archbishop Ralph's emissary had moved to Southwark; the manner of the palace guards was far from friendly. We began to worry.

The guards refused us entrance to the palace until they heard back from the Archbishop. Eliza became frustrated.

'We have been twice received by Archbishop Ralph at his request and come here at the express bidding of the Queen of England. We are not some baseborn varlets come to pester His Excellency. The nature of our condition means that much unwelcome attention is given by those who see us, and as word spreads of our arrival in Canterbury, there will be great disorder as we walk the streets back to the nunnery after our audience. Pray, let us stand inside your walls, away from prying eyes. Only then will the disruption of our presence be kept to a minimum.'

The guards reluctantly agreed, but we were told to stand no more than five paces from the entrance. Harry was not allowed inside. The hours passed like years. I am slightly taller than Eliza and so have to bear some of her weight. Standing became more and more painful as time went on. Just as I thought I could take no more discomfort, a guard returned with the news. The Archbishop could not see us today, we were told, and we should return on the morrow after Vespers to be granted an audience.

Eliza tried to console me as we returned to St Sepulchre's. 'We have come unannounced, and it is impertinent of us to think the Archbishop of Canterbury should be so free of his time as to meet with two country maids upon their arrival. We should not read any ill will into his actions.'

'The delay does not trouble me,' I replied. 'We are here on a great mission, and the path to fulfil Adeliza's wishes will be fraught with difficulty. But I am concerned about what today tells us about Archbishop William. He may not be as enamoured with us as his predecessor was.'

We spent the rest of the day following the nuns in their daily routine. The oblates were involved in tending the vegetable garden and doing the washing and cooking for the nunnery; the obedientiaries spent their day illustrating manuscripts – small devotional books, compendiums of prayers, guides for religious contemplation and treatises on the meaning and relevance of visions. Everything stopped every few hours for one of the eight canonical hours, when the nuns said prayers for those who had made donations. In the evening we listened as the oblates received training and education from Mother Abigail and the obedientiaries. It stirred old memories of a simpler time in our lives, when we did no more than play with our dolls in the abbey at Malling.

That night as we lay in our bed, a simple pallet filled with straw, I thought about what I had seen.

'The skill of the obedientiaries,' I said quietly, so as not to be overheard, 'in illustrating these manuscripts is far greater than the crude drawings I make on my goatskins. They could produce drawings of the plants which could be easily identified, even by those not knowledgeable in the skills of an apothecary. St Sepulchre's Nunnery could produce the *Physica* with fine drawings and with words from Ymbert's *Summarium Heinrici*, but augmented by my own discoveries. This *Physica* could be sent to monasteries and nunneries throughout the land, where they could make their own copies for physic gardens to be set up in the towns and villages near to them. God's servants could be put to good use, creating documents for healing, not just for devout contemplation. I will ask the Archbishop not only to grant me access to *Summarium Heinrici*, but also to entreat the nuns to help me with more detailed drawings for my *Physica*. Surely, God would be pleased at such talents being put to such practical use.'

'He would indeed,' replied Eliza. 'And such a document produced by the hand of skilled monks and nuns will be much coveted and will endure through the ages. Your plan will produce a legacy that will make you immortal.'

I smiled and ran my fingers down to where our bodies joined. 'We will be immortal anyway,' I said. 'But now it can be for our deeds rather than our condition.'

The next day we were back at the Archbishop's palace and were ushered into the same receiving room we had been in before. In Archbishop Ralph's time it had been richly decorated and welcoming – a gold leaf triptych on one wall; an ornate painted crucifix on another; a painting of the Virgin Mary on a third. Now the walls were bare, except for a single small carving of Christ on the cross, and the fire was unlit. A simple table and two benches were the only furniture in the room.

William entered the room without ceremony. The contrast between him and his predecessor was remarkable. Archbishiop Ralph had filled the room with his presence, his glance piercing into your soul as if he could read your every thought. William had the energy of a damp log, his eyes the glazed indifference of an elderly ewe. He gave us no greeting but only genuflected in front of the cross before turning to confront us.

'You are the joined women I have heard about? Tell me your business.'

Eliza and I had experienced many different reactions from those meeting us for the first time – fear, awe, astonishment, curiosity – but William's was something new. Complete disinterest. As he sat down, he glanced over at the door, as if he was already contemplating leaving.

I took a deep breath to steady my nerves. Eliza would sense me doing so and remained silent. I gave a small cough and started speaking.

'God bless you, Archbishop William. My sister and I are humbled by your presence. We had the great privilege to meet Archbishop Ralph and I trained at the feet of Ymbert the Wise to take his great learnings and apply them to my physic garden in Biddenden; thereafter to the ones in Tenterden and Appledore.' I paused, waiting for a reaction.

There was none, so I continued, speaking faster this time. 'We travelled again to Canterbury to discuss with Archbishop Ralph a great scheme for physic gardens in every town, so that any who were ill or infirm could find treatment close at hand. But shortly after our arrival, he was struck by the apoplexy, from which he never recovered. There might it have ended, except that Queen Adeliza has embraced our cause and has instructed me to write a great book on healing, *Physica*, a copy of which is to be given to the apothecaries of all new physic gardens in the land, so they can tend their gardens properly instructed and treat the sick with full understanding of the balance of the humours.'

William's gaze wandered around the room as I spoke. There was a long pause before he responded.

'And you bring a letter from Queen Adeliza, requesting that you access the great chest of learning here in Canterbury? Pass it to me now, child.'

I had not been called a child these last ten years, but I let it pass. I handed over the document. William looked at it for barely a moment before folding it away.

'I was a chaplain here when you met with Ralph d'Escures, so I am familiar with your story,' he said. 'And I was present when he discussed his plan with Ymbert the Wise for Kent physic gardens, before your second visit. It was Ymbert's view that a project of this importance should not be given a woman, and he told Archbishop Ralph so. Ralph's plan would have been opposed by his advisers and he would eventually have had to agree to look elsewhere for someone to achieve his dreams. Your journey at that fateful time would have been a fruitless one, even without the archbishop being stricken down after your meeting.'

Eliza could contain herself no longer. 'But it was Archbishop Ralph who summoned Mary here to discuss that very idea. Surely he did not agree with Ymbert's view?'

I winced at her interruption.

William showed no anger. 'Your interjection shows to me the wisdom of Ymbert's words,' he said to Eliza, his voice never wavering from the same dead tone. 'Women are highly emotional creatures, and should not be entrusted with a task of such seriousness and importance. Producing guides on religious contemplation is a more suitable task to occupy their time. I do not know the mind of my predecessor, but I am sure he would have been guided by Ymbert's sage advice. But that matters not. If the Queen now ordains that a *Physica* be written, then it shall be done by the hand of that most learned of practitioners, Ymbert himself. Let that be the end of the discussion.'

I did our little silencing movement to Eliza before I replied.

'Of course, Your Excellency. I bow to your great wisdom. I will tell Queen Adeliza of your decision.' It was as much of a challenge as I dared.

William gave an almost imperceptible shrug. 'This matter will be far from her mind at the moment. The King's quelling of the Norman insurgents will be all that occupies the thoughts of those around him. She has but one duty to perform as his wife, and she will be well advised to concentrate on fulfilling it. Henry needs a son and heir to bring peace to the Kingdom.'

'Then I will return to my physic gardens,' I replied. 'And I wish well on Ymbert the Wise – may he produce a great *Physica* that will edify and inform all who read it.'

William plucked at his beard. 'You may still be of use in this project, Mary Chulkhurst. Prepare a copy of your words for Ymbert's consideration. Any novel treatments you can describe will be considered to see if they merit inclusion in the *Physica*. Once they are copied in the hand of Ymbert the Wise they may travel far across the land.' A humourless smile crossed his lips. 'Perhaps your trip to Canterbury will not have been in vain.'

We returned to the nunnery saddened and frustrated. As I watched the nuns go about their selfless duties, I became annoyed at my mood.

'It matters not whose hand writes the *Physica*,' I said to Eliza. 'And I am committing the sin of vanity when I covet acclaim as the author. What matters is that the sick and infirm are healed. If it means a great man such as Ymbert the Wise must be given the task to achieve that, I should not do anything to stand in the way.'

'Ymbert may be wise, but he is lazy and arrogant,' Eliza replied. 'He may simply transcribe your words and achieve glory with little effort, but he will not produce the great encyclopaedia of knowledge that you would have done. It takes diligence and hard work to complete such a task, and he will be easily distracted by affairs of state. Queen Adeliza may be disappointed her dream will not come true.'

I sighed. 'Adeliza's heart is big, but she has little worldly knowledge of these matters. With every action there are political calculations to be made – who to support, what to oppose. We made enemies of William de Ashford and Robert de Crevecoeur with our foolishness. Her command to go to Canterbury with her letter of instruction was issued on a whim, with no counsellor present. It may be a blessing that we are spared involvement in the intrigue that might surround it.'

We headed back to Biddenden the next day. In many ways it was good that I had little to show for our visit. The next few weeks were busy, as Eliza prepared for the quarter-day feast at Ashford Manor; and she still had her poem to write, praising William de Ashford. And then there was *The Romance of King Henry*. I smiled ruefully. Eliza was only commissioned to write it so that I would not intrude on her when writing my *Physica*. Now it would be I who had to sit quietly while she scratched out her words.

ELIZA TRIED TO MAKE a start on *The Romance of King Henry* by seeking the advice of the learned men in the village who kept up with current affairs, and passing travellers who brought the latest news from London. It had not helped. She heard only tales of Henry's ruthlessness; seizing the English crown when his father died, before his elder brother Robert could intervene; imprisoning his brother for life after battling him on the fields of Normandy. Leading a debauched life full of mistresses and prostitutes, and having, by all reckoning, over a score of illegitimate children to his name. Castrating and mutilating those who crossed him. But most worrying of all was his morbid fear of humiliation. Masci had narrowly escaped punishment by making Henry show weakness at how devastated by grief he was when 'The *White Ship* Lament' was sung in his presence. Eliza was growing more and more fearful what reaction there would be to a full account of his life.

But these fears had to wait until after the quarter-day feast at Ashford Manor. William de Ashford had already sent a messenger asking about the readiness of the eulogy he had asked Eliza to write for him.

'I beg your master's forgiveness,' Eliza had told the messenger. 'Tell William that as his life has been so full of greatness, it is a lengthy task to chronicle all the tales of his good deeds that can be told to do justice to the glory of his being. Ask Baron William to be patient. The story will soon be ready.'

But in truth, she had written nary a word. There were only three things William de Ashford cared about – power, riches, and being more popular at court than Robert de Crevecoeur. If honouring the life of King Henry was proving difficult, singing the praises of William de Ashford was even more so.

The day of the feast approached and things went from bad to worse. Father had become increasingly frail; a palsy had seized him and he was subject to bouts of paralysis and involuntary tremors. Mary treated him with galingale, with half as much nutmeg and spike lavender, which she pulverised with female fern and saxifrage and sprinkled on bread for him to eat. But it had little effect, and he was too ill to travel with us. He bade Mother accompany us, but she decided to stay and nurse him. It showed how serious she thought his ill health to be. She would never otherwise have passed up an opportunity to be at such an august social gathering.

WHEN IT CAME TIME for Eliza's performance, we looked out at a sea of unfamiliar faces. The hall was packed with lordlings and reeves who had travelled from West Kent,

Sussex and Surrey just to have the chance to see Eliza and myself. There were a few familiar people there – Deorwin was one, along with some other village elders. But everyone else was pointing at us, making no pretence at disguising their stares; talking about us, loudly, not caring that we could hear. Questions that no-one had ever dared to ask in our presence were being shouted from one table to the next. 'How do they piss?' 'Do they have two cunnies?' 'Are they one or two?' We heard somebody call us 'it'. To those who had travelled far to view us, we were a curio, an oddity; they cared no more for our feelings than they would for a dancing bear. I had never realised how much it meant to have Mother and Father with us at these occasions.

I felt very vulnerable and alone.

Eliza began playing, the sound of her vielle soaring around the room. The conversation dropped, then slowly built again. As usual, I had little to do, apart from tapping out the beat on my timbrel. I looked out at the crowd. Almost all were talking about us to whoever they were next to. No-one was listening to the music. Eliza played louder and louder, putting all her energy and passion into the music. She finished with a flourish, then paused and dropped her bow to her side.

There was a muted applause from the audience and the buzz of conversation continued. William de Ashford looked bored. 'Sing "The *White Ship* Lament",' I whispered to Eliza. 'None will dare displease the King by showing disrespect to the memory of his son.'

Eliza had said she would never perform the piece again after hearing what had happened to Masci, and I had tried to convince her that as long as it was not played in the presence of the King, no-one had ever come to harm by performing it at social gatherings. She had said no then, but now she saw the merit in my idea to grab the crowd's attention.

'God bless King Henry,' she said, in as loud and strong a voice as she could muster. That brought the conversations to a halt. 'We all know the tragedy of the *White Ship* disaster. Let me tell it to you in song.'

Eliza played the vielle as she sang, creating an exquisite sound that blended with the poignancy of the words. The crowd was silent – at first because no-one dared to speak over the account of the death to the heir to the throne, but then because they became captivated by the performance. The applause at the end was stronger, but then the buzz of conversation grew again.

Eliza played a few more songs, the audience's attention wavering more and more with each one. It was time for the guests to return to their revelry.

'I will finish with a new poem,' Eliza announced after more lacklustre applause. '*The Laudation of William de Ashford*. Let us praise our generous host.'

An expectant murmur ran through the crowd. William leaned forward in his chair, looking to his left and right, smiling at whoever caught his eye. Eliza gave a nervous stoke across the strings of the vielle and started on a jaunty piece of music. After three beats of my timbrel, she started to sing.

Good William of Ashford, let the world know,
Of the gardens of healing you intend to bestow.

No tongue there is able to fully express
The depth of our joy, our true thankfulness;

With many a curtsey, and bow to the ground,
Such barons as you are few to be found.

She went back to playing the vielle. I struck my timbrel with extra strength, harder and harder as William's mood blackened. With a few final bow strokes, the music was finished.

There was generous applause, but William remained seated, waving down the shouts of acclaim with the palm of his hand. His steward looked over to him to see if he would address the crowd, and got his answer with a shake of the head. The steward stood up and thanked Eliza for the evening. William walked off without a word to either of us.

We headed off to our room. There was no joy after our performance.

'No-one cared about my singing tonight,' Eliza said. 'All they cared about was seeing us joined together. When we were little known, we were not subject to such scrutiny. Now rich merchants and noble families make a journey of many days to see us, and only our appearance matters to them. The more notoriety we attract, the less people care about what we do.'

I agreed. 'Our most joyous times are when you sing in the villages where we are known: Biddenden, Tenterden and Appledore. We have yet to hear whether William de Ashford considered your song tonight did justice to his greatness, but I fear your words did not sit kindly with him. If we have twice offended him, it would be wise not to tempt fate and risk another affront in future. Perhaps it is best we stay true to our own people, who love us for who we are and what we have achieved, rather than be the playthings of the rich and powerful. Our dealings with nobles have always ended in sorrow and frustration. Perhaps we would be happier with a simpler life.'

When we went to bid him farewell the next day, William was still furious.

'I have been a generous sponsor to you both, indulging these physic garden fancies and having you perform in front of the better men of Kent. And you repay me with nothing but humiliation, first by scorning me in favour of Robert de Crevecoeur and now by insulting me with such modest praise, when I had told all in attendance they were to hear a great laudation of my heroic deeds. You will not perform at Ashford Manor again, Eliza Chulkhurst, and be grateful I am a man of mercy and do not banish you from the Lathe of Scraye for your lack of respect.' His face reddened as he turned and glared at me. 'And you, Mary Chulkhurst. Despite my generosity of land and coin, my steward tells me when you journeyed to meet my loyal lieutenants Colin and Savaric, you were most disrespectful of their fine physic gardens. Eliza's rebellious blood flows through you also. I dare not risk upsetting Henry's queen by putting an end to her follies in the south of my lathe, but there will be no coin for more foolishness in the north. Leave now for home, and pray I do not hear of any further insolence on your part. You will not find me so forgiving again.'

We journeyed to Biddenden depressed and despondent. William's words had been harsh, but they had taught us a lesson. He could send us from his presence with a few words of rebuke, and no more than bruised feelings as a result. Were we to offend King Henry, the consequences would be far more serious.

1126

~

Chapter 26
Eliza

Over the next two years, Father's tremors became worse and I gave up trying to write *The Romance of King Henry* in order to help Mary care for him. He was rarely able to leave the longhouse after we returned from Ashford, and soon was too weak to do more than walk to the privy and back. Mary had Gerbert and Gaston take nets into the woods and capture as many titmouse birds as they could find. They only fly in clean air and have healthy flesh, and when cooked in water with butter, a healing soup for palsy can be made. Father had a bowl of such soup every day, but to no avail. On a cold blustery afternoon on the shortest day of the year, he closed his eyes for the last time.

His funeral was well attended. I played a plaintive air on my vielle, which brought me some inner peace. After the burial, we walked home with Mother. When we arrived at the longhouse, we cleared away his bed and sat by the light of a single flickering candle. Exhausted, yet unable to fall asleep.

I heard Mother's voice in the gloom.

'I have thought long and hard about this day,' she said. 'All of us knew your father would never recover.' She picked up Father's coif and gently stroked the flat woollen cap. 'He gave me a good life, and I tried to repay him by giving him my love and caring for him these twenty-two years.'

'He loved you very much,' I told her. 'Just as Mary and I do also.'

Mother gave a wistful smile. 'It was a great sadness that your father and I never had any children to grow up alongside you,' she said. 'But perhaps it was for the best. I could focus all my love on you and Mary, and be as proud as any mother could be, seeing you grow up and achieve such great standing amongst the villagers, and indeed so far afield.' She smiled again, a smile of relief this time, as if a great weight had been lifted from her. 'And now you are two strong, independent women, who can live your lives as you want, knowing that your great gifts of healing and entertaining mean that you are revered by all the good people of Biddenden and beyond. It is now fitting that you begin the next chapter of your lives and not be burdened by having to care for me as my body grows infirm, as you had to take care of your father in his years of decline.' She poked the fire for a moment before continuing. 'Once I am satisfied that there is no more I can teach you on how to manage a household, I wish to leave this farm and all Thomas's worldly possessions to the two of you. I will send a messenger to Malling Abbey, to see if Mother Agnes will accept me into her order. I can think of no better place to live out the rest of my days.'

I was shocked, and I could feel Mary's shudders going through me. It had never occurred to us that Mother would leave. There were many widows in Biddenden who managed their husband's affairs after their passing. Mother was more than able to do the same.

'Why, Mother, why?' I asked. 'It is the natural order that a wife should take over a husband's farm if there is no able son to take charge. This farm is yours to manage. Do not leave us to tend to it ourselves.'

'I must,' Mother replied, her voice barely more than a whisper. 'I have grown to love you, Eliza and Mary. But my heart was not always so open. When I first saw you at Malling, I'm ashamed to say I counselled your father against bringing you back to Biddenden. I even hatched some dark plots to ensure you never reached this place. I am ashamed of my thoughts and my actions from that time and have bitterly regretted them with the passing years. Now I want to redeem myself in the eyes of the Lord. And there is no better way to do this than to return to the place of your upbringing, to serve Him until the end of my days, reflect on my sins and ask forgiveness for them.'

I was uncomfortable hearing these words. Mary and I had heard rumours over the years about how the old village priest, Drogo, had tried to get us banished and many people had hinted that Mother was his accomplice. I had refused to believe such a thing, and so Mother's words were painful to hear. If there had been such a plot, it must have all have been Drogo's doing.

'You have been a wonderful mother to us,' Mary cried. 'Please do not leave.'

Mother smiled and stared off into nothing. 'It is what my heart tells me to do. But it will take some time to make ready for my move and we need to prepare for how the farm will be run when I leave. You would find it difficult to work in the fields – your days are already full tending to the physic

361

gardens. Let us see if Gerbert and Gaston can help with the farm when I'm gone.'

When Father had become unable to work, he had asked the two brothers to help out, paying them a penny every day they helped manage the farm. They now lived in a sunken hut in the village with their wives and Gaston's two children, but they had worked at the farm so often since Father's illness, they felt like family. The idea of their becoming our tenant farmers helped ease the thought of Mother's departure.

The three of us headed off to their hut the next day to discuss the plan, only to be met by a terrible sight when we arrived. Gerbert had been struck down with the sweats, along with Gaston's two children and their wives, and was unable to move. Gaston was on his feet, but he looked exhausted as he tried to care for them all.

He looked alarmed when he saw us. 'Eliza and Mary, Mistress Chulkhurst, stay away from this house,' he said, his voice croaking over his troubled breathing. He burst into a bout of coughing and wiped away some bloody sputum from his mouth. 'Stay away, do you hear?' he said, louder this time. The two children whimpered softly; groans came from Gerbert and the two women.

We ignored Gaston and stepped into the hut to see things more clearly. The children were drenched in sweat, yet also shivering with a fever chill. The two mothers were wiping the children's foreheads, despite the fact they could barely sit upright. We stepped back outside, as both families started coughing again.

'When did this malady strike?' Mary asked Gaston. While she waited for him to stop coughing, she gestured to Mother, who was standing a few feet away. 'You are not close enough to have been touched by the miasma. Go and tell Deorwin and the other elders what we have found here, and have them approach only if they are covered in goose fat and swaddling to protect them from the airy spirit that has taken hold of this family. Eliza and I will stay here and trust to God's mercy that we will be spared.'

There had been talk of the sweats approaching again, but this was the first time it had reached our village. When Deorwin arrived, Mary told him of Gerbert and Gaston's plight.

'I heard two other families coughing inside their hut in the distance I have walked to reach here,' he told Mary. 'The cursed spirit has visited our village again.'

This time, it was easier to arrange for everyone to stay isolated in their houses as they all remembered what to do from before. And the memory was still fresh of how it had spared them from the worst ravages of the disease. Mary and I walked with Deorwin as he gave each villager their instructions to remain isolated from each other. Mary answered any questions they might have, and by the end of the day all was in readiness for Biddenden to become a village in hiding again.

'I will not touch anyone or their possessions,' she told Deorwin, 'now that Eliza and I have entered the house of Gerbert and Gaston where the airy spirit has already taken hold. I have observed it takes a day or two for the spirit to manifest itself in another poor soul. We have acted quickly and forcibly to sit out this visitation. Hopefully that will mean even more will be spared this time than last.'

Her confidence was dashed when we returned to Gerbert and Gaston's house to check on their condition after all the villagers had been alerted. One of the children was already dead and Gerbert's wife had fallen into a stupor from which she could not be roused. Mary's eyes were wide as she took in the scene from the threshold of the hut. She stepped outside again and turned to address Mother.

'They will all be dead on the morrow if they are not given constant treatments.' She gripped my hand as she spoke, and I tensed as she did so. That was a signal she needed me to agree with something important. 'They need to be cared for at our longhouse. I have found that our blood is strong when dealing with imbalances of the humours spread by infection; we do not take so ill as those who are not so commonly exposed to these diseases. Gather some things and stay at Ada's alehouse while the spirit is in the air. Tell her I give this my blessing and that you have kept away from any danger. We will take these unfortunates to our longhouse and care for them until they recover. Gerbert and Gaston have been kind to us over the years and this way we can repay them.' Then she spoke to me. 'Do you agree, Eliza? We must do all we can to save them.'

Of course, I said yes. We went into the sunken hut to tell Gerbert and Gaston our plan, only to find the brothers even more distraught than they had been but a few minutes earlier. Gerbert's wife had taken her last breath and was lying pale and still on the hut floor. There was no time to lose.

'We shall return and give your child and Gerbert's wife a Christian burial,' Mary said to Gaston. 'But first we must get the rest of you to a place of safety. Harness the oxen and your brother and his wife and child can ride on the cart to our home, where I can treat your imbalances and restore you to health. Are you strong enough to do this?'

Gaston gave a dazed nod, and we set about moving everyone out of the hut. Mother had not come back, so we assumed Ada had agreed to take her in. After a sad, slow journey to our farm, we arrived at the longhouse as the sun was setting.

Bela helped us organise the longhouse before she returned to the nearby sunken hut– the arrangement that had been put in place the previous year when Bela had married Harry, the guide who had taken us to Canterbury all those years before. Gaston and the others took the space where Mother and Father used to sleep. Then we went to the far end of the room and covered ourselves in goose fat. Mary cooked some basil leaves in wine and honey, and made some cinquefoil cakes to draw out the bad humours from the body.

All we could do now was wait and see what fate had in store for us all.

We were woken in the night by cries and wails. Our worst fears had been realised. Gaston's wife and remaining child had died and, despite his own weakness, Gaston sobbed uncontrollably. For the first time, a stab of fear went through my heart and I realised how foolish we had been, bringing the sickness into our home. This version of the airy spirit was even more evil than the ones that had gone before.

An ox cart came in the morning, two bodies already laid out upon it, as the village collected the dead for burial in a communal grave.

'How many?' Mary asked the driver, and was told the toll had risen to twelve in the last full day.

The rest of the day we spent in silent despair. We washed the sweat off Gerbert and Gaston's bodies in the evening, to make them more comfortable for the night ahead. It was strange seeing these two strong men so helpless. They had been young when we first arrived in Biddenden, no more than two score years of age, but they had seemed so old to us then. We were now older than they had been then, six-and-twenty years of age, and the years between us seemed fewer. But they were far too young to lose their wives, and for Gaston's children to have died was an unimaginable cruelty. As we finished cooling down their fever with a cloth soaked in psyllium-infused wine, I noticed both brothers' breathing had become less laboured.

'They are fighting off the spirit,' I whispered to Mary. She nodded. For the first time there was hope of their survival.

In the morning, they were well enough to sit in the fire-side chairs, looking so much better, but still with a look of desolation in their eyes. 'Curse that evil spirit,' Gerbert said, the first words he had spoken in days. 'It has spared Gaston and me from its deadly touch, but taken all we hold dear. How can we return to our home, when it is full of such happy memories that will now fade away? I will journey to Chatham, to see if Robert de Crevecoeur needs a fighting man to join his army at Leeds Castle. With good fortune, I may find myself slain on some foreign battlefield before the year is out.'

Gaston was the less bitter of the two. 'We should not be so quick to throw away our lives. Eliza and Mary have risked theirs to nurse us through these cursed times and tried everything to save our loved ones.' He turned to look at us. 'It is to you we should give thanks and I will stay here in Biddenden until I have repaid my debt to you. And that day will be long in coming.'

'You owe us no debt,' Mary replied. 'If I am blessed with the knowledge and skill to heal others, it is my duty to do so. Now rest and recover your strength, and let us pray for your lost loved ones. Soon you will be able to return home and put these days behind you.'

Gaston shook his head. 'There I must agree with my brother. Our home has no happiness left in it now. It was once a joyous place, but now every moment I spend there will bring back a memory of the loss I have suffered. I will find another place to dwell. I cannot face being surrounded by recollections of my loved ones for ever more, haunted by memories of former happiness.'

After Gerbert and Gaston found the strength to head back to their sunken hut, I told Mary of an idea that had been growing in my mind.

'Let the brothers live in the longhouse instead of us,' I said to her. I could feel Mary's shock at my suggestion. 'Mother is at Ada's alehouse and, once she is free to travel, she has decided to journey to Malling, to spend the rest of her life at the abbey where we were raised. We have no need for this longhouse and would be just as comfortable in Bela and Harry's sunken hut. Harry will easily find another in the village, with our sponsorship. Gerbert and Gaston could not only be our tenant farmers, they could also provide us with the support we need until we become accustomed to living without Mother and Father. For their part, our company may also give them some comfort and solace.'

'Two men and two women living so closely will cause many a fishwife's tongue to wag,' Mary replied. 'It would be a scandal so soon after the brothers have been widowed, and would bring shame and dishonour on our name.' She paused.

'And it would be a humiliation beyond measure were we to make such a proposal to them and they refuse.'

'They have never recoiled from our joining, even though they were the first outside the elders to see us when we arrived at Biddenden. We have always felt at ease in their company, and they ours. They are distraught at their loss and are at the point of giving up on life. We could help them through their pain and they could help us at a difficult time in our lives. I think it behoves us to at least inform them of the possibility of such an arrangement.'

Mary thought for a moment. 'It pains me to think that in their despair they could bring about harm onto themselves.' She gave a curt nod. 'Your plan is a bold one, sister, and has much to commend it. Let us see what the brothers make of it.'

We headed off to their sunken hut, and the greeting was warm as usual.

'We travelled to meet with you,' I explained, 'to ask you both to move here and to become tenant farmers of our father's land, paying us only the rent we need to continue our lives as a healer and a performer. If you want to start a new life, you do not have to travel to faraway and unfamiliar places to do so. You can do so here in Biddenden. We will move into Harry and Bela's sunken hut – it will not take long to find them a new home nearby. Then you can stay in our longhouse and work our farm, and we can be companions together, helping each other through the dark days that lie ahead.'

Gerbert and Gaston looked at each other, their faces a mixture of surprise and confusion. 'We are simple peasant folk,' Gerbert said at last. 'We are not worthy of living in such a grand longhouse.'

'And you would need to consider your reputation,' added Gaston. 'Many would find much to gossip about in such an arrangement.'

'Let us ask Fordwin the priest for his blessing,' I replied. 'He will know it is an arrangement of convenience, nothing more. If he says yes, it will silence any scandal.'

'It would certainly provide protection for your good name,' Gerbert said. He looked at his brother, who nodded, and Gerbert continued, with more conviction this time: 'It does bring a certain cheer to my heart, which I never believed I would feel again. Let us hear what Fordwin has to say. If we are denied, we will speak no more of it and no harm will be done to your character.'

We all visited Fordwin the next day. He pondered long and hard about the arrangement, and in the end he agreed.

'You must vow all to return to your own homes every evening,' he told us. 'You are devout and pious good people and yet again the village is in Mary's debt for having devised a way for us to avoid the worst of the sweating sickness. But Gerbert and Gaston are of an age where they could wed again, and once their grief subsides their manly desires will return. You must all agree not to break the trust the village would be placing in you.'

In truth, many couples lived in close proximity out of wedlock, but none would attract the attention of Mary and myself. We made a solemn promise of chastity, and the brothers also swore an oath to Fordwin to honour our promise.

Mother also gave her blessing when she returned from Ada's alehouse, and helped us prepare the longhouse for the brothers to move in. A lifetime of memories were revisited over the next few days, as we gave to the deserving poor those of Father's possessions that Gerbert and Gaston would have no need of, and Mother's belongings that she would not be taking to Malling. Bela and Harry were found a new sunken hut to live in, close enough to the farm so they could still be called upon to help out if required, although with Gerbert and Gaston tending the farm we would not need to rely on them as much as we had done when Father was alive.

Mother's messenger had returned in two days with the news that Mother Agnes would most willingly accept her to take her vows to become a nun. She cried as she heard these words, shedding tears of joy. 'Mother Agnes has truly forgiven me for all my heartless actions in the past. The abbess is a saint among women and I am honoured that she has accepted me into her order.' Mary and I smiled our agreement with these last words, but also felt a dullness in our hearts as she spoke. We still did not like to be reminded of whatever Mother was so ashamed about from those early days.

Finally, the longhouse was ready for Gerbert and Gaston, and Mary and I moved into the sunken hut. It was time for Mother to say her goodbyes. Mary and I stood at the entrance to the farm, Bela on one side, Gerbert and Gaston on the other, as Harry prepared to set off with Mother to carry the few things she was taking with her all the way to Malling. We waved our farewells as the two of them set off on their long march. Just as they were about to disappear out of sight, Mother turned around one last time and shouted from the distance.

'Goodbye Eliza, Goodbye Mary. I love you.'

And with that, she took a few more steps and was gone.

I stood motionless, staring at that last point where we had seen her before she disappeared into a dip in the track, not able to accept that it would be the last I saw of her. I stared and stared, hoping that she would suddenly reappear and say she would return and live with us. But there was also a small frisson of excitement at the thought of our new life ahead, and of sharing it with Gerbert and Gaston.

Finally, I felt Mary's body shift, which told me she was finding my weight uncomfortable after standing so long. I put my hand around her waist and without a word we turned and walked towards our new home.

GERBERT AND GASTON worked in the fields all day, instructing our farm hands what tasks needed to be undertaken, and we spent the evenings together in the longhouse before retiring to our sunken hut. There was never any more than that, but it didn't stop a lot of disgusting speculation in the village. That didn't trouble any of us. After the feast at Ashford, invitations for me to perform came from every corner of England, but I always said no. We had made a good life for ourselves in Biddenden, simple and true. When I did play my vielle, it was to a handful of friends and neighbours in the village. I finally abandoned writing *The Romance of King Henry*, and dreaded Adeliza's return to England, I would have to disappoint her. But until then, every day was filled with contentment.

I wished these days would last forever.

1129

~

Chapter 27
Mary

We had been living alongside Gerbert and Gaston for three years, when the white palfrey arrived at our farm. Sitting astride the horse was Adeliza. Still as beautiful as ever, but now with the faintest of wrinkles to add character.

'All hail, Adeliza of Louvain, Queen of England,' her two stewards shouted in unison. Our startled hens went into a flutter. Her arrival may have lacked the pomp and ceremony of her first visit to Biddenden, but it still had an impact. Eliza and I scuttled over to greet her, calling out to Gerbert and Gaston to join us from the field nearby.

Adeliza had already dismounted when we reached her.

'God bless you, Queen Adeliza,' I said hurriedly, and winced with frustration that I had forgotten to use the formal French greeting that had so impressed her at our first meeting, seven years ago.

'*Diex vos sait*, Queen Adeliza,' Eliza said, a little too smugly. 'Had you sent word of your arrival, we could have prepared a welcome. You catch us in clogs and working smocks, with only a cauldron of pottage simmering on the fire.'

'Henry is impatient to get back to court and has granted me but a short leave before returning to his presence at tonight's resting place,' Adeliza replied. 'I have told him many times of the wonder of you living in his kingdom, but he is too preoccupied by affairs of state and matters of war to digress from his passage to London.'

Gerbert and Gaston had joined us by now, and I could see that Adeliza sensed the easy familiarity between us. Her eyes twinkled, and for a moment the young girl returned. 'I see it is not just at court that things have changed. Pray introduce me to these companions of yours.'

'This is Gerbert. This is Gaston. Two brothers who are our tenant farmers now that our father has passed away and our mother has gone to live in a nunnery. Since their families succumbed to the sweats, they have rented the longhouse from us. Eliza and I reside in that humble wooden hut.' I pointed to our home and a tingle of embarrassment sparked between Eliza and myself.

Gerbert and Gaston bowed and mumbled their greetings. No-one was sure what to do next.

Adeliza took the lead. 'I would very much like to see the physic garden,' she said to me. 'Then hear about other gardens and how *Physica* is progressing.'

Gerbert and Gaston returned to their labours. I wisely ignored the last part of Adeliza's request and showed her the cupboard in the longhouse where the various tinctures, ointments and dried herbs were stored.

'My apothecary cupboard is dry and cool,' I explained, 'and in the chest is the sheaf of goatskins describing the exact quantities of every remedy I know. They contain the instructions on how best to deal with any ailments that have occurred before, so no matter how long it is until one returns, the knowledge of how to deal with it is not forgotten.'

We stepped out of the longhouse. 'The garden is but fifty paces away, and is tended by Bela, the Biddenden healing wife,' I told her as we headed off there.

Bela turned at the sound of our voices. When she saw Queen Adeliza, she went into a panic and started wiping the dirt from her face as she tried to tidy up the things around her. It was not really necessary – the garden was meticulously laid out and Bela was punctilious at caring for the plants, removing every weed and obstruction to their growth.

Adeliza picked up the goatskin Bela was using to give her planting information. She frowned. 'I would have thought *Physica* would have been more elaborate. Does William de Corbeil not provide the services of monks to make more detailed copies? The monks of Canterbury would have no hesitation in doing the Archbishop's bidding.'

I took a deep, deep breath, then another, before speaking.

'Eliza and I journeyed to Canterbury to meet with Archbishop William, and presented your instructions to write a great *Physica* for the nation, but he told us such an undertaking could only be performed by one who had been more formally trained. He charged Ymbert the Wise with the responsibility of fulfilling your command. For many moons, I sent William goatskin documents containing the latest remedies I had perfected, but have never received a response. Now I write out my remedies and instructions and store them here. That way, I know they will survive me.'

Adeliza frowned. 'I have learnt to my cost when it comes to great matters of state, that it is not what is right or wrong that matters, but the multitude of calculations and sensitivities that need to be taken into account. My first thought is to make my displeasure towards Archbishop William known to the King.

But William de Corbeil is an important ally and Henry will not take action against him, despite his failings.' She sighed. 'The King's first queen was adept at navigating these subtleties and sensitivities. I know what my heart desires, but I do not know enough of the ways of the world to achieve it.'

I was shocked that the Queen of England would talk so openly. I sensed a great weariness in her words, as if the high-spirited young girl who had married the King of England full of youthful enthusiasm had become ground down by the reality of the great burdens that had been placed upon her.

I tried to speak of the positives of her plan. 'William de Ashford granted coin and land to support my physic gardens. Many lives have been saved, and many more have made speedy recoveries from ailments that would otherwise have blighted their lives. No queen has ever done more to ease the pain and suffering of her subjects.'

Adeliza smiled. 'You have done well, Mary Chulkhurst, and I do not wish to belittle your achievements. You have shown how much can be achieved in treating the sick and I will entreat my husband to encourage others to emulate your work. Can you prepare for me one further copy of your most important goatskin drawings and have them delivered to me at court? I may yet achieve my dream by guile, rather than by command.'

I readily agreed, and with Adeliza's mood brightened, Eliza also saw her chance to tell her of the unfinished manuscript.

'Your Majesty,' she said, 'we too find matters of state fear-ful to contemplate. And here I have a terrible confession to make. When last we met, you did me the great honour of commissioning me to write the story of your husband, our

King. But every time I picked up my pen, I was torn by doubt and uncertainty about what to say and what not to say. How to avoid offence and how to best praise his magnificence. I was commissioned to write such a piece for William de Ashford, which I dutifully performed. And he threw such a rage at the words I wrote, I feared I would never see my home again. I have tried again and again to tell of Henry's great deeds, but this terror always fills me, and stays my hand from writing a single word. I fear I must also disappoint you this day. I am not a fit author for so important a task.'

Tears welled in Adeliza's eyes and she turned away a little. 'I have imagined this day many times during my long stay in Normandy. When I would see the joyous results of two great enterprises I had commissioned as queen. Something that would endure – not the choosing of the flowers for a banquet or the colour of the robes I would wear at court. These have been great disappointments today, but I also disappoint myself by indulging in such flights of fancy, making such appointments on a whim and without due regard for the rigour and formality of due process.' She took a second to gather herself. When she spoke again, she had regained her regal composure. 'I discharge you both from the obligations you made to me. Let us never speak more of these follies again. Do you swear an oath of silence on these matters?'

We both knelt down and made our promises.

The sun was dropping lower now and the sky filled with birdsong. Adeliza watched the starlings cleave the air, before settling on a nearby oak.

'Oh, to be so free,' she muttered under her breath. She turned to look us, a forced smile on her face. 'Let us not end this visit on a note of disappointment,' she said, blinking as she spoke. 'It has been six years since we last met, and I am curious to know what has befallen you since then. Tell me of the adventures of the Maids of Biddenden.'

Eliza told her how I saved the village from another outbreak of sweating sickness, which claimed the life of Gerbert and Gaston's families, and how they had come to be our companions these last few years. I told of Father dying, and Mother choosing to become a nun at Malling Abbey, which Adeliza took much interest in. Then she asked Eliza to play 'The Fair Maid of Brabant'. She needed no persuasion to produce her vielle and sing the words of praise to her again.

'You inspire me to do great things with my life and not to dwell on my disappointments,' she told me when I finished. 'Your mastery of the vielle and the beauty of your words show me that no matter how difficult a life someone is forced to lead, there is always something they can do and succeed at. It may be that I too will be more blessed in spirit than in the flesh.'

I knew she was talking about failing to produce an heir and that she too was subject to great burdens in her life. Despite her high-born status and great wealth, she was surrounded by Henry's illegitimate children occupying high positions at court. If she herself were not fertile, Henry's only legitimate heir was his daughter, a year or two younger than Adeliza. It was not a treasonable thought to imagine that Adeliza would spend many years as a widow, constantly reminded of her failure to bear a child.

There was an emptiness inside me as I watched Adeliza ride off, but also relief. The life of two simple country maids was all we wanted. We would never aim so high in our ambitions again.

1134

~

Chapter 28
Eliza

Five years had passed since Adeliza visited us in Biddenden. Once, we heard that Henry was to travel through Kent to Normandy, and we hoped she would stop and visit us. But no. Gaston told me the talk in the alehouse was that Henry had made his nobles swear an oath of allegiance to Adeliza when she reached London after we last saw her, in the hope of quelling the growing dissatisfaction that she was failing to provide a new male heir to the throne. But the queen remained barren, and the King was taking up mistresses again, siring two children with Isabel de Beaumont, who was even younger than Adeliza.

'When Henry dies, we will have either a woman on the throne or a bastard,' Gaston told me. 'Many nobles will want to choose neither. If Adeliza does not produce a male heir while her childbearing years are still with her, there will be great unrest, maybe even civil war.'

It was strange, even disrespectful, for a country maid to feel pity for a queen, but it once again confirmed that we had been wise not to be drawn into the strong currents of power and influence that we would have had to navigate, had our dreams of writing the *Physica* and performing at court come to reality. In Biddenden, we had everything we wanted. Two loving companions – Gaston for me and Gerbert for Mary. Although that love was never consummated, that meant little to any of us. They had long ago ceased to be our tenant farmers, and we all slept together in the longhouse, Mary and I at one end of the living quarters, the brothers at the other. I am sure they had to endure much teasing and speculation when they went to the alehouse, but if they did, they never talked about it. No-one ever spoke about these matters to our face. Had they ever done so, there were enough villagers who would have shamed them out of the town.

Mary's skill as a healer continued to grow and, after she had made a copy of the goatskin drawings for Adeliza, she started again writing down her new treatments and sending them to Archbishop William in Canterbury, hoping Ymbert the Wise would incorporate them into his own *Physica*. No words of acknowledgement ever returned. It looked as though the Canterbury *Physica* would never materialise.

The Biddenden Lady Day fayre had grown into a grand event, honouring Mary and myself, with the villagers giving thanks for being twice spared the ravages of the sweats. In the early days we tried to resist the attention, even threatening not to attend one year, so we could retain our humility. Gerbert and Gaston told us we were silly. It was a day to celebrate the joy and life we had brought to the village, and a salute to our remarkable existence. After that, we took part and enjoyed the day, handing out the special horsebread cakes the villagers made. More recently, I had even been tempted to sing and play my vielle at the gathering, but I was always embarrassed by the applause for me, when it was Mary's healing skills we were honouring.

Our appearances at the fayre meant that many outsiders turned up on the day, to have a chance to spy the Biddenden Maids. We didn't mind as long as they weren't rude and didn't gape too much, and there were always a few burly villagers to take care of any who became troublesome. So I shouldn't have noticed one stranger, standing alone and watching proceedings with an amused, detached air. But my eyes kept getting drawn to him. There was something very special in his manner.

I pointed him out to Mary, but she just teased me about how handsome he was, and that I'd better watch I didn't offend Gaston with my observations. I resolved to think no more about him, but I couldn't help but snatch an occasional look. I could see him examining us, coolly and authoritatively, rather than throwing the half-embarrassed, half-astonished glances we usually received when people saw us for the first time. But he never came near. I calmed my unsettledness by telling myself he would be gone on the morrow.

But instead, he turned up at our longhouse, a ruffled Deorwin standing next to him.

'We did not know we had a great and noble visitor in our midst at the fayre,' Deorwin told us. 'Let me present Rahere, from the court of King Henry. He is here to talk to you about the hospital of St Bartholomew's.'

I had heard of a hospital – a 'house of spittle' to give it its full title, so named because of the jugs of spittle collected and poured away from those who were treated there.

Rahere proceeded to tell us his story. It was too incredible to believe.

'I must apologise for my silence yesterday, Eliza and Mary. And to you too, Deorwin, for not having the courtesy to inform you, the reeve of Biddenden, of who was in your midst. In truth, I wanted to grant myself a day of peace, so I could observe unfettered by attention the wonder of what this village celebrates each year. I hope you forgive my selfish indulgence.'

He bowed to Deorwin, who looked flustered as he waved away the apology. I had never seen Deorwin so in awe. It was obvious this Rahere had already made a big impression.

Rahere sat down, uninvited; but such was his presence it would have been churlish to object. 'I was born of humble origins, in a village much like yours,' he told us. 'But I enjoyed the good things of life and soon found myself at the court of King Henry. I was an entertainer at court – I made it my business all day long to attend spectacles, banquets, jests and the rest of the trifles of the court. With shameless ambition, I secured for myself the high office of court jester.'

He stood up and gave a little bow at this point, twirling his hand in an exaggerated gesture of acknowledgement. It looked so out of character, given his solemn and majestic demeanour, that Mary and I burst out laughing, as much in surprise as anything.

'So, you journeyed far to watch a fellow entertainer?' I said, half-teasingly. 'I hope my vielle playing was worth the journey.'

'Your playing was indeed a pleasure on the ear,' Rahere replied. 'But I mean no disrespect to you when I say it was Mary I came here to meet. Mary the Healer, guardian of the Kent physic gardens and scribe of the *Physica* skins, am I correct?'

Mary looked at me, confused, before replying. 'I have been spoken of thus,' she replied. 'But what is this to you?'

His gravitas returned and he spoke in a more solemn tone. 'Let me tell you some more of my story. I came to question the life I led, one devoted to pleasure and indulgences. Then two events had a profound effect on me; the death of Henry's first queen and the *White Ship* disaster. I became challenged by grief and came to realise there was much more to life than round after round of pleasure and merrymaking. I left the royal court and set out as a humble pilgrim on a long and perilous journey in the hope of finding enlightenment. I arrived in Rome and was staying on the island of St Bartholomew on the River Tiber, when I became ill with Roman fever, a terrible scourge that manifests itself in warmer climes. I made a vow to God that were He to spare me, I would return to England and devote my life to healing the poor.'

I was transfixed by the passion with which he spoke these words. Mary interrupted him and briefly broke the spell.

'So you have created a physic garden, just as I have done in Biddenden?'

'Much, much more than that.' He laughed, half in embarrassment. 'Not to diminish the good you have done here, Mary the Healer.'

I sensed that his story was far from complete and so urged him to continue. 'Was it you who built the hospital? That would have been a great undertaking to complete.'

'Indeed,' he said. 'And it was only because of the Biddenden physic garden that I was able to achieve it.'

Mary's head must now have been in as much a whirl as mine.

'Let me say why,' Rahere continued. 'I planned my return to court to coincide with Henry and Adeliza's from Normandy, in the year 1129.'

The year we last met Adeliza.

'On my journey back to England, I had a dreadful vision in which I was carried by a winged beast to the edge of a horrible abyss, into which I was about to plunge. As I cried out in terror, a figure appeared beside me, a being of wonderful beauty and imperial authority. It was Saint Bartholomew, and he directed me to found a church and hospital in his name, at Smithfield in London. He said I should have no doubt or anxiety concerning the expenses of this work, but should merely apply myself diligently to my appointed task.'

Rahere smiled to himself before continuing. 'When I presented my proposals at court, I found the reason for the Saint's confidence. Adeliza had told King Henry of your plan to go from the humble beginnings of a physic garden in Biddenden to create gardens in every town in England, each caring for the sick using the teachings of a *Physica* which would be provided to them. Adeliza told the King it was a good plan, but that you had lost the desire to see it through after being belittled by Archbishop William.'

We both felt a tremor of shock at this news, and Rahere noticed our discomfort. 'Do not worry, Mistresses Chulkhurst. With the unrest in the north, and William an ally of the King against Thurstan, Archbishop of York, Henry did not dare challenge him. But my proposal to build a teaching hospital, to both cure the sick and spread the word of how best to treat the most common maladies, was well received, and King Henry granted me a royal licence to proceed.' His eyes danced as he recalled that day. 'Now the hospital is open, and every day is saving poor souls from entering the gates of Heaven – or Hell – so I wanted to journey to Biddenden to give thanks to you for the inspiration you gave the Queen to make St Bartholomew's prophesy come true.'

Mary was lost for words. Gerbert, who like his brother had remained in the shadows during the meeting, came forward and gave her an embrace.

'You must forgive Mary for her lack of response,' he said. 'It is beyond comprehension that a simple garden in our village could have had such consequences.' Gaston stepped forward and stood next to me.

Now it was Rahere's turn to be surprised, as he realised Gerbert and Gaston were more than just our tenant farmers.

'Gentlemen, I must apologise for the slight. I thought the Maids lived alone.'

Normally, Mary and I are offended when strangers assume there is an intimacy between us and the brothers, but Rahere had such an easy charm, it was hard to be annoyed with him.

Gaston explained. 'My brother and I are companions of Eliza and Mary, nothing more,' he said. 'There is no need to seek our permission to continue your discussions. There seems to be much you need to discuss with each other. Let us leave you to it. We will be the fields if you need to find us.'

We spent the rest of the day talking to Rahere. He was a most unusual person. If Mary's and my skills had been combined into the one body, with him they were combined in the one mind. He spent hours going over Mary's goatskin treatments, debating the finer points with her and telling her of new ideas which had been tried out at his hospital.

Then the entertainer took over from the healer. 'There is a new way to play the vielle,' he told me, 'which only those most skilled in the playing dare attempt. Bring yours to me and I will explain it.'

He took the instrument from me delicately, as though a new-born child had been handed to him. 'Your playing soars like a bird, but a simple adjustment will give it more depth,' he told me. 'Add a new string, the bourdon, using the thickest of cat gut, placed off the fingerboard and attached to the side of the pegbox, to give a low pitch. Pluck with your left thumb, so that it produces a pleasing beat to your music.' Then he turned to Mary. 'You are a fine healer,' he said, 'but may I be so bold as to say the Chulkhurst musical skills reside only with your sister. As she plucks the bourdon string, take that as your cue to strike your timbrel. It will give better purpose to your efforts.'

Rather than be insulted, Mary merely laughed. 'Sire, many will thank you for saving their ear from my efforts.'

Rahere, he told us, had established an annual cloth fair at Smithfield the previous August, which had been extremely popular and raised all the funds to run the hospital for the year. There had been a myriad of entertainment – jugglers, fire eaters, jesters, minstrels, storytellers and many more, and Rahere confessed that he himself would sometimes amuse the crowds with his juggling. That evening Gerbert, Gaston, Mary and I watched him perform.

There was more joy and laughter in our house than any of us could ever remember.

But it was as he was leaving the next day that he told us his biggest surprise. 'I will return to court and tell Adeliza that I found you in good spirits and held in much esteem by your villagers. She has spoken to me fondly of the time she spent with you.'

'I am honoured to hear that,' I replied. 'Our last meeting was marked by sadness that we had not fulfilled the commands she had given to us. We hope every day that we may see her again in happier times.'

'Then your wish will be granted,' Rahere replied. 'I have saved the best of my news to cheer my departure from you. King Henry and Adeliza are to return to France when the autumn leaves arrive and will stay for a time at Robert de Crevecoeur's grand new castle at Leeds, a day's march from here. Robert has pledged to support the claim of Empress Matilda, Henry's only legitimate child, to accede to the throne on Henry's death, and Henry wanted to give thanks that the owner of such a formidable barrier to Norman invasion was on his side. There is to be a feast day in celebration, the greatest the shire of Kent has ever seen. I have been privileged to be asked to perform, and I would want to pay honour to Mary's physic gardens and also invite you to perform alongside me, Mistress Eliza. What say you? Will you have mastered the bourdon string by then?'

'We have vowed to live a quiet life in Biddenden for the rest of our days,' Mary said, before I could reply. I felt the shock of disappointment. To my surprise, Mary then laughed. 'Do not worry, dear sister, I jest. The granting of such honour is the most wondrous news.' She turned to Rahere. 'Usually my sister has to use all her powers of persuasion to make me agree to attend such events. To this one, I go willingly. You have achieved so much to help the sick, and have created something that will last forever. It would be an honour to celebrate whatever small part I have played in making it happen.'

After Rahere left, Mary and I discussed what our own legacy would be.

'Your remedies will surely outlast the songs and poems I have been able to write,' I told Mary. 'Songs have been sung since before Greek time, with only a few ancient tunes still being performed today. But your wisdom in matters of balancing the body's humours will survive for as long as your words on the goatskin scrolls are able to be read.'

'The success of our farm means that we have acquired much land in the last few years,' Mary replied. 'But one day, we will be gone. If Gerbert and Gaston are still spared by then, they should continue to work the farm, in appreciation for all their years of companionship. We have no heirs, and they are now of an age where it is likely that they will also leave no descendants. Let us arrange that when Gerbert and Gaston join us in Heaven, our lands are managed by the village elders to provide an annual dole of bread and cheese to the needy of the village. What do you say, dear sister? Should we leave such a bequest to the good people of Biddenden?'

Of course, I agreed, and we went to seek out Deorwin to tell him of our decision.

'A most worthy gesture, and one that will ensure that your wondrous life is never forgotten,' Deorwin said, when we outlined our plan to him. 'The "Bread and Cheese Lands" I shall call your estate, and bread and cheese will be handed out, paid for by the rent from these fields, for as long as Biddenden remains in existence. But let us hope that it will be many years before that first bounty will be granted. There is much good for you still to do, with the time you have left on this Earth.'

Deorwin drew up the documents detailing our endowment and Gerbert and Gaston witnessed our signing, but

Deorwin's confidence about our good health turned out to be unfounded. I adapted my vielle to add the bourdon string Rahere had told me about, and I was looking forward to practising on it over the summer months. But then a lingering melancholic decline settled on Mary. Her skin became pale, her eyes sunken but luminous, and she was struck down with fever. Soon the same condition took hold of me. I was constantly sweating; my extremities were cold and could only be warmed with great difficulty. We took to our bed and continued our listless decline. Mary started coughing, and to her horror saw blood mixed all through her sputa.

'I am down with phthisis, the white plague,' she told me. Gerbert and Gaston looked on, concerned. 'You are safe, dear companions,' she said to them. 'Unlike other forms of plague, this is not carried in the miasma. But if it is indeed the white plague, it is deadly news indeed. I need to be sure.' She paused, steeling herself for what she would say next. 'Gaston, will you do me a great kindness? Come with your knife and make a small cut on my skin. I need to express some blood, so I may examine it. If it has changed colour to a bright red, that will tell the awful truth I fear.'

Gaston came over, full of tears. He looked into Mary's eyes. She nodded, and Gaston stroked the edge of the dagger across her skin. Mary gasped with the pain, but smiled at him as the blood ran.

She collected a small measure in a bowl, while Gaston tied a cloth tightly around the cut arm. Mary stared at the blood, her face showing the crumpled look of defeat.

'It is bright red; thin, sharp and hot,' she concluded. 'Its heat will consume my lungs, and yours too, dear sister, until they can provide no more life force to our body. With every day, we will waste away, our bodies becoming thinner, until our souls leave our bodies. This is a cruel blow indeed.'

Gaston wailed in despair. 'Is there no remedy to this evil? Surely, with all you know of the humours of the body, there must be something you can do?'

Mary forced herself to smile. 'There are limits to what even I can do,' she replied. 'But yes, my dear Gaston, I know of treatments. Eliza and I will take expectorants and purgatives, to drive this evil from our bodies, and every evening you must perform a blood letting on Mary and myself. Find some brooklime from the edges of streams and ditches and cook it in lard with the mushrooms next to willow trees. This will slow the attack on our bodies.' She looked away before she spoke again. 'Maybe long enough so that we may recover.'

'That is great news,' I said, forcing myself to sound positive. Mary could hide the truth from others, but she could not hide from me how she felt inside. 'Come, Gerbert, prepare some wholesome pottage for us. We shall fight this thing together.'

It was not until night had fallen that I finally had a whispered conversation with Mary about our fate.

'There is no cure, is there?' I said, fearing to hear her words in reply.

'None.'

The word stabbed my heart, like an icy dagger from a poisoned well.

'None my physic garden can provide.'

Suddenly I had hope. 'Then there is something that can be done? Tell me, sister. What can it be that you cannot administer yourself?'

'There is a monk in Wiltshire, known as William of Malmesbury. He is the most revered scholar in the land, a man who has written great books on history and healing. His works mention a cure for this disease – the King's Evil, he called it. I had dismissed it from my mind until now.'

I was confused. 'But have there not been others in the village who suffered this disease? Why did you not perform the cure on them?'

Mary managed to find the strength to laugh. 'Because William's cure is the King's touch. Only if the monarch lays his hand on an afflicted subject can the evil be lifted. That is not something I can grow in my garden.'

I kept my whisper, but said my words with grim determination. 'Then we know what we must do, dear sister. We shall fight off this white plague with all of our strength until Henry arrives in Kent. If, as Rahere says, he comes to honour us, we can beseech him to perform this act. It is only three weeks away. We can survive until then. We must.'

Three weeks was but a short time, but it felt like eternity. Each day, we slipped deeper and deeper into a black void. Our urine became thin and colourless, our bowel movements pungent. Every evening, before the bloodletting, we tried to perform some exercise that would make our lungs breathe more deeply, but this became more and more difficult. By the end of the second week, we could not even stand upright. Mary had Gaston make some cakes from the roots and leaves of the cornflower mixed with fresh deer tallow and we tried to eat them as much as we could, to suppress the hot and moist humours growing within us.

Then Mary fell into a deep sleep from which she could not be wakened. Were it not for the slow rising and falling of her chest, it might be thought she had already departed. It went on for one day, then a second. On the third, her eyes opened again. She lay for a few moments, exhausted by the effort of keeping them open, before she could summon the strength to speak.

'I am sorry, dear sister, I am failing you,' she said, slipping again into sleep.

Gerbert had made arrangements for a cart to carry us to Leeds Castle. He decided he could wait no longer. Leaving Gaston to care for us, he made off to prepare it for the journey. Gaston sat beside us, holding Mary's hand.

'Bring me Adeliza's mirour, so I can see my sister's face at peace,' I said, my voice rasping with the dryness of my throat.

He held the mirour over me, angling it until I caught Mary's reflection. Her skin was transparent, very white and fair, with a blooming red in the cheeks. She had never looked so beautiful.

Then, in an instant, the bloom disappeared, replaced by a dull pewter blue. I screamed, a cry that used up every ounce of strength in my body. 'Mary! Mary!'

Gaston took a blanket and covered Mary's face, tears pouring from his eyes. Gerbert walked into the room and saw immediately what had happened. He came over.

'There is no time to lose,' he said, his voice shaking. 'I must cut you free. Mary's dead blood will be flowing into your body. With your bodies separated, there is still a chance the King's touch can work its miracle.'

I looked over at Mary's dead body. For a few moments, for the first time in my life, my body was mine alone.

I finally spoke. 'As we came together, we will also go together.'

I closed my eyes, seeing only darkness. With every passing moment, I felt heavier and heavier. Then the sun started shining and I was alone, climbing a tree, looking out over the people of Biddenden, waving and cheering. I was riding a horse at full gallop, Mary on the horse next to me, feeling the wind blowing through my hair. I felt the icy chill of the river as I swam, effortlessly, from bank to bank, the skin on my naked body tingling with pleasure. I was running, running up a hill, nothing now to hold me back.

I kept on running forever.

THE STORY OF THE MAIDS

According to local history, Eliza and Mary Chulkhurst were conjoined twins born at the beginning of the 12th century to a wealthy family from the village of Biddenden in Kent. They lived until the year 1134, when Mary fell ill and died. Eliza was asked if she wanted to be surgically separated from her twin, but said the words quoted at the end of this story: 'As we came together, we will also go together.' She endured this Mezentian existence for six hours before she died. Although the Maids die of tuberculosis in this novel, their actual cause of death is unknown.

In their joint will, the Maids left twenty acres of land to the church wardens of the parish; the rent from these fields, called the Bread and Cheese Lands, to provide support for the elderly and poor. This tradition continues into the present day, with donations to the needy made every Easter; along with Biddenden cakes made using a mould showing two women joined together. They are brick-hard and store well, but are almost inedible.

There were numerous contemporaneous mentions of a pair of conjoined twins living in the twelfth century. A poem called *'De Contempu Mundi'* by Bernard of Morlaix, an Anglo-Saxon monk at Cluny, contained a reference to conjoined twins born in the English countryside. The *Chronicon Scotorum*, an Irish medieval historical chronicle from that time, told that in 1099, a woman gave birth to 'two children together, in this year, and they had but one body from the breast to the navel, and they were two girls.' *The Annals of the Four Masters* had an almost identical description, although it was stated they were born in 1103; in *The Annals of Clonmacnoise*, their birth was given as 1100.

The first mention of the rent from the Bread and Cheese Lands being used for charitable purposes was in 1605, when the Archdeacon of Canterbury, after visiting the Biddenden parish at Easter, wrote to his superiors to complain about the unruly mob that crowded the church, eagerly awaiting the distribution of bread, cheese, cakes and beer. A court case in 1645 contained depositions from witnesses saying these lands had originally been donated by 'two Maidens that grew together in their bodies', showing the story was well known in the seventeenth century. The cakes in the form of an effigy of the Maids were first mentioned in 1775; in 1808, the first broadsheet on the Chulkhurst twins was printed and sold outside the church at Easter for two pence. One of these broadsheets survived and is in the Wellcome Museum in London.

In 1820, a new account was printed. It stated that the Maids' gravestone could be seen in the church in Biddenden, though it was worn by time to the point of being unrecognisable. It was thought it was lost or destroyed when the church was later rebuilt, although there is an unmarked ancient gravestone near the rector's pew which has a diagonal line etched on it, which some think signified that it contains two joined bodies. A memorial to the Maids in the church was described with these lines from an unknown poet:

A SHORT AND CONCISE ACCOUNT OF

ELIZA & MARY CHULKHURST,

Who were born joined together by the Hips and Shoulders,

IN THE YEAR OF OUR LORD, 1100,

At Biddenden, in the County of Kent,

COMMONLY CALLED

THE BIDDENDEN MAIDS.

THE READER will observe by the Plate of them, that they lived together in the above state Thirty-four Years, at the expiration of which time one of them was taken ill and in a short time died; the surviving one was advised to be separated from the Body of her deceased Sister by dissection, but she absolutely refused the separation by saying these words,—"As we came together we will also go together," and in the space of about Six Hours after her Sister's decease, she was taken ill and died also.

By their Will, they bequeathed to the Churchwardens of the Parish of Biddenden and their Successors Churchwardens for ever, certain Pieces or Parcels of Land in the Parish of Biddenden, containing Twenty Acres, more or less, which now let at 40 Guineas per annum. There are usually made in commemoration of these wonderful Phænomena of Nature, about 1,000 Rolls with their Impressions printed on them, and given away to all Strangers on Easter Sunday after Divine Service in the afternoon: also about 300 Quartern Loaves and Cheese in proportion to all the Poor Inhabitants of the said Parish.

THOMSON, PRINTER, TENTERDEN.

Property of the Wellcome Institute, London.

The moon on the east oriel shone;
Through slender shafts of shapely stone,
The silver light, so pale and faint,
Showed the twin sisters and many a saint,

Whose images on the glass were dyed;
Mysterious maidens, side by side –
The moonbeams kissed the holy pane,
And threw on the pavement a mystic stain.

The Maids were now famous. By the mid-nineteenth century, almost 1000 cakes and 300 loaves of bread and cheese were given away every Easter Sunday and the tradition was reported as far afield as the *New York Times* in June, 1895.

The likeness of the Maids corresponds closely to the type of conjoined twins known as pygopagus twins, where they are joined at the hip. Pygopagus twins account for eighteen per cent of all conjoined twins and it is certainly medically feasible that twins born this way could live to the age of thirty-four, even in medieval times. However, some historians have cast doubt on the story of the Maids, most notably Edward Hasted in 1778 and George Clinch in 1900. Hasted was by all accounts a noted historian but also an unpleasant man who despised 'vulgar traditions', and many of his statements on the traditions he wrote about have been proven to be wrong. Clinch believed the Maids to be real, but from a detailed analysis of the moulds, concluded they were dressed in clothes from the reign of Queen Mary and so dated them to the sixteenth century. Despite these reservations, no historian has ever come up with a theory as to why the inhabitants of a rural village, living such an arduous life, would invent or embellish a story to explain a tradition going back centuries, and how they could get the medical details correct.

Photograph by Sir Benjamin Stone, 1906.

The Chulkhurst name lived on in Biddenden until the eighteenth century. The first photographs of the customs associated with the Maids was taken by Sir Benjamin Stone in 1906, showing the widows of the parish queuing at the window of the Old Workhouse, along with a photo of the cakes. In 1907, the Bread and Cheese Lands were sold for housing, raising £564. This allowed the annual dole to expand considerably, and provided for cheese, bread and tea to be handed out at Easter and cash payments to be made at Christmas.

Today, the modern housing estate built on the Bread and Cheese Lands is entered via Chulkhurst Close and a sign, showing the Maids side by side, greets visitors when they arrive at the village. Biddenden cakes continue to be given out each Easter, and are sold as souvenirs.

Photograph by Sir Benjamin Stone, 1906.

As regards the other characters in the book, most were imagined in the writing of this fictional biography. However, the following were all real-life historical characters and all the historical dates and facts about them are true: King Henry I and Adeliza of Louvain; Avicia, Prioress of Malling; Gundulf, Bishop of Rochester; Archbishops of Canterbury Anselm, Ralph d'Escures and William de Corbeil; William de Ashford; Robert and Rohaise de Crevecoeur; Rahere, founder of St Bartholomew's hospital. Of course, none have ever been known to have met Eliza and Mary.

St Bartholomew's is the oldest hospital in the world and today is a centre of excellence for cancer and cardiac care, still operating on the site where Rahere built it, almost nine hundred years ago.

King Henry died in France in December 1135, from eating a surfeit of lamprey eels. He and Adeliza never had any children, despite Henry earning the dubious distinction of having more illegitimate children, twenty-four by most counts, than any other English monarch. He was succeeded, not by his legitimate daughter Matilda or any of his illegitimate offspring, but by his nephew, Stephen of Blios. This led to the civil war that many had feared, the Anarchy, which would have undoubtedly led to the destruction of any Kent physic gardens. The unrest eventually ended when Stephen besieged Leeds Castle in 1139, to quell Robert de Crevecoeur's support for Matilda.

Adeliza did commission a flattering account of Henry's reign, similar to Eliza's *The Romance of King Henry*, from the Welsh poet, David, and had it set to poetry and then to music. She also popularised the writing of secular books written in the Anglo-Norman vernacular, just as Mary's *Physica* would have been, the most notable one Philippe de Thaon's *Bestiary*, which contains a dedication to Adeliza. She also founded her own hospital, for leprosy, at Fugglestone St Peter in Wiltshire.

Ironically, perhaps Adeliza's most lasting legacy was that Henry added the lion of her family crest to his own, with his grandson Henry II doing the same with the lion on the crest of his wife, Eleanor of Aquitaine. That brought the number of lions on the royal crest to three – the Three Lions of the England football shirt.

Adeliza finally found her love match when she married William d'Aubigne in 1138. They went on to have seven children, deepening further the mystery as to why her marriage to Henry was childless.

ACKNOWLEDGEMENTS

Thanks to all my author friends for their encouragement for me to write this book, and particular thanks to Elena Kravchenko for her advice and friendship. And most of all, thanks to Agnes for her loving support, not just in the writing of this book but also for our life together.

Thanks to my editors, Debi Alper, Sheena Billett and Michael Faulkner; Michael Campbell at MC Writing Services for the typesetting; Robin Kinsman-Blake for the historical map of Kent; James Willis at Spiffing Covers for the book cover.

FURTHER READING

Many thanks to the authors of my source material.

For information on Eliza and Mary Chulkhurst: *The Biddenden Maids: A Curious Chapter in the History of Conjoined Twins*, J Bodeson; *The Story of Biddenden*, Biddenden Local History Society.

For insights on conjoined twins: *One*, Sarah Crossan; *The Girls*, Lori Lansens; *The Less You Know, The Sounder You Sleep*, Juliet Butler.

For information on twelfth-century England: *Medieval Lives*, Terry Jones and Alan Ereira; *Life in a Medieval Village*, Frances and Joseph Gies; *A Journey to Medieval Canterbury*, Andy Harmsworth; *Malling Abbey 1090–1990*, Anne M Oakley; *The Pillars of Earth* and *The Evening and the Morning*, Ken Follett.

For information on health and healing in the twelfth century: *Physica*, Hildegard von Bingen, translated by Priscilla Throop. Hildegard von Bingen was a twelfth-century healer, visionary, artist and poet. All of Mary's remedies in this book are detailed in Hildegard's *Physica*, although none are advised to be used for treatment today. Hildegard also wrote the love poem which is the basis of Eliza's ode to Masci.

Eliza's 'The *White Ship* Lament' is loosely based on *The White Ship* poem by Dante Gabriel Rossetti and 'The Fair Maid of Brabant' is my semi-modernised translation of part of *The Faerie Queen* by Edmund Spencer. Eliza's dreadful laudation to William de Ashford is all my own work.

GD Harper
www.gdharper.com